THE GREY MAN

The Grey Man

by
S.R.CROCKETT

Alloway Publishing
AYR

1984

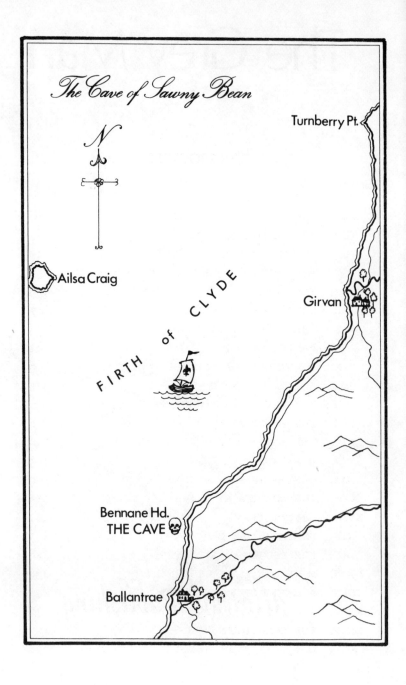

The Cave of Sawny Bean

N

Turnberry Pt.

Ailsa Craig

FIRTH of CLYDE

Girvan

Bennane Hd.
THE CAVE

Ballantrae

CONTENTS

THE GREY MAN

CHAPTER I

THE OATH OF SWORDS

WELL do I mind the first time that ever I was in the heart-some town of Ballantrae. My father seldom went thither, because it was a hold of the Bargany folk, and it argued therefore sounder sense to give it the go-by. But it came to pass upon a time that it was necessary for my father to adventure from Kirrieoch on the border of Galloway, where we dwelt high on the moors, to the seaside of Ayr.

My father's sister had married a man named Hew Grier, an indweller in Maybole, who for gear's sake had settled down to his trade of tanner in Ballantrae. It was to his burying that we went. We had seen him snugly happed up, and the burial supper was over. We were already in a mind to set about returning, when we heard the sound of a great rushing of people hither and thither. I went aloft and looked through a gable window upon the street. Arms were hastily being brought from beneath the thatch, to which the laws of the King had committed them under the late ordinance anent weapons of war. Leathern jackets were being donned, and many folk cried 'Bargany!' in the streets without knowing why.

My Aunt Grisel went out to ask what the stir might be, and came in again with her face as white as a clout.

'It is the Cassillis folk that are besieging the Tower of Ardstinchar, and they have come near to the taking of it, they say. Oh, what will the folk of Ballantrae do to you, John, if they ken that you are here? They will hang you for a spy, and that without question.'

'That,' said my father, 'is surely impossible. The Ballantrae folk never had any great haul of sense ever since

7

Stinchar water ran; but yet they will hardly believe that Hew Grier, decent man—him that was your marrow and lies now in his resting grave, poor body—took on himself to die, just that I might come to Ballantrae to spy out the land!'

But my aunt, being easily flustered, would not hearken to him, thinking that all terrible things were possible, and so hid the two of us in the barn-loft till it should be the hour of the gloaming.

Then as soon as the darkening came, putting a flask of milk into my pocket and giving a noble satchel of cakes to my father, she almost pushed us out of her back door. To this day I remember how the unsteady glare of a red burning filled all the streets. And we could see burghers' wives standing at their doors, all looking intently in the direction of the Castle of Ardstinchar upon its lofty rock. Others set their heads out of the little round 'jaw-holes' that opened in each gable wall, and gossiped shrilly with their neighbours.

My father and I went cannily down by the riverside, and as soon as we turned Hew-the-Friar's corner, we saw all the noble tower of Ardstinchar flaming to the skies—every window belching fire, and the sparks fleeing upward as before a mighty wind, though it was a stirless night with a moon and stars floating serenely above.

Down by the waterside and straight before us we saw a post of men, and we heard them clank their war-gear as they marched from side to side and looked ever up at the castle on its steep, spitting like a furnace, flaming like a torch. So at sight of them my father turned us about sharply enough, because, in spite of what he had said to my Aunt Grisel, he had much reason to fear for his neck. For if, on the night of a Cassillis raid, one of the hated faction should be found in the town of Ballantrae, little doubt there was but that a long tow and a short shrift would be his fate.

We climbed the breast of the brae up from the waterside, intending to make a detour behind the castle. My father said that there would be an easy crossing at Heronford, where he knew a decent man that was of his own party. Thence we could make up the glen of the Tigg Water, which in the evil state of the country was as good and quiet a way back to Minnochside as one might hope to find.

It seemed a most pitiful sight to me, that was but a young lad (and had never seen a fire bigger than a screed of muirburn screeving across the hills with a following wind at its tail), to watch the noble house with all its wealth of plenishing and gear being burned up.

I said as much to my father, who swung along with his head bent to the hill slope, dragging my arm oftentimes almost from the socket, in his haste to get us out of such unwholesome company as the angry folk of Ballantrae.

'It is an enemy's house!' he replied very hastily. 'Come thy ways, lad!'

'But what harm have the Bargany folk done to us?' I asked. For this thing seemed strange to me—that Kennedy should strive with Kennedy, burn castle, kill man, harry mow and manger, drive cattle—and I never be able to make out what it was all for.

'Hold your breath, Launcelot Kennedy!' said my father testy with shortness of wind and going uphill, 'or right speedily you will find out for what! Is it not enough that you are born to love Cassillis and to hate Bargany?'

'Are the folk of Cassillis, then, so much better than the folk of Bargany?' I asked, taking what I well knew to be the chances of a civil answer, or of a ring on the side of the head.

It was not the civil answer that I got.

And, indeed, it was an ill season for query and question, or for the answering of them. In time we got to the angle of the castle, and there we were somewhat sheltered from the fierce heat and from the glare of light also. From the eminence we had gained, we could look away along the shore side. My father pointed with his finger.

'Boy, do you see yon?' he whispered.

I looked long and eagerly with my unaccustomed eyes, before I could see in the pale moonlight a dark train of horsemen that rode steadily northward. Their line wimpled like a serpent, being pricked out to our sight with little reeling twinkles of fire, which I took to be the moon shining on their armour and the points of their spears.

'See,' said my father, 'yonder goes our good Earl home with the spoil. Would that I were by his side! Why do

I live so far among the hills, and out of the call of my chief when he casts his war pennon to the winds?'

We looked all round the castle, and seeing no one, we made shift to get about it and darn ourselves among the heather of the further hillside. But even as we passed the angle and reached a broken part of the wall, there came a trampling of iron-shod hoofs. And lo! a troop of horsemen rode up to the main castle gate, that which looks to the north-west. It was all we could do to clamber out of sight over the broken wall, my father lifting me in his arms. There we lay flat and silent behind a pile of stones, just where the breach had been made—over which we could look into the courtyard and see the splotched causeway and the bodies of the dead lying here and there athwart it in the ruddy light of burning.

Just as the foremost horseman came to the gate, which the riders of Cassillis had left wide open, the roof of red tile fell in with an awesome crash. The flames again sprang high and the sparks soared. Soon all the courtyard was aglow with the red, unsteady leme which the skies gave back, while the moon and stars paled and went out.

'Hist!' whispered my father, 'this is young Bargany himself who comes first.'

I looked eagerly from behind a stone and saw the noblest figure of a young man that ever I saw or shall see, riding on a black horse, sitting framed in the dark of the gateway, the flames making a crimson flicker about him. After a moment's pause he rode within the deserted close, and there sat his horse, looking up sternly and silently at the leaping flames and hearkening as it were to the crackling of the timbers as they burned.

Then another and yet another horseman came riding within, some of whom my father knew.

'See you, Launce, and remember,' he whispered; 'that loon there is Thomas Kennedy of Drummurchie, Bargany's brother. Observe his fangs of the wolf. He of all the crew is the wickedest and the worst.'

I looked forth and saw a gaunt, dark youth, with a short upper lip drawn up from teeth that shone white in the leaping flame which harvested the goodly gear of the house of Ardstinchar.

'There also is Blairquhan the Simpleton, Cloncaird of the Black Heart, and Benane the Laird's brother—a very debauched man—and there, I declare, is my Lord Ochiltree. Upon soul and conscience, I wonder what he does here thus riding with the Barganies?'

As soon as the fire died down a little, some of the party began to search about among the defences and outhouses, and a few even entered into the inner part of the tower. In twos and threes they came forth, some bringing a wounded man, some a dead man, till, on the cool, grey stones of the court, there rested five that lay motionless on their backs, and two that moaned a while and then were still. The more lightly wounded were cared for in a chamber within the gate. Then we could see all the gentlemen of the Bargany side dismounted from their horses and standing about those five that were killed.

'Alas for young Girvanmains!' I heard one cry, for we were very near. 'What shall we say to his father? And here also is Walter Pollock, the cunning scrivener—and James Dalrymple, that was a kindly little man and never harmed anyone—the Lord do so to me, and more also, if I write not this killing in blood upon the walls of Cassillis!'

The crowd thinned a little, and I saw it was the Laird himself that spoke.

Then this same young Bargany, who was taller by a head than any there, called for room. So they made a ring, with the dead men in the midst, and Bargany standing a little before. He bent him over the body of Walter Pollock, the young clerk, and drew forth a book from his breast.

'Listen!' he cried, 'all you that love Bargany, and who now behold this deed of dule and cruelty. Here lie our dead. Here is the Book of God that I have taken from one of the servants of peace, cruelly bereft of life by our enemies!'

'I warrant he drew a good sword when it came to the fighting, clerk though he might be,' whispered my father, 'I know the Pollock breed!'

Bargany looked at the book in his grasp and again at the hand which had held it.

'This falls out well,' he said. 'Here in the presence of our dead, upon the Bible that is wet with the blood of the unjustly slain, let us band ourselves together and take oath to be avenged upon the cruel house—the house of over-trampling pride—the house that has ever wrought us woe! Will ye swear?"

He looked round a circle of faces that shone fierce and dark in the lowe of the furnace beyond. As he did so he unsheathed his sword, and pointed with it to the topmost pinnacles of Ardstinchar. In a moment there was a ring of steel all about him, for, quick as his own, every man's hand went out to his scabbard, and in every man's grip there gleamed a bare blade. And the sight thrilled me to see it, ay, more than all the religion I had ever been taught, for I was but a boy. And even though religion be learned in youth, the strength and the use of it comes not till after.

Thus Bargany stood with the brand in his right hand and the Bible in his left, to take, as the ancient custom in our countryside, the solemn oath of vengeance and eternal enmity. And thus he spake,—

'By this Holy Book and by the wet blood upon it, I, Gilbert Kennedy of Bargany, swear never to satisfy my just feud against the bloody house of Cassillis, till of all their defenced towers there stands not one stone in its place, remains alive not one scion of its cruel race. I who stand here, in the presence of these dead men of my folk, charge the Kennedies of the North with the blood on my kin, the spoiling of my vassals, and the heart-breaking of my father. In the name of God I swear! If I stay my hand and make not an end, the God of Battles do so to me, and more also!'

Gilbert Kennedy kissed the book which he gripped in his left hand, and then with sudden gesture of hatred he flung down the sword which he had held aloft in his right. It fell with a ringing dirl of iron upon the stones of the pavement beside the slain men, and the sound of its fall made the flesh creep on my bones.

Then the Laird's wicked brother, Thomas, called the Wolf of Drummurchie, came forward, hatred fairly sparkling in his eyes, and his teeth set in a grin of devil's anger.

'I swear,' he cried, 'to harry John of Cassillis, the enemy that has wrought us this woe, with fire and sword —to cut off him and his with dagger and spear, to light the thack and to lift the cattle. I will be an outlaw, a prey for the hunters for their sake. For Cassillis it was who first slandered me to the King, chased me from my home, and made me no better than a robber man upon the mountains.'

And in turn he kissed the Book, and his sword rang grimly on the pavement beside his brother's. So one by one the men of Bargany took the solemn band of eternal and bloody feud. Presently an old man stood forth. He held a spear in his hand, being, as my father whispered, but a tenant vassal and keeping to the ancient Scottish yeoman's weapon.

'By the blood of my son that lies here before me, by this spear which he held in his dying hand, I, that am but the poor goodman of Girvanmains, before death takes me to where all vengeance is Another's, I swear the vengeance of blood!'

And he cast the spear beside the swords of the gentlemen. Then issuing forth from the chamber over the gate, and leaning heavily upon the arm of a young page boy, there came creeping the strangest shape of a man—his countenance thrawed and drawn, his shrunk shanks twisted, his feet wambling one over another like those of a mummer's bear. Bowed double the man was, and he walked with a staff that tapped and rattled tremblingly on the pavement as he came. The men of war turned at the sound, for there had been stark silence among them after old Girvanmains had let his spear fall.

Like one risen from the dead, the old man looked up at the tower which was now beginning to show black against the dulling red glow of the dying fire.

'Thou tower of Ardstinchar,' he cried, lifting up a voice like the wind whistling through scrannel pipes, 'they have burned you that erstwhile burned me. Curse me Cassillis and the Lords of it! Curse me all that cleave to it, for their tender mercies are cruel. I, Allan Stewart, sometime Abbot of Crossraguel, lay my curse bitterly upon them for the cruel burning they gave me before their fire

in the Black Vault of Dunure. But bless me the House
of Bargany, that rescued me from torture and took me to
their strong tower, wherein I have to this day found in
peace a quiet abiding chamber.'

'Mark well, boy,' whispered my father; 'remember this
to tell it in after days to your children's children. Your
eyes have seen the Abbot of Crossraguel whom the King
of Carrick, the father of our Earl John, roasted quick in
the vault of Dunure—a deed which has wrought mickle
woe, and will yet work more.'

And even as my father spoke I saw the old cripple
hirple away, the young Laird himself helping him with
the kindliest courtesy.

Then, last of all that spake, came a voice from one
who had remained in the gloomy archway of the gate, by
the entering in of the courtyard. He that broke the silence
was a tall man who sat on a grey horse, and was clad from
head to foot in a cloak of grey, having his face shaded
with a high-crowned, broad-brimmed hat of the ancient
fashion.

'Give me the Book and I also will swear an oath!' he
said, in a voice which made all turn towards him.

'Who may that man be? I ken him not,' said my
father, for he had named all the others as they came within.

So one gave the man the blood-stained Bible, and he
held it in his hand for a moment. He was silent a space
before he spoke.

'By this Christian Book and among this Christian
people,' he cried, 'I swear to root out and slay utterly all
the house of Cassillis and Culzean, pursuing them, man,
woman and child, with fire and sword till they die the
death of pain and scorn, or I who swear die in the accom-
plishing of it.'

The unknown paused at the end of this terrible oath,
and gazed again at the Book. The dying flame within
the castle flared up for a chance moment as another rafter
caught fire.

'Fauch!'' said he of the grey cloak, looking at the
Bible in his hand, 'there is blood upon thee. Go thou into
the burning as the seal of our oaths. A bloody Bible is no
Christian book!'

And with that he threw the Bible into the red embers that glowed sullenly within the tower.

There broke a cry of horror from all that saw. For though in this dark land of Carrick deeds of blood were done every day, this Bible-burning was accounted rank blasphemy and ungodly sacrilege. But I was not prepared for its effect upon my father. He trembled in all his limbs, and I felt the stones shake upon which he now leaned breast high, careless who should see him.

'This is fair devil's work,' he muttered. 'The fires of Sodom, the brimstone of Gomorrah shall light upon us all for this deed!'

He would have said more, but I never heard him finish his words. Sudden as a springing deer, he tore from the covert of the wall by my side and bounded across the court, threading the surprised group and overleaping the swords and the bodies of the slain men. He disappeared in a moment through the door into the tower, within which the flames still glowed red, and from which every instant the crash of falling timber and the leaping flames answered each other.

Ere my father sprang back, his figure stood plain and dark against the fire within, like that of a smith at his forge seen in the bygoing upon a snowy night. He held the unburned Bible clasped to his breast, but his left hand hung straight down by his side.

A moment after he had swung from a window and fallen upon his face on the pavement with the Bible beneath him.

A dozen men ran towards him and seized him—Thomas of Drummurchie the first among them.

'A traitor! A spy!' he cried, lifting a sword from the pile with clear purpose to kill. 'To the death with him! It is John Kennedy of Kirrieoch—I ken him well, a rank Cassillis thief!'

And he would have slain my father forthwith, but that I ran among his legs and gripped him so close to me that he fell clattering on the pavement among the swords. Then I went and took my father's hand, standing by his side and crying out the while,—

'Ye shallna, ye shallna kill my father. He never did ye harm a' the days o' his life!'

'Who are you, and what do you here?' asked young
Bargany in a voice of command, when they had set my
father on his feet.

'I am John Kennedy of Kirrieoch on Minnochside,
and I came to Ballantrae to bury the corpse of my sister's
man, Hew Grier, merchant and indweller there, that was
this day laid in the earth.'

So, right quietly and calmly, my father spoke among
them all.

'But what seek you in my burned Castle of Ardstinchar
and alone with these dead men?' asked the young Bargany.

With a quietness that came of the hills my father told
the chieftain his plain tale, and his words were not words
that any man could gainsay.

Then Bargany answered him without consulting the
others, as none but a great chief does whose lightest word
is life or death.

'Ye are here within my danger, and had I been even as
your folk of Cassillis, ye should have died the death; but
because ye stopped devil's work and, it may be, kept away
a curse from us for the burning of the Holy Book, ye shall
not die in my house. Take your life and your son's life, as
a gift from Gilbert Kennedy of Bargany.'

My father bowed his head and thanked his house's
enemy.

'Bring a horse,' cried the Laird, and immediately they
set my father on a beast, and me in the saddle before him.
'Put the Bible for a keepsake in your winnock sole, turn
out the steed on Minnochside, and come no more to
Ballantrae in time of feud, lest a worse thing befall you!'
So said he, and waved us away, as I thought grandly.

Some of the men that had sworn enmity murmured
behind him.

'Silence!' he cried, 'am not I Lord of Bargany? Shall
I not do as I will? Take your life, Kirrieoch. And whenever a Bargany rides by your door, ye shall give him bite
and sup for the favour that was this night shown you in
the courtyard of Ardstinchar.'

'Ye shall get that, Bargany, and welcome, whether ye
let me gang or no!' said my father. And pressing the Book
to his bosom, and gathering up the reins in his un-

wounded hand, we rode unquestioned through the arch of the wall into the silence of the night. And the hill winds and the stillnesses without were like God's blessing about us.

But from a knoll on the left of the entrance the man of the grey habit, he who had thrown the Bible, sat silent upon his horse and watched. And as we looked back, he still sat and watched. Him my father took to have been the devil, as he said to me many times that night ere we got to Minnochside.

Also ere we left the clattering pavement behind, looking out from the postern door we saw the thrawn visage of him who was Allan Stewart, the tortured residue of the man who had once been Abbot of Crossraguel, and in stature like a square-shouldered tower.

And this is the way my father brought home the burnt Bible to the house of Kirrieoch. There it bides to this day, blackened as to its bindings and charred at the edges, but safe in the wall press at my father's bed-head, a famous book in all the land, even as far as Glencaird and Dranie Manors upon the Waters of Trool.

But it brought good fortune with it—a fortune which, God be thanked, still remains and grows. And as for my father, he never lifted sword nor spear against the house of Bargany from that day to this, because of the usage which Gilbert Kennedy gave him that night at the burning of Ardstinchar.

Nevertheless, for all that, he exercised me tightly in the use of every weapon of war, from the skill of the bow to the shooting of the hackbutt. For it was his constant intent to make me an esquire in the service of Sir Thomas Kennedy of Culzean,* reputed the wisest man and the best soldier in all the parts of Carrick and Ayr. As, indeed, I have found him.

And this saving of the burning Bible was, as I guess, the beginning of my respect for religion—which, alas! I fear this chronicle will show to have been both a late-garnered and a thin-sown crop.

*Culzean is pronounced Culayne, as though to rhyme with 'domain.'

CHAPTER II

THE LASS OF THE WHITE TOWER

Now, as the manner is, I must make haste to tell something
of myself and have by with it.

My name is Launcelot Kennedy, and I alone am the
teller of this tale. In a country where all are Kennedies,
friends and foes alike, this name of mine is no great head-
mark. So 'Launcelot of the Spurs' I am called, or sometimes, by those who would taunt me, 'Launcelot Spurheel.'
But for all that I come of a decent muirland house, and
Kennedies of Kirrieoch, who were ever lovers of the Cassillis
blue and gold—which are the royal colours of France, in
memory of the ancient alliance—and ever haters of the red
and white of Bargany, which we hold no better than
butchers' colours, bloody and desolate.

The story, or at least my own part in it, properly begins
upon the night of the fair at Maybole—whither to my
shame I had gone without troubling my master, Sir Thomas
Kennedy of Culzean, with the slight matter of asking his
permission. Indeed, none so much as knew that I had been
to the town of Maybole save Helen Kennedy alone; and
she, as I well knew (although I called her Light-head Clatter-
tongue), would not in any wise tell tales upon me. There
at the fair I had spent all my silver, buying of trittle-trattles
at the lucky-booths and about the market-stalls. But upon
my return I meant to divide fairly with Helen Kennedy,
though she was fully two years younger than I—indeed,
only sixteen years of her age, though I grant long of the
leg and a good runner.

So, being advised of my excellent intentions, you shall
judge if I was not justified of all that I did to be revenged
on the girl afterwards.

It was the early morning of a March day when I came to
the foot of the Castle of Culzean. I went with quiet steps
along the shore by the little path that leads to the coves
beneath. I carried the things that I had bought in a napkin, all tied safely together. Now, the towers of Culzean
are builded upon a cliff, steep and perilous, overlooking
the sea. And I, being but a squire of eighteen (though

for my age strong and bold, and not to be beaten by anything or feared by any man), was lodged high up in the White Tower, which rises from the extremest point of the rock.

Now, as I say, I had not made mention of the little matter of my going abroad to Sir Thomas, both because it was unnecessary to trouble him with so small a thing, and also on account of the strictness of his opinions. It was, therefore, the more requisite that I should regain my chamber without putting lazy Gilbert in the watch-house at the gate to the trouble of letting fall the drawbridge for me. I did not, indeed, desire to disturb or disarrange him, for he would surely tell his master, being well called Gabby Gib-cat because he came of a race that never in their lives has been able to hold a secret for a single day in the belly of them—at least, not if it meant money, ale, or the good-will of their lord.

So it happened that before I went to Maybole I dropped a ladder of rope from the stanchions of my window, extremely strong and convenient, which came down to a ledge someway up among the rocks, at a place which I could easily reach by climbing. Thither I made my way while, as I tell you, the night was just beginning to dusk toward the dawning. I had all my buyings in my arms, tied up well and that tightly in the napkin, just as I had carried them from the lucky-booths of Maybole. I tied the outer knot of my bundle firmly to the last rung of the ladder, praying within me that Sir Thomas might be fast asleep. For I had to pass within three feet of his window, and, being an old man, he was somewhat wakerife in the mornings, easily started, and given to staring out of his lattice without method or sense, in a manner which had often filled me with pain and foreboding for his reason.

But by the blessing of God, and because he was some-what tired with walking in the fields with his baron-officer the night before, it happened that Sir Thomas was sound asleep, so that I was nothing troubled with him. But immediately beneath me, in the White Tower, were the rooms of his two daughters, Marjorie and Helen Kennedy; and of these Helen's room was to the front, so my rope ladder passed immediately in front of her window, while the chamber of Marjorie was to the back, and, in this instance, concerned me not at all.

So as I scrambled up the swinging ladder (and, indeed, there are not many that would venture as much on a cold March morning) I passed Helen Kennedy's window. As I went by, the devil (as I take it) prompted me to scratch with my toe upon the leaden frame of her lattice, for the lass was mortally afraid of ghosts. So I pictured to myself that, hearing the noise at the window, she would take it for the scraping of an evil spirit trying to find a way in, and forthwith draw the clothes over her head and lie trembling.

Pleasing myself, therefore, with this picture, I scraped away and laughed within myself till I nearly fell from the ladder. Presently I heard a stirring within the chamber, and stopped to listen.

'She has her head under the clothes by now,' I said to myself, as I climbed on up to my own window, which I found unhasped even as I had left it. I entered, gripping the edge of the broad sill and lifting myself over with ease, being very strong of the forearm. Indeed, I had won a prize for wrestling at the fair that day, in spite of my youth—a thing which I intended to keep secret till Helen Kennedy should begin to taunt me with being but a boy and feckless.

It chanced, however, that I, who had been thus victorious with men older than myself, was now to be vanquished, conquered, and overset, by one who was two years younger, and she a lassie. Then being safe in my chamber, I began to pull up the ladder of cords with all my goods and chattels tied at the end of it. And my thoughts were already running on the good things therein —cakes and comfits, sweetmeats, some bottles of Canary wine, and gee-gaws for the adorning of my person when I rode forth—the latter not for pride, of which I have none, but in order that I might ride in good squirely fashion, and as became the gentleman attendant of so great a lord as Sir Thomas Kennedy of Culzean, Tutor of Cassillis, brother of the late, and uncle of the present Earl of that name.

I drew up my rope ladder all softly and with success, because from the stanchions it swung clear of the walls of the castle, for the reason that my turret jutted a little way over, as is the custom with towers of that architecture. And so all went well till my bundle came opposite the window of Helen Kennedy's room. There it was suddenly caught and gripped tight, so that I could in no wise pull it further. Nevertheless I wrestled with it so strongly, even as I had done with grown men at Maybole, that the cord suddenly gave way. And what with the stress and pith of pulling, I fell *blaff* on my back, hitting my head upon one of the low cross-beams of my little chamberlet.

This made me very angry indeed, but I leave you to judge how much more angered I was, when I found that the cords of my rope ladder had been cleanly severed with a knife, and that my bundle and all it contained had been most foully stolen from me.

I looked out of the window, rubbing my sore head the while with my hand.

'Nell Kennedy!' I called as loudly as I dared, 'you are nothing but a thief, and a mean thief!'

The lass put her head out of the window and looked up at me, so that her hair hung down and I saw the soft lace ruffle of her night apparel. It was long and swayed in the wind, being of a golden yellow colour. (The hair, I am speaking of, not by'r Lady, the bedgown.)

'Mistress Helen Kennedy from you, sirrah, if you please!' she said. 'What may be the business upon which Squire Launce Spurheel ventures to address his master's daughter?'

'Besom!' said I, taking no heed of her tauntings; 'thief, grab-all, give me back my bundle!'

My heart was hot within me, for indeed I had intended to share everything with her in the morning, if only she would be humble enough and come with me into the cove. Now, there is nothing more angering than thus to be baulked on the threshold of a generous action; and, indeed, I was not given to the doing of any other kind— though often enough frustrated of my intention by the illsetness of others.

'Thou wast a noble ghost, Spurheel,' she cried, mocking me. 'I heard thee laughing, brave frightener of girls! Well, I forgive thee, for it is a good bundle of excellent devices that thou hast carried for me all the way from the fair at Maybole. Everything that I craved for is here, saving the brown puggy-monkey wrought with French pastry and with little black raisins for the eyes which I heard of yesterday!'

'I am glad I ate that by the way,' I said, in order to have some amends of her; for, indeed, there was no such thing in the fair, at least so far as I saw.

'May it give thee twisty thraws and sit ill on thy stomach, Spurheel!' she cried up at me. For at sixteen she was more careless of her speech than a herd on the hill when his dogs are not working sweetly.

Nevertheless she spoke as though she had been saying something pleasant and, by its nature, agreeable to hear.

For I do not deny that the lass was sometimes pleasant-spoken enough—to others, not to me; and that upon occasion she could demean herself as became a great lady, which indeed she was. And when no one was by, then I took no ill tongue from her, but gave as good as I got or maybe a kenning better.

I could hear her at the window below taking the packages out of the bundle.

'Ye have good taste in the choice of cakes!' she said, coming to the window again. ' The sweetmeats are most excellent. The pastry melts in the mouth.'

As she looked out, she munched one of the well-raised comfits I had bought for my own eating. At Culzean we had but plain beef and double ale, but no lack of these. Also puddings, black and white.

'See, it flakes tenderly, being well readied!' she cried up at me, flipping it with the forefinger of her right hand to show its delicate lightness. She held the cake, in order to eat it, in the palm of her left hand.

At which, being angered past enduring, I took up an ornament of wood which had fallen from the back of an oak chair, and threw it at her. But she ducked quickly within, so that it went clattering on the rocks beneath.

She looked out again.

'Ah—um—blundershot!' she said, mocking me with her mouth. 'Remember you are shooting at a rantipole cock-shy at Maybole fair.'

'Give me my property,' I replied with some dignity and firmness, 'else in the morning I will surely tell your father.'

'Ay, ay,' cried she, 'even tell him about Maybole fair, and coming home through the wood with your arm round the waist of bonny Kate Allison, the Grieve's lass! He will be most happy to hear of that, and of the other things you have been doing all the night. Also to be thy father confessor and set thee penance for thy deed!'

'It is a lie!' I said, angry that Nell Kennedy should guess so discomfortably near to the truth.

'What is a lie, most sweet and pleasant-spoken youth?' she queried, with a voice like Mistress Pussie's velvet paws.

'The matter you have spoken concerning the Grieve's lass. I care nothing for girls!'

And I spoke the truth—at the moment—for, indeed, there were things bypast that I was now sorry for.

She went in and explored further in my bundle, while I stood at the upper window above and miscalled her over the window sill as loudly as I dared. Every little while she ran to the window to examine something, for the light was now coming broad from the east and flooding the sea even to the far blue mountains of Arran and Cantyre.

'Ribbons—and belts—and hatbands, all broidered with silk!' she cried. 'Was ever such grandeur known in this place of Culzean? They will do bravely for me, and besides they will save thy back from the hangman and the cart-tail whip. For thou, Spurheel, are not of the quality to wear such, but they will do excellently for the pearling and ribboning of a baron's daughter. Nevertheless, heartily do I applaud your taste in taffeta, Spurheel, and let that be a comfort to thee.''

'Was there ever such a wench?' I said to myself, stamping my foot in anger.

Last of all Nell brought to the window the three bottles of Canary wine, for which I had paid so dear.

'What is this?' she cried, with her head at the side in her masterful cock-sparrow way. 'What is this? Wine, wine of Canary—rotten water rather, I warrant, to be sold in a booth at a fair? At any rate, wine is not good for boys,' she added, 'and such drabbled stuff is not for the drinking of a lady—woulds't thou like it, Spurheel?'

She ducked in, thinking that I was about to throw something more at her—which, indeed, I scorned to do, besides having nothing convenient to my hand.

'Look you, Squire Launce,' she said again, crying from the window without setting her head out, 'you are something of a marksman, they say. There never was a nonsuch like our Spurheel—in Spurheel's own estimation. But I can outmark him. Fix your eye on yon black rock with the tide just coming over it—one, two, and three—!'

And in a moment one of my precious broad-bellied bottles of wine played clash on Samson's reef two hundred feet below the White Tower. I was fairly dancing now with anger, and threatened to come down my rope ladder to be even with her. Indeed, I made the cord ready to throw myself out of the window to clamber down. But even as I did so, the glaiked maiden sent the other two jars of Canary to keep company with the first.

Then she leaned out and looked up sweetly, holding the sash of the window meantime in her hand.

'You are going to visit my father in the morning, doubtless, and tell him all about the bundle and the Grieve's lass. Good speed and my blessing!' she cried, making ready to shut the window and draw the bolt. 'I am going to sleep in Marjorie's room. The gulls are beginning to sing. I love not to hear gabble—yours or theirs!'

But I leave you to guess who it was that felt himself the greater gull.

CHAPTER III

THE SECOND TAUNTING OF SPURHEEL

Now I shall ever affirm that there was not in all this realm of Scotland, since the young Queen Mary came out of France —of whom our grandfathers yet make boast, and rise from their chairs with their natural strength unabated as they tell—so lovely a maid as Marjorie Kennedy, the elder of the two remaining daughters of Sir Thomas, the Tutor of Cassillis. Ever since I came to the house of Culzean, I could have lain down gladly and let her walk over me—this even when I was but a boy, and much more when I grew nigh to eighteen, and had all the heart and some of the experience of a man in the things of love.

And how the lairds and knights came a-wooing her! Ay, even belted earls like Glencairn and Eglintoun! But Marjorie gave them no more than the bend of a scornful head or the waft of a white hand, for she had a way with her that moved men's brains to a very fantasy of desire.

For myself, I declare that when she came down and walked in the garden, I became like a little waggling puppy dog, so great was my desire to attract her attention. Yet she spoke to me but seldom, being of a nature as noble as it was reserved. Silent and grave Marjorie Kennedy mostly was, with the lustre of her eyes turned more often on the far sea edges, than on the desirable young men who rode their horses so gallantly over the greensward to the landward gate of Culzean.

But it is not of Marjorie Kennedy, whom with all my heart I worshipped (and do worship, spite of all), that I have at this time most to tell. It happened on this day that, late in the afternoon, Sir Thomas, my master, came out of the chamber where ordinarily he did his business, and commanded me to prepare his arms, and also bid the grooms have the horses ready, for us two only, at seven of the clock.

'That will be just at the darkening,' I said, for I thought it a strange time to be setting forth, when the country was so unsettled with the great feud between the Kennedies of Cassillis and the young Laird of Bargany and his party.

'Just at the darkening,' he made answer, very shortly indeed, as though he would have minded me that the time of departure was no business of mine—which, indeed, it was not.

So I oiled and snapped the pistolets, and saw that the swords moved easily from their sheaths. Thereafter I prepared my own hackbutt and set the match ready in my belt. I was ever particular about my arms and of those of my lord as well, for I prided myself on never having been faulted in the performing of my duty, however much I might slip in other matters that touched not mine honour as a soldier.

Once or twice as I rubbed or caressed the locks with a feather and fine oil thereon I was aware of a lightly-shod foot moving along the passage without. I knew well that it was the lassie Helen, anxious, as I judged, to make up the quarrel; or, perhaps, with yet more evil in her heart, wishful to try my temper worse than before.

Presently she put her head within the door, but I stood with my back to her, busy with my work at the window. I would not so much as look up. Indeed, I cared nothing about the matter one way or the other, for why should a grown man and soldier care about the glaiks and puppet-plays of a lassie of sixteen?

She stayed still by the door a moment, waiting for me to notice her. But I did not, whereat at last she spoke. 'Ye are a great man this day, Spurheel,' she said tauntingly. 'Did ye rowell your leg yestreen to waken ye in time to bring hame the Grieve's lassie?'

I may as well tell the origin now of the name 'Spurheel,' by which at this time she ordinarily called me. It was a nothing, and it is indeed not worth the telling. It chanced that for my own purpose I desired to wake one night at a certain time, and because I was a sound sleeper, I tied a spur to my heel, thinking that with a little touch I should waken as I turned over. But in the night I had a dream. I dreamed that the foul fiend himself was riding me, and I kicked so briskly to dismount him that I rowelled myself most cruelly. Thus I was found in the morning lying all naked, having gashed myself most monstrously with the spur, which has been a cast-up against me with silly people ever since.

Now this is the whole tale why I was called 'Spurheel,' and in it there was no word of the Grieve's daughter— though Kate Allison was a bonny, well-favoured lass too, and that I will maintain in spite of all the gibes of Helen Kennedy.

'I will bring you the spoons and the boots also to clean,' she said, 'and the courtyard wants sweeping!'

In this manner she often spoke to me as if I had been a menial, because when I did my squire's duty with the weapons and the armour, I would not let her so much as touch them, which she much desired to do, for she was by nature as curious about these things as a boy.

So for show and bravery I tried the edge of my own sword on the back of my hand. Nell Kennedy laughed aloud.

'Hairs on the back of a bairn's hand!' quoth she. 'Better try your carving knife instead on the back of a horse's currying comb!'

But I knew when to be silent, and she got no satisfaction out of me. And that was ever the best way of it with her, when I could sufficiently command my temper to follow mine own best counsel.

So the afternoon wore on, and before it was over I had time to go out into the fields, and also towards evening to the tennis-court—where, to recreate myself, I played sundry games with James and Alexander Kennedy, good lads enough, but ever better at that ball play which has no powder behind it.

At the gloaming the horses were ready and accoutred for the expedition. The Tutor of Cassillis and I rode alone, as was his wont—so great was his trust in my courage and discretion, though my years were not many, and (I grant it) the hairs yet few on my chin. It was still March, and the bitter winter we had had seemed scarcely to have blown itself out. So that, although the crows had a week before been carrying sticks for their nesting in the woods of Culzean, yet now, in the quick-coming dark, the snowflakes were again whirling and spreading ere they reached the ground.

As we rode through the courtyard and out at the gate, I heard the soft pit-pat of a foot behind us, for I have a good ear. I heard it even through the clatter of the hoofs of our war horses. So I turned in my saddle, and there behind us was that madcap lass, Nell Kennedy, with her wylicoats kilted and a snowball in her hand, which she manifestly designed to throw at me. But even as I ducked my head the ball flew past me and hit Sir Thomas's horse 'Ailsa' on the rump, making him curvet to the no small discomfort of the rider.

'What was that, think ye, Launcelot?' my master asked in his kindly way.

'It might have been a bat,' I made answer—for it was, at least, no use bringing the lassie into the affair, in spite of what she had done to me that morning. Besides, I could find out ways of paying my debts to her without the telling of tales, and that was always one comfort.

'It is a queer time of year for bats,' answered Sir Thomas, doubtfully. But he rode on and said no more. I kept behind him, ducking my head and appearing to be in terror of another snowball, for the ground was now whitening fast. Nell Kennedy followed after, making her next ball harder by pressing it in her hand. So we went till we came to the far side of the drawbridge and were ready to plunge into the woodlands.

Then I gave the whistle which tells that all is well on the landward side, and is the signal for the bridge to be raised. Gabby Gib-cat heard and obeyed quickly, as he was wont to do when his master was not far away. At other times he was lazy as the hills.

The bridge went grinding up, and therefore the Gib-cat would immediately, as I knew, stretch himself for a sleep by the fire. So there I had Mistress Nell on the landward side of the drawbridge and the gate up, with the snow dancing down on her bare head and her coats kilted for mischief.

I lagged a little behind Sir Thomas, so that I could say Nell, whose spirits were somewhat dashed by the raising of the bridge, 'Step down to the water side and bring up the three bottles of Canary or go over to the farm and keep the Grieve's lass company. She may perchance be lonely.'

So waving my hand and laughing, I rode off and left her alone. I hoped that she cried, for my heart was hot within me because of the good things on which I had expended all my saving, and which I had in all kindliness meant to share with her.

Yet we had not reached the great oak in the park before she was again by my side.

'Think ye I canna gang up the ladder in the White Tower as well as you, Spurheel. It is just kilting my coats a kennin' higher!'

And I could have bitten my fingers off that I had forgotten to pull it in again to my chamber. For in the morning I had mended and dropped it, not knowing when it might be needed.

CHAPTER IV

THE INN ON THE RED MOSS

AND now to tell of sterner business. For light-wit havering with a lass bairn about a great house is but small part of the purpose of my story—though I can take pleasure in that also when it chances to come my way, as indeed becomes a soldier.

We rode on some miles through the woods. It still snowed, and straying flakes disentangled themselves from among the branches and sprinkled us sparsely. It grew eerie as the night closed in, and we heard only the roar of the wind above us, the leafless branches clacking against one another like the bones of dead men.

It was not my place to ask whither we were going, but it may be believed that I was anxious enough to learn. By-and-by we struck into the moorland road which climbs over the Red Moss in the direction of the hill that is called Brown Carrick. The snow darkness settled down, and, but that once I had been friendly with a lass who lived in that direction, and so was accustomed to night travel in these parts, I should scarce have known whither we were going.

But I understood that it could only be to the lonesome Inn of the Red Moss, kept by Black Peter, that Culzean was making his way. As we began to climb the moor, Sir Thomas motioned me with his hand to ride abreast of him, and to make ready my weapons, which I was not loth to do, for I am no nidderling to be afraid of powder. When at last we came to the Inn of the Red Moss, there were lights shining in the windows, and looking out ruddy and lowering under the thatch of the eaves. It was ever an uncanny spot, and so it was more than ever now.

But for all that the Red Moss was populous as a bees' byke that night, for men and horses seemed fairly to swarm about it. Yet there was no jovial crying or greeting between man and man, such as one may hear any market day upon the plainstones of Ayr.

The men who were meeting thus by dark of night, were mostly men of position come together upon a dangerous and unwholesome ploy. As soon as I saw the quality of the

gentlemen who were assembled, I knew that we had come
to a gathering of the heads of the Cassillis faction. Nor
was it long before I saw my lord himself, a tall, well-set
young man, inclining to stoutness and of a fair complexion
with closely-cut flaxen hair.

The Laird of Culzean, my master, lighted down and took
the Earl by the hand, asking in his kindly way,—

'Is it well with you, John?'

For in his minority he had been his tutor and governor,
and in after years had agreed well with him, which is not
so common.

'Ay, well with me,' replied the Earl, 'but it is that
dotard fool, Kelwood, who has gotten the chest of gold
and jewels, which in my father's time was stolen from
the house of Cassillis by Archibald Bannatyne, who was my
father's man. He died in my father's hands, who was not a
cat to draw a straw before. Nevertheless, even in the Black
Vault of Dunure he could not be brought to reveal where he
had hidden the chest. But now Kelwood, or another for
him, has gotten it from Archie's widow, a poor woman that
knew not its worth.'

'But Kelwood will deliver it, John. Is he not your man?
Trouble not any more about the matter,' counselled the
Tutor, who was ever for the milder opinion, and very
notably wise as well as slow in judgment.

'Nay,' said the Earl, 'deliver it he will not, for Bargany
and Auchendrayne have gotten his ear, and he has set his
mansion house in defence against us. I have called you
here, Tutor, for your good advice. Shall we levy our men
and beset Kelwood, or how shall we proceed that I may
recover that which is most justly mine own?'

For it was ever the bitterest draught to the Earl to lose
siller or gear. The Tutor stood for a moment by his beast's
neck, holding his head a little to one side in a way he had
when he was considering anything—a trick which his
daughter Nell has also.

'How many are ye here?' he said to the Earl.

'We are fifteen,' the Earl replied.

'All gentlemen?' again asked the Tutor.

'All cadets of mine own house, and ready to fight to the
death for the blue and gold!' replied the Earl, giving a cock

to the bonnet, in the side of which he had the lilies of France upon a rosette of blue velvet, which (at that time) was the Cassillis badge of war.

As the Earl spoke, I, who stood a little behind with my finger on the cock of my pistol, saw my lord raise a questioning eyebrow at me, as if to ask his uncle who the young squire might be whom he had brought with him.

'He is the son of John Kennedy of Kirrieoch, and with us to the death,' said my master.

For which most just speech I thanked him in my heart.

'The name is a good one,' said the Earl, with a little quaintish smile. And well might he say so, for it was his own, and my father of as good blood as he, albeit of a younger branch.

Presently we were riding forth again, seventeen men in our company, for the Earl had not counted the Tutor and myself in his numeration. We rode clattering and careless over the moors, by unfrequented tracks or no track at all. As we went I could hear them talking ever about the treasure of Kelwood, and, in especial, I heard a strange, daftlike old man, whom they called Sir Thomas Tode, tell of the Black Vault of Dunure, and how lands and gear were gathered by the tortures there. His tales and his manners were so strange and unseemly, that I vowed before long to take an opportunity to hear him more fully. But now there was much else to do.

Betimes we came to the tower of Kelwood and saw only the black mass of it stand up against the sky, with not a peep of light anywhere. Now, as you may judge, we went cannily, and as far as might be we kept over the soft ground. The Tutor bade us cast a compass about the house, so that we might make ourselves masters of the fields, and thus be sure that no enemy was lying there in wait for us. But we encompassed the place and found nothing alive, save some lean swine that ran snorting forth from a shelter where they had thought to pass the night.

Then I and the young Laird of Gremmat, being the best armed and most active there, were sent forward to spy out the securest way of taking the tower. I liked the job well enough, for I never was greatly feared of danger all my days; and at any rate there is small chance of distinction sitting one's horse in the midst of twenty others in an open field.

So Gremmat and I went about the house and about, which was not a castle with towers and trenches, like Dunure or Culzean, but only a petty blockhouse. And I laughed within myself to think of such a bees' byke having the mighty assurance to dream of keeping a treasure against my Lord Cassillis, as well as against the Tutor of that ilk and me, his squire.

There was no drawbridge nor yet so much as a ditch about Kelwood Tower, but only a little yett-house with an open pend or passage, that gave against the main wall of the building. Within this passage, could we gain it, I knew that we should be well protected, and have time to burst in the wall, even if the door withstood us. For once within the archway, I could not see how it was possible for those in the house to reach us, in any way to do us harm.

Gremmat and I therefore went back to our company with the news, but the best of it—the part concerning the yett-house—I kept to myself. For the Laird of Gremmat, though a tough fighter, was not a man of penetration, so that I well deserved the credit of telling what I alone had seen.

When I told the chiefs of my discovery, my Lord of Cassillis said nothing but turned abruptly to the Tutor, thinking nothing of my tidings or of the danger I had been in to bring them. Nevertheless Sir Thomas, my master, turned first to me, as was his kindly custom.

'It is well done of you, Launcelot. The sheep herding on Kirrieoch has given you an eye for other things,' he said.

And at that I think the Earl gave me a little more consideration, though all that he said was no more than, 'Well, Tutor, and what do you advise?'

'I think,' said the Tutor, 'that you and the younger men had best take Launcelot's advice, and conceal yourselves in the pend of the yett-house, with picks and, perhaps, a mickle tree for a battering-ram, while I and a trumpeter lad summon Kelwood himself to surrender. In that clump of trees over there we shall be out of reach of their matchlocks.'

So the Earl took the advice, and in a little we were in the black trough of the pend, with an iron-bolted door in front

and the rough, unhewn stones of the wall on either side
of us.

Then the Tutor's trumpet blew one rousing blast and then
another, till we could hear the stir of men roused out of their
sleep in the tower above us. But we ourselves held our
breaths and keeped very quiet.

Once more the trumpet blew from the clump of oak trees
over against the main gate.

'Who may ye be that blaws horns in the Kelwood without
asking leave of me?' cried a voice from the narrow window
in the wall above us.

And my master, Sir Thomas, answered him from the
coppice,—

'It is I, Kennedy of Culzean, that come from your liege
lord to demand the treasure that is his, stolen from his
house by his false servant and now reset by you, Laird
Currie of Kelwood.'

The Laird laughed contumeliously from his turret
window.

'An' the Earl wants his treasure, let him come and fetch
it,' said he.

At which answer it was all that we could do to keep the
Earl quiet. He was for setting the squared tree to the door
at once.

'Kelwood,' again we heard the voice of Sir Thomas,
'I ken well who has deceived you in this matter. Listen
to no glossing words. No man can strive with the Kennedy
and prosper in all these lands 'twixt Clyde and Solway.'

'Which Kennedy?' cried Kelwood, from his window,
fleeringly. And this set the Earl more bitterly against him
than ever, for it was as much as to say that the Bargany
Kennedies were equal in power and place to his own house
of Cassillis.

'Lift the trees and to it!' he cried, and with that, being
a strong man of his own body, he garred a great fore-
hammer dirl against the iron of the door. And though he
had many faults, this forwardness should be minded to him
for good. Then there was a noise indeed, coulters and fore-
hammers dinging merrily against the door, while from aloft
came shouts and the rolling of heavy stones down about us;
but by my strategy there was not one came near to hurting

us. The defenders might have been so many sparrows
fyling the roof, for all the harm they did to us. But nevertheless, they banged away their powder and shouted. We
that were with the Earl shouted none, but kept dourly to
our work. Stark and strong was the bolted door of Kelwood,
and all the might of our men could do it no injury, nor
so much as shake the hinges. It must have been the work
of a deacon among the hammermen.

But I felt that we were against the wall of the kitchen,
for one side of the passage was warm on my right hand, and
the other clammy and cold. So I cried on them to leave
the door and pull down the stones of the jamb on my
right. Then since I had given them good advice before,
and they knew that I was of the household of the wise man
of Culzean, they were the more ready to take the counsel,
though they thanked me not a word, but only lifted the
tree and drave at it.

'Make first a hole with the crowbars,' said I. 'Pull down
the stones; they are set without lime under the harling.'

So they did it, and we found the first part of the wall
as I had said, not difficult of conquest; but the inner, being
cemented with shell lime, was like adamant. Therefore,
with a shout, we set the tree to it, swinging it in our hands.
After many attempts we sent the butt of it crushing
through, and then, before the enemy could come to the
threatened place, we had made a hole large enough for a
man to enter on his hands and knees. I was leaping
forward to be first within, but Gremmat got in front of
me and crawled through. Whereat the Laird of Kelwood
himself came at him with his gun, and shot Gremmat in
the kernel of the thigh, so that he dropped in a heap on
the floor, and was ever thereafter unable of his legs. But
I that came second (and right glad was I then that I had
not been first) rose and set my point at Kelwood, for he
was tangled up with the reeking musket. I had him
pierced before ever he had time to draw, and was set in
defence for the next that might come, when the Earl and
the other gentlemen came rushing past us both, and completely invaded the place of Kelwood, so that all within it
immediately surrendered.

Then the Earl was like a man gone mad to find the

chest, and questioned the Laird, who, as was somewhat
natural, could do nothing but groan on the floor, with
my sword-thrust through his shoulder. But in a little
they found the box in a cunning wall-press under his bed,
where it could not be reached except by moving the whole
couch from its place and sliding a panel back—which being
done, the secret cavity was made plain.

It had been a harder task to transport young Gremmat
back with us than it was to take the treasure—which was
in a small enough compass, though heavy beyond belief.
But after going a mile or two we left the young wildcap
at the house of a good and safe man, who made himself
bound to the Earl for his safe keeping till he should be
whole of his wound.

CHAPTER V

THE THROWING OF THE BLOODY DAGGER

INDEED it had been no likeable job to deny Cassillis that
night. For with the fighting, the treasure, and the reproaches of Kelwood, whom he could hardly be kept from
finishing with his own hand, his spirit was apt for wars and
stratagems—all the more that he himself had as yet had
little experience of blows or the smart of wounds. Kelwood
we left with those of his dependents that had been in the
tower with him. His wound proved not so serious as it
might have been, and in a month he was safe with the
Laird of Kerse—which thing occasioned a most bitter
quarrel between Cassillis and the Craufords, as indeed hereafter ye shall hear.

It was already greying for the dawn when we reached
the House on the Red Moss. Black Peter was at the door,
and within the kitchen a large fire was blazing, which,
because the night was chill and the sweat of fighting hardly
yet well dried on us, we were right glad to see. We laid
down the chest in a little trance at the back of the kitchen,
setting it upon an oatmeal ark which stood there.

Black Peter went out to hold our horses while we talked
together, and left his daughter, a well-favoured lass of about
my own years or thereby, to wait upon us. So meeting
the lass in the dusk of the trance, on pretext of seeing that

the treasure was safe, I took occasion of a kiss of her—not
that I liked it over much, or that her favours were precious,
but because such like is held a soldier's privilege at an inn,
and no more to be disregarded than the reckoning—indeed,
somewhat less.

But the wench dang me soundly on the ear for it, so that
my head echoed again. Yet I liked her better for that,
because it made the adventure something worth attempting.

'Go,' she cried, 'grow your beard before ye set up to
kiss women. I would as soon kiss the back of my hand as
a man wanting the beard to his face.'

Thus she gave me also the woman's buffet of the tongue,
and I could have answered her, and well, too, but that I saw
behind me my Lord Cassillis himself, and right heartily he
was laughing—which, I do admit, disconcerted me no little,
and brought me to silence.

'Ah, lad,' he said, 'have ye not learned from your experience of this night that women are just like castles? Ye
must reconnoitre them circumspectly before ye can hope to
take them by direct assault.'

He went by, giving me a clap on the shoulder, as one
that had sympathy both with the winning of castles and
of women. And I think he liked me none the worse for
it in the long run. But I hoped that he would not make
a jest of it nor tell the Tutor of the matter. For my master,
Sir Thomas of Culzean, being a grave man and reverend,
was not apt to look upon the follies of youth with so
kindly and comprehending an eye.

Within the kitchen of the Inn of the Red Moss there was
routh of liquor, and all the Cassillis faction were gathered
there, quaffing and pledging one another. They were
flushed with their success, and several were even keen for
assaulting some of the Bargany strongholds at once.

But the Tutor cautioned them.

'Mind what ye do. Young Bargany is as a lion compared to that braying ass we left groaning behind us at
Kelwood; and John Muir of Auchendrayne has at once
the wisest head and the evilest heart in all this broad
Scotland. Be patient and abide. We have gotten the
treasure. Let us be content and wait.'

'Ay, and by waiting give them the next score in the

game!' said the young Earl, scornfully—for he, too, was hot
with success.

So they stood about the kitchen with drinking-cups of
horn in their hands, while the Earl unfolded a plan of the
great house of Bargany, and began to explain how it
might be taken.

'But,' he said, 'we must wait till, by some overt and considered act of war, Bargany gives me the chance to execute
justice with my Balliary of Carrick, as is my legal right.
Then swiftly we shall strike, before that Bargany can reach
us with the sword, or John Muir of Auchendrayne foil us
by getting at the King with his fox's cunning.'

Hardly were the words out of his mouth when a silence
fell upon us. The Earl ceased speaking and inclined his
head as though, like the rest of us, he were harkening eagerly
for the repeating of a sound.

Then we who listened with him heard something that
was like the clattering of horses' feet at a gallop, which
came nearer and nearer. There arose a cry from the front
of the house—that wild, shrill scream, the unmistakable
parting cry of a man stricken to death with steel. Then
broke forth about the Inn of the Red Moss, the rush of
many horses snorting with fear and fleeing every way,
the while we, that were in the house, stood as it had been
carved in stone, so swift and unexpected was this thing.

The Earl remained by the table in the centre, with his
hand yet on the plan of the house of his enemy. Sir
Thomas was still bending down to look, when all suddenly
the glass of the window crashed and a missile came flashing through, thrown by a strong man's hand. It fell with
a ring of iron across the paper that was outspread on the
table. It was a dagger heavily hilted with silver. But
what thrilled us all with fear was, that the blade of it was
red nearly to the hilt, and distilled fresh-dripping blood
upon the chart.

Then was heard from without something that sounded like
a man laughing—but as of a man that had been long time
in hell—and again there came the galloping of a single
horse's feet.

The first in all in the house to run to the door was no
other than the young lass I had tried to kiss. She flung

the door open and ran to a dark, huddled thing, which lay across the paving stones of the little causeway in front of the inn.

'My father—oh, they have slain my father!' she cried. We that were within also rushed out by the front door, forgetting all else, and filled with dread of what we might see.

The dawn was coming red from the east, and there, in the first flush of it, lay Black Peter, plain to be seen, a dark tide sluggishly welling from his side, and his young daughter trying pitifully to staunch it with the bit of laced napkin wherewith she had bound her hair to make her pleasant in the men's eyes.

When Peter of the Red Moss saw the Earl, he tried to raise himself upon his elbow from the ground. One feeble hand went waveringly to his head as if to remove his bonnet in the presence of his chief.

Cassillis sank on his knees beside him and took the hand. There was a fragment of a leather rein still clasped in it, cut across with a clean, slicing cut.

'Peter, Peter, poor man, who has done this to you?' he asked.

The man that was about to die turned his eyes this way and that.

'My lord, my lord,' he said, struggling with the choking blood that rose in his throat, 'it was—it was—the grey man—!'

And the Earl listened for more with his ear down to Peter's mouth, but the spirit of the man who had died for his master ebbed dumbly away without another word. So there was nothing left for us to do but to carry him in, and this we did in the young sunshine of a pleasant morning. And the maid washed and streeked him, moaning and crooning over him piteously, as a dove does that wanteth company.

I went, as it happed, into the trance to fetch her a basin of clear water. The top of the meal-ark stood empty!

'My lord—the chest!' I cried, and all save the maid alone rushed in. The treasure of Kelwood was gone! Without the door, on the trampled clay and mud, there

were the steads of naked feet many and small. But of
the treasure-chest for which we had ventured so much
that night, we saw neither hilt nor hair, clasp nor band.

Only in the kitchen of the house on the Red Moss there
was a dead man, and a maid mourning over him; on
the table a dagger, red to the guard, and from it fell slowly
the drip of a man's life blood, blotting out with a bitter
scorn the plans of our wisest and the enmity of our proudest.

CHAPTER VI

THE CROWN OF THE CAUSEWAY

I RODE forth from Edinburgh town with infinite glee and
assurance of spirit. No longer could I be slighted as a boy,
for that day I, even I, Launcelot Kennedy, had been put to
the horn—that is, I had been proclaimed rebel and outlaw
at the Cross of Edinburgh with three blasts of the king's
horn, 'Against John, Earl of Cassillis, Sir Thomas of
Culzean, called the Tutor of Cassillis, and Launcelot
Kennedy, his esquire!' So had run the proclamation.
I wondered what that unkempt, ill-tongued lassie, Nell
Kennedy, would say to this. But the honour itself even
she could not gainsay.

It is true that there were others forfaulted as well as I—
the Earl himself that was a sitter in the King's council
board, Sir Thomas, my master, and, indeed, all that had
any hand in the great contest in the High Street of
Edinburgh. How close had every leal burgess kept within
doors that day and how briskly screamed for the watch!
How the town guards sequestered themselves safe behind
bars, and were very quiet, for there was hardly a man to
be seen from the castle to Holyrood-House that was not a
Kennedy, and trying to kill some other Kennedy—as indeed
is ever the way with our name and clan.

We of Cassillis had ridden hot foot to Edinburgh to
denounce the Bargany faction to the king, in the matter of
the treasure and the killing of Black Peter. Not that we
knew for certain that it was Bargany who had any hand in
the murder and reiving. But it was necessary to make a
bold face for it, and, at all events, we knew that the thing
had been done in Bargany's interests. So we went, all

prepared to declare that the active criminal was Bargany's brother, Thomas of Drummurchie, a bold and desperate villain, who had been outlawed for years for many a crime besides murder in all its degrees. Also we hoped that if the king were in a good humour towards us of Cassillis, who were always the men of loyalty and peace, he might even attaint Bargany himself. So that our Earl, being the Bailzie or chief ruler of Carrick under the King, might get his will of his house foe, and thus put an end to the quarrel. For there was no other hope of peace, save that our enemies should be laid waste.

But we found King James in aught but a yielding mood. The ministers of Edinburgh, and in especial one, Mr. Robert Bruce, a man of very great note, and once a prime favourite with the king, had been setting themselves against his will. So at first we got little satisfaction, and it did not help matters that, on the second day of our visit, the Bargany Kennedies and Mures rode into the town in force—all sturdy men from the landward parts of Carrick, while we were mostly slighter and limberer lads, from the side of it that looks towards the sea.

The next day, as I went down the Canongate with the gold lilies of Cassillis on my cocked bonnet, I declare that nearly every third man I met was a Bargany lout, swaggering with his silly favour of red and white in his cap. But, for all that, I ruffled it right bravely in despite of them all, letting no man cock his feather at me. For I had a way, which I found exceedingly irritating to them, of turning the skirt of my blue French cloak over my shoulder when I met one of the other faction, as if I feared defilement from the contact of their very garments. This I did with all of the underlings—aye, even with Mure of Cloncaird. Indeed, I had already had my long sword three times out of its sheath by the time I got to the guard-house at Holyrood.

It was just there that I met young Bargany himself, coming direct from the King's presence. But I practised my pleasantry not with him. For a more kingly-looking man did I never see—far beyond our Earl (shame be to me for saying such a thing!), and, indeed, before any man that ever I saw. But Gilbert Kennedy of Bargany was the bravest man that was to be gotten in any land, as all men that saw him in his flower do to this day admit. And hearts were like water before him.

He was of his stature tall and well-made, with a complexion black but comely, noble on horseback, and a master both of arms and at all pastimes. And when I beheld him, it came upon me to salute him—which, though I had small intention thereof till I saw him, I did. It was with some surprise, perceiving, no doubt, the Earl's colours, that he returned my greeting, and that very graciously. The moment after I looked about me, and right glad I was to observe that none of our folk had been in the place before the palace to observe my salutation.

After this we of Cassillis went in parties of three or four, and our swords were in our hands all the day, in spite of the watch—ay, in spite even of the King's Guard, which His Majesty had sent to keep the peace, when he himself had gone off to Linlithgow in the sulks, as at this time was oft his silly wont.

For me, I went chiefly with Sir Thomas, my master, as was my duty; but being allowed to choose my companion, I chose Muckle Hugh from Kirriemore, which marches with mine own home of Kirrieoch on Minnochside. Hugh was the strongest man in all Carrick, and had joined the command chiefly for the love of me—because he had once herded sheep for us, and my mother had been kind to him and given him new milk instead of skim for his porridge.

And I warrant you when the two of us took the crown of the causeway, we stepped aside for no man, not even for Bargany and his brother Drummurchie had we seen them (which by good luck we never did). But others we saw in plenty. It was 'Bargany thieves!' 'Cassillis cairds!' as we cried one to the other across the street. And the next moment there we were, ruffling and strutting like gamecocks, foot-to-foot in the midst of the causeway, neither willing to give way. Then 'Give them iron!' would be the cry; and in a clapping of hands there would be as pretty a fight as one might wish to see—till, behold, in a gliff, there on the cobble stones was a man stretched, and all workmanly completed from beginning to end, while the clock of St. Giles' was jangling the hour of noon.

For the matter of the killing of Black Peter, and the way
that lassie his daughter held his head as she washed him,
abode with us, and made our hearts hot against the Barganies. That is, the hearts of the younger of us. For I wot
well that the elders thought more of the lost box of treasure,
than of many men's lives far more famous and necessary
than that of poor Black Peter, who died in his duty at the
house door of the Red Moss—and that is not at all an ill
death to die.

But there came a day when the ill blood drew to a head.
It was bound to come, because for weeks the two factions of
us Kennedies had been itching to fly at each other's throats.
The Barganies mostly lodged together in the lower parts of
the town beneath the Nether Bow, in order to keep us
away from the King when he was at Holyrood House,
and also to be near the haunts of those loose characters
of the baser sort with whom, as was natural, they chiefly
consorted.

We, on our part, dwelled in the upper portion of the town,
in the well-aired Lawnmarket and in the fashionable closes
about the Bow-head. For none of us, so far as I knew,
desired to mix or to mell with loose company—save, an'
it might be, the Earl himself. That being 'the custom
and privilege of the nobility,' as Morton said to his leman,
when he wished to change her for another.

Now, we had among us of our company one Patrick
Wishart, an indweller in Irvine and a good fighter. He was
an Edinburgh man born, and knew all the town—every
lane and street, every bend and bow, every close and pend
and turning in it. He also knew that which was even more
valuable, where the King's Guard were, and how to shut
them up till we had done our needs upon our foes. He was
well advised besides where each of the leaders among the
Barganies dwelt.

On the day appointed the Earl gave us all a meeting-
place by the back of Saint Giles' High Kirk, beneath the wall
of the Tolbooth. And there we mustered at ten of the
clock one gay morning. It was a windy day, and, spite of
the sun, the airs blew shrewdly from the eastern sea, as is
their use and wont all the year in the High Street of
Edinburgh.

Now our young Earl had ever plenty of siller though afterward he parted with it but seldom. Yet for the further-ance of his cause he had spent it lavishly during these days in Edinburgh, so that all the common orders in our upper part of the town held him to be the greatest man and the best that ever lived. And as for the vices he showed, they were easy, popular ones, such as common folk readily excuse and even approve in the great—as women, wine, and such-like.

So as we swung down the street all the windows of the armourers' shops in the booths about the Kirk of Saint Giles' were opened, and as many as desired it were supplied with spears and pikes and long-handled Highland axes, each with a grappling hook at the back, such-like as had brought many a good knight down at the Red Harlaw.

And these were afterwards a great advantage to us, for though we were much fewer in numbers, yet we had longer weapons of assault and also the upper side of the street to fight from.

Then we sallied forth crying, 'A Kennedy!' And the streets were lined to see us go by, many a douce burgher's wife, knowing our good intentions and our not companying with the riotous troublers of the town, but rather, when we could compass it, with honest, sonsy women, giving us her blessing from an upper window.

Patrick Wishart advised that we should stop up all the alleys and closes as far down as the Blackfriar's Wynd with barracadoes of carts, barrels, and puncheons, to prevent the enemy sallying forth upon us from behind. It was a good thought, and but for a foe without, whom we knew not how to reckon with, it had been completely successful. Down by the Nether Bow, where the street narrows, was the place where we first saw the misleared Bargany faction drawn across the street to resist us and contemn the King's authority.

When we observed them we gave a mighty shout and heaved our weapons into the air, that they might see the excellence of our arming. They sent a shout back again, and I saw in front of their array Bargany himself with a casque on his head, the sun glinting the while on a steel

cuirass which covered him back and front. Then I gave
the word to blow up the matches; for by this time I was well
kenned for a good soldier and proper marksman, and had by
my lord himself been put over the hackbuttmen, which was
a great honour for one so young. Thus we advanced to
the onset. But first my Lord of Cassillis, going to the front,
cried to Kennedy of Bargany to know why he withstood
him in the highway of the King's principal town.

'Because ye have lied concerning me to the King. Because ye have slain my men, hated my race, and sought to
bring me to my death!' answered back young Bargany in
a clear, high voice.

'Ye lie, man! Have at you with the sword!' cried
our Earl, who was never a great man with his tongue,
though sometimes masterful enough with his hands.

So with that I gave the order, and our hackbuttmen shot
off their pieces, so that more than one of the wearers of the
red and white fell headlong.

'A Kennedy! A Kennedy!' cried the Earl. 'To it,
my lads!'

And in a moment we were on them. By instinct we
had dropped our matchlocks and taken to the steel, so that
the first thing that I knew, I was at Thomas of Drummurchie's throat with my borrowed pike. He roared an
oath, and leaping to the side, he struck the shaft with his
two-handed sword, which shore the point off near to my
upper grip. And there is little doubt but that I had been
spent ere I could have drawn my sword, had not Muckle
Hugh of Kirriemore brought his broadsword down upon
the steel cap of the Wolf of Drummurchie, so that with the
mighty blow he was beaten to the ground, and, being
senseless, men trampled upon him as the battle swayed to
and fro. Yet I have never forgotten that, but for Hugh,
I was that day almost sped, which should have been a
lesson to me not to trust to a weapon of which I had no
skill, even though it might be an ell longer in the haft
than my sword. Also I was thankful to God.

'A Kennedy! a Kennedy!' cried we. 'We are driving
them. They give back!'

For we felt the downward push upon the hillslope, and
that gave us courage.

And the crying of 'Bargany' was almost silenced, for now the wearers of the butcher's colours had enough to do to keep steeks with us, with their faces braced to the brae, and so needed all their breath.

By this time I had my arm cleared and my sword out, and, certes, but the fray was brisk. Now, when it is hand to hand I fear no man. Once I had a chance of paying my score in the matter of Drummurchie, for as I passed over him he cut upwards at me with a knife. But I spared only long enough from the man I was engaging at the time (who indeed was no swordsman or I dared not have done it) to slash the Wolf across the wrist, which, I am given to believe, has troubled his sword-hand all his life—and for no more than this he has borne me a grudge unto this day, so malicious and revengeful are some men.

Thus we drove the Bargany faction into the Canongate in spite of the swordsmanship of their chief, who fought ever in the forefront. It was, indeed, all over with them, when suddenly, from behind us, there came rushing a rabblement of men with weapons in their hands, all crying 'Bargany!' Able-bodied scoundrels with long hair and pallid faces they were, and they laid about them with desperate vigour. Now, it is no wonder that this was a terrible surprise to us, and, hearing their cry, the broken Bargany folk down the streets and closes took heart of grace to have at us again. We were not discouraged, but part of us faced about, so as to fight with our backs set one to the other. Nevertheless, I saw at once that unless some help came we were overpowered.

'Into the lanes!' I cried, though, indeed, I had no right to give an order, but, in the pinch of necessity, it is he who sees that should lead.

So into one of the narrow lanes which led to the ford and down by the stepping-stones across the Nor' Loch we ran, but not in the way of a rout. Rather we retreated orderly and slow—withdrawing, grieved at heart to think that we had to leave so many of our sick and wounded behind us. Yet, because of the love they bore us as peaceable men, we knew that the town's dames would succour them—also lest we should be bloodily revenged on their husbands when we came back, if they did not.

At the edge of the Nor' Loch, six or seven of us made
a rally, and having wounded and captured one of the long-
haired desperadoes whose assault had turned the tables
against Cassillis, we brought him with us, thinking that my
Lord might wish to question him with the pilniewinks.

Now not many of the Bargany faction pursued; some
because they knew not whither we were gone, some because
both their chief and the Wolf of Drummurchie were
hurt, and others again because the rabble which had fallen
on our rear, not knowing one party from another, had
turned their weapons upon their friends.

Nevertheless, it was a patent fact that we good men of
Cassillis had been baffled and put to shame by the thieves of
Bargany in the open High Street of Edinburgh. It has
not happened to many to be victorious and pursuing, and
again broken and defeated, all within the space of half-
an-hour.

When we were safe from pursuit on the other side of
the Nor' Loch, we questioned the varlet whom I and others
had captured, as to what was his quarrel against us.

'Nothing,' he said. 'I and the others were lying in
the Tolbooth, when suddenly the gates were opened, and
there stood one at the door, clad in grey, who gave a sword
or a pike to each man, as well as a piece of gold, telling us
that there were other ten of the same awaiting each good
striker who should fall on and fight those whom he would
show us.'

'What like was this man?' said Sir Thomas, my master.

'An ordinary man enough,' said the fellow; 'grey of
head and also clad in grey, but with armour that rattled
beneath his clothes.'

Then we looked at one another, and remembered the
dying words of Black Peter—'It was—it was—the Grey
Man—!'

Once more such a man had crossed the luck of Cassillis.
By what golden key he had bribed the warders and opened
His Majesty's Tolbooth, we knew not; but assuredly he
had clean beaten us from the field.

Nevertheless, I was much cheered to hear on the next
day that the name of Launcelot Kennedy, called 'of
Kirrieoch, or Launcelot of the Spurs,' was among those

that were 'put to the horn,' or in plain words declared rebel and outlaw at the Cross of Edinburgh.

For I knew that Nell Kennedy would never flout me more. Even fair Marjorie would, perhaps, not disdain speech with me now, and might perchance let me walk by her side in the garden some summer evening.

CHAPTER VII

MY LADY'S FAVOURS

IT was as I had foretold. Those that had flouted me for a beardless boy, now scorned me no more. I mean chiefly Nell Kennedy. Indeed, for some days it was as much as I would do even to speak to her. She would make shift oftentimes to pass me in the pleasaunces of the house of Culzean, when I walked abroad in the sunshine with my hand on my sword—as was my duty—to receive her father's guests. For there was a great repair of people to our castle ever since the outlawing, the cause of which was considered most fortunate and honourable to all concerned.

Nell Kennedy, as I say, would often pass me in the orchard or in the Italian garden, which her father had made with great expense. And as she went by, she would kick with her foot a stone in front of me. But of this I took no heed whatever, no more than if I had not seen it. Because, for my own part, I was resolved never to think of maids and such light matters again, but rather to concern myself solely with glory, as became one who at eighteen had been out-lawed for rebellion and other deeds of military prowess.

Once it happened that we were all in the garden—Marjorie, the loons James and Alexander Kennedy, and little David, Sir Thomas's youngest son. Also Nell Kennedy was there. Sir Thomas himself was walking to and fro at the garden's end, all by his lone, with his hands clasped behind his back, as was his custom.

Then Nell, who, being angry, desired above all else to put a slight upon me, called me to come to her, speaking roughly as though I had been a servitor, and bade me take a misbehaving puppy dog of hers within doors.

But I was equal with her, and beckoned to me Sandy, her brother, who played about on the grass plots.

'Who may this little girl be that hath the messan dog with her?' I asked of him.

'Thou art a great blind colt-head not to know my sister Nell!' he answered, and ran again to his play with his brothers.

'Ah,' said I, looking over the heads of those that stood near by, 'now I do remember to have seen the little maid playing with her dolls before I went to the wars!'

And with that I marched off, and walked to and fro on the terrace near to my master. Presently he came and walked with me, as I had hoped he would, in sight of Nell and of them all, speaking low and kindly the while. And I listened as though it were an affair of State and policy he had been confiding to my private ear, though indeed it was only concerning our greatly increased expenses with the vast number of guests who came to see him, and his fear that the buttery might be running low.

When Nell Kennedy had betaken herself away in an access of anger and despite, I made my bow to Sir Thomas, her father, and went to the Italian pleasaunce once again. Presently the young Lady Marjorie came walking by, fairer of face than the flower of the hawthorn hedge on a moonlight night, but with hair tossed about her temples blacker than the sky on a night of stars. Her eyes were bright and large when she turned them on me.

'Launcelot, come and walk with me awhile,' she said kindly, 'unless you have something better to do—with your arms and war gear as it may be,' she added. And her way of speaking thus of my calling as a soldier pleased me. Also in spite of my renunciation of all pleasure in women's society, my heart gave a great stound at her marked favour. Perhaps, also, at the way she had in walking, which was with her head high and her bosom set well forward in its open work bodice of fair linen, and all her sweet body swaying lightly to the side as a willow wand that bends in the wind.

Her voice, the voice of Marjorie Kennedy, sounded like the running of deep water in a linn under the dusk of trees, with undercurrents of sobs and pitifulness in it, for all that it was so proud. For even thus, in her youth, walking as the fairest maid the sun shone on, Marjorie seemed ever to be 'fey,' trysted to some lot beyond that of maids who are to be good men's wives and mothers.

But enough of speaking about her. Better that I should tell what she said to me as we walked up and down, while the young buds were cracking open that gracious May gloaming.

'It was a good fight, I hear, and well fought,' she said.

'Which fight may it please you to speak of, my Lady Marjorie?' said I, making as though I had been in many.

'The battle in the High Street of Edinburgh,' she made answer, and methought smiled as she said it. But there was no bairnly scorn or raw coltish ignorance in Marjorie's smile, as there mostly was in the face of her sister—who was nothing but a child at any rate, and still wore her hair without a snood, flying daft-like about her shoulders.

Then I told Marjorie Kennedy of all the fight, and she listened with face turned away from me to the sea, looking to the the hills of Arran that were so blue in the distance, so that for a space I thought she hearkened not to what I said.

But in a little she interrupted me. 'And you speak thus with admiration of Gilbert Kennedy of Bargany, he that is an enemy to our house and name! How say ye then that such an one is noble and worthy?'

For I had been telling her of meeting him coming from the king's palace.

'Ay, noble and generous is Gilbert Kennedy of Bargany, as well as the handsomest man that walks, with a spring to his feet as one that goes upon the deep twigs of the pine trees in the woods. He can twirl a lance in one hand on horseback—for I myself have seen him—never was there such a man!'

For I had given him all my heart and admiration, being then young—or at least not very old in years—and I wished with all my strength that such an one had been chief of our side and Earl of Cassillis, instead of he that was. Though my lord is a good man also, and I deny it not.

Then it was that my Lady Marjorie showed me the greatest favour that ever she showed to any man, and caused my heart to beat high with love and hope. For she took my hand in hers, holding it to her side as she walked—ay, and

stroked and touched it gently with her other hand as we
went along, being hidden by the screen of the leaves in
the pleasaunce hedges. Now this was so sweet to me and
precious, that I slept with my right hand in a glove of silk
for many days—ay, and even forbore to wash it. For I
bethought me that though, as a man of war, I had for-
sworn the society of silly girls, yet every true knight had a
lady for his heart's mistress, whose colours he might wear
in his helmet, and whose lightest word he might treasure
in his heart.

Thus we two walked and talked, while the sun was
going down and the colours of a dove's breast crept over
the water from the west.

'And this Gilbert of Bargany—tell me of him—for,
being the great enemy of our house, I desire to hear more
of him,' she said.

So I told her, being nothing loth to speak of so brave
an enemy.

'Was he at all hurt in the combat, think you?' she
asked again, carelessly, as one that thinks of other things.

'Wounded? No,' I replied, with a laugh; 'on the
contrary, he pursued us down to the ford of the Nor' Loch,
and defied us all to come back and have it out. But I
think that not he but another, had a hand in the craven's
trick of letting loose on us the offscourings of the prisons—
Highland catherans and Border hedgethieves.'

'And who might that other be?' she asked.

'That,' I replied, with dignity, 'I am not at liberty to
tell. It is yet a secret under trust.'

'Tell it me,' she said, bending her eyes on me, that
were beautiful as I know not what.

And this, indeed, I should very gladly have done at that
moment, but truly I knew nothing of the matter. So I
made haste to answer that I would readily die for her, but
that it was a soldier's duty that he should keep the secrets
with which his honour had been entrusted.

'Then tell me what you can,' she said, so quietly that I
was ashamed of my subterfuge. Though that is the way
that all wise men must talk to women, so as to keep the
peace, telling them (mostly) the truth, but seldom the
whole truth.

'It was,' said I, 'the Grey Man!'

'Ah,' she replied, quickly drawing away her hand, and laying it upon her heart, 'the Grey Man!'

'What ken ye of the Grey Man?' I asked her, in surprise.

'Nothing,' she said, giving me back her hand; 'I know not why, but for the moment something came upon me, and I felt as it had been a little faint. It is nothing. It has already passed.'

Then I wished to bring her a cup of wine from the house. But she laughed more merrily than ever I had heard her, and tossed back the lace kerchief which confined her hair, so that it lay about her white neck with the ends dropping over her bosom.

'Let us two walk here yet a space, Launcelot,' she said, 'for it is lonely within the great house.'

A saying which made my heart swell with gladness and pride, for she had never thus distinguished any man before, so that I forgot all about my vows and about forswearing to company with women. But this was indeed very different.

'My Lady Marjorie,' I said (I much desired to say 'My sweet lady' as they do in the stage plays, but dared not), 'My Lady Marjorie,' I said, 'I, even I, will be your true knight, and fight for you against all, if so be that coming home I may see the pleasure in your eyes.'

'Ah, will you truly?' she asked, and sighed. Then she was silent for a moment but drew not away her hand, which I took of be a good omen.

'No, you must not—you must not. It would not be fair!' she said.

'I love you with all my heart!' I whispered, trying to reach her hand; but somehow, though it was very near, I could not again take it in mine.

She seemed not to hear me speak.

'Well,' she said at last, as if to herself, 'perhaps it will be good for the lad.'

I could not conceive what she meant.

'Launcelot,' she continued, and her voice had music in it such as I never heard in any kirk or quire, at matins or at laud,—'Launcelot, do not think of me, I pray you—at least, not if you can help it—'

'Help it I cannot,' answered I; 'it is far beyond that!'
And so I thought at the time.

'But, Launcelot, my sweet squire,' she said again, 'hast
thou already forgotten thy vow? It is better for thee to be
a squire of arms than a squire of dames! At least,' she
added, smiling, 'till you win your spurs.'

'I will win them for your sake, an you will let me,
Marjorie!' I cried.

'Win them, then, Launcelot,' she made me answer,
suddenly breaking from her reserve, 'win them for my sake
—and see, meantime you shall wear my colours.'

And she undid a brooch of gold whereon were the lilies
of France, that were the badge of her house, and setting it
on the velvet collar of my coat she gave a little dainty pat
to the place where she put it.

'It sets you well,' she said, pushing my hair to one side
to look at me; 'two such I have. Wear you one and I shall
wear the other—for Marjorie Kennedy and the honour of
Culzean.'

It sounded like a sacred oath rather than the posy of
a love-gift: '*For Marjorie Kennedy and the honour of
Culzean!*'

Then most humbly would I have lifted her fingers to
my lips and kissed them, not daring more; but she put
her hand on my head, for she was tall (though not as tall
as I), and bent sweetly to me.

The blood of all my heart fled insurgent to my ears,
deafening me, as I also stooped toward her.

'No, not there,' she whispered, and kissed me gently
on the brow.

'My laddie,' she said, 'be brave, true, noble, and one day
you shall know root and branch what the love of woman is.'

And waving me not to follow her, she went in with her
head turned away from my sight.

So there for a great space I stood in the dusk of the
arbour, mazed and bewildered by the strange, undreamed-of
bliss—ennobled by the touch of her lips, ay, more than if
the King himself had laid his sword on my shoulder in the
way of accolade.

Then at last I moved and went in also, dragging tardy-
foot away from the sweet and memorable place.

At the garden gate I met Nell Kennedy, and made to pass without seeing her. But she stood in the middle of the way.

'I know,' she said, pointing scornfully with her finger, 'Maidie has been talking to you behind the hedge. She has given you the French brooch she would not give me yesterday, though she has another.'

Then I walked silently past her, with as great dignity as I could command, for that is ever the best way with forward children.

But she turned and cried after me, 'I know who will get that other.'

A saying which did not trouble me, though I could not quite forget it, for I knew well enough that it was only Nell's spite, because her sister had not given her the golden badge which she coveted.

High in my room in the White Tower I sat and looked out to the sea. There I sat all night, sleepless, till the sun rose over the woods and the chilly tops of the waves glittered. I bethought me on all that had happened, and I remembered with shame many things in which I had done not wisely—especially in the matter of the Grieve's lass, and my convoying of her home through the wood. For now, with Marjorie Kennedy's badge against my lips, all things had become new; bitterly was I ashamed of my folly, and right briskly did I repent of it.

CHAPTER VIII

THE LAIRD OF AUCHENDRAYNE

IT is not to be supposed that the taking of the treasure of Kelwood was permitted to pass without the Earl, a man keener for red siller than any other man in Scotland, casting about him for the reivers of the gear he had so confidently counted his own. His old grandmother of a Countess, whom, though a young man, he had shamefully married for her tocher and plenishing, flustered about the house of Cassillis like a hen dancing on a hot girdle when she heard of the loss. It was but the other day that she had had to draw her stocking-foot and pay down eight thousand merks, that her man might be permitted to resign the office of High

Treasurer, lest all her gear would be wasted in making loans to the King, who had great need of such. And so the further loss of this treasure sat wondrously heavy on my Lady Cassillis, as indeed it did on her husband.

The Earl himself rode over to Culzean to hold council concerning it with his uncle, the Tutor. He cherished a wonderful affection for Sir Thomas, considering, that is, what a selfish man he was, and how bound up in his own interests.

So after they had talked together a while, pacing up and down in the garden (while I walked apart and pressed the hard brooch-pin of Marjorie Kennedy's trysting favour to my breast for comfort), they called me to them.

So with all respect and speed I went, and stood with my bonnet off to hear their commands. I thought that it was some light matter of having the horses brought. But when I came the Earl was looking keenly at me, and even Sir Thomas paused a little while before he spoke.

'Launcelot, you are a brave lad,' he said, 'and I know that you desire to distinguish yourself even more than you have done, though you have shown your mettle already. Now my lord and I have a matter which it needs a man to perform—one of address and daring. I hear from all about me that you are a ready man with your wits and your tongue. Will you bear my lord's cartel of defiance to his enemy, David Crauford of Kerse?'

'Ay, my lords, that will I, and readily!' I replied, knowing that my good fortune stood on tiptoe.

'I am not eager,' the Earl said, breaking in upon my reply, 'for reasons which I have given to the Tutor, to send one of my own folk. I would rather accredit one more kin to Culzean here, one who is a gentleman of good blood and a brave Kennedy, such as I observed you to be on the day of the tulzie in Edinburgh.'

'I will serve Cassillis till I die,' I replied, making him a little bow—because I wished him to see that, though I was of the moorland house, I had yet manners as good as he had brought back with him from France. Besides, I saw Marjorie looking down upon us from the terrace, which made me glance at my shadow as it lay clearly outlined upon the gravel.

And I was glad to observe that the point of my cloak fell with some grace over the scabbard of my sword. Now this was not vanity, God knows, but only a just desire to appear point device in the presence of the heads of my clan and of the lady of my heart—which is a thing very different. For all things I am not vain, nor given, after the manner of some, to talking greatly about my own exploits.

'So,' said the Earl, 'you will go to David Crauford of Kerse at his own house as my messenger. You will not give him a written but a spoken message. And in token that you come from us who have power to speak, you must exhibit to him our signet rings, which we now entrust to you to guard with your life.'

So, giving me the rings, which I put under my glove upon the first finger of the left hand, he communicated to me the cartel for the Laird of Kerse, which he made me repeat carefully thrice over in their hearing. Then he dismissed me to go my way.

And as I went, I saw the lads roistering in the garden with the young Sheriff of Wigton, who had married their eldest sister when she was but a lassie. And I smiled as I thought within me, 'Had I been so born to lofty estate, I might even have been playing at golf and pat-ball, instead of riding on the errands of Cassillis and Culzean, with an Earl's message in my mouth and an Earl's signet on my finger.'

And I do not think that the pride was an unworthy one, for since I had none to push my fortune for me, it was the more necessary that I should be able to do it for myself.

I went to get my war-horse, for after the affair of Edinburgh, Sir Thomas had given me 'Dom Nicholas,' a black of mettle and power, well able to carry me even had I been clad in full armour, instead of merely riding light as I now meant to go, with only my sword and pistolets.

At the seaward corner of the White Tower, going by the way of the stables, I met my Lady Marjorie, and my heart gave a bound at the seeing of her. She came gravely forward to give me her hand. Yet not to kiss, as I knew by the downward weighting of it, and by her taking it quickly again to herself.

'Whither go you, grave man of affairs?' she said, smiling with pleasantry.

'I go with an Earl's cartel and defiance,' I replied, telling her, perhaps, more than I ought. But then she was my lady.

Marjorie became very pale and set her hand on the stone parapet of the sea wall where she stood.

'To Bargany?' she asked, breathlessly, for it was natural she should think that the quarrel with the family had broken out again.

'Not to Bargany,' I said, smiling to reassure her. 'I cannot now tell you where, but it is out of Carrick that I ride—Carrick for a man—Kyle for a cow. I ride to the land of sweet milk cheese!'

'God speed you, then,' she said. 'Take care of yourself —beware of the dairymaids. I have heard they are dangerous.'

'For your sweet sake,' cried I, waving my bonnet to her as I ran down the path.

But before I went fairly out of sight I turned and looked back, for, indeed, I could not help it. And Marjorie was still standing under the archway where I had left her, but with so sad and lost a countenance that I had run back to ask her what was her grief. Then she seemed to awake, kissed the tips of her fingers to me, and turning her about, walked slowly within.

When I was fully arrayed, I rode past the front of the house on pretext of knowing if my lords had any further commands for me, but really that the maids might see me upon Dom Nicholas in his fair caparison of beaten silver. She whom I wished most to see I saw not indeed; but there at the great gate, with a foolish spraying branch of hawthorn in her hair, was Nell Kennedy, of whom during these last days I had scarcely so much as thought.

And with her, to my burning shame and amaze, was Kate Allison, the Grieve's daughter. The two girls stood with their arms about one another's waists, as maids that are yet half bairns are wont to do. But neither of them looked at me. Only when I made Dom Nicholas caracole by, they turned disdainfully aside as though they were avoiding the path of some poisonous toad or asp. And so, wholly without word, they passed down one of the leafy avenues that beset the place of Culzean, which thing in a moment rendered all my full, sweet cup empty and bitter.

At this I was much dashed and crestfallen, so that I had no spirit in me. For I was sure, by the attitude of the maids, and their demeanour to me, that they had gotten to the stage of the confiding of secrets. And if that were so, I had a good guess that it would be as well for me to avoid the Grieve's house by the shore for some time to come. Which thing, indeed, last evening's tryst with Marjorie had made me resolve on before. But it was not the matter of Kate Allison's anger that troubled me; it was rather that the clattering minx, Nell Kennedy, would certainly tell her sister of my past boyish affairs with the pretty young lass, and specially of our home-coming from the March fair so late at night.

But the stir of going through the town of Maybole—the lasses running to the doors to admire, the 'prentice lads envying and hating me, so worked on me that, for a space, I forgot the ill-fared memory of the two maids linking down through the greenwood together. Yet the thing came again into my mind and stuck there, before I had o'ertaken half the way to Dalrymple, by which I was behoved to go.

As I rode along I practised pulling at the wicks of my upper lip, where I was persuaded that my moustache was certainly beginning to grow apace. For so I had seen the soldiers of the King's Guard do in Edinburgh, and mightily admired them at it.

The way went pleasantly by, there being many folk of all degrees and qualities on the road. And as many as saw me come, stepped aside and stood respectfully at gaze, if they were on foot; or courteously saluted me as an equal if they were on horseback. Both which things pleased me well.

So I went on smiling to myself for the pleasantness of my thoughts, in spite of the incident of the lasses. Suddenly, however, I came upon a horseman like myself, that rode down a loaning from the muirside. I saw no weapon that he had about him, yet he was no mere landward minister or merchant, by the sober richness of his habit. He was dressed in fine cloth of Flemish blue, with a plain edging of silk, but without lace or any broidery. His face, when I saw it, was pleasant, and there was on it a smile that spoke of good cheer. He seemed to be tall of his person, and, from the manner in which he reined his horse easily with his left hand, I knew him to be strong. A well-appearing, sober, conditionable man of fifty I should have taken him to be, fit to be head of a house or to sit at a king's council table.

But his occupation was the strange part of his sudden appearing. He was employed in reading a little book which he held in his right hand, riding easily all the while with his horse at a brisk walk—a thing which I never saw anyone do before. Then was I sure that he was a man of religion, by his busying himself thus with his devotions. At which I was the better pleased, since religion is a thing I was ever taught to reverence above all else, for that is the habit of the moorland folk who get but little of it. On the other hand, they tell me that in Edinburgh, where there are as many as seven ministers, the folk pay little heed to their privileges; and are, as indeed I have seen, given over to following all manner of wickedness and that with greediness.

As my fellow-traveller came down the loaning he looked up, and seeing me, he wheeled his horse alongside of mine, and very courteously gave me 'Good-day.'

Then, as well he might, he admired Dom Nicholas, letting his eyes stray smilingly over my equipage. Yet even at that moment I marked that it was a set smile, and methought that there was a busy brain behind it.

'You ride like a soldier that hath seen the wars, young sir,' he said.

'Ah,' I replied, lifting my bonnet of steel as to an elder, 'but little enough of these, my Lord, for I am but a youth.'

'You will mend of that last, I warrant,' said my companion, 'and in the end more swiftly than you will care about.'

'You were busy with your book of devotion,' said I, with respect, for I care not to force my conversation on any man; 'let me not interrupt.'

'Nay,' he said, 'I fear I am no great churchman, though for my servants' sake I have reading and worship daily in my own house, and generally I may claim to be very well affected toward the Almighty.'

'Are there no churches in your part of the country,' I asked him, 'for I perceive by your habit you are not a hereaway man?'

'There are indeed kirks there, but I cannot bide to be hampered and taken in a snare within walls, in the present unsettled state of the country. A peaceable man does well to worship in the open. What sense is there in being shut weaponless in a kirk, and shot at through the windows, as happened not long ago?'

I asked how that could be.

'Have you not heard how in the north country the Craufords beset the Kennedies in Dalrymple Kirk, taking them at an advantage without their weapons of war—so that a Kennedy now goes no oftener to kirk than the twenty-ninth of February comes into the calender.'

'How strange it befalls in a small world,' said I, laughing, 'for I am a Kennedy, and I ride to visit the Craufords of Kerse.' Then he looked at me more closely than ever.

'My name,' he said courteously, 'is John Mure of Auchendrayne.'

So I told him my name and style, and also the knight's name to whom I was squire, for after his giving me his own I could not do less.

'You have been in Edinburgh lately?' he said. 'And I doubt not, by your looks, bore yourself well in the sad broil in the High Street. Indeed, I think that I heard as much. Though being a man of good age, and one that is of quiet ways, I neither make nor mell with such tulzies, which are for young, lusty folk at any rate.'

After a little riding in silence and thought, he asked me if I had ever spoken to Gilbert Kennedy of Bargany, and it was with a loath heart that I answered 'No.'

Then he spoke long of him and his noble prowess, comparing him to the Earl of Cassillis, to his great advantage—which I grant it was easy enough to do. But since I could not wear a man's signet ring on my finger and deny him even by my silence, I spoke up for my colours. And that is good enough religion, as I read it.

'I am Cassillis man,' said I, with my hand on my sword, 'and I care not who knows it.'

'Hush you, young sir,' replied the Laird of Auchendrayne, soothingly, 'mind that you are now in an enemy's country. I warrant that Currie of Kelwood has travelled this road not so long before you.'

'I am not one who cares whether folk know my opinions,' I cried. 'See, I wear them on my collar. And I have on my finger a double safe-conduct.'

Whereupon I let him see the rings, drawing off my gauntlet that I might show him the signets.

Then he redoubled his respect and rode nearer to me, which made me glad that I had showed him the seals with their crests.

'You are young to ride so far alone on such great folk's business,' he said softly. 'Even I, that am old and sober, am not so trusted.'

'Laird Auchendrayne,' I replied to him, 'you do jest with me because of my youth. For you yourself are of the great ones, their kinsman and equal at muster and council-board, and but lately, in the Earl's absence, Bailzie of Carrick!'

Then he went on to speak of the Earl, mocking at him as one greedy-tooth for land and siller like his father, and warning me that when he had done with me he would cast me off without fee or reward, like an old glove.

'Nay, worse,' said he, 'for he will save the worn glove to sell over again to Granny Nish of the Luckenbooths.'

'Light-hand or luck-penny,' said I, 'Launcelot Kennedy is not the man to change his colours for goods or gear.'

'And who bids you?' said he. 'Tush, man! you are at the horn and outlaw. Any man may take your life and be the freer for it. The sneckdraw Cassillis and the old wife Culzean are not fit mettle for a gallant like you to ride beside. Hear ye, man; I will tell you a secret which none knoweth yet, but which, if you are wise and bold, will make your fortune with the King. Bargany is to marry one of the Queen's bower-maidens—one too that carries the King's name—*and he is to have the Earldom of Carrick!*'

Here he hushed his voice and leaned towards me, setting his hand on the arch of Dom Nicholas's neck.

'And that,' he whispered, 'will mean knighthood and an estate—besides a fair maid with a tocher, to every good man that can draw a sword and lead a company. What

think ye of that? Be not hasty, man. I tell you Bargany
will crumple up Cassillis as I crumple this bit of paper.'

And he threw a crushed sheet of writing into Doon
Water as we rode beside it.

Then I faced about upon him, and set myself very straight
in the saddle.

'Sir,' I said, 'you are an older man, a richer man, a
better learned man than I. But let me tell you, sir, that I
am an honester man than you; and maybe I shall win
though none the worse of that at the long and last. But if
what I have said offend you, I am willing to give satisfaction
on horse or foot, now or again, either to you or to any
younger man of your name. I bid you good-day, sir, for
I count you not good company for leal gentlemen.'

And with that I turned my back on him, and rode on
my way.

'Go your own gate,' he said, rather regretfully than
angrily. 'You have thrown away a kindly offer for an old
song and a sounding phrase. You are a mettle lad, but with
much wind in your belly.'

So I rode on, thinking that I had done with him—which
was very far indeed from being the case.

CHAPTER IX

CARTEL OF CONTUMELY

Now, the place where I took my leave of that pleasant
reputable treason-breeder, John Mure of Auchendrayne, was
within a quarter of a mile of Dalrymple Bridge, where it
strides across Doon Water. I am persuaded that when I
left him a little behind, I saw him heave up his hand, for
I got just a waft of it with the tail of my eye. Yet though
I could not swear it conscience-clear in any court in the land
(unless absolute need were), I am still persuaded in my
mind, as much as I was then, that the douce and gracious
man intended that I should fall into an ambush, if I
proved overly hard-bitten for his projects and temptings.

So as I came near to the bridge-end, I looked very warily
about, and methought that I spied the black muzzle of a
hackbutt, where there was no need of such like. Now
hackbutts do not, even in Carrick, grow on hedges, though

in these days a man might somewhat easily make the mistake of thinking so. I judged, therefore, that there would be an ugly face behind the gun, and a finger on the slow match that intended me no good.

As I paused, turning about on my saddle, I saw a fellow rise out of the copse-wood before me, and run like a rabbit to the bridge-end. That was enough for me. Fighting is well enough, and I can be doing with it, for it is the path of glory and of fortune. But black treachery I cannot stomach.

So being mightily angry, but resolved like steel to show John Mure and his butchers that I despised them, I turned Dom Nicholas's head and set him straight at the deeps of Doon Water, where ford there was none. In a moment we were splashing in the pool, and in another Dom Nicholas had thrown back his head and taken to the swimming like a duck. It was but a little way across, but far enough for me, for I saw the fellows running along the bank from the end of the bridge, blowing on their matches and bidding me stop. Now that was not a likely thing for me to do, being, praise the Lord! in my sober senses.

But when I got to the other shore, and set my horse to climb the steep (which was by a mill on the waterside), I was somewhat dashed to find one sitting quiet on his horse, within ten paces of me, with his fingers on his sword and his pistol bended in his hand.

I apprehended in a moment that this must be James Mure the younger of Auchendrayne, and I thought that I was as good as dead. Yet I held up my hand and cried, 'Herald!' and 'Safe-Conduct!' Though I knew that with such men as the Mures I might just as well and usefully have cried 'Bubbly Jock!' or 'Pigeon Pie!'

The young man in war-gear who sat his horse above me, did not move nor lift his weapon to fire.

'Tell me,' he said calmly, 'who may you be that cried "Safe-Conduct!" and "Herald!" on the lands of Kerse?'

I answered him that I was Launcelot Kennedy—and to effectuate something with him I added 'of Kirrieoch.' For I thought it was unlikely that he would know the hill country well enough to remember that my father was still alive. Which I take to have been an innocent enough deception, in that it hurt no one.

And in this I was right, for he answered at once,—

'I am David Crauford the younger of Kerse, but what said you of safe-conducts?'

So I showed him the rings, and told him that my business lay by word of mouth with his father. Thereafter I laid before him the matter of the scoundrels running at me nigh to Dalrymple bridge. Indeed, we could even then see them retiring in a group.

'Let us ride to the bridge head now, and see if they will molest us?'

And this we did, but none stirred nor showed themselves.

'So,' he said, 'let us ride on to Kerse.'

As we went our way we had much excellent discourse of the news of the countryside, and also of Edinburgh and its customs. I found David Crauford a fine and brave fellow, and regretted heartily that he was not on our side of the blanket—a thing which, indeed, I was too apt to do. I considered it an unfair thing that all the shavelings should be ours, and all the paladins theirs. Yet I was comforted by the thought that it was easier to be distinguished among the men of Cassillis than with Bargany—for in the kingdom of the blind the one-eyed man is king, as the saw hath it.

Thus we came at last to the place of Kerse. It was a handsome tower, with additions that made it almost a castle, standing upon a rising ground by a loch, and over-looked at a safe distance by some high rocks and scaurs, which David Crauford told me were called the Craigs of Kyle.

It was the slowest time of the afternoon when we arrived at the ancient strength, and David, saying that his father might not be wakeful, slipped on ahead, in order to assure me a proper reception—so, at least, he said.

And at the doorway I was met by many men-at-arms, with pikes in their hands and feathers in their bonnets. And there came forth to meet me eight of the twelve brothers of Kerse, all bareheaded and with swords at their sides. In the background I could see the cause of my adventuring— Currie, the Laird of Kelwood—bowing and smirking like a French dancing-master. But I never so much as looked his way.

'From whom come you, and in peace or war?' said David Crauford, just as though I had not told him—which was quite right and proper, for these commissions of diplomacy should be carried out with decorum and observance.

'I come,' said I, 'from the Earl and also from the Tutor of Cassillis, and am commissioned to speak with the Laird of Kerse in their name and on their behalf.'

With that I was conducted through a lesser into a greater hall, at the upper end of which was a raised platform, two feet or so above the floor. The hall and dais were alike strewed with yellow bent grass, such as grows upon the sides of the hills and on the seashore. On the dais stood a great oaken chair with a hood about it, and in it there sat the noblest old man that ever I saw. He seemed by his beard and hair to be ninety years of age at the least, yet his natural colour was in his cheek, and he was gleg both to hear and to speak.

So they introduced me, and I went up to the old man of Kerse to show my credentials, bending my knee, but not near to the ground, in token of courtesy.

'Come hither, David, and tell me what are the posies on the rings.'

So David came near, and, looking at my hand, he read that motto of the Earl of Cassillis—'Avise a fin !' it read.

'Ay, ay, that will do. Let the lad speak his message,' said the old man.

Then in the midst of three-score Craufords I set myself, with my shoulders squared and my hand on my hip, to speak the message of my lord. I do not deny that I liked the job well enough, for it was the sort which enables a man to make a figure—thus to stand alone among a host of enemies, and speak a challenge of defiance.

'Master David Crauford, Laird of Kerse and Skeldon,' said I, giving out his titles like a herald, 'I bear you greeting and worship from John, Earl of Cassillis, and Sir Thomas Kennedy of Culzean, Tutor of that ilk.'

The old man bowed in token of respect for the formal courtesy. 'My principals bid me say that they request and demand as their right, that you shall deliver up to them the Laird of Kelwood, their liege vassal, presently rebel and fugitive; and also that you render back the box of treasure and the stones of price which they have good reason to believe their vassal aforesaid hath concealed with you. These things being done, they assure you of their friendship and support in all your undertakings.'

So I gave it out clearly, formally, dispassionately, and without heat, as one that is accustomed to high commissions.

As I spoke I saw the old man grip his staff as though it had been a sword, and ere I had done, he had half risen from his seat as though he would have struck me to the ground.

'And you dare, you beardless birkie, to bring such a message to Crauford of Kerse, in his own hall and among his own folk?'

But I stood still with my hand on my side as before, looking at him with a level brow, knowing that without a weapon in my hand, and with a double safe-conduct on my finger, I had by far the best of it, ay, though there had been a thousand Craufords in the hall.

'Father, father,' said David from behind, as one accustomed to soothe the old man's anger.

'I ken—I ken bravely. The laddie has to bring his message, but Scraping Johnny of Cassillis shall rue this day. Tell him,' he cried, his voice rising to a wild scream, 'that I have seen no doit of the dirty money which he howks out of every dub with his swine's snout. The Laird of Kelwood indeed, I have with me, and here he shall bide while it likes him—not for his own sake, for he is small credit either to Kennedy or Crauford (to his face I say it), but because Kerse is an eagle sitting on high, and it has not yet come to it that he must, forsooth, throw down so much as a well-pyked bone at the bidding of Cassillis.'

I bowed to the ground as having gotten my answer. But I had another part of the piece still to play, and the doing of it liked me ever better, for I saw that this time I should anger not only the old man but the young.

'Then,' said I, 'in the name of John, Earl of Cassillis, whom ye call swine's snout, I am charged to tell you that if ye will not deliver the man and the thing that are his just right, then will my master come and gar ye be fain to deliver them—'

Then there went a murmur of scorn and anger all about the hall, and the white locks of the old man fairly bristled on his head. But I spoke on, level as a clerk that reads his lessons.

'Hearken ye to the word of Cassillis—the last word— gin ye refuse he will come on Lammas day proximate, and in token of ignominy and despite, he will tether a brood sow upon the lands of Kerse, and not a Crauford shall steer her for the length of a summer's day.'

What a shout of anger went up from about the hall! The blades of the young men fairly blazed from their sheaths. The old man rose in his chair and lifted his staff by the middle. Two tall servitors that stood at the back of the hall, lighting the dusk with torches, sprang forward ready to catch him should his strength fail. There were at least thirty swords pointed at my breast, and one great lout threatened me with a Lochaber axe.

But with my heart swelling I stood still and calm amid the graceless tumult, like one of the carven stones which look out from the niches of Crossraguel. Motionless I stood as I had done from the first, for I was a herald with an Earl's message.

'An insult! an insult! an insult in the hall of Kerse. Kill the black Kennedy!' they cried, gnashing on me with their teeth like wild beasts.

I declare I never was happier in my life, knowing that I had made that day a figure which would not be forgotten, and that my bearing among them would be spoken of over all Carrick and Kyle. How I wished that Marjorie Kennedy could have seen me. And I smiled as I thought how little it mattered after this, whether or no Nell Kennedy turned tale-pyet.

'I will take the smile off his black Kennedy's face with a paik of this Lochaber axe!' cried my great lout. But indeed I smiled not at him nor any of his sept, but at the thought of Nell Kennedy.

Then when they had roared themselves out in anger, they became, as I take it, some deal ashamed of the hideous uproar, and of a sudden were silent—as with a stave thrust in the joint and a twist of the wrist one may shut off a noisy mill-lade.

So I got in my last word.

'Thereafter, John, Earl of Cassillis, bids me say that he will leave not one standing stone in the house of Kerse upon another, for the despite and contempt done to him as its overlord.'

Then the loud anger gave place to silent, deadly hate, and it was some time before any could speak. David the younger would have spoken, but his father waved him down, fighting for utterance.

'Hear ye, sir, and bear this message and defiance to your master. He has put a shame on us in this our own house. Tell him that he may bring his swine to Kerse every Lammas day, and fetch with him every swineherd Kennedy from every midden-head betwixt Cassillis and the Inch. There are plenty stout Craufords here in Kyle that can flit them. Ay, though this hand, that was once as the axe-hand of the Bruce, be shrunken now, and though I lean on these bearers of torches because of mine age, tell him that there are twelve stout sons behind me who can render taunt for taunt, blow for blow, to King or Kennedy. And tell him that Crauford of Kerse knows no overlord in earth or heaven—least of all John Kennedy, fifth Earl of Cassillis!'

Then I bowed as one might before some of the glorious pagan gods of whom Dominie Mure has tales to tell. For, indeed, that was an answer worth taking back, and, being a man, I know a man when it is given me to see him. So, with my face to him still, and my bonnet in my hand, I made my way off the daïs. There I turned me about, and, as an Earl's spokesman should, set my steel bonnet on my head to go out alone through the crowded hall.

But the old man stayed me.

'Launcelot Kennedy of Kirrieoch,' he said, courteously, 'to you and not to your master, I say this. Ye have well delivered an ill message. May ye never get your fill of fighting, and at the last may you die in harness. I would to God ye were my thirteenth son!'

So I bowed again, and for respect I walked backwards to the door of the great hall with my head again bare. Then I helmed myself and passed without to Dom Nicholas.

There was now a full muster of Craufords in the court-yard—a hundred of them, I should say, at least. But no murmur arose among them as, helped by a groom, I mounted and moved slowly through the throng, having saluted David the younger and his brothers with my hand.

Then, as I rode through the gateway, the feet of Dom Nicholas clattering on the stones, I was aware of a troop of twelve that followed me, all well-accoutred men riding in order. And I knew the author of that guard. It was David, who had resolved to see me safe across Dalrymple bridge, and so gave me the attendance of a prince.

Then knew I how excellent a thing it is to have to do in peace or war with gentlemen. For to do them justice, the Craufords of Kerse were neither landloupers nor ambuscaders.

CHAPTER X

SIR THOMAS OF THE TOP-KNOT

My guard of honour did not leave me till I was within sight of the towers of Cassillis, when David Crauford and his men parted from me with silent salute. Nor had the dyke-back hiding gentry so much as ventured to show their faces. So I rode down to Cassillis yett, a well-kenned place and famous in story. Down a smooth, green mead I rode to it. At the gate the porter, a surly rogue, bade me stand.

'Stand thou, hang thee, pock-faced varlet!' I cried; 'haste thee and up with the gates, or thine ass's ears shall answer for it, nailed incontinent to a post!'

Whereupon, seeing him wondering and still wavering, I drew off my glove and flashed the Earl's broad signet ring at him. I declare he laid hold of the pulley like one demented.

'I trust, noble sir, that ye will not mention the matter of my hasty greeting to my lord,' he said to me as I passed, for the rascal was shaking in every limb.

'Let it learn you to be better scraped as to the tongue for the time to come,' I answered sharply, for I was none

sorry once for all to read the villain a lesson. There is
nothing better than a man who worthily and for his office's
sake magnifies his office, but there is nothing more scunner-
ing than that a menial knave, in pride of place, should beard
his betters.

In the hall of Cassillis, while I waited for my lord, I
met the old man of strange aspect, who had been with us
upon the Red Moss. He was dressed in a long, lank robe
like a soutane, and he carried a book with him, very filthy
and tattered. In this he read, or pretended to read, by-
whiles, muttering and mumbling the words over to himself.

Seeing me stand alone, he came over and began to speak
to me about matters that I knew not of—something that
concerned the Black Vault of Dunure, so I understood him
to say.

But his appearance as he talked caused me to laugh,
though, being an old man, I did not let him see it. His
head appeared as bald all about as is a hen's egg. But on
the very crown there was an oval place of a hand's breadth
or thereby, from which dropped a crest of yellow-white
hair, very laughable and ludicrous. For as the old man
talked the silly cockscomb on his crown waggled, and being
toothless his jaw waggled also. So that the nut-cracker jaw
underneath and the waggling plume aloft might well have
made a cat laugh.

'I am Sir Thomas Tode,' he mumbled, when I began
to get a little familiar with his shambling speech—'ay me,
Sir Thomas Tode' (he pronounced the word as though it
had been the name of the foul beast that squats on its
belly), 'the famous Sir Thomas Tode am I. Ay, dear
mother Mary—I mean Christian friends, but a feck of life
it has been my lot to see.'

I thought within me what a strange old scare-the-crows
this was, to have the name and style of knighthood. So I
asked him what were his ancestral possessions.

'I am only poor Sir Thomas Tode, chaplain to two mighty
Earls,' he said, shaking his head and waggling his top-knot,
till he looked more like the father of all the apes that ever
were, than a sober cleric.

'Even so,' he went on, 'I was bred to Holy Church—I
mean brought up in ignorance, to serve the Whore that

sitteth on the Seven Hills. I was chaplain to the old Lord
Gilbert, the father of the Earl John that is. Ah, many a
time did I shrive him soundly, and none needed it more.
Faith, but he was a ripe, crusted old sinner—'

And Sir Thomas Tode chuckled a senile laugh at his
memories of the bygone wickednesses of the great.

'Faith, I doubt shrewdly that he fries for it now. For
in these days there are no prayers to hoist men out of
purgatory by the telling down of the good broad bonnet
pieces—more's the pity for poor honest churchmen! Ah
me, the times that were! The times that were!'

The old man paused a moment to think the matter over,
and then very visibly his mind went wandering after some
greater and yet choicer wickedness which he might retail
to me.

'Have you ever heard,' he said at last, 'of the roasting
of the Abbot of Crossraguel? Man, I was there—yes, I
was there—Tom Tode was there, and turned him on the
iron brander till I burned my fingers!'

And the ancient rascal beat merrily on the floor with
his stick and charked together his toothless gums.

'Now sit ye down, and I shall tell you all that took
place in the Black Vault of Dunure—'

Just then I saw a sonsy, red-faced woman, ample of
bosom and with many plies of wylicoats pleated and
gathered about her, rise from the black stair head—even
as Dominie Mure fables that Venus (a heathen goddess, but
one of whose ongoings I own it diverts me greatly to hear)
did from the sea. With three strides she came across the
hall and caught Sir Thomas Tode by the shock of yellow-
white hair on his crown.

'Be you at it again?' she cried. 'I will give you your
fill of the Black Vault of Dunure, doddering old bletherer
that ye are. Who is to turn my spit, I would have you tell
me, gin you waste your time yammering to wanchancy
lazybones of the Black Vault of Dunure? "Black Vault of
Dunure" indeed! You have told your lies till I declare you
grow to believe them yourself!'

So without a word of protest from the knightly lips of
Sir Thomas Tode, he was led below, his head nodding and
bowing as his captor shook the yellow top-knot.

After the pair were gone, I laughed both loud and long, so that they had to fetch me nigh on a gallon of strong ale to recover me of my access of mirth, and prepare me for the presence of the Earl.

And right certainly did I vow within my heart, that it would not be long before I renewed acquaintance with Sir Thomas and his tyrant, for it seemed a strange and merry thing to see an Earl's chaplain so used. It was, indeed, many a day since I had seen such sport.

At last I was led in to the Earl. He sat in a rich dressing-robe, flowered with gold, and a leather-bound book with knobs and studs of brass lay open beside him. It was the account book of his estates and overlordships.

'What was that loud mirth I heard a moment since?' he asked, for the Earl John did not seem to be in the best of tempers. Indeed he was said never to be canny to come near, when he was in the same house as his wife, a thing passing strange and but not wholly without precedent.

I answered that I laughed at a good story of Sir Thomas Tode, his private chaplain.

'My what!' he cried. 'Oh, ye mean old Tode of the Top-knot! Was his story about the Black Vault of Dunure?'

And without stopping for an answer he went on with one of his proverbs, just as though he had not sent me on an errand, and that in peril of my life. I never met a young man so broadened on wiseacre saws and proverbs in my life. It was clean ridiculous, though well enough in a gap-toothed grandfather, no doubt.

'The loud laughter of the idle gathereth no gear,' said Earl John.

'No,' replied I, 'but since it cheers the heart, it costs less than your good strong ale.'

'Ay, but,' he said, breaking in and looking pleased, 'but you have had some deal of that too. I can smell it.'

Then he looked briskly up, as if delighted with himself for his penetration, and catching me with my hand held guiltily before my mouth, he smiled.

'Well,' he said, 'can you not come to the point—why stand so long agape? What of your mission?'

So, being nothing loath, I told him the whole matter, much as I have related it in this place. And though at the beginning he sat calmly enough to listen, long before I had finished he was striding up and down the room gripping at his thigh, where for common he wore his sword—for, after all, Earl John was a true Cassillis, and neither craven nor hen-hearted.

'And they roared upon you, standing still. Nay, you did well! I wish it had been I! Man, I will give you the horse you rode upon, and all the caparison. I declare I will!'

For which I thanked him in words; but in my heart I said, 'It is an easy present to give that which is your uncle's, and hath indeed been mine for weeks.'

Then he seemed to remember, for he said, 'But give me back my signet. Ye have done well, and on Lammas day ye shall do better. Will ye take a ring or a sword for a keepsake?'

A moment only I divided my mind. A ring, if good, would indeed buy many swords. But Cassillis was not the man to give a ring of price. Contrariwise a sword was a thing that all men had good skill of, and for very shame's sake a good sword would he give.

'I crave a sword,' said I, briefly.

'Ye have chosen like a soldier. I shall not grudge you the wale of swords,' the Earl made reply, smiling upon me, well pleased.

So with that he went out into the armoury, and came back with the noblest sword I had ever seen. Blade, hilt, and scabbard were all inlaid with scrolled Damascus work of gold, thin limned and delicate—I never saw the like. And my blood leaped within me—I declare to my shame, nigh as hotly as it did when Marjorie Kennedy kissed me on the brow in the arbour of the pleasaunce at the house of Culzean.

'Buckle it on, and take it with you,' said the Earl, 'lest looking long upon it my heart should smite me, and I want it back again.'

So I thanked him and presently was gone without great ceremony, lest, indeed, it should be so.

'Stay the night at Cassillis,' he cried after me. ' I have a letter to send to my eame the Tutor in the morning.'

CHAPTER XI

SWORD AND SPIT

THE house of Cassillis is not a great place for size, to be so famous. But the Earl has many castles, to which he goes oftentimes—specially to the grand house of the new style which he is building at the Inch, and from which he means to assert his overlordship of the Lairds of Galloway, which, as I see it, is likely to breed him trouble—more than if he had stayed here at home and flairdied his old gammer mistress into good humour.

So, leaving his presence, I went to see that Dom Nicholas had the best of food and bedding, passing through the grooms and men-at-arms in the bravery of my Damascus sword, walking carelessly as though I wore suchlike every day—a thing I liked well to do. I also made them change the straw for better, though, indeed, there was little to find fault with. But it is always best when one goes first into the stables of the great to speak loud, to cry, 'Here, sirrah, what means this?' And then order fresh bedding to be brought, and that instantly. Thus I made myself respected, and so walked out, while the grooms bowed, pulling the while at my moustache and pressing upon the hilt of my sword, so that the point stood out at the proper angle behind with my cloak a-droop over it, as I have said.

Then, on my way back to the house, I must needs pass —or so I made it appear—through the kitchens, where I found my tyrant Venus-of-the-fiery-face in the act of cooking the supper.

Seeing me lean against the baking board, dressed so *cap-à-pie*, she came and brushed me a place to sit upon. Then she asked, 'Would I be pleased to drink a cup of sack—rare and old?'

So, seeing her set on it, I denied her not; but sat down, unbuckling my weapon for ease's sake, and throwing it down with clank of blade and jingle of buckle on the clear-scoured boards of the great deal table in the midst. The Lord forgive me for caring so mightily about these things and so little for going to church! Some good day, doubtless, I shall change about. And in the meanwhile, what would you?

Were you that chance to read never eighteen and thought you not well of yourself, having a new sword? If not, the Lord pity you. It is little ye ken.

But all the while I longed to hear more of Sir Thomas Tode, and if it might be, to see him. So I asked of the lady of the pans where her husband was.

She set her thumb over her shoulder, pointing to a narrow door as of an aumrie or wall press.

'He is in there,' she said shortly.

'And what else is there in there?' said I, laughing, for what was I the wiser?

'Half a bullock is in there,' she said, laughing also. 'That is the meat-cupboard. It is fine and caller, and he is not troubled with flies upon his miserable bald head.'

'The meat-safe,' cried I, much astonished; 'and what does a reverend chaplain and a knight in the meat-safe?'

'The old dotard will not quit his maundering about the Black Vault of Dunure to every one that comes near. He got hold of a silly chapman in the yard that came with fish from Ayr, and I declare he must sit down and prate by the hour of the Black Vault of Dunure. So I shut him up in the meat-safe. Faith, I will give him Black Vault of Dunure ere I have done with him. The Black Vault of Cassillis and the company of the dinner roast will set him better.'

'And what says my lord to your using his chaplain so?'

The lady gazed at me a moment in a kind of wilderment. Then she broke into the vulgar speech of the country, which, because I learned to write English as those at the Queen's Court do, I have used but seldom in this chronicle—though, of course, not for lack of knowledge.

'Sain me,' she said, 'this may be a queer, uncanny world, but it is surely no come to that o't yet, that a wife mauna check and chastise her ain man. Guid Lord, no—life wadna be worth leevin'—see till this—' she said.

And taking a key from her pocket she rapidly unlocked the door of the meat-closet.

Sir Thomas was discovered sitting most forlornly within, upon the corner of a great chest, with many pieces of meat depending from hooks about his head. His wife, reaching

in from the step, took him by the top-knot of hair as by
a handle, and pulled him out upon the floor of the kitchen
with one movement of her arm.

'It's a guid's mercy,' she cried, 'that yince ye war a
papish monk wi' a shaven crown, for the place that ye
keepit bare sae lang has ripened late, after a' the lave o'
the crap has been blawn awa' wi' the wind.'

I had been endeavouring to explain to myself the strangeness of the wisp upon Sir Thomas's head, but the words of
his wife made clear the matter. It was but the retarded
growth of his long fallow tonsure.

'An' it's a de'il o' a queer thing,' said Mistress Tode,
'that turning your coat ootside in should turn your hair
inside oot! Heard ye ever the mak' o' that?'

'It was all owing to—' began Sir Thomas Tode, looking
at his wife with a cringing shamefacedness that was most
entertaining.

'Oh, I ken,' interrupted his wife, 'it was owing to the
Black Vault o' Dunure, nae doot! I declare I canna haud
ye aff it. I jaloose that it maun hae been owing to the
Black Vault o' Dunure that Mary Greg, a decent cook
woman and a deacon in her trade, took up wi' the likes o'
you—that mak's yoursel' nae better than a mountibank wi'
your yammer-yammering like a corn-crake aboot black
vauts and roasted abbots. Fegs, I declare I could roast ye
yoursel'. Ye are that muckle thocht and care to me, but
ye wadna pay for the trouble. Even the Earl himsel'
couldna mak' a profit oot o' you—an' a' folk kens that he
wad drive a flea to London market for the sake o' the
horns and hide!'

'Wheesht, wheesht, honest woman!' said Sir Thomas
Tode, 'wha kens wha may be listenin'—maybe the Countess
her very sel'.'

'Faith, an' I carena,' cried the brave cook, tossing her
head, 'she is a backstairs body at ony gate, but she canna
fear me—na, brawly no'. I ken ower muckle. I ken
things the Earl doesna ken. Certes an' serve him richt—
a young man like him—but three-an'-twenty, to mairry his
grandmither. Though guid kens Mary Greg is no the
woman to speak, that mairried nocht better than an auld
skeleton hung on strings—for nae sounder reason than that

it is the custom for the cook in a decent big hoose to tak'
up wi' the chaplain.'

The kitchen began to fill, and I bethought me that I
should be going; for it was not seemly that a gentleman
and a squire should collogue overly long with all the orra
serving-men and women in a great house. But before I
could lift my sword and depart, there came in a dark, burly
man with a sharp-cleft eagle's face on him, his eyes very
close together, and a contemptuous sneer that was liker a
snarl, on his face.

'Good e'en to ye, John Dick,' said the cook. 'Mind
ye keep the peace, ye wull-cat, for there are to be no
collieshangies in my kitchen!'

A voice called something querulously down the stairs.

'Coming the noo, my leddy,' cried Mrs. Tode, the cook
of Cassillis, 'I am juist pittin' on the pot—'

And she vanished up the stair.

As soon as she was gone, Sir Thomas appeared to wake
up from a dream. He looked eagerly around him.

'She will no be back for a while,' he said. 'I might
have a chance. I maun tell you of the roasting of the
abbot. Man, I saw it—I was there. I held him on the
ribs o' the grate. I set him on the brander, and poured the
oil on him that he might be roasted in sop. Oh, man, ye
think I am a fool. Ever since that day, never hae I been
alone without seeing the face o' him, crying out for them
to ding whingers into him, or blaw him up wi' powder to
ease him—the auld Earl grinin' at him like a wild cat, and
hunkering low to watch, with his hands on his knees. Oh,
young men, never you put your hand to the torture of
man, for it bides with you in the brain—just as, asleep or
awake, night or day, I see the Black Vault o' Dunure!'

'Good life,' cried his wife, entering briskly at the
moment, ' is it possible that the auld fule is at it again?
The very de'il's in the craitur. He thinks that he was at the
roastin' o' a man, whan a' the roastin' he has done in his
life has been turnin' the spit in this decent hoose o' Cassillis.
Come awa', ye doitered auld loon, what did I tell ye the
last time?—Into the keepin' chamber wi' you!'

And she caught him by the top lock to lead him away
once more. But I pled for him, saying that I had never

heard of his fantasy, and had indeed encouraged him to begin.

The tall man who had been called John Dick, the fellow of the hateful countenance, in whose eyes there was the insolence of challenge, at this point stalked up to the table on which my sword still lay. He took it in his hand with a contemptuous air, examined the Damascus work of fine gold, and was about to draw the blade from its sheath.

'That sword is mine,' said I, scarcely looking at the fellow, 'and does not leave its scabbard save when I draw it.'

'And then,' quoth he, with a bitter sneer, 'I opine it will not do much damage. 'Tis but a bairn's plaik at any rate! And in fit hands!'

'It may be that you would like to try, sirrah,' said I, slipping my hip off the table and buckling on my sword with one movement.

'Very willingly,' said he of the sneer. 'Come out to the green.'

But before I could move to end the matter, there arose from the corner, where he had been lying on an oaken settle, a tall, slender lad of foreign aspect and distinction. He had on him a green suit like the Royal hunting liveries. A long, plain sword in a black leather scabbard swung by his side.

'Launcelot Kennedy of Kirrieoch,' he said, bowing to me, 'I am Robert Harburgh, and though for the time being I serve here as little better than a cullion, I am yet of some blood and kindred. Therefore I shall do you no shame. And you, sir,' said he, turning to John Dick, who stood lowering, 'being your equal here, I can serve your turn to cross swords with—and spare this gentleman the discomfort of defiling his sword of honour with such black ignoble blood as yours.'

And with that he whipped out a long, straight sword which glittered in the firelight. John Dick turned up his lip wickedly, so that we saw his teeth, and the black, curly fringe of hair about his face stood out, till his visage was like that of an angry ramping bull of Galloway.

There were only men in the kitchen when the *fracas* arose, for Mistress Tode had gone to do some errand for the Countess.

'You are surely a stark man,' said John Dick, 'to mell

or meddle with me. Ken ye that I have wounded more men with my whinger than I have fingers on my right hand?'

'And how many may that be?' said the young man who had espoused my cause.

'Why, four,' said John Dick, surprised at the question.

'Then in a little while you shall have one less—and that is but three. Guard yourself!'

And there in the red dusk of the kitchen they cleared themselves for fighting, and their blades met with so stern a clash that sparks were driven from the steel. But Harburgh, my young and melancholy Dane, forced the fighting from the first, driving Dick before him round the narrow and enclosed place, countering and attacking with such dexterity and fury as I had never seen, though for years I myself had been a sound swordsman. But such fighting as this I saw not—no, not in the schools which the King has set up in Edinburgh to be used instead of golf and siclike foolish games, which the men of the east country love to play in their idle folly and wantonness.

They had not gone far when my champion, using a snicking undercut I had never seen, severed the little finger of his opponent, at the second joint just where it overlaid the hilt, so that the tip of it fell on the floor. Whereat Sir Thomas Tode lifted it and wrapped it with care in two sheets of clean scrivening paper which he took from his pocket.

But John Dick, who after all was a man, though a crab-grained and ill-conditioned one, only called a halt for a moment and wrapped his wounded finger in a napkin, drawing the cincture close with cord. And he was in the act of continuing the fight, and pressing his adversary for revenge, being resolved to kill him for the affront, when, with a loud outcry, Mistress Tode rushed down the stairs. She seized a huge spit, and with the sharpened end so briskly attacked both the combatants, battering them soundly about their heads, that they were compelled to desist.

And it was most comical to see these fierce and confident fighters drop their swords' points and shield their heads with their hands to ward off the blows of the stick.

'Varlets!' she screamed. 'Briskly I will learn you to fight and tulzie in my kitchen. Out with you,' she cried, giving John Dick the sharpened end of her weapon in his wame, 'out with you, for it was your de'il's temper that began the fray.'

And so, having opened the door, she fairly thrust him out into the night. But she had not time to close it again before one whom none of us had seen came within the circle of red light. He was a man of a dignified countenance, dressed in black, and he held a plain staff, also of black, in his hand. On his head there was a broad hat with a cord about it. Upon his coat he wore no ornament save a broad, black silk collar which lay upon his shoulders, and over that again there fell another collar of fair soft linen, very white and well dressed.

'What means this tumult in the house of Cassillis?' he asked, speaking as one that has authority, and has been accustomed to wield it unquestioned for many years.

Now there was not a man there but longed to ask, 'And who may you be that speers?' But none answered rudely, for the awe that was upon them.

Then at last Robert Harburgh said to him, but courteously, 'Sir, you ask of the tumult. It was a matter that concerns those only that fought upon their own proper quarrel. It concerns neither you nor yet my Lord Cassillis, in whose house ye presently are.'

'Lead me to my lord!' he said, as one who had only to speak that the doors might be opened.

But Robert Harburgh withstood him and would not suffer him to pass.

'Let me see the Earl of Cassillis instantly!' said he.

'The Earl is at supper,' said Robert Harburgh, 'and cannot be disturbed.'

'I will eat with him,' said the stranger, calmly.

Then when some scullion laughed, for of custom those who ate with the Earl of Cassillis entered not by the kitchen door, the unknown made a gesture of extraordinary contempt and yet withal of a marvellous dignity.

'Go, instantly,' he commanded, pointing to the stair door with his finger, 'and tell your master that Robert Bruce, Minister of Edinburgh Town, would see him in the name of the Lord and of His Highness the King of Scots.'

And Robert Harburgh, who had just outflouted John Dick, the ruffler of camps, bowed before him. And as for me I took my bonnet off my own head and saluted, for there was no one of us who had not heard of the famous and well-reputed minister, to whom the King had committed the rule and governance of all the realm during the half-year he was in Denmark busy marrying of his queen.

So with Robert Harburgh leading and myself following, the minister passed up the stair with due attendance, and into the supper chamber where the Earl and Countess took their meal at even, mostly without speech each with the other. And when through the open door I saw the Earl welcome his guest as he would have done the King himself, and especially when I heard their serious and weighty conversation, the thought came to me that it was well that there were men in Scotland able to make religion so to be honoured. Then again I laughed, thinking of the mighty difference that there was between Maister Robert Bruce, Minister of Edinburgh and sometime ruler of Scotland, and poor Sir Thomas Tode, domestic chaplain to the Earl of Cassillis and the well-pecked husband of Mary Greg, his cook.

CHAPTER XII

THE FLITTING OF THE SOW

IT was Lammas day, and the strange wager of battle was about to be fought. Maister Robert Bruce, who had composed so many quarrels (and made so many more in the doing of it), had altogether and utterly failed to make up this one. So he had passed south to his friend and favourer the Laird of Bargany, who for all his soldiership was ever great for the honour of the Kirk. I hope that the Minister of Edinburgh made more of him than he made of Earl John, of whom he gat nothing but fair speeches and most indifferent drink, which were indeed in my time the staples of Cassillis hospitality.

Now, it so happened that Sir Thomas Kennedy, my master, could not move from his chair, much less sit a horse, because of that old income in the knee, which ever in the hot season of the year caused him so much pain and trouble. Thus it fell to me to lead our small levy from the lands of Culzean, for we were near to the country of the Barganies, and it would not do, in the absence of an armistice, to denude our head castle of all the fighting men that were thereabout.

The morn of Lammas was one that promised to open out into a day of fervent heat, for the mists rose lazily, but did not dissolve as the sun climbed the skies. Yet it was a morning that pleasured me beyond telling, as I buckled on my new sword of price, and rode out to fight. I am not averse from fighting, but I own it is the riding out in array that I chiefly love.

What a heartsome sight it was when we turned our faces towards Cassillis Yett, and saw the companies of Kennedies come riding and running over every green knoll—long, upright men of the South who had started the night before from far Minnochside and Auchneil, shoulder-bent shoremen who came over the edge of Brown Carrick, pikemen, spearmen, and hackbuttmen, together with a multitude of limber, pranksome lads with only a leathern jacket and a whinger.

When we came to Cassillis Yett, there by the road-end was Sir Thomas Tode, who was charged to tell us that my lord had gone before us with many soldiers and horsemen. They had taken also with them a trail-cart, being a box with shafts like a carriage, but without wheels, mounted on a great brush of branches and twigs, which stuck out behind and scored the ground with a thousand ruts and scratches. This was for the conveyance of the sow, which from sundawn to sunset was to be tethered, in despite and contempt, upon the lands of the Craufords of Kerse. For that was the wager of battle between the Kennedies and the Craufords.

The place where we found the Earl and his tethered sow was well chosen. It was a three-cornered piece of land, of which two sides were defended by the Doon Water sharply bending back upon itself, while across the broad base of the triangle there ran a moss. The beating of the drums and the playing of pipes were on all the hills; and so gay and cheerful was the scene that it might have been a fair or a weapon-shawing, for the sound of merrymaking and deray that there was all about.

The Doon, that should run so red or sunset, now sparkled pure and clear in the light of morning, and the speckled piets and pigeons scudded here and there among the coppices. We had not been long established on this tongue of land with our tethered sow when there arose a crying among the outposts, and word was brought that from all the Craigs of Kyle, and out of all the country of the east, the Craufords and their allies were gathering to the trysted fray.

Presently we saw them top the brae in ordered companies. It was bonny to see them come stringing down the sides of the hills, now going singly like cattle along a path in the steep places, and now forming into squadrons and companies on the plain ground. The sunshine sifted through the thin clouds as through a sieve, and made a strange pale glittering on their war gear, so that all the country round was lit up with little sparkling flashes of fire, like the wave tops when the sun rises out of the eastern sea.

They had their drums also, though it was the latest of many affronts that the Kennedies had put holes in all the Crauford drums which were in the town of Ayr upon the last market day. And this quarrel also had to be settled. Presently we could see all twelve of the stalwart sons leading on their vassals from the brown hills. They were a sunburnt company, because it was about the Lammastide, when the muirmen are wont to be out all day at the watersides at the winning of the meadow hay—the crop which is hard to grow, ill to mow, bu: worst of all to gather into barn, as the saying goes in the parts of the outland hills.

It was nine of the morning when the Craufords moved to the attack. All this while the loathly sow, that was at once provocation and offence, lay upon a little mound in the midst of our camp, grunting and grumphing most filthily. The Earl had set a little snipe of a raggetty loon to stir her up with a pointed stick, so that she should not go to sleep, but should grunt and disport herself as she ought. Being thus encouraged, the boy did his work to admiration, and the old grouting wretch kept up such a snorking and yellyhooing that she could be heard almost from Dalrymple Kirk to the Mains of Kerse.

Then there was a pause for parley. Of this I will not write at length, because it was for the most part but rudeness and dirtiness that were bandied about and between—each party miscalling the other for greater thieves and worse murderers than their neighbours. Even in this I do not think we had the worst of it, for John Dick (whose finger-stump was well healed) spat out oaths as if for a wager. And Muckle Hugh miscalled the Craufords in a voice like thunder, as though they had been dogs that would not run aright upon the hillsides of Kirriemore, in that dear land which looks towards Galloway.

Now, I cannot say that I was keen of this particular quarrel. For though there was some pleasure in making a figure in the great hall at Kerse, I foresaw but a brawling of clowns and the splattering of confused fighting without honour or chivalry, in this affair of swine and blundering melées. Yet, because I was there in the place of my knight, I could do no more than just bear the brunt and abide.

Presently the Craufords came on with their horsemen first and the pikemen behind. But the mounted men came not far, for the bog laired their horses, and they sank deeper and deeper at every step. Then the footmen came between them and charged up to our foremost lines, so that we were hand-to-hand and hard at it in a trice. It was not, however, the work of many minutes to gar them turn about and run, for our front was solid and broad, while the hackbutt shooters had fine rests for their guns, so that on a still day they could bring a man down at thirty yards or more. A good many Craufords were already splattering like wounded waterfowl in the moss which protected our front.

After this we had time to look across the Doon Water, from which there was a crying. And lo! there on the bank stood our late guest, Maister Robert Bruce, the Minister of Edinburgh.

But our Earl was now too hot to think of courtesy, so he bade the Minister stop where he was, or come over and take a pike by the end; and this greeting made me sorry, for he was a grand-looking man, with his long black cloak and his noble black horse, which, they say, had once been the King's own charger.

So I took the great risk of drawing the Earl aside, and urged upon him that he should call a parley and see what the Minister wanted. This, very reluctantly, he did, and we could hear Master Bruce speaking from over the Doon Water clearly, as if he had been in his own pulpit.

'In the King's name I bid you cease,' he cried; 'and in God's name I debar and forbid you. If ye persist, I shall deliver you to Satan, so that ye may learn that it is dangerous to despise authority.'

'Hoot toot, Maister Bruce, the days of curses are by with,' said the Earl, 'and, besides, the most of us have ta'en a heap of risks afore noo. We can e'en afford to take another.'

'I wish to speak,' said the Minister, 'with Crauford of Kerse.'

'Then gang farther up the waterside and gie a cry. There's nae Craufords here except dead anes!' said the Earl, who had his daft coat on him that day, so that we feared he had been bewitched.

But the young men of the Craufords would have nothing to say to him, having, as I suspect, no goo for a Minister meddling in the bickerings of men.

So he returned and asked Cassillis for one to take him to Kerse.

'Go, Launcelot,' said the Earl, 'and guide him. We will manage somehow to keep the battle up among us till you return.'

So, nothing loath to get away from gruntling horror on the knowe top, I set Dom Nicholas's breast to the river, and was beside the Minister in a trice.

As I passed up the waterside I came quite near to David Crauford the younger. He stelled up the cock of his pistol to shoot at me, but I held up my hand.

'I am going to the Kerse to see your father. Have you any word?' I cried to him.

For in these quaint times the friendliness and complaisance with which killing was done will scarce be believed— often with a jest, and, as one might say, amicably.

'To see my father?' cried David across the water. 'Ye'll find him bird-alone. Then tell him that we'll flit the Cassillis sow or it be dark yet.'

He turned again to where his brothers were standing in council, looking often south and north, as though they expected some reinforcement. Then something came into his mind.

'Gangs the Minister to Kerse wi' you?' he cried down the wind. I told him ay.

'Then,' said he, laughing, 'he is likely to hear my father at his devotions.'

I had at that time no inkling of David Crauford's meaning, but before all was done I learned.

So Master Robert Bruce and I rode daintily and cannily along the riverside, till we came to the ford of the mill which is beneath the house of Kerse. As we rode our horses through the water and slowly up the bank, and even as we set our heads over the edge, we heard the loud and wrathful crying of a voice that shook the air. It sounded just as when, straying by quiet woodland ways, one turns the corner of a cliff and comes suddenly upon the sea edge, and lo! the roar and brattle of the waves on the long beaches.

As we neared the house of Kerse we noted that the words rose and fell, swaying like the voice of a preacher who has repeated the same prayer times without number.

'Did not the young man mention that his father was at his devotion? Heard ye ever tell that he was a religious person?' asked the Minister of me.

I answered him no, but by all accounts the contrary. I told him that I had once been in the house of Kerse, and that none there (including myself, I might have added with truth) seemed to be greatly oppressed with any overload of the Christian virtues.

When we came near we were aware of a wide and vacant house, all the doors open to the wall, stables and barn alike void and empty. Not so much as a dog stirring. But from the house end that looked down the water, there came the crying of this great voice of one unseen. Midnoon though it was, and I with the most noted minister in Scotland by my side, I declare that I felt eerie. Indeed, I have never cared for coming on a habited house, when it stands empty with all the furniture of service left where the folk laid them down, and finding no one therein. Such a place is full of footfalls and whispers, and a kirkyard at midnight is not more uncanny, at least not to my thought.

'It sounds much like a man blaspheming his Maker,' said the Minister.

We rode round an angle of the wall, where there was a flanking tower; and there, straight before us, sitting on a high oaken chair under a green tree, was old David Crauford

of Kerse, his head thrown forward, his hands clenched, his
eyes fixed on the brown of the hill over which his sons had
gone—while from his mouth there came an astounding
stream of oaths and cursings, of which, so far as one could
grasp it, the main purpose seemed to be the sending of
every Kennedy that ever drew the breath of life directly and
eternally to the abodes of the damned.

We dismounted leisurely from our horses, and reined
them loosely to the rings in the louping-on stone at the
house end. Then Maister Bruce strode forward and stood
in front of the old man, who had never for a moment noticed
us nor ceased from his earth-shaking cursings.

Not until the tall and dark figure of the Minister had
blotted out the point of the hill towards which he looked,
did the old man intermit his speech. Then he drew his hand
slowly across his brow, and threw his head back as if to
distinguish whether it were indeed a living man who
stood before him.

'I am Robert Bruce, Minister of the Town of Edinburgh,'
said my companion, 'and I come from His Majesty the
King of Scotland, to bid you make an end of this evil
and universal regardlessness, which has polluted the whole
country with cruelty and dissension, with public factions
and private deadly feuds—'

Old David Crauford leaned forward in his chair and set
his hand to his ear, as though he had not heard a word of
the Minister's speech.

'What say ye, man?' he cried, testily, like one who is
stayed from his purpose by childish pranks.

'I say,' said the Minister, stoutly, 'that the disquieting
of the lieges with jacks, breast-plates, plate-sleeves, and
pistols is as much dishonouring to God as it is distasteful
to His Majesty the King—'

'Hear ye me, my man. Hae ye done?' said old David,
glowering at him.

'Are you a Christian man?' said the Minister, sternly,
'or,' he added, as if on second thoughts, 'a loyal subject of
King James the Sixth?'

'Christian!' cried the old man with great indignation.
'Do you speer me gin I am a Christian? Man, do ye no
ken that I am an Ayrshireman? An' as for a loyal subject

of King Jamie, man, I hae been four score year and ten in the world, and proud am I to say that three score and sax o' them hae been at the King's Horn for rebel and outlaw—an' never a penny the waur o' either, being ever willing and able to keep my ain heid and haud my ain land again baith prince and Providence!'

'Old man,' said the Minister, sternly, 'ken ye that ye speak blasphemies. Know ye not that for every word ye utter, God shall enter into judgment with you?'

'Verra likely,' said David Crauford, drily. 'Stand oot o' my licht, man, I canna see through ye. Gin ye dinna, this pistol will enter into judgment wi' you.'

The Minister stepped aside—not, as I think, at all for fear of the pistol, but despairing of reaching the conscience of such a seared and battered heathen.

Then suddenly the old man rose from his seat as one that sees a heavenly vision. His face appeared transfigured and shining, and, with his white hair falling on his shoulders, I declare he looked like the Apostle Andrew in the Papish window of the High Kirk of Edinburgh.

'I see him! I see him!' he cried. 'He comes with the tidings of battle.'

I looked where he pointed with his eyes, but could see nothing save a black dot, which seemed to rise and fall steadily. Nevertheless, the old man spoke the truth. It was, indeed, a swift rider making straight for the house of Kerse.

As the man came nearer we saw him spur his horse till it stumbled and fell at the park dykes, weary or wounded, we could not tell which. This roused David Crauford, and he shouted to the man who now came on lamely on foot.

'Man, is the sow flitted?' he cried.

The man, peching and blown with his haste, could not answer till he came near.

'Is the sow flitted?' again shouted the old man.

'Oh, Laird Kerse,' cried the messenger, the tears trickling down his face, 'pity this sorrowfu' day! There has been a waesome slaughter o' your folk—ten o' them are dead—'

'Is the sow flitted?' cried Crauford, louder than ever. 'Can you no answer, yea or nay?'

'Oh, Kerse, hear me and weep; your braw and bonny son Jock, the flower of Kyle, is stricken through the heart, and lies cauld and dead on the ground.'

'Scoundrel, dolt, yammering calf, answer or die. Is the sow flitted?' The patriarch stood up on his feet, fiercely threatening the messenger with his staff.

'The sow is flitted,' cried the man. That and no more.

The old man fairly danced in a whirling triumph, cracking his fingers in the air with joy like a boy.

'My thumb for Jock!' cried he, 'the sow's flitted!'

And with that he dropped slack and senseless upon his great chair.

The Minister took my arm and led me to the louping-on stone.

'Come away,' he said sadly, 'it is no use. Ephraim hath too long been joined to his idols. Let him alone. It is as guid Maister Knox foretold. The Word of God is indeed made of none effect in Kyle and Carrick.'

CHAPTER XIII

THE TRYST AT MIDNIGHT

FROM Robert Harburgh I got the tidings of the disaster that had befallen the Cassillis' arms soon after I had ridden away with the Minister of Edinburgh. The Craufords were in no hurry to come on in spite of all the taunts of the Earl, and the disordered noise of the foul beast which for despite he had tied on their lands.

But they kept outposts on the hills about, and they looked often this way and that way—even I had seen them. Then began a waving of flags and crying of words, till once more their line settled into place, and from the north and the south at once fresh bands of horsemen came riding towards us. And as they came nearer, the Cassillis folk saw that they from the North were led on by James Mure the younger of Auchendrayne, and from the south there came the band of outlaws and robbers that called Thomas of Drummurchie their captain. On two sides these beset us, with only the river between, and the Craufords began to gather more closely than ever on our front.

Then the Earl remembered that what Dom Nicholas

and I had done so easily in the crossing of the Doon, other men as determined might also do. But being, as I have said, by nature a brave man, he first awaited the event. Nor was it long before, at a given signal, Drummurchie and young Auchendrayne set their horses to the water and came at us through the bends of the river, in spite of the shots that rained upon them, and the men that dropped from their seats and spun down the flooded Doon. For it was soon after the time of the Lammas floods, and the water was yet drumlie and wan.

In our front the Craufords raged, and altogether in a trice our position was wholly turned.

'This is not well done,' cried our Earl to Thomas of Drummurchie, as he laid stoutly about him. 'Thy brother had not so have treated his chief, when he strove with the enemies of the clan. Wolf should not tear wolf, nor Kennedy Kennedy!'

In a little it was seen that the promontory could not be kept in face of a force three times our number, and specially when those of our own name and ancient alliance were striving against us.

'Out of the neck of the bottle, and keep together!' cried the Earl, who on stricken field was no shaveling.

So with that, Earl John led his people straight across the water at the point of the land that jutted between the forces of Auchendrayne that came from the north, and Drummurchie's desperate riders who beset us on the south. So swiftly was this done that before they could close or the Craufords come on, most part of the Cassillis folk had passed Doon water. Though there were twenty at the least who were either drowned or else wounded to death, where they had fought the wager out on the fair holms of Dalrymple.

It so befel as the Minister and I were riding home, that we came on our little company of Culzean lads riding with tired horses and slack reins shorewards. And God be thanked for His ill-deserved mercy, in the quarrel that had been so evilly settled, there was no loss to Culzean. For we came not home with a single empty saddle, nor was there so much as a pike staff left behind. The last of it that they heard was the shouts of the Craufords as they flitted the sow over the water to the lands of Kennedy, thus clearing their own borders ere set of sun, according to their boast and promise.

On the morrow's morn there came to each Kennedy's gate a little squealing pigling with the Cassillis colours of blue and gold tied in derision to its curled tail. And round its neck was this motto, 'The flitted sow of Cassillis hath pigged, and Crauford of Kerse sends the litter home!'

And so in like manner was done at the house of every Kennedy that had men at the fight of the sow-flitting, whether they lived near or far. But who left them at the yetts, none saw. All which was more likely to be a ploy of Thomas of Drummurchie or John Mure's than of the Craufords—who, to do them justice, had small skill in aught save hard strokes, but plenty of that. For even to this day there is small civility or scholarship about Kyle Stewart and King's Kyle.

Now there was no mistaking but that we came home with our fingers in our mouths, and the countryside jeers at us of Cassillis and Culzean were many as the leaves of the summer trees. Nor could I win belief that I had been, by command of the Earl, at the house of Kerse along with the Minister, instead of on the green inch of Dalrymple by Skeldon haughs. For, believe it who will, there are many right willing to have a catch at me; though, God knows, I had never gone out of my way to put a slight upon any man, nor yet thought more highly of myself than I ought to think.

In time, however, the bitterness died down, and at Culzean things went their wonted quiet way. It is true that Nell Kennedy never so much as looked the way I was on. I heard that she went about telling everyone whom she thought would carry the tale to me, that I had gotten the Earl's sword for procuring the sow of Skeldon, and carrying her over Doon water on my back. But this was no more than spite, easily seen through, and I minded it not. For everyone in Carrick knew the cause why I had gotten the blade from the Earl, who, indeed, is not a man to give aught for naught, nor yet to bestow where, with honour, he might withhold.

But to balance the beam, Marjorie was kinder to me

than ever she had been, so that I thought of a surety that
her heart had at last been touched by love. But as it
chanced, I was to get news of that before I was greatly
older.

As the thing fell out, one night I had been somewhat
late out of bed, visiting of a friend whose name it does not
advantage to set down here. And in the morning, while
yet it was dark, I was returning by the rough shore tracks
to the coves, from whence I had to clamber warily up, in
order to reach my ladder of rope which depended, as of old,
from the overhanging turret of the White Tower.

As I stood to breathe a while in the quiet of the cove,
I was aware of voices that spoke above me, for the sea was
quiet and the moon dipping down to the setting. My
thoughts were running at the time on treasure-seeking, for
among the things I had had on my mind that night there
was the matter of the losing of the Kelwood treasure in the
House of the Red Moss. Thinking that I might learn something of importance, I hasted to clamber in the direction
from which came the voices. And as I glided along the
foot of the rocks in the black shadow, I came almost without warning upon two who stood close together.

I could not go back. I could not go forward. I could
only retreat sideways as far as the rock would let me, and
even then I stood within a few feet of the speakers.

At the first words I knew them. It was Marjorie
Kennedy of Culzean talking with Gilbert of Bargany, the
enemy of her house and of us all. The blood settled sharply
chill about my heart, and the bitterness of death seemed to
come upon me. The maid to whom my heart had gone out,
to whom I had looked up as my liege lady, was standing
here in midnight converse with the sworn enemy of her
race and of her father.

But I had no time for consideration—none for deciding
what I should do. I was no eavesdropper, yet for my life I
could not go forth and confront them.

I could hear Gilbert Kennedy's words. They were
pleading and passionate words.

'Hear me, listen to me, Marjorie,' he said, and I could
see his uncovered head turned towards her where she stood
black between me and the sea. 'I love no one but you. I

have sought none but you. Ever since I was a stripling lad,
like your young Launcelot Kennedy, have not I given you
worship and service? Why then do you hate me, despise
me, turn away from me?'

As I listened my heart rose again in hope. 'Your
Launcelot Kennedy,' he had said. It might be that I, even
I, was the cause why Marjorie turned from him as he said.

'Gilbert,' said Marjorie Kennedy, and her voice was like
the still waters of a sheltered sea lapping on the wet sands,
'I do not turn from you. I am not proud with you. If I
were, would I be here to-night? But in spite of this I am
trysted to another fate. If there is to be any use in my life,
it is that I may become the sacrifice that is to compose this
quarrel. And it cannot be with you for husband.'

'And wherefore not?' said Bargany fiercely, striking
one hand into the hollow palm of the other.

Marjorie put out one of her own hands as if to restrain
him.

'I will put you to the test,' said she; 'if I were Lady
Bargany, would you submit to John, Earl of Cassillis, and be
his man, setting aside all your ancient quarrels, and acknow-
ledging him as your liege lord?'

'God forbid!' said Bargany, promptly.

Marjorie put out her other hand for him to take.

'And I like you the better for it, Gilbert,' she said
impulsively.

Bargany set her fingers to his lips, and held her hands as
if he could never let them go.

'Then,' said she, 'since this bitter strife and the killing
of friends must somehow be stopped, and since you would
not stop it even for me—who am I that I should not be at
my father's command, to give and to take, to be sold and
bought like a beast in the market-place?'

'Who talks of buying and selling?' interrupted Bargany,
roughly. 'Give me but a look of your eyes, and I will carry
you to my house of Bargany, and see if any dare to take
you from the safe keeping of Gilbert Kennedy.'

'And my father?' said she, speaking very quietly, but
clearly, so that I heard every word.

'Your father,' answered Bargany, 'is a good man—too
good for such a crew. He has married one daughter to the

young Sheriff of Galloway. Wherefore not another to his cousin of Bargany? Is not Kennedy of Bargany, even though he be an enemy, better than any noltish Galloway laird?'

'Ah,' said Marjorie Kennedy, softly, 'but there is another reason—'

'Tell it me and I will answer it,' said Bargany, with a swift fierceness, for I think he imagined that he was making head against her scruples. But I had heard her speak in that still way before, and could have told him different.

'Isobel Stewart, bower-maiden to the Queen, and the Earldom of Carrick—they are surely reasons enough!' said Marjorie Kennedy.

Bargany started as though an adder had stung him. For a moment he seemed bereft of speech.

'Who has been lying to you of me?' he said, almost under his breath, as though the night air had suddenly made him hoarse.

'Nay, think again,' said Marjorie; 'is it not true? Better a soiled bower-maiden of the King's court and an earldom with her, than poor Marjorie Kennedy of Culzean in her smock!'

I never heard her say a spiteful thing before nor since— but when it comes to the matter of the Other Woman, all women are alike.

Bargany stamped his foot in very anger.

'A fig for dignities, and a rotten fig for Isobel Stewart,' he cried. 'I love but you, Marjorie Kennedy! Will you come to me, so that you and I may face the world together? For it is a black world and needs two hearts that can stand by each other.'

Then betwixt me and the sea (as I have said) I saw Marjorie knitting and clasping her hands as if her spirit were wrestling within her.

'Yea, Gilbert,' she said, very gently at last, 'it is as you say, a black, black world. But neither you nor I are going to better it by the breaking of trysts and engagements!'

'And what tryst have you?' he demanded sullenly.

'I am trysted to sorrow,' she answered, 'trysted for ever to want that which most I desire, and to have that which most I hate. Gilbert Kennedy, take my hand this once and hearken. You and I are too greatly like one another to be happy together. We are not mates born for smooth things. Sorrow is our dower and suffering our weird, and the pity of it is that we must dree it apart. I think we are both "fey" to-night,' she said, breaking off with a chance of tone. 'We had best go within.'

'Within?' said Bargany, scornfully, for he bethought him that he could never enter the house of Culzean as a friend.

'Now, Gilbert,' said Marjorie, 'be a man and forgive. Be a man also to Isobel Stewart, that she may know you a truer man than she has ever met in King's courts—ay, truer and nobler, as I think you, than the King himself. And let me go my way. . . .' She covered her face with her hands and stood a space silent and bowed. 'Let me go my way!' she said again. And so would have gone from him.

But Gilbert Kennedy had her in his two arms and was kissing her mouth, and that often and passionately.

'No,' he said, 'I will not let you go. I will take you in spite of all—though there were at Culzean a thousand fathers—at Cassillis a thousand earls!'

She withdrew herself from him with quiet dignity, yet without anger.

'But you will not take me in spite of one Marjorie Kennedy,' she said.

Then at this, quick as a musket flash, Bargany turned on his heel and tramped angrily down the shingle of the shore, his sword clanking and his spurs ringing, as careless who might hear as if he had been crossing the paved court of his own house of Bargany.

And Marjorie Kennedy stood still and watched him go, her hands pressed to her bosom, as though it needed both to still the dreadful beating of her heart.

'I love him! I love him!' she cried to the stillness, when he was quite gone. 'Oh, that he might trample me, that his hand might slay me, so that in death he might lift up my head and say once again, "I love you."'

And so she also passed away within.

Then I, in my corner, where I had been an unwilling hearkener, set my face between my knees and thought that the world would never be bright again. For I had heard that which I had heard, and I knew now that Marjorie, my

Lady Marjorie, would never know love for me while the world lasted.

Nevertheless, I rose up and clambered aloft to reach my rope ladder. I climbed over the rocks, thoughtlessly, heedlessly, and I scraped my shoe so that it sounded loud in the still night. Suddenly I saw something bright above me, the flicker of a white robe. I had nearly fallen, thinking that the appearance might be a spirit of the darkness.

'Dinna be feared, night-raker,' said a voice I knew well; 'it is only Nell Kennedy. Think ye that none can climb up the White Tower besides yourself?'

I was so greatly astonished that I could not speak at once.

'What may you be doing there at this time of the morning, Nell?' I said at last.

'Just like yourself—trying to find a quiet way to my bed,' said she; 'but I must hasten, or I shall be late to let in Marjorie.'

'What Marjorie,' said I, pretending that I knew nothing of the matter.

'Lie to other folk gin ye like, Spurheel,' said the madcap, contemptuously, 'but dinna think ye can lie to Nell Kennedy. I saw ye come from the hole down by the Cove.'

'But what do you here, Nell?' said I, for it might be that the mad lassie had a lad, and it seemed a terrible thing that she should be so misguided at her age as to meet him alone by night.

'Maybe I was down by seeing Kate Allison, the Grieve's lassie,' said she. 'Do you honestly think, Spurheel, that Helen Kennedy would permit a sister of hers to gang jooking here and there about the shore wi' a bonny young man at the dead of nicht all be her lone? It is not very likely.'

I said no more. It was not easy to argle-bargle with Nell Kennedy.

'And now betake yourself up the rope to your garret,' she said, 'and I will follow after, for I must let our Maidie in by the east door or it grows light.'

I motioned her to go first, but she turned on me in great indignation.

'Hear ye, Spurheel, up wi' ye! And if ye so much as set your nose oot o' your window when I am on the rope, it will no be telling you.'

So I climbed up and shut-to the window, and long before I was settle in bed I heard the two sisters talking softly together in the room beneath. So I knew that Nell Kennedy had carried out her mad ploy.

CHAPTER XIV

THE ADVENTURE OF THE GARDEN

I NEED not tell all the reasons why my well-beloved and kindly master, Sir Thomas Kennedy, had grown to be hated with a deadly feud by all the ill-conditioned of the Bargany faction, saving indeed by Gilbert Kennedy of Bargany himself. For one thing, my master was the man of the best and wisest counsels among all the supporters of Cassillis. He had many virtues, being well-liked wherever he went for kindliness and courteousness. Also he was a man of good principles and religion, so far as the times permitted, and indeed somewhat beyond, as he found to his own bitter cost or all was done.

Still more, my master Culzean was never one to suspect evil of any man, and was ever prone to cover wrack and ruin by over-trust and graciousness.

The first act of a great and wide conspiracy to compass his death was now to be played, for Thomas of Drummurchie, the brother of young Bargany, was not of so lofty a spirit as his chief. Indeed, to speak plainly, he was no better than an assassin and a common bully. He caused all the country-side to lie in terror for fear of him, being great with none, save only with the Lairds of Auchendrayne,— which was a strange thing considering their outward profession of strict honour.

It happened that there was a worthy knight, an indweller in the town of Maybole, Sir Thomas Nisbett by name, who was a crony of my master Culzean. Now, it was the practice for the gentry of the neighbourhood during the winter, to enter in and dwell within the town of Maybole in many pretty and well-built houses of freestone, diverting themselves during the dead time of the

year with converse together in each other's houses. These
stand for the most part in the chief street of Maybole,
and have fine gardens attached to them. Of them all,
that of the Earl of Cassillis, is the largest, but the one
belonging to my master Culzean is but little behind it in
beauty and convenience.

But Sir Thomas Kennedy bode little about his house in
Maybole, chiefly because his lads and lasses loved most to
remain at Culzean, where the cliffs are and the sea spreads
wide, clattering pleasantly on the rocks, and with the birds
blithely swirling and diving about it all the year round. And
of this I also was glad, for to live in a town is a thing I
cannot abide for any long time, being bred to the life of
the hills and to the wind in my face.

Now, on this New Year's Day, it so happened that this
Sir Thomas Nisbett had invited my master, being, as I say, a
crony of his own, and of an age with him, to sit down at
supper in his house in Maybole. So Culzean took horse and
a small attendance, of whom I was the chief, and rode over
to bide the night in Maybole town, meaning to lodge in his
own house, and in the .morning return to his Castle of
Culzean.

My master was a mightily curious man in one particular.
He could not abide any repair of people coming and going
with him on his journeyings. And if in a quieter time he
had gotten his will, he would have ridden here and there
without any attendance whatever—so kindly and unsuspicious of evil was his nature. On the New Year night he had
bidden me to remain within doors, because, as he said, he
knew his way home full well from Sir Thomas Nisbett's
house. Also, I suspect, he wished me not to observe
whether he retained his usual walk and conversation, after
seeing the New Year in with the Provost and the other
Sir Thomas, for the custom of Maybole was exceedingly
hospitable.

New Year's Day had been dark and gloomy. The
promise of oncoming foul weather was in the feel of the
raw, drooky air. No sooner was it dark than a smurr of
rain began to fall, very wetting and thick, so that even with
torches it had been impossible to see many places. We
reached our lodging at the town house of Culzean before

the night had set in, and as the supper was at six of the clock, it was no long time before my master took his way to Sir Thomas Nisbett's house. He left me seated by the fire with a book of chronicles of the wars to read. As soon, however, as he had issued forth upon the street, I took my bare sword in my hand, and by another door I sallied forth also. For in such a town as Maybole there are always ill-set folk that would gladly do an injury to a well-kenned and well-respected man like my master. And much more now when the feud had waxed so hot and high.

But it chanced that Sir Thomas, so soon almost as he set foot over the doorstep, greeted his fellow-guest, the Provost of the town—who, as became his office, had with him one to hold the tail of his furred gown out of the clarty mud, and also a lad with a torch running before him. Nevertheless, I followed on in that darker dusk which succeeds the glare of a torch. On our way we had to pass through the garden behind the house of Sir Thomas Nisbett, which was full of groset bushes, divided by high hedges of yew and box. I came softly after them, and abode still by the gate when the Provost and his train had passed through with our good knight in their midst. The pair of them were talking jovially together as they went, like men with toom kytes that know they are going in to be filled with good cheer.

'I declare I am as hungry as a moudiewort in a black frost,' said the douce Provost. 'I haena seen meat the day. What wi' hearkening to auld wives denouncing ane anither for kenned and notour witches, and sending men of the tribes of little Egypt to the Tolbooth, my life has no been my ain.'

My master laughed loudly and heartsomely.

'It is weel to be hungry and ken o' meat,' he replied, in the words of the well-kenned proverb.

And the pair of them laughed with their noses in the air, easily mirthful like men that strengthen themselves with the comfortable smell of dinner blown through an open door.

But I question much whether they had laughed so heartily if they had seen what I saw at that moment. And that was a face looking over the height of the yew hedge—a face wrapped about the mouth with a grey plaid and with a grey brimmed hat pulled close down over the eyes. As the flickering of the torch died out at the entering in of the house door, I saw the man raise his hand in a warning and forbidding gesture, as though he made a signal to men who could see him, but who were hidden from my sight.

This was enough for me. I resolved that those who plotted evil behind backs should have to war with Launce Kennedy, who, at least, was no mean foe, and one not given to wearing his eyes under his coat.

Not for a moment after this could I leave the garden, for one of the villains might have gone to the window and shot at my master through the glass—as one had done years before to good Maister John Knox (who, as I have heard tell, reformed religion in this land) on an evening he sat quietly reading his book and drinking of his ale in his own house in the High Street of Edinburgh.

So I got me into an angle of the garden and climbed a wall, which, being grown with ivy, was a good and safe post of vantage. From thence I could overlook the whole enclosure. After a little my eyes became better accustomed to the darkness. The lights from the windows also made a faint glimmering athwart the hedges, and I could distinctly see men darning themselves into their hiding-places, and getting ready their pistols and hackbutts.

Even as I sat there on the wall and froze, a plan came into my head which sent the blood surging through my veins, like the tide scouring the gut of Solway. I remembered that Sir Thomas Kennedy was at no time very active on his legs, and what with the income in his knee and the good wine under his belt, he would assuredly be in no key for running when he issued forth.

Also they were certainly many who lay in wait for him. I counted at least five moving about in the faint light. So I mounted the top of the ivied wall, and slid down the outside, landing heavily on my hinderlands in a ditch. I stole round to the gable door of Nisbett's house, and told the manservant that I had come to see my master, whereupon they permitted me to go up to the room on the first storey, where the guests were already set down at the banquet. I knew well that it was no use speaking to my lord, but I did venture to call out the host, Sir Thomas

Nisbett, whose head was stronger and whose heart more readily suspicious than those of the Laird of Culzean.

Him I told how the matter stood, whereupon he wished to speak to the Provost and to call the town officers. But I assured him that these determined assassins in the yard could render an account of the town guard twice told over.

'So,' said I, 'I have this to propose to you in a word. When the time comes for the guests to depart, you will detain my master—and the Provost, too, if you can.'

'Ere I have done with them they will not move far to-night, or my name is not Thomas Nisbett,' said the host, nodding his head, for these were the manners and hospitalities of the time.

'And you will lock them in a secure place till the morning!'

'But,' said Nisbett, 'will not the villains attack my house? If it be as you say, they have assurance for everything.'

I told him that they might very well do that, but that if he gave me a mailed coat with plate sleeves, and also kneecaps of steel, together with my arms and cap, I though I could make a race for it and carry them all off along with me.

'But, laddie,' he cried, 'ye gang to your death!'

I told him not so, for that even when accoutred I was a notable runner, and could course like a hare.

'And in any case, better Launce Kennedy be dead than Culzean, or the Provost and yourself, Sir Thomas Nisbett. What would happen to the town and countryside then?'

'Ay, better that,' he said very sententiously, at which I could scarce forbear but smile, for the very simplicity of the man was such that he not only counted his life worth more than mine, but expected me to do the same. However, it was not concerning him, but of my master and my master's children that I thought. What mattered little to a Kennedy of Kirrieoch, mattered greatly to Sir Thomas Kennedy, Tutor of Culzean. Yet I know not that I had any great fear of failure, for I had thus far won off scotfree, even when in the general engagement our faction had gotten the worst of it. And so I thought to do always.

The evening wore on like eternity, and I had many a thought in my heart, though but few of them were sad or waesome, for I was too young. Most of all I prayed that I might bear myself well, and in some shape at least carry the matter through without dishonour.

When the Provost and my master had well drunken and eaten yet more, their host stole away from them on a pretext, and came to the chamber where I sat in darkness, planning how to make my way through the garden.

He brought me presently the equipment of which I had need, and of his own accord added another pistol of admirable French workmanship. For France is ever the country for good ordnance of all sorts—from the pistolet which Sir Thomas Nisbett gave me to the cannons that dang down the Castle of Saint Andrews about the heads of Normand Leslie and his crew.

'Gin ye live ye kin keep the pistol,' he said, as one that did me a vast kindness.

Then over my steel cap I set the great broad hat of Sir Thomas of Culzean, and did his cloak about me.

It was now the time to go, and I tell you true, my heart beat a pretty tune to dance to as I stood at the back of the door—with my host hiding well in the rear, lest they should nick him by firing as the light within showed me plain in the doorway.

So I ordered the lamp to be removed and the door to be opened. Then my host bade me adieu in a loud, hearty tone, and said that he would come round and visit me in the morning. It was with a bitter sort of joy, not wholly unpleasant, that I heard the door clash sharply to behind me. I had my sword in my right hand and my pistol ready bent in the other. And I bethought me how many would have risked the same wager of battle.

There was a light flickering somewhere in the town— belike a party passing homeward with torches from a merry making, or some of the bonfires lighted for the inbringing of the New Year. I could see my friend of the beckoning hand now standing erect with his plaid about him. He was the same I had seen at the burning of the Bible when I was but a boy in the courtyard of Ardstinchar, and, I doubted not, the Grey Man of our later troubles.

I knew that the sharpshooters would be placed in the alleys of the garden. Indeed, I had seen them pass to their situations, and observed that they had their hackbutts carefully pointed at the path along which I must pass. So instead of walking directly down the main road to the gate, I made believe to stumble on the threshold, and to recover myself with an exclamation of pain, in order that I might divert them into waiting till I should come their way. For I must perforce pass by the mouths of their muskets so close that they could not miss.

But instead of taking the main avenue, I darted sideways along the narrower path which led round the garden's edge, and there, cowering in the angle, I waited for what should happen. In their hurry and surprise I heard one hackbutt go off with a crash, and the light from the touch lit up the garden. Then in the darkness that followed I ran further down the walk towards the outer gate. In the midst I came upon a fellow who kneeled with his musket upon a stick, trained upon the middle path by which they had hoped that Culzean would come. Then with my sword I stuck the hulking villain through that part of him with which I came most readily in contact. What that might be, I declare that I know not until this day. Only I judged that it could not have been a very mortal one, by the vigour with which he cried out.

Then indeed there was confusion and deray to speak about. I saw the form of the Grey Man, whom I had observed directing the ambush, rise from the further dykeside. He spoke sharply like one that cries orders, and at the word many men came rushing pell-mell to see what was the cause of the hideous outcry on that side of the garden where I was.

But I overstepped the carcase of the rascal into whom I had set my good blade, and most circumspectly made my way down the side of the wall unseen of any.

But when I had advanced as far as the way out by the single gate, my fate came, as it were, to the stern and deadly breach. For there were marksmen who had their pieces trained on that place. With my own eyes I had seen them set themselves in position. Nevertheless, the noise behind waxed so imminent that I drew a long breath, and sprang at the opening. As I went through, ten or twelve pieces at the least, both pistolets and hackbutts, were loosed off against me. I heard the bullets splash, splash all about my legs and body, and one that had bounded from the lintel of the door-post, dunted me on the breast-plate, which it was a God's mercy I had minded to wear. Yet for all I escaped wholly unscathed.

Outside the gate there were two fellows that withstood me, and I had small time to ask whether they were friends or foes. So, to make siccar, I speered no catechisms of them, but only shot off my pistol into one of the thickest parts of one, setting the muzzle almost to his belt, and with yet more gladness gave the other a sound iron thrust in the shoulder. For all my life I have loved the point more than the edge—and a thousand times better than the powder and lead—which is an uncertain hit-or-miss thing at best.

I cleared the yett, sprang through, and there I had it down the High Street of Maybole with the bullets spelking about me like hailstones, and chance night-wandering burghers scudding for their doors like conies on the sandy knowes.

I heard the fierce rush of men behind me, and looking over my shoulder I saw some ten running my way with their swords drawn in their hands. So I knew that it was likely there would be one among them who could outrun me, having war-gear upon me and that not all mine own. With that I undid the cloak of the Laird of Culzean, my master, and let it fall; and so much lightened I sped on till, near to the house of one Matthew M'Gowan, they fairly ran me to earth.

CHAPTER XV

A MIDNIGHT LEAGUER

THE place of my refuge was a summer-house set in a garden, and mostly made of wood. But it had three feet of stone-work about the walls, which chance fortifications, as I think, saved my life. Then I praised the forethought with which I had brought with me abundant powder and shot in the horns I had slung at my girdle. I also remembered to thank Providence for misdirecting the bullets as I ran out of the garden door.

Here in this small child's playhouse it was my fortune to stand such a siege as mayhap never man stood before. And of that I shall tell, so that all may judge and see whether the reward which the Earl of Cassillis afterwards obtained for me, was at all out of keeping (as some allege) with the services which I, Launce Kennedy, sometime esquire, rendered to him and his house.

Yet I did the thing for love and by no means for reward. Ay, and largely without thought also. For such was the spirit of the times, that wagers of battle were accepted lightly to spite one and overpass another, like children that play Follow-my-leader upon the street.

So I lay in my summer-house, behind the low breastwork of stone, while above me the bullets rattled through the frail woodwork like hailstones that splash into still water.

Lying thus prone, I charged my pistols—a thing which from long practice, I could do very well in the dark, and gazed out through the open windows that looked every way. What I suffered from most was the want of light upon the approaches of my castle at the top of the garden. For I was placed upon a little hill, and the ground sloped in every direction from me. Yet even this advantage of position did me little good, for the light was too uncertain to show me those that might come against me. And more than all, this uncertainty put me in a sweat lest I should shoot at shadows and allow the real enemy that came to invade and slay me to pass harmless, so that they would break upon me before I was aware.

Occasionally, however, the light that burned somewhere in the town cast glimmerings over the garden, and then I could see dark figures that crouched and scuddled behind and sheltered ayont the trunk of every leafless tree. After that God-sent illumination grew brighter, I think it is not too much to say that each time I got a fair chance at an enemy, there was one rascal the fewer alive—or at least one that had a shot the more in him. It cheered me to see them crawling out of the range of my ordnances as if they had been few and I a host.

Most of all I aimed, with the deadliest and most prayerful intent to kill, at the tall man in the cloak, whom I had seen from the first directing the ploy. Time and again I believed that I had him, but upon each occasion it was some meaner rogue that bore the brunt.

Thus I held my own with Sir Thomas's French pistol laid aside ready for them if they came with a rush, and my own for common use to load and fire again withal, till the barrels almost scorched me with the heat. Also I kept my sword ready to my hand, for when it comes to the edge of death, I put more confidence in my blade than in all the ordnance in the land. Though Heaven forbid that I should speak against the pistolet, when that very night I had so often owed my life to it. My chief hope now was that the Provost of the place, who had been a guest with Sir Thomas, might escape and rouse the townsfolk. The people of Maybole loved not the Barganies greatly, but, on the contrary, were devoted to the service of my master Culzean, because of his kindliness of disposition, and the heartsome way he had of calling them all 'Sandy' and 'Jeems,' according to their Christian name, a thing which goes a far road in Scotland.

It so happened just then that the fire that did me so much good—which, as I afterwards learned, was lighted by one of my enemies for frolic in the wood-yard of one Duncan Crerar, millwright—burned up a little and cast a skarrow over the garden where I was. When it was at its brightest, there came four fellows, running up the brae all with their swords bare in their hands, so that it seemed that I was as good as dead, for it was manifestly impossible that I could withstand them all. But I minded the saying of a great captain of the old wars, 'Stop you the front rank, and the second will stop of itself.' So I took good and careful aim with my pistols at the two fellows that led the charge, and fired. The first of them tossed his blade in the air, spun about like a weathercock and fell headlong, while the other, lamed in his leg, as it appeared, tried to crawl back down the hill again. The two that came behind were no little daunted by this fall. Nevertheless, they still came on, but I cried out as loud as I could, 'Give me the other pistols, Sir Thomas, and I shall do for these two scoundrels also!'

At which they gave back in great astonishment and ran, I make no doubt, to tell their masters that they had to do with more than one old man well lined with sack and canary. Then in the breathing space I charged my pistols again, and cried to the fellow that was limping along the ground by the back of my summer-house,—

'Link it, my lad, back to your master, or I shall put another bullet in ye, in a place where it will stop you from groaning and hirpling there at my lug!'

For I understood well that he desired to take me in the rear.

At this moment there happened a thing surprising. I saw a tall, dark figure overleap a wall at the side from which the shots came thinnest. I saw it stoop and lay fire to something that was darker than itself, when instantly there arose from the pile of millwright's shavings and kindling wood a clear light which caused all the garden to be seen without any difficulty.

Then the tall, unknown figure, which seemed yet unaccountably familiar to me, walked slowly up the middle walk towards the summer-house, the pistols cracking all about, and the bullets splashing faster than ever upon the roof and sides of my shelter.

Then I saw who it was.

'Run for it, Robert Harburgh,' I cried. 'Man, you are mad.'

But I declare he never altered by a single pulse-beat his deliberate advance. At the door he paused as one that upon the threshold would turn to kick a yelping cur. Then giving the sharpshooters a wave of his hand in contempt, he entered and shut the door.

'Saint Kentigern's fish and a thousand devils,' said I, 'I am not feared of any man, but there is no sense in foolhardiness, Robert. Come in out of reach of their bullets this moment, thou fool!'

'Ah,' he returned to me, 'I had as lief die and be done with it.'

'But then I would not, for my stomach is in good order,' replied I, swiftly, 'so lie down on thy belly and at the least help me to keep alive, for I am most consumedly anxious to keep my body from proving leaky by the entering in of bullets.'

So, obediently he laid him down, watching one side of

our cunning defences. He told me that he had heard what was a-doing—how that the Mures and Drummurchies, together with Sawny Bean, the savage carl that was called of the common people 'The Earl of Hell,' had gotten the Laird of Culzean in a little summer-house in a walled garden and were there worrying him to death.

'So,' said Harburgh, 'having nought better to do, I primed my pistols and came.'

The firing upon us grew hotter than ever. We seemed at times to be closed within a ring of fire. Yet neither of us were the least hurt, save that a chip from the edge of a stone, driven off by a bullet, had struck me on the cheek and made it bleed.

When the fire which Robert Harburgh had lighted burned up, we that were marksmen lost no chances at any who showed so much as an arm or a leg. And many of those murderous rascals whom we did not kill outright (not having a fair chance at them from their lying in shelter and other causes), were at least winged and sore damaged, so that we judged that there would be some roods of lint bandage required about Drummurchie and Auchendrayne on the morrow.

Outside we heard a great and growing turmoil and the sound of many voices crying 'To the death with the murderers! Break down the doors!'

It was the noise of the people who had risen in the night and were coming to help us. For in a moment the gate of the yard was broken down, and a rout of men in steel caps and hastily-donned armour came pouring in. And it had been comical to watch the array, if our urgent business had allowed. For some had put on a breastplate over their night gear; some fought like Highlandmen in their sark-tails, which, on the night of the New Year, must have been breezy wear; while others again had snatched a hackbutt and had forgotten the powder, so that now they carried the weapon like a club by the barrel.

Before these angry levies our cruel invaders vanished like smoke, as though they had never been, clambering over walls and scurrying through entries. But it is reported that several of them were sore hurt in thus escaping—indeed, here and there throughout the town were no fewer than five dead and six wounded, chiefly in the two gardens where I had been compelled to discharge my pistols.

Robert Harburgh stepped out of the summer-house before them all, stretching his limbs.

''Tis a cramped, ungodly place, friends,' he said. 'After all, it is better to fight in the open and risk it!'

'Where is the Laird of Culzean?' cried some that knew him not. 'If ye cannot show us the laird, ye shall die forthwith!''

'Nay,' replied Harburgh, 'concerning that I ken not. 'Tis not in my provinc(, being general information. My parish is fighting, not the answering of questions. Come hither, Launce, and tell them of thy master!'

Whereat I came forth and told them of the cruel plot and the attack upon Sir Thomas at Nisbett's house. But they would not be satisfied till they had gone there and found him. Nothing would do but that he should show himself unhurt and speak a word to them at the window. Which, being of short-grained temper and with a monstrous headache, he was most loathe to do. But Robert Harburgh, who had experience of suchlike, being before his marriage a great man of his cups, poured water upon his head, and, having dried it by rubbing, he brought him to the window, where he spoke to the people as his kindly friends and neighbours, and thanked them for their affection.

'Nay,' cried one, 'thank your own young squire, who has to-night ta'en your life upon him.'

So the people of Maybole, for the honest and honourable love which they bore us, abode under arms till the morning, and searched all the town for the murdering ruffians of Drummurchie. Yet they found them not, for such always have a back door to escape by.

In the morning, Sir Thomas called for his hat and cloak, and when they were brought he started in wonder and cried, 'What, in the name of the shrunk shanks of the Abbot of Crossraguel, is the meaning of this hole?'

Then Robert Harburgh said, ''Tis but an airy summer suit that Launcelot wore last night, when he went forth among those that sought to kill the Laird of Culzean.'

My master stared without comprehending. But when he fully understood, he clasped me in his arms.

'God knows,' he said, ''I would give my right hand, if I could believe that I had a son who would ever do as much for me. Those I have are good for naught but golf and stool-ball.'

Wherein by his hasty words he did his honest, silly lads much wrong.

CHAPTER XVI

GREYBEARDS AND DIMPLE CHINS

ONE Sabbath morn there came an unwonted message to me, as I sat lingering and idle in the armoury of Culzean. I had cleaned my own graith and oiled the pistols—which I regularly did on the Sabbath morning whenever I did not go to the kirk at Maybole. Now, this particular day of which I speak, I was idly conning the leaves of a song-book full of trifling, vain, and amatorious lilts and catches—some of them very pleasant, however, and taking to the mind. It ought to have been my psalm-book that I was at, God forgive me; but since ballad-book it was, why, even so will I set it down here.

And the message that came was by the mouth of a kind of jackal or lickpot of John Dick's—who, for reasons of his own, hated me, chiefly because I took no share in the foulness of him and his subservient crew. This youth was of so little worth, that in all the transactions of this book he has not once come into the narrative—though as I now remember he was at the tulzie in Edinburgh, and also at the flitting of the sow. On both occasions he was the first to run.

The name of him was Colin Millar, an ill-favoured, envious, upsetting knave, compact of various ignorances and incapacities. And there needs no more to be said about him.

'There is a man wanting to see you down at Sandy Allison's, the Grieve's,' he said.

Then he looked at me with the cast in his eye as crooked as a paddock's hind leg, and says he, 'The fat will be in the fire now, I'm thinking. They tell me that it is the Minister!'

I knew very well what the ill-tongued hound meant. So right gladly without a word I set the knuckles of my hand, Sabbath morning though it was, against his ugly face in a way that would leave a mark for a day or two.

'Take you that, dog,' I said to him, 'and learn to keep a more ruly member in your insolent head. Think not that you are John Dick, though you carry his dirty slanders. As the wild boar gnashes its tushes, so the little piglings squeak!'

And as he went away, lowering and snarling, I had a mind to go after him and give him something more than my knuckles. For the thing he meant was a lie of the devil, lighted at his furnace and spewed out of the reek of his pit.

But as I went to the door there came a poor lad from the stable with the same message—that there waited one for me at the house of Sandy Allison, the Grieve.

So I knew that the dog Millar had not invented the whole matter. Whereupon I looked carefully to my gear, did a new doublet upon me (because it was the Sabbath day) and girt me with a sash of blue, coft in Edinburgh and never before worn. Then setting my sword in its sheath, I went out through the woods, which were now grown leafless and songless.

There was a brisk air of winter, crisp without rawness, in the breeze, and I was glad to be out of doors; for since the matter of the meeting with Gilbert Kennedy, which by ill chance I had seen, both Marjorie and Nell came seldom my way. Which is, perhaps, why I looked so well to my apparelling ere I went to the Grieve's house. For a lad wearies for the speech of women-folk, and if he gets not one kind—why, he will seek another.

But now, when I come to think of it, I need not have troubled so to deck myself. For after the corner is turned and the long lane leads straight to the garden of roses, a woman cares not whether a man be clothed in dishclouts or whether he glitters like a bridegroom in cloth of gold.

So when I came near to the house there issued forth to meet me Kate Allison, which seemed to me like ancient days come back, and my heart beat in a fashion I never thought to feel again. For a burnt stick is easily lighted, and Kate Allison was, without doubt, both bonny and kind. She was waiting for me at the corner of the barn like one that has an assignation. So when she came near me she put her hands roguishly behind her, and said, 'Launce

Kennedy, you are a false, deceitful lad, and no true lover. But think ye not that I care a pin, for I have gotten a braw lad of my own, and no thanks to you. Ye can get the Lady Marjorie to convoy hame next year from the Maybole Fair.'

And her speech made me glad, for she dropped me a courtesy and pretended to march off. So I knew full well that if she had not been heart-whole and at ease about all doubtful matters, she would have greeted me very differently. So, as I say, I was glad. Yet presently I liked it not so well as I expected, for though men are often false to their loves, they never understood how their loves can change from loving them. I knew well that Kate would, if not meddled with, immediately return to tell me what had befallen, and why it was that they had sent for me.

Which indeed was just what she did.

'We have gotten a mighty grave man here with us, who came to our house last night at e'en. We wanted to send word to the castle to Sir Thomas; but the man said that he had had enough of the Kennedies to last him his lifetime, and that he would put up with us, if we could make shift to give him a bed. He is a man of a majestic and noble countenance, and when he had come within, he took a Bible from his wallet, and tairged us tightly on the histories of the wars of the Jews and on points of doctrine.'

'Ye would be fit for that,' said I to her, laughing, 'for most of our discourse has been upon points of doctrine and practice—though I mind not that we touched upon the wars of the Jews. We had ever wars enough of our own. Was it not so, sweet Kate?'

And I would have taken her by the waist, for that is ever the way, as I have just been reading in my song-book, to punish a woman, when like a pretty scold, she slanders her love. So, as the London stage catch hath it, I forgave her for it. Yet for all she would by no means permit me to come near her—which I was mortally sorry for. Because though I wanted her to change, I desired her not to change so mightily as all that.

'Na, na,' she said, 'and that's by with. Kate Allison needs no general lovers. Wear you your own lady's favours; I can get them that loe me and none other, to wear mine.'

I pursued the subject no further at that time, meaning, however, to return to it. For a man likes not to see the things which have been freely his slipping from him like corn through a wide-meshed riddle. It makes his mind linger after things long past, and he begins to think them sweeter than any favours that ever he had, even when all the garden was most fully his to wander in and cull at his lordly pleasure.

Too soon for my liking, therefore, we came to the door of the Grieve's house, which was but a wide kitchen with two smaller rooms off it. I heard a voice uplifted as it seemed in prayer, and I bethought me with shame of my so late mean and earthly thoughts; but I looked at Kate Allison, and she was so pleasant to look upon that I found excuses for myself.

Then the prayer being done we went in, and they told the man in the inner room that that same Launcelot Kennnedy, for whom he had inquired, was come.

So in a moment there came forth from the inner chamber, even as I had expected, Maister Robert Bruce. He wore his long, black cloak, and his fine, cloth coat showed soberly beneath it. His hat was on his head, which he doffed for a moment to Kate Allison and her mother, and then set on again. He bade them excuse him, for that he had much business to talk with me. I followed him out, and as I passed Kate, methought she looked disappointed that I should go thus soon. So, the corners of her mouth being down, and her mother's back turned, I put my hand beneath her chin, and plucked at the loose slip-knot of her bonnet, which was a pretty quipsome thing that haymakers use, but prettier on her than on any of them. Whereat she flashed forth a great, sharp pin and set in spitefully in my arm, which also was a pleasing habit of hers. But all was innocent and friendly enough, and my only excuse for thinking more of daffing with Kate Allison than of listening to the grave converse of Maister Robert Bruce, is that then I was nearing nineteen years of my age—which, as you all do know, is a time when maids' dimples are more moving than the wisdom of the sages.

That is all mine excuse, and, as well I wot, but a poor one. Yet when once Maister Bruce had me in the wood, taking me by the arm, the majesty of his countenance and the moving fervour of his voice so worked upon me that in good sooth I thought of naught but what he said.

He told me that he was resolved to depart out of this land of Carrick and Kyle, which might have been the Garden of Eden if it were not inhabited by devils. He had come no speed at reconciling the parties at feud, even as I could have told him before he began.

'When I had thought,' he said, 'that I had made some way in softening the heart of Gilbert Kennedy, who vaunts himself to be sincerely attached to me—and I do believe it —I said to him that he ought, for the settling of the quarrel, to give in his submission to his liege lord, the Earl of Cassillis. In a moment comes the fire into his eyes, the anger grows black in his heart, and all my good words are undone. I think you Kennedies are all of you possessed with evil spirits, even as it was in the days of the Gadarene out of whom Christ cast many devils.'

He paused a moment, and then continued,—

'So the name of the devils of Carrick is Legion, for they are very many!'

Then, being sorry that he should so speak of those who, after all, were my master's kin and in a manner my own —for all the world knows that a blood feud is a thing acknowledged in the Bible, as one may see when David lay on his deathbed—I asked him how I could serve him, in order that I might stay his abuse of that which he did not understand.

'You may wonder,' he went on, 'that I choose to speak in confidence to one that is but an esquire, and, I hear, as ready with his sword in the quarrel as any of them. But at least you are not like the rest, occupied entirely with the safety of your own skin, and unwilling to look the matter in the face.

I told him that I did not wonder at all that he was willing to speak to me, for that I could keep my counsel truly and well.

'Faith, and I believe that,' he cried, 'if it were only your self-conceit of being able to do it.'

But I understood not at all what he meant, for if there is anything that I am conspicuously lacking in, it is this very quality of self-conceit.

'Hear ye, then, and mark well my words,' said the Minister of Edinburgh. There is a man in this country who is at the root of all the blood and all the slaughter, and who, if he be not curbed, will yet do tenfold more mischief. Your master thinks that he can bribe him to friendship; well, I am no judge of men, if the man is to be bribed at any price beneath the sole power and sway of all this wild country of the west.'

'It is Gilbert Kennedy of Bargany that you mean,' said I, for I own I was jealous of his good name, enemy though he was.

'Gilbert Kennedy is but a hammer in this man's hand. Your good knight here at Culzean is but a spoon for him to sup with. And the only man that sees through him (and that but partially) is your jolter-headed Earl, whose keen care for the merks, the duties, and the tacks, makes him somewhat clearer in the eye than the rest of you.'

'And who is this plotter?' said I.

He stopped and looked about him to see that none was listening. Then he laid his lips almost to my ear.

He whispered a name which, in this place, I must not write, though afterwards it will be plain enough.

'It is simply not possible,' said I; 'the man you mention is but a bonnet laird, as one might say, with a peel-tower and a holding of half-a-dozen crofts. Why, my master could eat him up saltless, without turning out more than half a parish of his fighting men.'

'Nevertheless,' said Robert Bruce, 'that is the man who stands behind and makes the miracles work, as in Popish days the priests were wont to do behind the altar. Ye are but a set of jigging fools here in Carrick, and the man that pipes to you is the man I've told ye of!'

Then I thought over the matter—all that I knew of the man.

'In truth,' said I, 'I am none so sure that you may not be right.'

Robert Bruce smiled as one that waxes aweary of a babe's prattle.

'For,' said I, 'I mind that I heard him endeavour to win one by promises to the side of Bargany—'

'Pshaw,' said the Minister, 'he would as readily try to

win Bargany to the Earl's side, if it suited him to murder them both together. It is his plan to make them fight each other till there are none left—to cut off the heads of the taller poppies as in the ancient tale of Rome. I tell you this man has no side but his own, no desire but his own profit, no end but to make himself supreme in Carrick.'

'And what can I, that am but a squire and a youth, do in the matter?' said I.

'You are on the spot, Launcelot,' said the Minister, kindly. 'I am in Edinburgh, and if things march as evilly as they have been doing of late, it is likely I shall be even further afield than Edinburgh. But you can watch—you can judge whom it boots to warn. You can put in a word—'

'I shall put in a sword,' said I, stamping my foot; 'put it in deep—to think of such deceit and guile in a mere vassal and understrapper of my lord's.'

'Launcelot,' said the Minister of Edinburgh, 'you begin to make me sorry I trusted you. I should have spoken to a graver man.'

'Nay, sir,' I said, 'you mistake me. I but mean that if it came to the bitter bite of iron, the time for words might go by.'

'Ay,' he replied thoughtfully, 'there is some sense in that, but give not up the judicious words too early.'

So we betook ourselves gravely and staidly out of the wood, and at bidding him farewell I received his benediction, which he gave me with his right hand stretched out. And though I am tall and stand as erect as any man, yet the Minister of Edinburgh overtowered me by half a foot. But I minded that not in him.

So I went to the castle armoury to bethink me, for after what I had heard maids and bonnet strings were not to be more in my thought that day.

CHAPTER XVII

THE CORBIES AT THE EAGLE'S NEST

ONE snowy day, I mind it was a Thursday according to the day of the week, I had ridden to Girvan by the shore road. I journeyed unmolested save that one sent a shot after me as I passed the tower of Girvanmains. But this not so much, I think, with intent to do me an injury, as because they saw my Cassillis colours, and could not let them pass unchallenged by a yett of the Bargany folk.

But upon my return I got one of the greatest surprises of my life, for as I rode gladly into the courtyard of Culzean, lo! there was my lord out on the steps, with the noble courtesy and distinction which none could assume so well as he, being indeed natural to him, bidding farewell to a pair of guests whom I never looked to see in the courtyard of Culzean, save as it might be coming in decently, heels first, for the purposes of Christian burial.

The two strangers were John Mure of Auchendrayne and the young Laird, his son. The old man was dressed as I first saw him—in plain, fine cloth of blue without decoration. He wore no arms or any armour that was visible—though by the square setting of his body as he came down the steps I judged that he wore a stand of chain mail underneath. His son James, a cruel, loutish, hot-headed, but not wholly ill-looking young man, was clad in the gayest fashion. He wore the wide, falling lace collar which Prince Henry had brought in from France, and a pointed doublet and wide breeches of the newest English mode.

It was John Mure who was speaking, for his son was but a lout, and had little to say all the days of him. He waved his hand to the steps, by the door of Culzean, whereon there stood Marjorie Kennedy, with her arm on Nell's shoulder, both being pale as death, and seeming more dowie and sad than I had ever seen them look before.

'It is to be the burying of strife,' cried Auchendrayne; 'in this loving cup I drink it. The day of our love is at the dawning, and the auguries of the time to come are of the happiest. To our next and sweeter merrymaking!'

And Sir Thomas, with his face one beaming smile of pleasure, bade him a loving farewell, and told him to haste back, for that cousins thus joined in affection could not be too often together.

And all the while I sat Dom Nicholas as one that is sunk fathoms deep in blank astonishment.

As Auchendrayne rode through the gateway, he waved his hand to me, and turning to Culzean, where he stood looking after them, he cried in the hearing of them all,—

'You have there the handsomest and the boldest squire in all the south country, Culzean. This is the bruit that I hear of this young man everywhere I go.'

And so, still smiling and bowing, he rode away with his son half a length of his horse behind him.

But I gave him no greeting, neither yea nor nay—but regarded him with a fixed countenance. For my heart was like stone within me, because of the sorrow that I saw coming on the house and could noways prevent.

Now the bitterness of this winter did not come till some time after the New Year. It was about the midst of January when the frost bit most keenly, and the snow began to fall most deeply. The Culzean lads, James, Alexander and little David (who was my favourite), caused the court and out-buildings to ring with happiness. Joy and peace seemed indeed for a little to have come back to Culzean. This was the first snow since David had donned the trunks, and laid by the bairn's kilts—which are indeed mortally cold wear in the winter season when it comes to rolling in the snow.

David, as I say, was my favourite, and continually in my loneliness a comfort to me, though I have not hitherto often mentioned him, seeing that the young lads of Culzean come not into my tale greatly, saving at this time. Though, in the coming day, they may into the tales others shall tell, when we that now prank it so gaily are no better than the broken shards of a drained pottle-pot. But little Davie was a merry lad, and I am glad that there is occasion for me to name him in this history.

Davie was now manfully equipped in doublet and trunk hosen of duffle grey homespun so thick that his brothers feigned that with a little trouble and propping they stood up very well by themselves, when their daily tenant had untrussed him and gone to bed.

And ever the snow came down. It lay deep on all the face of the country, but more especially it had swirled into the courtyard of Culzean, so that the very steps of the door were sleeked, and great wreaths lay every way about the court. The lads made revel in it, borrowing shovels from the stables and throwing up the snow on either side, so as to make narrow passages between the different doors of the castle and the offices about.

I cannot set down, because that there is press of matters more serious yet to be related, a tithe of the merry pranks the rogues wrought in their madness. They revelled in the smother of the snow like whelps that are turned loose. Yet because there is none too much of merriment in this chronicle, I shall make shift to tell somewhat of their quip-some rascaldom.

It chanced one morning that Alexander, who was of a mirthful mind, stood by a little door which led into the house wherein our peats and turfs were kept for the fires, so that it might not be necessary to bring a supply each day from the peatstacks on the hill where the greater store was.

Whether Sandy's head ached from having eaten too many cakes at the time of the New Year, I know not, but suddenly it came into his mind that it might be a desirable thing and a cooling, to stick his bullet head into a mighty snowdrift which lay in front of the peat-house door. So accordingly, for no particular reason, he bent himself into an arch and thrust his head neck-deep into the snow.

At this moment came his elder brother, James Kennedy, upon the scene, and his mood was also merry.

'Bless the rascal,' quoth he, 'whither hath his tidy lump of a top-knot betaken itself to?'

So without loss of a moment the rogue made him a large ball of snow, well compacted, and caused it to burst upon the stretched trusses of Sandy's breeches, with a noise like the breaking of an egg upon a wall.

Sandy snatched his head from the snow swift as a blade that bends itself to the straight, and stood erect. There was no one in sight save little Davie, who danced at a distance and laughed innocently at the jest. For James, the doer of it, had instantly dropped into a deep snow passage. Whereat Sandy, cured as to his head, but villain-ously stung in the breech, turned him about in fierce anger, seeking for someone to truncheon. The lad Davie's laugh annoyed him, and Sandy, being an adept at the palm play, sent a snowball at his young brother, which took him smartly upon the cheek.

Instantly Davie, poor callant, set up a cry of pain, which brought his sister Nell upon the scene with all the furies in the tangle of her hair.

'Ye muckle, good-for-nothing calves!' she cried, addressing both her unseen brothers, whom she well knew to be lying hidden somewhere among the snow passages of the courtyard, 'I will bring Launce Kennedy to you with a knotty stick, and that by my father's orders— clodding at a bairn that gate, and garring him greet. Ye think I canna see ye, but if ye dinna come oot decently, I will come and bring ye. Ye may think black shame o' yoursel's!'

And this I do not doubt that James and Sandy did. For to be flyted upon by a lass, lying prone the while upon one's stomach in a snow bank, does not make for self-respect. So both the lads began to crawl away as best they might from Nell's dangerous neighbourhood. It jumped greatly with my humour to watch them from the upper window of the armoury which looked abroad over the court. All unwitting they approached the one to the other with their heads down, and at the corner, each running with full speed upon his hands and knees, they knocked their skulls together soundly, with a well-resounding crack which pleased me. Instantly they clinched and fought like wild cats, biting and fisting in the snow—till their father attracted from the hall by the noise, came down and laid upon them both right soundly, with the great whip wherewith the dogs were beaten when they were trained for hunting.

All this was excellent sport to me, but the best was yet to come. In a little thereafter I saw Nell, who was a merry lass when there was nothing upon her mind, come quietly out of the side door that led to the kitchen places, with David in her hand. She set him within a small flanking tower, which in old days had been loop-holed for arrows. Then she locked the door upon him, taking the key with her. Before she went she handed the boy two or three snowballs made from the wet, slushy snow, where the sunshine had caused some drops to melt off the roof and fall from the eaves.

Thus she went to the corner, I watching with joy the while from the window of the armoury.

'Jamie, Sandy,' she cried, 'come hither, lads. There's something here for your private ear!'

At first the boys would not move, still smarting and sulky from their father's training-whip. But in a little they came, and Nell enticed them with the repeated promise of 'something for their private ear' (the artful minx!), till she had them exactly opposite the little window where David was posted with his weapons of offence.

Suddenly from the arrow-slot there came a discharge of artillery. The providence that helps the weak put pith and fusion into little David's arm. As though it had been the smooth stone of the brook that sped whizzing to the brazen front of Goliath, the first moist shot of David's ordnance plumped with a splash into the ear of Sandy. In an instant I lay upon the floor in the laughter which comes only from beholding silly things. For there below me were James and Sandy Kennedy each dancing upon the point of their shoon, and with their little fingers digging in their several ears to excavate from thence the well-compacted slush wherewith little David had taken his fitting revenge.

Nor was the occupation made easier for them by the vexatious commentaries of their sister Nell, who repeated over and over again to them, between her bursts of laughter, 'Did I not tell you that if ye came to the corner of the tower ye would get something for your private ear? This will learn you to let wee Davie alane!'

CHAPTER XVIII

BAIRNS' PLAY

THERE remains yet one other of their pranks to be told, and that only because it is knit into the story, and so must be unravelled along with it.

The pair of elders, after this defeat at the hands of Nell and little David, took counsel together, and might sooner have hit upon something to their mind, but that James, as was usual with him, stood in an attitude of cogitation, having his mouth very wide open. Whereat Sandy, whose wits were brighter, could not, even for the sake of the alliance between them, refrain from dropping therein a snowball which he had ready in his hand for any purpose

that might arise. This he did with the same neatness and
adroitness with which he would have dropped a ball of
worset yarn, when the caps were on the green for the game
royal of Bonnet-Ba'.

It took some time and a mighty deal of struggling on
the ground before this treachery between friends could be
arranged. Also much thrusting of snow down the backs of
doublets and holding it there till it melted—together with
other still more unseemly and uncomfortable proceedings.

Then the reconciled allies entered the castle together,
promising peace, and fell into talk with young Davie, who
stood within the great door in the inviolate safety of the
hall.

'Do you want a merk?' said Sandy, tempting him with
the sight of one, which at that day was great wealth. 'It
will buy store of peaches, and pears, and baked apples at
Baillie Underwood's in the High Street, preserved cherries
also, and marmalit of plums.'

Then said Davie, 'A merk I want, indeed, as does
everyone, but you are not the fellow to give it me. Therefore quit your pother, for I know that you would only make
friends to get me apart, and so work mischief upon me.'

A wise boy David.

'As I live I lie not,' said Sandy, taking a great oath. 'I
will give you the merk, if ye go down after dark to the
barn, and passing through the great door to the lesser door
at the back, shut and bolt it with its bar of oak, and so
return the way ye went. If ye do this, sure as death, I lie
not, I will give you the merk.'

Little David, who had ofttimes been deceived of his
brothers, considered upon the offer a while, and at last he
said to Sandy,—

'As sure as death ye might lie, though twice ye have
said it; but give the merk into the keeping of Launce
Kennedy, that will not tell lies, at least not for such freits,
and then I will take your dare, and go shut the further
door of the barn.'

They came up therefore to me to the armoury, James,
Sandy and David all together; and as soon as I heard them
coming I went from the window and sat by the fire, that
they might not suspect I had observed aught of their mat-

ters. Then, when they revealed the plot to me, I bade Sandy be careful what he did, for it was growing dark, and I misdoubted that they meant to fright the child. So I feared them with the threat of their father, and as little David lingered while his brothers went lumbering and shouting down the armoury stair, I put into his hand a short blackthorn cudgel which the young Sheriff of Galloway had brought with him over from Ireland.

'If ye see anything more than common, hit it as hard as ye can with that,' I bade him.

And so little David passed out. I could not see him far across the yard because of the fall of the gloaming, but on his return, all a-drip of sweat and in a quivering tremble of agony, he told me what had befallen him.

'It was bitter cold,' he said, 'and I will not say that I was not feared, for I was. Yet, so long as the door stood ajar, there came a ray of light through it, and my heart was cheered. But presently it was shut to, and I had all the way to go alone.

'But I heard the cows in the byre rattling at their hemps through the rings, and as I kenned, pulling at the meadow hay in their stalls. And that at least was some company. So I went on and the frosty snow squeaked under my feet. I came to the great door of the barn. It stood open, vast and terrible as the mouth of a giant's cave. But I thought of the marmalit of plums, and in I went with my heart gulp —gulping high in my throat.'

I nodded at the little fellow, for many a time had I felt the same, and said nothing about it—when I was much younger, of course.

'So,' said he, 'I went through the barn in which was such hay and straw, till I came to the midst of it. Here I stopped to listen, for I could hear a noise, indeed many noises. However, it was only the black rattons firsling among the straw. I felt a thousand miles away from home, an orphan, and very lonely—nor did thinking on marmalit of plums now bring comfort—at least, none to speak of.

'But, nevertheless, because I thought of the taunting and japing of James and Sandy, I took my way to the further door that looketh upon the old orchard. The black corn-stacks shut out many of the stars, but those that were left tingled and shone cold. I thought I had no friend nearer than one of these. I was much afraid.

'Yet nevertheless I shut the back door and barred it—barred it good and strong with both bolts, and set a corn-measure at the back for luck. This being done, I turned and took but one step towards the great door, through which I could see the snow shining like a mist. Then my heart stopped, and I tried to cry out very loud, but, alas! I could not cry out at all.

'For there was Something in the doorway. I could see it against the snow. Something that crawled on the ground with dull, horrid eyes, set wide apart, and that turned a shapeless, horned head slowly from side to side, moaning and yammering the while.

'I thought I should die. Then I feared that I should not die before the thing took me, for it slowly invaded the barn till it filled all the doorway. By this I knew that I should indeed be devoured. Nevertheless, I minded what it was you said before I went. So I thought that, having a stout stick in my hand, I might as well die after having smitten a good stroke as not—'

'Bravo, young David!' cried I; 'that is the right spirit of battle.'

'So I took the blackthorn in both hands,' he went on, 'and swung it about my head as you showed me in the hagging down of trees. With that I struck the horrible thing fairly between the eyes. Then leaping over it I ran, how I know not, for the house door—where I laughed and wept time about till Nell brought me here that you might bid me stop. Now I want the merk.'

So I gave him the merk, took down the dog-whip from the nail where it hung, and went out to look for Jamie and Sandy—for well I knew that this had been one of their tricks to frighten the boy, and I was resolved that they should take a thrashing, either from me or, what they would less desire, from their father—who, though a kind enough man till he began to lay on, was apt to be carried away with the exercise, and to forget bowels of mercy.

But when I got upon the snow by the door, Sandy came running to me, fairly crying out with terror. He had the hide of a muckle bullock, which had been killed that day, trailing from his waist. His face, in the light that fell from the lamp in the hall, was a sight to be seen. There was a lump on his brow, between the eyes, as large (to a nearness) as a hen's egg. All his face was a-lapper with blood, so that for the moment I thought that the lad had really been killed. But when I pulled him up to the armoury, and got him washed, I found that the blood was only that of the bullock, whose hide he had wrapped about him in order that he might crawl on the ground and fright his brother David.

And I had there and then taken him to task with the dog-whip (for indeed he might have bereft the child of reason), but the sight of his own wordless terror smote upon me, so that I desisted—for that time at least.

For a while Sandy could not speak by reason of the fear which blanched his face, and caused him to hold by my coat even when I went across the room. At last however he found tongue.

'There is a man,' he stammered, 'a man with a drawn sword, standing at the barn end in a grey cloak, and a wild beast crouching beside him.'

'Barley-break, flim-flam,' said I, for I believed not a word of it, 'your head is muzzy with your carrying the bullock's head and horns, and serve you right had David given you a warble on it twice as big.'

'No,' gasped Sandy, 'it is not fantasy. I saw the man clearly. He stood against the sky in a grey cloak, and the beast crouched and held a lanthorn by him. Oh, Launce, I fear I have seen the Black Man, and that I shall die.'

'Seen your granny's hippen-clouts!' said I, roughly, for I was angry at his senselessness. 'Lay raw beef to your beauty-spot, my man, sleep here with me, and I will forgive you the licking with the dog-whip.'

So by little and little I got Sandy soothed down till he went to sleep on my bed, moaning and tossing the while. Then I set me down to think, alone, on the window-sill about the courtyard, for I had long since handed David over to the care of Nell. Sometimes for convenience, I slept in the armoury, for Sir Thomas had trusted me with everything since I had proved myself in the wars.

I saw well that evil was somehow intended against the house of Culzean, and that something terrible walked in darkness. I resolved that I should find out what it was or die. Yet I liked not stealthy adventure so much as plain cut and thrust, and wished that I had had Robert Harburgh with me. But I knew that, though brave as a lion, he somewhat lacked discretion, and so might spoil all. There was nothing for it, therefore, but to go out alone.

CHAPTER XIX

FIGHTING THE BEASTS

HAVING shut and locked the armoury door behind me, I stood a great while very still on the steps in the black shadow; for nothing could I see, though I looked till my eyes ached. So I set out with my sword bare in my hand, and my left hand hafting an easily-drawn dagger. I declare if I had only known for certain that the thing which troubled the house was naught but flesh and blood, I had not cared the tickling of a Flemish poulet. For I was growing to rejoice in adventure, believing that my own luck was to win through in safety whatever might befall to others. Indeed I never loved a leg-lagging, grease-collecting life, like that of a burgher or a cellarer. But rather to strip and lay on till the arm dirls with striking—that is, in a just cause, of course. Although sometimes, if your chief so command, one must strike without inquiring with too queasy a conscience, like a mere yea-forsoothing knave, what may be the cause for which ye are set to drive the steel. For it is soldierly to strike first and inquire the cause after—that is, if the man live.

But I ride the wild mare whenever I lay the reins on the neck of my goose-quill. And since I love to keep the pages even and the lines straight, anything that will serve to fill up the tale of my day's doing goes down. But pleasant writing maketh not always good or full-mattered reading.

I stood therefore awhile outside the armoury door and saw only the drifted snow and the line of white roofs against a dark sky. So, having little hope of discovery by waiting like a dancer outside a ring, I stepped lightly down, being shod in soft double hosen without leathern shoon, so that my feet made no noise on the frosty snow. About the house I stole, gliding from shelter to shelter, till I came to the edge of the cliff, where I could hear, but not see, the breaker waves crisping and clapping upon the shore. At such time the sea is black. But so much blacker was the night that I saw it not even when I looked straight down upon it.

Turning, I made the circuit of the castle, but still found nothing. Then I minded me how it was by the barn that Sandy had seen the vision which had affrighted him. So I set teeth and gripped blade tighter, and took my way to the barn door. It stood wide and vacant, gaping at me like an open sepulchre.

I will admit that it required all my courage boldly to go in, for it is hard to enter that which is the blackness of darkness to you, with the knowledge that all the while you stand the fairest of targets in the doorway. But because, as my father had told me, it is ever better to pursue than to flee, I stepped within with elbow crooked for the thrust, and dagger arm cleared of the cloak.

But it was as silent in the barn as elsewhere. I did not even hear the rats of which my little David had spoken. I began to think that I had been as needlessly and as childlessly alarmed as he. Then all at once and quite clearly I heard voices speaking together at the outer corner of the granary.

So I went near to a convenient wicket that I might listen, and my very heart and life chilled and thickened, because that the voices were those of our Marjorie and someone else who spoke low and sober—not quick and high like Gilbert Kennedy.

Then was my heart full of disgust that I should find her whom I had loved and worshipped engaging in another midnight tryst, and one that might be no better than a paltry intrigue.

So angered was I that I stole to the door, meaning to break out upon them in violent speech, caring little in mine anger what should happen. But as I came to the edge of the hard-beaten threshing-floor, Marjorie Kennedy came to the door swiftly. Turning in front of the barn, and standing with the shawl thrown back from her head, she spoke to the man she had left, whom as yet I saw not.

'Remember,' she said, 'I promise no more than the bare fact. I tell you I choose the grave before a bride-bed, the worm before such a husband!'

But the man to whom she spoke uttered no word, though he had come nearer to where in the dusk of the doorway I stood with my sword bare in my hand. I could see him plainly now—all but his face, for the tide of darkness was on the ebb. He was the tall, cloaked man whom we knew as the Grey Man.

Behind him, at the angle of the wall, crouched a black mass which yet was human—because, even as I looked, it took something from under a coat, and rose erect beside the Grey Man. As Marjorie vanished these two figures moved towards my hiding-place in the barn. I had no time to do more than glide within, pull a sheaf or two from the mow, and thrust myself, like a sword into its scabbard, within the hole I had made amid the piled grain.

Even as I looked, their dark figures filled up the square of greyness which the open barn door made against the snow. I saw them enter, feeling with their hands, as though to grasp something, yet not making any light to guide them in finding it.

Then indeed I was disquieted, and my very bones became as water within me. For if there is anything trying to the flesh of mortal man, it is to lie still and be groped for in the dark by unknown and horrible enemies. I had a nightmare sense of powerlessness to move, of impotence in the face of peril. I knew that when the blind groping inhuman horror took me by the throat, I should not be able even to cry out. It was like a dream of fever made real.

A moment after I heard a man's voice speak in a fierce whisper.

'Ah, here it is! Give me your hand and put strength to it.'

Then in a moment, like the breaking of a dam, the fear quite went from me. They were but common-place robbers after all, and I a craven and a coward to lie still while my master's goods were being stolen before my eyes.

I leaped out upon them without waiting to think, for I was not feared of a dozen such.

'Hold!' I cried. 'Stand for your lives, gutter-thieves, or I will run you through!'

I stood in the doorway with my sword and dagger in hand, and as soon as I felt one come against the point of my blade, I let him have it with all my might, for it was not a time for half-measures. Then, though I heard the answering cry of wounding, there was no time for further action, for something came at me with a rush like a wild beast of the wood, and the snarl of the springing heather cat. Now there are many things that a lad of eighteen or nineteen may do—things of worth and daring—but he cannot stand against the weight of a strong and well-grown man when he leaps upon him. Therefore I cannot count it to my shame that now I was overcome and overborne. Once and again was I smitten, till I felt the iron, as it had been fire, strike me here and there. And though I felt no pain, there was something warm, which I divined to be my own blood, running down. Then I knew no more.

When I awoke I was in the Grieve's house, lying on a bed. Sir Thomas Kennedy, my master, and the Earl himself were bending over me. They had unclasped my hand, and now stood back in wonderment at what they found gripped in it.

'It is the key of the treasure chest of Kelwood—the key with my father, the King of Carrick's seal graven upon it! Where could the lad have gotten it?'

Yet of a certainty they had taken it out of my tightly-clenched hand, which had been fixed upon something ever since they found me on the barn threshing-floor, where I lay senseless in a pool of my own blood.

CHAPTER XX

THE SECRET OF THE CAIRD

IT was, I can avouch, a strange experience for me to lie on my back in the Grieve's house all through the long days of spring and summer. Kate Allison and her mother were tirelessly kind. The Grieve himself generally set his head past the door as he went and came from his meals, crying

mayhap something of the day—that 'it was warm,' or that
it was 'a wat yin,' and thinking it the height of a jest to
say to me, 'An' what kind o' weather hae ye below the
blankets?' For with kindly-natured country folk a little
jest goes a great way, and serveth as long without washing
as a pair of English blankets.

Then in the forenoon Sir Thomas would come in from
the castle, opening the hallan door and walking across the
Grieve's kitchen as unceremoniously as he would have
done in his own house.

'My lad, they have made a hand of you, but we will
dowse them yet for that!' was one of his stated encourage-
ments to me. 'Let me see the clours—hoot, man, they will
never mar you on your marriage day!'

And so, kindly and smiling, he would pass out again,
walking with his hands behind his back as far as I could see
him along the arches of the woodland.

Then would Marjorie come to the door, and inquire for
me of good Mistress Allison. But she never accepted of
her hearty invite to remain—or, at least, to enter and see the
invalid. Gently would she ask after my well-being, and
being assured of it, as gently would she go her way—her
fair face looking so white and sorrowful the while, that I
was wae for her, and for the unkenned secrets of her heart
into which God forbid that I should pry.

But that which cheered me most, I think, was the kindness and warm-heartedness showed me without stint, both
by Nell Kennedy and Kate Allison. They were no longer
flighty and sharp of tongue in speaking to me, but rather
spoke freely and sat much in the kitchen, with the door of
my room open so that I could see them, nipping and scart-
ing at one another like kittens in their wantonness, which
was a great diversion and encouragement to me on my
weary bed. And there we had no little merriment, for
Nell Kennedy would be saucy and miscall me for my
laziness and sloth—also for my lack of appetite, which she
called 'dainty and dorty,' meaning thereby that I wanted
finer meats than they had to give me.

Also, though she was no maid for gossip, Nell would
bring me all the clash of the castle-town and farm-town, all
the talk that was gone over in the mill, while the thirlage

men waited for their grist. Where she got it to tell me I cannot imagine, but it was all like sweet wine to me that could hear naught most of the day and night, but the birds singing without and Mistress Allison clattering wooden platters within.

Also (and that was the kindliest thing she could have done, and touched my heart most of all), she brought to me all my war-harness and accoutrements. My sword, which she had cleaned herself after the scuffle in the barn; the dagger I had dropped when I caught and clutched the key of the Kelwood treasure, wherever that had been gotten—the pistols; the fine new hackbutt which had just come from the town of Ayr, and which Sir Thomas had given me for mine own, as he would have given a child a toy.

'Give the bairn its plaiks, then,' said Nell, as she laid them on the bed. 'Would it love to play with them? Then it shall!'

She spoke in an enticing and babyish way that diverted me, and warmed me too, when I thought she had so much kindliness for me.

So I said, 'It is monstrously well done of you thus to divert me.'

'Hoots,' she said, 'see what else I have brought you.'

And with that she took from her pocket all the apparatus of cleaning my pieces and sword, besides the links and buckles of Dom Nicholas's harness and equipment, the sight of which put me in a fever to see him again. Never was anything kindlier done. Also, she brought me from her father's scanty library such books as she thought I might care to read; though, indeed, I read but little, never having been greatly given to lear—save, as it might be, books of songs, troll-catches, wits' recreations and such like.

But amongst others she brought me a French manual of fence, which gave me infinite pleasure. For with her help I could spell out the instructions, and the plates of positions I was fain to imitate with my two rapiers, till I had hacked and scarred all the four posts of the bed most grievously. And Mistress Allison declared that it was not safe for any-one to come within the outer door.

But one day my bed-fast practice-at-arms stood mine hostess in good stead, for which afterwards she gave me full thankfulness. It chanced on a certain noontide of heat that all were at the hayfield. Even Kate and Nell had gone to toss the hay, which is a pleasant thing to do in good company, but, i' faith, ill enough to think on as I lay tossing my weary body, and cursing the luck that tied me here in a dull room—vexed with heat, the weight of bedclothing, and the broad buzzing flies which would light on the corner of one's nose, each time that sleep was on the verge of flapping down silently with his black wings to bring a welcome shortening of the weary hours. Mistress Allison stole about the kitchen on bare, broad feet, flapping and slapping the flags with them as she carried her cakes to the girdle plate, or swung it from the cleek above the clear baking fire of brown peats. She thought me asleep, for I had cleaned all my arms till I could see myself sitting up in bed, with my pale face and towsed haystack of a head, in every square inch of them.

Kate had brought me that day a book called *The Whole Duty of Pilgrims*, but finding it full of religious reflections and not tales of the Crusaders as I had hoped I laid it aside for the Sabbath day, as being more reverent and fitting.

All at once the outer door of the Grieve's house was thrown back on its hinges, and a great sturdy caird entered —mayhap an Egyptian sorner, or bold robber, such as were vexing the realm at the time, or perhaps only a common muddy rascal of the road.

'Mistress, I bid you good-day,' he said. 'I am hungry and would have meat!'

Plain and quite short he said it—even as I have written it down.

'In this Grieve's house of Culzean even gentry folk say "An it please you," and "By your leave!"' replied, with some indignation, the mistress of the dwelling.

'But then I will e'en help myself, without please or leave either,' cried the villain. And with that he opened a leathern wallet that he had slung over his shoulder, and began to thrust therein, not only the scones, but anything about the dresser and tables that his thievish fancy lit upon.

'Now, mistress,' said he; 'let me have any siller you have in the house, and a well-pleased kiss of your weelfaured moo' therewith, or else I must do my needs with you!'

And with that he opened a great gully knife, as though he would run at her. Mistress Allison cried out with a strange cry of woman's fear, which I who had been in battle never heard the like of before. Just at this moment I pushed the bedroom door open with the point of my toe, and sat there looking straight at the man, with a pistol bended in each hand, and both of them trained point blank on the rascal's heart.

I make bold to say that in all this realm of Scotland there was not any man so exceedingly astonished as this particular sturdy thief at that moment.

'Drop the knife, sirrah!' I commanded, as one that cries his orders in a battle.

And the knife rang obediently on the stone floor.

'Kick it into the corner with your foot— No, not with your hand.'

And reluctantly he kicked the knife away from him.

'Now, my excellent good man,' said I, 'sit you down and put your hands behind you. There and thus, be still where you are, quite in the middle of the floor and not elsewhere.'

So he sat him down, and, keeping my pistols dead upon him, I bade Mistress Allison tie his hands firmly with cord, and give him a settle to lean against. Thereafter I comforted him with stern philosophy.

I told him of his wandering and uncertain life. I showed him conclusively how that he went ever in danger of the hangman's whip, and that at the end there could only be awaiting for him a shameful death. I told him also that our overlord of Culzean had the power of pit and gallows, and that, on the return of the haymakers, he should be brought out—when in an hour there would be an end of all his misery upon the dule-tree, or tree of execution, which stands by the great gate and bears medlars at any season, but only for an hour at a time.

''Tis the most cruel and unjust treatment of poor, beset, far wandering men!' said the man on the floor. They were the first words he had spoken since he threw down his knife. I wondered he could speak so well.

'We have heard no complaints, so far,' I made answer, drily, for the man's former insolence stuck in my throat. And in especial the thought of what might have happened to mine hostess or the maids, had I not been there upon the bed with my weapons beside me. So I kept him in torment of mind for a space.

At last, as the afternoon ebbed away, and the hour of sundown and homecoming wore on, his anxiety waxed pitiful. He turned and twisted to free his hands, so that the only way I could quiet him was to lift a pistol and point it at him. But even that did not appear to soothe him for any length of time.

At last he raised his head.

'Master,' said he, sullenly, but speaking not that ill, 'ye have me, I grant, in the cleaving of a stick. Now I will tell you a thing you greatly desire to know. Will ye promise to let me go, and I will never meddle you more?'

'I do not mean that you should,' said I, 'nevertheless, what is the thing that you can tell me? And when I know, I shall judge its worth—on the honour of a gentleman.'

'I can tell you,' said he, 'where you will find the treasure of Kelwood!'

'What bald-crowned blethers!' I cried scornfully. 'Pray, how am I to know that you speak the truth? Ye may tell me that it is with the gold cup, at the end of the rainbow!'

'It is true,' said the man, 'I might lie to you; but I will not, for I need my life. It is sweet to me as yours to you.'

'How can such a life be sweet?' I asked, daffing with the man in my power—which was 'bad form,' as John Mure himself sayeth in his history of the troubles.

'It is not a time to argue,' said he, "but my life is as pleasant as the trees that toss their branches, and as the free life of the forest.'

'Too free altogether,' said I, 'thus to come in and threaten the life and honour of a decent woman. We must have such freedom trussed and stretched on a tow rope.'

'I did but fright her,' said he, sullenly.

'That is as may be,' replied I, keeping my pistol trained

for his left eye-hole, 'and in any case it will be all the
same in two hours.'

'But,' said he, 'hear me concerning the treasure of
Kelwood. Ye have conquest the key. I can tell you
where the box itself is. For if I win clear this time, I must
escape over seas from the vengeance of the Grey Man.'

'But you may lie even as you have stolen, and I fear me
murdered also, for by your talk you are one of a murderous
set.'

'Of the lying you must e'en take your chance—even as,
after telling you, I must take my chance of your cutting
my bonds and letting me go.'

'You have a gentleman's word,' I answered him.

'And how much is that worth in Carrick this day,' he
said harshly and bitterly, 'even with a bond to back it?'

'Mine,' said I, with what dignity I could muster, 'is
worth as much as truth itself'—which, I grant, was but a
windy saying.

'I believe it, and I will trust it,' said he. 'The treasure
of Kelwood is in the cave of Sawny Bean, on the seashore
of Bennanbrack, over against the hill of Benerard.'

And not another word would he say.

So when Mistress Allison had locked herself in the milk-
house, and advised me that the haymakers were in full
sight, I caused my man to roll himself to the door of the
bedroom. There with my sword I cut the bonds.

'Now,' said I, 'take the door sharply, without so much
as going to the other side for your bundle or your knife,
and then the woods are open to you and the world wide.'

'I thank you, master,' he said civilly. 'When you go for
the treasure, I counsel you do not call on Sandy by your
leasome lane.'

And with that caution he betook himself into the glades
of the wood.

CHAPTER XXI

MINE ANCIENT SWEETHEART

AFTER he was gone I cast about in my mind, and, for the
life of me, I could not decide whether the fellow had been
lying to me or not. It was indeed a thing to be wondered
at, how this chance scoundrel should know (what I had

thought known only to my Lord Cassillis and my master)
that after the fight in the barn I had carried away, clenched
in my hand, the key of the treasure chest of Kelwood.

Now, as was natural after this encounter, the goodwife
of the Grieve's house could not make enough of me. Indeed,
if anything, she made too much of me, for, instead of suffering her daughter and Nell to entertain me as before, while
she went about her work, she thought it her duty as soon
as one of them came in and sat down, to leave that which
she was about, and come and sit with us for company. Now
Mistress Allison was a good woman and agreeable of her
tongue, but I did not feel the necessity for this byordinar
kindness.

Yet it was not easy to alter it. Then in the evenings
came Robert Harburgh to see me. At first he came once
a week while my wounds kept me weak and fretful. Then,
as I grew better, he came twice. And when I was able to
sit up, it came about that he would arrive every night and
bide till bedtime—so that at last I was almost shamed to
have him sitting there and feared that he might be burden
some to Kate Allison and her mother.

For Robert Harburgh had but little to say, but he ever
looked and proved kindly. Also he brought me many
things from Maybole and elsewhere—oranges and wine
that had been shipped to Irvine from foreign parts,
neckerchiefs also for Kate and her mother. A quiet,
down-looking fellow was Robert, something dull of the
uptake, and with little to say for himself; but a most
noble sworder, and wholly without care for his body
when it came to the fighting.

Now it seems a strange thing that I, who had so long
played the lover to Kate Allison, should be laid by the heels
in her father's house, hearing the whip and frisk of her gown
about the chambers all the day. And I still loved to hear it,
for she was a bonny lass—and kind, kind to me. Also her
eyes were pleasant, and had both mischief and tears in
them—not like Nell Kennedy's, that held only mischief
and scorn—save once, as it seemed to me, a little while
when I was deadly fevered, and when Dr Low of Ayr,
the Earl of Cassillis's own physician, ordered me herb-
drinks, and shook his doting wiseacre's head over me like

a most melancholious billy-goat. Then for a little Nell's eyes were quiet and sorrowful.

But it did not last. For by the time that I could get a scheme laid to take advantage of the gleam of kindness, she was again but mine own ill-set lassie-boy of a Nell, and we were throng at the sparring and quarrelling just as usual. But, as I say, Kate Allison was wondrously kind to me. Many a night when the weather was hot, and my wounds paining me as though they would break again open, would she sit by me with clear caller water from the spring, tirelessly changing the soft linen cloths. And when the drops of fever-sweat stood on my brow, she would touch them gently away, and lay her own cool cheek against my forehead. Ay, and when I put my hand up and drew down her face, she would kiss me right frankly upon the lips. Yet, as I judged, not quite as of old. But I thought it might be the illness that made the difference, for with being sick in body and feverish in mind, nothing tastes the same. And so I thought it might be also with kisses.

But after I had grown stronger, I shall ever mind me of one night when I got a horrid awakening. It was a quiet gloaming. Kate Allison and I had the house to ourselves—to which, speaking for myself, I did not wholly object. I lay stretched upon the long oaken settle, on cushions which Nell Kennedy had brought from the great house. Kate sat beside me on a stool and leaned an elbow on the oak's edge. She was unwontedly silent, and sometimes I touched her cheek lightly with my hand. It was a most pleasant night, and my mind was full of pity and consideration for her. I bethought me that, though doubtless I could have looked higher, I might do worse in time than think of settling down with a sweet and pleasant lass like Kate Allison. It was also touching to me that she should never have wavered from loving me, all the time that I had been forgetting her and thinking of others. But that, I said to myself, is the way of women.

We were silent a great while, with the silence that needs no speech, and my heart had grown melting and kindly to the young lass, even as it had been in old days. All of a sudden she spoke.

'Launce,' said she, 'I'm going to be married!'

She never moved her head off my shoulder, leaning with her elbow on the edge of the settle, and looking away from me out at the door. Neither did she draw her hand from mine, but rather settled it the more kindly, nestling it in my palm.

Yet anyone might have knocked me off the oaken settle with a straw.

'Married!' said I. 'Ay, Kate, lass, of course you are going to be married. 'Tis what you and I must come to. I assure you I oftentimes have been thinking about that. There are not the makings of an old maid about you!'

This I said and waited for the answer of her eyes, in order to laugh again and make my jest. But she did not look at me. I do not think she heard me.

'I am to be married on Thursday!' she said calmly.

'Kate Allison!' I said, trying to turn up her head that I might look into her eyes. I thought to see the make-believe in them. But as women know how to do, she evaded me without seeming to be conscious of it.

'Why, Kate Allison, sweetheart!' said I, 'how can I be ready by Thursday, laid here on my back, with only you to care for me?'

'I am to be married on Thursday to Robert Harburgh!' she said.

Then I drew my hand away, and sat erect and stern as the settle and my wickness would let me, for it is hard to appear dignified and like a soldier, lying on a couch and wrapped in women's shawls.

'I am deceived!' cried I, 'mine own familiar friend, in whom I trusted, has betrayed me, coming to steal that which was dear to me when I lay most weak and weary.'

And I think I made as if to rise, for I had an idea that I must go and get my sword—though what for, I cannot now imagine. But Kate Allison gently put me back on the pillows, and sat down beside me, taking one of my hands again, laying it against her cheek, and drawing at the same time her stool nearer to me.

I tried to withdraw my hand from hers, but being weak she masterfully kept it so that the tears sprang to my eyes for very helplessness and anger.

'You have played with me and deceived me, Kate Allison,' I cried, as soon as I could command my voice; 'you have forgotten the old days and all that we were to one another.'

Nevertheless Kate Allison never winced but let me say my say out. And by this I knew that the old days were gone indeed. She was mightily set in her mind.

'Launce,' she said gently, 'Launce, dear sweetheart, hearken—I am fond of you. No lass in Carrick but would like you for a lad and a lover, even for your very faults, which are what all may see.'

What she might have meant I have even yet no idea.

'Ye are perfect for a lad that comes courting, and I liked ye fine—ay, and like ye yet. But I saw lang syne that the lads that court best are not the men that marry best.'

'Women are all traitors!' said I, with indignation tingling through my body; 'they kiss and they forget. And then in a trice they go kiss another—'

'Ay,' replied Kate Allison, with a little more gravity, 'and I mean to have a short word with you on that very thing.'

She paused for a moment, and looked staidly and thoughtfully out of the window. I believed at nineteen that I wholly understood all women. But now I know that when I am twice that and more, the simplest seeming of them will be able to wrap me in her daidly-apron, and sell me in the market for green cabbage.

'Listen, Launce, my dear,' she said. 'I was but a Grieve's lass, and not unbonny of my face, so you courted me. You longed after kissing, being a heartsome lad with a way with you and a glint in your e'e. And so you kissed me, and in my youth and folly I said ye not nay. But you went over the hill to the Boreland and you kissed Grace, and you kissed the lass at the house of the Red Moss—and you thought that I would never know it. And more, you expected that none else should ever come near to kiss me. Ay, and would have waxed mightily indignant and flashed a brave sword had any dared, for that is the excellent way of the lads that come courting—but not at all the way of the men that wise women marry.'

I was mazed and confounded before her, but could not answer a word, for the thing was as true as if she had read my heart. Where had the young lass so learned the ways of men?

'Forgotten your kisses, Launce?' she went on. 'And what of them? I count kisses but as the X's and O's that bairns make on the flags with soft cam stone—gone when the game is over.'

'The home-coming from the fair at Maybole and the kisses that you and I then kissed,' said I, bitterly, 'were these X's or O's? I rede ye tell me!'

'Launce,' said Kate Allison, 'we dreamed a pleasant dream, you and I. We have awaked. It is a new day. We wash the night fantasies off our faces, and are ready to meet the morning with the sunshine in our eyes. Together we have sipped the cream. It is time to drink the milk. We have gathered the flowers—let us look to the fruit.'

'Kate,' said I, more kindly, 'when did you think all these things?'

For the lassie made me marvel with the aptness of her speech, and ashamed with her plain saying of things that I had hardly named within myself.

'Ah,' she said gently and wisely, 'the thoughts of a lass when a lad comes courting her, are more than she tells with her mouth. For many a kiss is honey-sweet on the lips, but bitter as gall in the heart. Yet so has it not been with yours and mine. We loved and we part, even as the way-gaun of the wind that kissed the apple blossom in the spring when the year was young and glad.'

She made to rise from her seat.

'I must go,' she said.

'To go meet Robert Harburgh and to kiss him. I thought I knew his whistle!' said I, with my heart raging angry and disconsolate in spite of her fine words, which I could not answer.

'Ay,' she said, rising and setting her lips tenderly to my brow, which I pettishly turned away, being weakly sullen, 'even so—to meet Robert Harburgh and to kiss him.'

And with that she passed to the door. She turned ere she went out to say a last word.

'And you, Launce, my lad, will also one day desire to leave kissing comfits and find abiding love. And you need not go far afield to look for it either.'

Thus I was left alone with a heaving heart. And I am not ashamed to say that I wept bitterly for poor Launce Kennedy, who had none to care for him in all the wide lone world, in which he was now so sore wounded and cast aside like an old shoe or a broken sword.

But even as I wept and pitied myself, Nell Kennedy danced in, merry as the morn, and brought a great spray of belated hawthorn to set in a dish of water to keep the room sweet.

And I declare I never knew the young lass look so winsome before.

CHAPTER XXII

A MARRIAGE MADE IN HELL

WHEN Robert Harburgh came in to see me in the evening, I was chill enough in my reception; but since he was of a calm temper, though so great a sworder, I might just as well have embraced him, for all the difference it made to him.

'So,' I said, without giving him more than time to sit down—for all my days I must ever fly headlong at a thing and have done with it—'so you are going to marry Kate Allison?'

'She was proposing so,' said he, as calmly as when he had walked across the yard to the summer-house, with the hackbutt bullets splattering about him and the guns going *crack-crack* down the hedgerows, like the thumbs of a class of bairns when the dominie asks a question.

'So,' said I. 'And you were thinking, maybe, that that was the action of a friend when your comrade was laid by the heels?' 'I was thinking so,' said he, looking out of the window at the trees.

'Did you not know,' I cried, for I was angered beyond words, being weak, and taking ill with the cherry being thus snatched out of my mouth, 'did you not know that Kate Allison was my lass before she was yours? Did she not tell you that?' said I.

Now, had I been myself, I should not thus have told left-handed tales on a lass, even though I believed with some reason that she had deceived me.

'I was not deprived of the sight of my eyes,' said he, very quietly.

'And you mean by that—?' said I, trembling with, anger.

'That I did not need telling that you had been court-ing the lass off and on for a year or twa, and that she took it not ill.'

'And, in spite of that, you made up to Kate Allison when I was lying sick unto death upon my bed?' I asked him bitterly.

'How long may you have kenned Kate Allison?' said Robert Harburgh to me in his turn.

'Six years or so,' said I.

'And did you ever, in all that time, ask her to marry you?' he inquired.

'No,' said I, not seeing what he was driving at.

'Then,' said Robert, very drily, 'I did, though I kenned her not six weeks. And I would not wonder,' he went on, as though deep in meditation, 'I would not wonder but that is the reason why she is going to marry me.'

So I turned over in bed, being deep in the sullens, and Robert Harburgh went away, saying only, 'Now ye are angry, Launcelot, but ye will find us both good friends, and blythe will we be to see you at the five-merk lands of Chitterlintie which my Lord Cassillis is setting to Kate and me.'

However, as things fell out, the wedding was not to be on the Thursday, nor yet for many Thursdays, for Robert was bidden ride with the Earl to the Inch, his new house in Galloway. Hither he went to set pressure on the country lairds, who were his feudal holders, to gar them pay the dues which he, Grab-siller John, thought had been too long overlooked by his forbears. As the business was likely to prove a troublesome one, he sent for Robert Harburgh to ride with him. So, without so much as stopping to dis-mount, for the message came when he had been on duty, Robert Harburgh rode away. And if you will believe it, he went without so much as kissing his sweetheart. He leaned down and shook hands with her! But as for me, I marvelled how she bore with that, for to my certain knowledge she liked the other not so ill.

Just as I was daily getting stronger, I received another shock which had, I think, even more effect on me than the other. One morning there came Sir Thomas down from the castle, and I could see that he was full to the teeth with news, for he walked with great confidence, and swung a little stick made of two twisted stems of ivy which I had given him, very quaint and curious.

'It is all done with now,' he said, as soon as ever he had gotten himself seated; 'there are to be no more ill times in Carrick, and kinsmen's blood shall not flow any more in the West. John Mure of Auchendrayne and I have settled it all between us. His son and apparent heir, James, is to marry to-morrow with my daughter.'

I stared at him, stunned and dumbfounded.

'Ay,' he said, 'it is short notice, but young folks, ye ken—and my daughter would not hear of a great wedding; only what was fitting and plain.'

'Your daughter?' I said, steadying myself, though my heart was like to break, for I thought all my friends were to leave me together.

'Ay, Marjorie,' said Sir Thomas, 'she is a quiet like lass and speaks little, but when I put the matter of the marriage to her, she said only, "If it will staunch the feud, I am ready to marry whomsoever you will—Sir Thomas Tode, gin you like!" But that was only her daffing, for, as we all know, Sir Thomas is married already. And even if he were not, marrying him would be neither here nor there in the matter of the Cassillis and Bargany feuds.'

For my good master never saw far into a whin bush all his days, though accounted by most to be a wise man.

On the morrow, which was the day of the ill-faured wedding, I put on my complete accoutrements for the first time. I had Dom Nicholas saddled, for I felt strong once more, and greatly desired to be away from the place. So I stood by the gate as the party from Auchendrayne came in, and saluted them, as was my duty. Then I was riding away alone down by the shore road, when I heard in the distance the sounds as of an approaching cavalcade.

Bridles were jingling, stirrups clicking, and spearheads making points of light, while the white foam went blowing back from the hard-ridden horses. When they rode up, I saw that they were as trenchant a set of blades as ever a man might wish to set eyes on. And at the head of them rode young Gilbert Kennedy of Bargany.

So, not knowing whether they came in peace or war, I set myself upright on the back of Dom Nicholas, who was of so great freshness with kicking of his heels in the park, that he was ill to keep at the stand. Nevertheless, stand I did in the midst of the outer gate, so that I should know whether they came in peace or war, and to have time to cry to the porter, even if they rode roughshod over me.

And though I was weak, and knew not what might happen, it was a joy untellable to be somebody again, and to gar men reckon with me.

But, being pale, I fear I made a poor figure to stand in the gate and withhold so many. For during my captivity the hair on my face had begun to grow in a manner that was surprising, and proved a constant trouble to me to keep shaven.

'Halt!' I cried to them. 'How come you to Culzean —in peace or boding in fear of war?'

'But to wish the Tutor luck on his birthday in passing,' said Gilbert, 'and then to ride on to the help of John, Earl of Cassillis.'

So, much astonished at what had befallen, and especially at his last saying, I fell in behind him, and the word was given to ride forward.

But Bargany called me to come beside him, and asked me of my health. I replied that I had been long time sick of a wound, but that I was now recovered, and above all things desired action, being sicker far of the doing of nothing.

Whereat he laughed, and said, 'Be cheerful, and if ye want blows, I will ask the loan of you as a hostage from your master.'

Then, seeing the stir about the doors, and the serving men running every way with flagons and dishes, he said, ''Tis a great stir for naught but the Tutor's birthday. What may be the occasion?'

Then, with my eyes secretly upon his, I told Gilbert Kennedy that the Lady Marjorie was to be married that day to James Mure of Auchendrayne. I never saw a man's countenance change so suddenly. The fire sprang to his eyes, and died out again like dead tinder. The heart blood flushed hot to his face, and, returning, left him pale as a maid in a decline.

Then I minded how I had taken the matter myself. Yet I was sorrier for him, because I knew that he had loved her longer and better than I. But nevertheless he tossed his sword hand in air, and cried, 'We are in time for a bridal, brave lads; this is more than we bargained for. Let us go greet the bride and wish her joy.'

And this I grant was a better way than sulking and self-pity in the greenwood, which would have been mine that day, had I been left alone.

With that he put the horses to the gallop, and we rode through the narrow pass of the drawbridge by two and two. The roar of the horses passing over was as the roar of the sea when the storm drives up from the west on the Craigs of Culzean.

As we came by the corner of the terrace, I saw him give a look at that window of the White Tower which faced to the landward. It had been the Lady Marjorie's, and now was to be hers no more. Then I saw him look down on the fretting sea, as it tumbled white on the pebbles and rocks by the Cove. And I knew why he looked there, and I knew more also, for I remembered what I had heard Marjorie say after he had gone clanking down the shore in his anger and pride.

Yet all the while Bargany rode light-hand upon his bridle-rein, the pride of his horsemen clattering behind him, gay with the music of hoofs and the dance of red and white pennons.

I wondered not that, as they said, he took the eyes of ladies wherever he went. So that the Queen's bower-women quarrelled concerning him, till Her Majesty said, 'I shall have no peace till I take him for myself. But what would James say if young Bargany were to sing "John, come kiss me now," beneath my bower window?'

But more than all ladies' favours I envied him such a brave repair of horse to follow him. For Culzean was too poor, and the Lord of Cassillis too near the bone to keep any such array of mounted gentlemen.

For hackbuttmen, and footmen with spears, were more

to our Earl's mind, being better in the time of war, and
a deal cheaper in the days of peace—which even in these
troubled years were so many more than the days of
fighting.

As we rode up, and the Bargany squadron halted with
a great spattering of sand and tossing of the heads of horses,
the wedding folk were just coming out. First of all there
issued forth the bride, our Marjorie, the Marjorie that had
been ours, on James Mure's arm—he that now was her
husband. And behind them came the Minister of Maybole
and Sir Thomas, walking together very caigy* and jocose.

But Marjorie's face was like stone, though the bitterness
of death overpast was gone from it. I trust mine eyes
may never see such a look of reproach and pain in any
human face, as was in hers when she saw Gilbert Kennedy
sitting his horse in front of the squadron, upon the gravel
stones from the seashore that were laid before the castle
steps. But Gilbert only saluted her, and cried aloud as was
customary, 'Luck to the wedding and health to the bride!'

Then ran Sir Thomas to him and took his hand, bub-
bling over with kindliness and pleasure.

'The feud is staunched indeed, when I see Bargany
once more in peace at the house of Culzean, even as my
good friend the Laird of Auchendrayne said it would be.
What might be your kindly errand? And will ye not
light off your beasts and bide to feast with us.'

'I cannot,' said Bargany. 'The Earl of Cassillis is
besieged in the house of Inch by the Lairds of Galloway,
and I ride to his assistance.'

Then she that had been Marjorie Kennedy turned to
him, and said, 'And will ye indeed consent to staunch
feud for John Mure's sake, that would not do it for mine?'

Which seemed to me a strange mode of speech to be
spoken in the hearing of a husband on his wedding day.
But I had forgotten that none held the key to the utterance
saving Gilbert Kennedy and myself.

'The staunching of the feud is neither yours nor mine,
Lady Marjorie,' said Bargany, bending very gently toward
her, 'but I cannot bide still in my house at the town of
Ayr while a Kennedy of Cassillis—my enemy though he

* Friendly.

be—is dared, outfaced, and threatened by a pack of Galloway lairds.'

'Are they, then, ill men and far in the wrong?' said she.

'On the contrary, they are good men and in the right. But that does not hinder me from standing for my name and house against every other, even though that house be foredoomed to fall, because it is divided against itself.'

Then he turned to my master, saying to him, 'For this one time, and as a pledge to my Lord the Earl John that I mean his good, will you permit Launcelot, your esquire, to ride in my company—he that hath so oft ridden well against my folk?'

'Gladly,' said Sir Thomas, 'but the lad has been ill.'

'It is no far ride, and the boy needs but change of air and foes of mettle to strengthen his sword-arm against.'

So in a trice I was ready to follow my house's enemy.

As I turned I saw John Mure of Auchendrayne standing, looking in the dignity of his white hair most like a saint, though contrariwise I knew him to be that which I will not name. I heard him say to my master, 'Ye see, did not I tell you? This marriage brings all good things already. And this is but the beginning.'

'Nay,' replied Sir Thomas, 'indeed it is most gratifying and well done of you. Who would have believed a week ago that to-day Bargany would have saddled his steeds and mounted his men to ride to the succour of John, Earl of Cassillis?'

And I saw my good, simple master raise his hand and clap Auchendrayne upon the shoulder. Then, for very hate and loathing, I turned away. Even as I did so I saw the eye of John Mure on the watch, and I knew that he understood. For his glance was like a rapier-thrust when your enemy means killing.

Ere the horsemen turned to ride away, Marjorie came down the steps to where Bargany sat his charger, and slipping a ring off her finger she handed it up to him.

'For your Isobel Stewart!' she said.

And though I saw it not, I am as certain as if I had seen the crest and posy upon it that the ring was his own, one which he had given her in some past day when they had far other hopes than to part in this fashion on her wedding morning.

Then, with a quick cry of command and the gallant clatter of hoofs, we rode away. And that was the last parting in life of Gilbert and Marjorie Kennedy, who had been lovers ever since they were bairns, and had linked themselves together for man and wife with chains of yellow gowans upon the braes of Culzean.

CHAPTER XXIII

A GALLOWAY RAID

As you may suppose, it was no grief, but the reverse, for me to ride away with Bargany to the South, and leave behind me the drear house of Culzean upon that dismal day of doom and sacrifice. Nell Kennedy I saw nothing of, though, as I learned in the aftertime, she saw me. For she too had fled from the house, being unwilling to have aught to do with such a deed of cruel wrong as the marrying of her sister, that was the flower of the West, to an oafish lout like James Mure.

'Not but what our Maidie can stand up for herself. And if she gets not her own way, sorry am I even for James Mure!' said she.

It was from the branches of a thick plane that Nell watched us ride away to the house of the Inch, and noted me as I cantered by Bargany's side. Of which, had I known it then, I should have been fain. For, wild ettercap as she was, I now counted Nell Kennedy almost the only friend I had left.

And as we went, Bargany told me of the Earl's message brought him by James Young, the Minister of Colmonel. And in especial how he had telled a great lie to win through the men of Galloway—in which sin it was then uncommon for a minister to be found out.

'Not but that my heart is with the lads of Galloway,' said Bargany, 'but after all, Gibby Crack-tryst is the first of the Kennedies, and I shall not see him put down, whatever be his deserts, by Garthland and the Sheriff. If Cassillis is to go down, Bargany shall go with it; and all Galloway, twice told, shall not accomplish that!'

Although I felt chilled by the dull, unheartsome day we had left behind us, I can tell you I thought no little of myself to be thus riding in comradeship with Bargany at my elbow. For though I had so ridden with the Earl once or twice, yet I counted ten times more on Bargany. Forty horsemen were of our company, and mine was the weariest body among them all. For it was my first long day, after my sickness with harness on my back, and pulses beat where my wounds had been, so that I feared that they would break out afresh, and I have to be left behind.

At last we stayed our steeds at a small tenant's house called Craigaffie, a little way from the Inch, where a vassal of Bargany's dwelt. Him we sent to meet the Earl and tell him that we were there—also to bid the Galloway men come to an arbitrament, if so they would. For they had enclosed the Earl back and front in his own house of the Inch, so that none could pass—save indeed one that knew the byeways and outgates as did this Peter Neilson of Craigaffie.

Presently there came back from the Earl a message most piteous, for he knew the men of Galloway had him fast; and he was afraid for the safety of the rents and mails that he had with him in silver and minted gold—far more, to do him justice, than he was anxious about his own skin. Bargany was his dearly-beloved cousin, his eame, his saviour. He would keep friendship with him more than with any friend he had all the days of his life, for this notable deliverance he had wrought. He was to come and put himself in the Earl's hands after he had sent the lords of Galloway about their business. The Earl's plighted word would be his security.

At this Bargany gave a smile, and set his thumb over his shoulder at the forty swords that were riding behind him.

'These,' said he, 'will be the best security that John, Earl of Cassillis, will not harm me when I go to visit him in his castle of the Inch.'

It was no long season before there came MacDowall of Garthland and Sheriff Agnew to represent the men of Galloway, and never in my life, save when I went as herald to the great house of Kerse, did I see such an exchange of high civilities. It was as the meeting of heroes, when compared to the double-dealing and deceit of our break-tryst Earl. More than ever, I wished that I had

been born on the other side of the score. But it hadna
bin to be.

Agnew the Sheriff was a tall man, with dark hair quickly
frosting to grey, a hawk's nose, a long arm good at laying
on, and a biting tongue which he knew well when to hold.
The Laird of Garthland, on the other hand, was red of
beard and brown of hair, altogether a man well set, beginning also to be well-stomached with good feeding and sleep-
ing on benches of the afternoons.

It was Garthland who saluted first, for he came of the
oldest race in Galloway—save, perhaps, it may be, the
MacCullochs of Ardwell. But the eagle-nosed Sheriff was
the chief spokesman.

'Greeting courteously to you, Bargany,' he said. 'This
is a pleasure unexpected. Over on our poor shire-side, the
erne of the hills neither mixes nor mells with the quarrels
of the carrion crow.'

'I greet you well, Sheriff,' said Gilbert Kennedy; 'but
say your say plain out, without bringing all the birds of the
air into the matter.'

'Plainly then,' said the Sheriff, 'the matter is this.
The Earl has moved the law against us for rights his
father granted us years agone, rights that have never been
questioned, and when we will not yield to him, he uses his
influence with the King to make us traitors. He sends his
low-born officers to remove us from our kindly homestead-
ings, and from the castles where for centuries our forefathers
dwelled—ay, before one stone of Cassillis lay on the top
of another.' And the fire glinted in the Sheriff's deep-set
eyes, till, with his eagle's beak, he looked himself the very
erne of which he had spoken. He went on. 'Then comes
he himself, with a force of forty horse, to reduce the un-
broken baronage of Galloway. He summons us to the
court of doom, and lo! we come to this yett with a hundred
gentlemen, and as many more footmen that but wait to
be called. We have obeyed his mandate to the letter,
whereat he sulks within gates. Then we send him word
that we are at the trysting-place, and that we will be most
glad to see his face. But for some reason or other that I
cannot guess at, he comes not; but withdraws himself into
the house of the Inch, where presently he remains. And we,

being bound to see that no ill befalls him within our borders, have set ourselves down to be the warders and the protectors of him and of the castle.'

So said the Sheriff, and made his courteous amend. And to him Bargany replied,—

'But, Lochnaw, ye know well that ye have no warrant thus to shut up the Earl of Cassillis, immuring your lawful feudal superior and defying ancient custom.'

Then spake the red-bearded Laird of Garthland.

'If it come to that, we are bound to you and not to the Earl, Gilbert Kennedy. Ye are bound to maintain us in our rights! Am I to lose my auld and kindly office and possession, which I have held in direct line from Uchtred, Lord of Galloway? Of a truth, no, Bargany! Ye are of a conscience overtrue for work of this kind. Ye will do to me your honourable duty, as your predecessors have ever done to mine in time past.'

And having said his say with dignity, the red Garthland held his peace.

I could see very well that Bargany was ill at ease. He liked not the errand he had come on. Blows were very well, but to be process-server sat heavy on his stomach. I heard him mutter,—

'That I, Gilbert Kennedy, should be doing John of Cassillis's dirty work! For none other sake than Marjorie's would I do this thing!'

But he took up his parable with the Lairds of Galloway.

'Hearken, Garthland and Lochnaw—if, as ye say, I am above ye, well do ye know that the Earl is by law above us both.'

He paused for a moment, wry-faced, as though he had swallowed the bitterest drugs of the apothecary. And I saw the Sheriff smile a smile as bitter every whit.

'Hearken to me. If my lord continue to do ye wrong, and will not use you kindly, by mine honourable word in the hearing of all these friends, I will not only leave his lordship—I will maintain you to the last drop of my blood. But if ye pursue my lord to take his life, seeing that he has sent for me to aid him, I will defend him to the uttermost of my power.'

Then said the Sheriff, 'Bargany, we are honourable

men and peaceful. We are not here to attack the Earl, but to defend ourselves in that thing in which he would do us wrong.'

'I will deal straightly with my lord,' said Bargany; 'be content, and leave the outcome to me.'

'We are content,' they replied, both of them as one. 'We ken a man when we front him, for we ourselves are men. We will abide your judgment, whatever you may command.'

So in a trice Bargany had gotten the Earl to promise all good things, and the Galloway men were satisfied. Thereafter they all dined together with my lord in the house of Inch, and parted very merry. And the men of Galloway convoyed us northward to the braes of Glenap, where the whole force and retinue of Bargany's servants and friends met us. Thus was the Earl released from durance, and his promises were loud and many, so that we were all well-contented. And I thought that the old feud was at last come to an end.

CHAPTER XXIV

THE SLAUGHTER IN THE SNOW

BUT, alas! I was never more disappointed, shamed, deceived in my life. For no sooner was our Earl back in his own messuages and domains, and behind his lines of hackbutt-men, than he resiled from all his promises—both to the Galloway men, who had done so honourably in the re-leasing and convoying of him, and (what seemed to me worse) also to Bargany, who had pledged himself in honour to satisfy the Sheriff and Garthland. For after all, a lie told to a loon of Galloway is not like one to a man's own kin and country. Though, of course, a man that is true all through the web, will not tell a lie to any. But such men are few, at least in the shire of Ayr where I dwell, and in Edinburgh to which I have at different times voyaged.

But Bargany, as was natural, was fierce in his indignation with the crack-tryst Earl.

'For,' said he, 'he has made me, that am a man of my word, break faith with men of a like pattern, even with Uchtred MacDowall of Garthland and the Sheriff of Galloway.'

So after all this tangled business, instead of peace, as my deeply-deceived master had supposed when he gave over his daughter to the traitors of Auchendrayne, there issued at the last naught but feud, more deadly and hateful than ever.

The Earl, who, to do him justice, was no coward as to his own skin, went hither and thither between Cassillis and Maybole, and even south to Auchneil, riding freely as though he had been within his own borders all the time. And the traps that were laid for him by Auchendrayne and Thomas of Drummurchie, the Laird of Bargany's barbarous brother, were too many to be told. Yet for the sake of the new alliance, such as it was, Culzean meddled not at all with the matter, though doubtless it was a source of infinite bitterness of spirit to him.

Then all of a sudden there came upon us the eleventh of December, which is a day yet remembered in Carrick, because of the many brave lads that pranked it in pride in the morning, and who yet lay stiff in their war gear or ever the early winter gloaming had fallen.

We at Culzean got our warning from the Earl's man, John Dick, on the night before, how it was the order that we were to gather at Cassillis yett and ride with them back to Maybole town all in a company. John Dick told us, but with even more than his customary surliness and unwillingness, that the cause of this raising of the clan was, that two days before Bargany had ridden past the gate of Cassillis, where the Earl was—stopping not at all, but riding by with pennons flying in despite, which was held a deadly insult to his feudal superior. So Earl John had sworn to be equal with him on his return.

It was such a day of snow (this eleventh day of December) that even in the midst of the fight, when the hackbutts were talking and the steel ringing, a man could scarce see whither he was going. At times so thick was the drift, that when a man struck at an enemy with his lance, he could not tell who it might be that opposed him, whether friend or foe.

But when, very early in the morning, we rode out to the muster, the oncoming storm had not yet begun. The air was bitter cold, blowing from the south-east, so that it drove in the faces of the Bargany folk all the day. Now, as of late years it had been customary with him, my Lord of Culzean was not able to ride with us. For the chill weather unmanned him, and he could do nothing but hurkle over the fire, with a lad to rub his swollen feet and stiff knee-joints.

So it befell that once more I had the leading of our good lads from the sea border. Right merry we were as we rode forth, for the matter seemed to us no more than a good adventure. None thought that the issue would be so grim and bloody as it proved. We were but half-way to Maybole when we came suddenly on Auchendrayne himself and John Dick, the Earl's messenger, in close converse—which I thought a strange thing, seeing that Auchendrayne was so great a favourer of the Bargany faction. So soon as they saw us come in sight they parted, and John Dick rode away over the fields, but Auchendrayne came towards us, riding easily and pleasantly as if to market.

'A good day to you,' he cried. 'Whither away, armed *cap-à-pie*, so early?'

'We ride to meet my lord, and to do his bidding!' I said, making my words brief and curt, because I liked not the man, for all his fine figure and commanding presence.

'Your master Sir Thomas, is, I hear, laid by with his ancient trouble. I asked John Dick concerning him. Tell him that I grieve to hear of it.'

'Without doubt you were on your way to visit him,' I said, with mockery in my manner of speech, for it was a strange thing to meet John Mure on the wrong side of the town of Maybole at daybreak of a winter's morning.

'Without doubt,' he answered readily; 'but now that I know of his weak state of health, I need not trouble him this day!'

'There is the greater need, Laird Auchendrayne,' I made reply, 'that you should go on and cheer him with your pleasant discourse.'

He answered to that not a word good nor bad, but turned his horse and rode away to the right, making, as

I guessed, a detour to avoid my lord and join our enemies of Bargany.

It was early in the morning of this famous eleventh of December (as I have been told) that there was a goodly stir and commotion in the town of Ayr. Gilbert Kennedy had resolved that he would ride that day to Bargany by way of the town of Maybole. Sorely and often they of his faction tried to dissuade him, but he was set immovably on it, as he was on anything to which he had once made up his mind.

'Think ye,' he said, 'that I am feared of John, Earl of Cassillis, or of all the Kennedies of the shore edge that ever scarted other folk's siller into their wallets like sclate-stanes?'

'Ye needna be feared,' said his brother Thomas, the Wolf of Drummurchie, 'but ye surely have enough of sense to take care of your pelt. Even a swine has that muckle. Do you think that Cassillis, and those that are with him, have not as much sense as we? They will be standing by some roadside where we have to ride by, and they will have holes cutted out, I warrant you, long or this, to shoot us in the by-ganging—even as we did for Earl Johnnie at the limekilns of the Dalgorrachies.'

But that debauched villain, the Laird of Benane, and his little-wit sister, moved him to that pride, to which also his own heart ever too easily inclined. So, in spite of all entreaty, Bargany leaped on his charger and rode forward himself, with only ten or twelve horsemen as a first vanguard. Behind him there came other seventy, making in all the number of fourscore armed men on horseback, all good riders of mettle. Some of these were such burghers of Ayr as had a soul beyond the ell-wand, and could follow a foray and bend the pull of a pistolet with any man. For I have learned that all townsfolk are not nidderlings, as once I thought in my hot youth and little knowledge.

Now, so soon as they were well mounted there were two at Bargany's muster who rode away to warn my Lord of Cassillis by which way Bargany should come, so that he might be in array. The traitorous names of them were William Cunningham and Hew Penandgow, against both

of whom Auchendrayne had warned Gilbert Kennedy.
But Bargany had taken no heed, for he said, 'Never
yet have I seen the time when my right arm could not
keep my head against kings and earls, let alone pock-
puddings and Penandgows!'

'Nor like I this day's work,' said Auchendrayne, 'for
I see not here the weight of men to do your turn and carry
you through.'

Yet all the time he was plotting that Gilbert Kennedy
should no more ride home to Bargany, and that John Mure
should rule the land in his stead.

It was not long before they came to the bridge of Doon.

There they stayed awhile, and Bargany set his fighting
men in array. And, as was the custom, he made an address
to them—of which I have heard much and often, for all
men minded it as the speech of a brave man.

'Sirs,' he said, so that they could all catch his words,
'I am here to protest, before God, that I seek neither the
life nor the dishonour of my lord. But I desire only to
ride home to my house in peace, if he well let me. But if
not, I look to you all to do your duty as becometh men.
He that is willing to do this, out of love and kindness for
me, let him tarry with me to the end. But if not, let him
leave me now at this present!'

And they all answered, 'We will die in your defence if
any dare hurt or pursue you!'

So being well agreed, they of Bargany rode forward.
They were divided into two companies, and their faces
were set toward the gate of the town. And now it befits
that I speak of the things which I saw with my own eyes,
and of the noble muster that we of the Cassillis faction
made on the knowes outside of Maybole.

I mind well how the Earl's spies came riding in with
the news that Bargany had ridden out of the town of Ayr,
and what joy was in the hearts of most of us that were
there, when we heard that with him he had but eighty
men.

Earl John was so full of pleasure that his countenance
shone, and he cracked his thumbs like a boy, seeing his
enemy already in his power. He rode here and there
among us, and saw to it that all the hackbuttmen had

good-going matches, and all the footmen practicable spears and pikes.

When we gathered in the High Street of Maybole the snow was just beginning to fall, and presently it came driving up from the south, so that we had it on our backs all through the fight.

I was put in the very forefront of the muster with my twenty horsemen. For, save and excepting those of Culzean, and the few that surrounded his own person and were his gentlemen (as Robert Harburgh and others), my Lord of Cassillis counted not many horsemen, but rather spent his means upon providing hackbuttmen with the latest species of ordnance.

Nevertheless, gallantly enough we rode forth from Maybole, with the hackbuttmen and spearmen coming on foot after us. The street was full of them as far as one could discern through the oncoming storm, rising and falling like the waves of the sea. Yet was our soldierly figure a little spoiled by the falling snow—at least to the eyes of the women that looked down upon us in droves from the upper windows of the houses. But, of course, a soldier cared nothing for such a trifle.

When once we got outside the town, my lord bade his men line the hedges and banks, so that the hackbuttmen might have both rests for their pieces and shelter for themselves. On the other hand, the Laird of Bargany had few hackbuttmen, for he said, 'It is not the arm of a gentleman. Comes a bullet of lead and be he lord, prince, or peasant, Childe Roland or base craven, there is no difference and no remead.'

No sooner were we set, all under cover, than our spearmen upon the left and we upon the right, discerned the host of Bargany beginning to crown the opposite knolls. And through the pauses of the storm I could see the leaden glint of their spears, and hear the words of command. It was indeed a picked day for a grim fight to the death.

At the head of all Gilbert Kennedy rode, behind him the Wolf his brother, and the Laird of Auchendrayne wearing a long cloak, for it was a stormy day and he no longer a young man like the others. Then it was that my heart rose against the fighting, and I had no such gladness in it as was usual with me, all for the sake of young Bargany whom I loved. Yet as soon as I set eyes upon John Mure of Auchendrayne, I felt the iron grow in my veins and the hot anger mount to my head. Of its own accord my hand gripped the spearhilt, for this day, by the Earl's command, I was again to lay a lance in rest. But I had now learned the game and art of it, and took lessons no longer from anyone.

'If the Lord prosper me this day, I will make an end of one false rogue!' So I vowed, solemn as if I had been in the kirk on a Sabbath day.

Then the two forces drew so close together that we could see and hear one another—that is, before the snow swept down, blotting out faces and forms, friend and foe alike.

Immediately there began the challenging and taunting, as is ever the way in these clan battles, where every fighter knows everyone else, and has met him at kirk and market a score of times.

Then Patrick Rippitt, that was ever a wild lad, cried out for provocation to the Laird of Bargany's younger brother, with whom he had some quarrel about a lass.

'Laird of Benane, Laird of Benane, this is I, Patrick Rippitt, that took your hackbutt from you! For thy latest love's sake, come down to the hollow and break a tree with me.'

For that was his manner of challenging his enemy to fight with lances. And again, 'Then for all thy loves' sake,' cried Patrick, which made a laugh, for Benane's loves were comparable to the snowflakes for number, and eke for the lightness—but by no means the whiteness of their characters.

'For all thy loves' sakes, come down, and I will gar thy harns clatter!'

But Benane was silent and returned no answer, albeit the moment before he had been giving Bargany counsel to ride forward at the charge. But Benane was a man, debonnair but feckless, a weighty man with his tongue, but thewless and unable of his hands.

Long ere this the men of Ayr were keen to be at the shooting. But Bargany held them in, saying, 'I will go to the length of my tether in eschewing all cummer **and** bickering, so far as I may.'

And with that he wheeled about his force off the knowes of the Lady Carse, and went down by the bogside of Dinhame, to see whether a way might be won in that direction, without coming to the bloody arbitrament **of** battle.

But my Lord the Earl cried out, 'Ware ye, there **on** the left. They would turn our flank and take us **at** unawares!'

So he spread out his hackbuttmen, and made them race down the ridges over against Bargany's men, till they won to the foot of the Bog of Dinhame. There on the edge of the moss was a wall of turf, or, as the country folk call it, a 'fail dyke,' so our hackbuttmen, coming to it, first lined it, and then began to fire on Bargany, who was somewhat disconcerted and taken aback at their alertness. I galloped round to the right, to make safe the wing with my little band of horse, for I feared we might be suddenly assaulted by the whole band of eighty.

However, as it happened, the sudden shooting of our musketeers threw their lines into confusion, some of them halting by a little burn-side that was at the bog-foot. This staying of the charge gave further courage to our musketeers, who had full time to plant their rests and make their matches ready. Our pikemen also gathered at the back of the turf dyke and levelled their weapons over the heads of the kneeling hackbuttmen, so that it had been as vain for the whole company to have charged upon us, as for them to have attacked the walls of Calais.

Nevertheless, I saw them muster again boldly and come at us. I caught the trampling of their horses as they gathered speed. The fire of our musketeers, flickered out here and there adown the line, for it was a dark afternoon and the flashes could clearly be seen. I saw sundry horses go down and heard men fall, the iron plates of their mail clashing on the frost-firmed ground. Some of those who started most gallantly reeled in their saddles, threw up their arms and fell backwards, while their horses galloped riderless away, for that is the manner of men's falling who are smitten by the bullet as they ride.

The Wolf of Drummurchie was down. I hoped that he would rise no more, for he was a most cruel beast and the bane of many lives. Indeed, from before the fire of our musketeers, all trained marksmen, the riders of Bargany who had been so proud, fairly melted away. Thus was Earl John justified of his dependence upon powder and lead.

CHAPTER XXV

MARJORIE BIDS HER LOVE GOOD-NIGHT

I WAS just rejoicing that the battle was well over, and that the victory remained with us without great shedding of blood, when to my infinite astonishment I saw a little dark cloud of five or six men disengage them from the deray, and charge straight at the thickest of us. They seemed to come suddenly out of the midst of the battling snowstorm, for the driven flakes beat so in their faces, that had it not been shed from their armour they would have been fairly sheeted white in it, as indeed were the trappings of their horses.

In a moment more they were amongst us—Bargany himself first of all, with Cloncaird and James and Andro Banatyne, and behind them, with his sword bare, Auchendrayne himself. Yet I opine he came not willingly, but that his horse, unaccustomed to noise, ran away with him. By what freak of madness they resolved thus to charge, as it had been an army in position, it is beyond me to tell. In a moment these five were in the midst of the slicing steel and the flame of ordnance—the snow-flakes driving in their eyes and their swords cutting a way through the white drift to reach the foe.

Never was there such a fight—at least, not in this land, for there were but five of them to near a hundred of us! So that I saw no honour in the battle, and besides, it went hard with me to have to smite that Gilbert Kennedy, at whose side I had ridden so blithely all the way to the house of Inch.

But I spurred Dom Nicholas forward with a kind of joy, toward the mound where Auchendrayne had managed to stay his horse just outside the heady rush of the fight. I saw that he meant to watch what the end might be, but

I was determined that I should give him more than he bargained for. So I couched lance, and crying, 'A Kennedy!' held at him, swinging a pistol point-blank as I came, and throwing it away as I gripped the spear. And this time at least I might well have been called Spurheel for I rowelled Dom Nicholas most vigorously. I came upon John Mure with a surge so that I clean overbore him with a lance-thrust in the thigh. I cared not a jot that he was old. The devil was older than he, and besides, if he wanted not to stand the chance of battle, he might even have bided at home for the quarrel was none of his.

And it had been telling all of us if I had stayed to finish him. When I think of the ill the man did afterwards, and how for years he had been bringing many to their deaths, I can bite my thumb for letting him off scot-free.

But, like a fool, I contented myself with the lance-thrust and the chance pistol bullet I sped at him in the heat of the fight. For I never could abide the cruel slaying of the wounded, which is practised even more in this private wars than in the great affairs of nations. And this over delicacy has often stood in the way of my advantage.

So I turned, and left Auchendrayne lying on the ground. As I came back I heard Bargany crying out, 'I fear we are too few! But have at them till we die!'

There was but one that fought with him, all his other companions being stricken down. And in a trice he alone was left on his horse. Nevertheless, it was with a light hand on the rein and a feat touch of the heel, that Gilbert Kennedy kept his head, though the blows fell like hail on his armour. There were three that he held at arm's length —all the while crying out for the Earl, and trying fiercely to break through the spearmen, who stood like a fence about the person of Cassillis.

'Where is my lord himself?' he cried. 'Let him now keep promise, and come out like a man to break a tree with me!'

So went the fight of the one against the many, and such deeds of valiance saw I never any man do in this realm of Scotland, though in my time I have seen so many brave and worthy things done. For Gilbert Kennedy attacked Patrick Rippitt and Quintain Crawford with strokes that

nearly dang them senseless, crying at each blow, 'Bargany!
Bargany! To the rescue, Bargany!' But ever as he raged
through the fight like a lion, I saw John Dick watching
him with a poised lance in his hand. And while Gilbert
was at blows with Rippitt and Big Quintain, Dick raised
the spear and sent it quivering at him, with an art which
I never saw any man master of, save only himself. Gilbert
Kennedy had taken no note of him—for, as I heard
afterwards, Auchendrayne had told all that were in the
camp of Bargany, that John Dick was his man, and his
paid intelligencer in the host of the enemy.

The poised lance struck young Bargany full in the neck
and stayed. So in the midst of his foes, and striking at
them to the last, he fell, who was the bravest man of his
age. And at his overthrow there fell a silence for a space,
and the battle smother cleared. Only the snow fell and
scarce melted on the face that was already white and
set in death.

We crossed our spears and made a bier with our cloaks,
whereon we laid him. Then very gently I drew away
the deadly lance, though the wound bled not much, but
inwardly, which was worse. We thought to bear him to
some castle of his own folk, as it might be to the house of
Auchendrayne. But the Earl John came and looked at
his foe and kinsman as he lay on the snow with his eyes
closed.

'Carry him to my castle at the town end of Maybole,'
said he, 'for that is near by.'

Now I thought that not the best place in the world for
the young man's recovery, but, being bidden, it was not
mine to reply, but only to obey.

We came to the portcullis gate of Maybole, and were
bearing him in upon our shoulders, when down the road
to the town there came, riding like the wind, first a lady
and then a man that followed hotly in pursuit. When
they came nearer, I saw that the lady was she who had
been Marjorie Kennedy, and that the man riding after
was her husband, James Mure. At sight of us who bore
the soldier's bier slowly on our spears, Marjorie leaped
from her horse, and left it to wander, bridle free, whither
it would. But a page seized and held it.

She came swiftly to where we were carrying our burden on the crossed lances.

'Is it Gilbert Kennedy?' she said.

We told her ay.

'Lay him down under the gate,' she commanded, 'I would speak with him.'

'But, my lady Marjorie,' I said, as gently as I could, 'I fear that he is dead already.'

'Then I would even speak to him dead,' she cried. 'Lay him down!'

Her husband came up to take her by the hand as if to remove her, but she turned on him in white anger, swift and flaming.

'You that have never yet dared to lay a hand on me, is it like that you shall begin now? Go, look to your father; cravens that shun the battle ought not to brawl with women in the gate!'

And without further remonstrance James Mure slunk away, like the very pitiful rogue that he was. I could have kicked the cur, and wished there had been fewer folk there —for I had done it too.

Then she that had been so proud and haughty to young Bargany when he was alive, took the fair, wounded head in her arms, crouching beside him in the dun, trampled snow, while the flakes blew in upon her unbound hair. She crooned and hushed him like a bairn, while we that had borne him stood wide from her, some turning away altogether. But, because I knew all and loved her, I stood near.

'Gilbert,' she said, 'noblest and dearest, never doubt but that I loved you—never loved but you. Though I flouted you oft, and ever sent you empty away, yet I loved you and none other. And I want the world to know that I loved him—ay,' she said, turning her face up to us all defiantly, 'ay, and loved him with clean hands, too, for he that is dead never knew it. But I desire you that were his enemies in life, to know that I, Marjorie Kennedy, honoured myself by loving the noblest man and the fairest—not that thing there, who by cozenance bought me, as cattle are bought in the market-place.'

She laid down his head very gently, taking a fine silken scarve, soft and white, from her own neck. And in the folds of that which was yet warm with the warmth of her pure and gracious bosom, she wrapped from common sight the head of him who had died without knowledge of her love.

Then she kneeled low down upon her knees, clasping hands and holding the last fold of the napkin ere she covered his face from sight.

'Ah, best beloved,' she said very gently, yet so that I could hear, 'fare thee well! So have I never said farewell before. But ever scornfully, being in fear of mine own heart's treachery. Lie you there that wert the noblest man the sun shone on, of adversaries the most fearless, of enemies the most chivalrous, of friends the truest, of loves the sweetest—lie you there. Those that hated you were many. But there was one that loved you—ay, and loves you, and ever shall love you! Lie you there, heart that never feared aught but God and dishonour and a lie— heart that never took favour from man nor refused one to a woman. See, I will touch your lips—those sweetest lips that never of my own will, have I touched before. The earth be kind to your body, sweet. The heavens receive your soul with honour, and the angels that warred with Satan and vanquished him, stand up at your entrance to give you room!'

She smoothed the cloth upon the face with mighty love in the caressing of her finger tips.

'Good-night, dear love,' she said, lifting it for the last time and kissing his brow. 'It is sweet, even thus in death, to tell thee that I love thee!'

Then, when Marjorie had done bidding her love fare-well, we lifted the crossed spears, and setting them again on the shoulders of men, we carried Gilbert of Bargany away.

CHAPTER XXVI

DAYS OF QUIET

I RAN back to bid Marjorie return with us to Culzean, where at least we could keep her safe. She stood where we had left her, looking at the place where her love had lain. The marks of the crossed spears and certain drops of blood alone remained on the snow.

At the sound of my voice she started as from a dream.

'Ah, Launcelot,' she said, looking at me strangely, as though I too had been dead and in a newer life had unexpectedly confronted her, 'do you think that I, who fear not fifty in the highway, fear one or two in the house of Auchendrayne? My work is not done there yet,' she added; 'till it be, there I shall bide.'

And with that she mounted and rode away. Never did I see a cavalcade ride home in such fashion after a victory. There was not a man of us from Culzean but went with his head hanging down like a little whipped cur. And when we told Sir Thomas he was like to break his heart, for he was a kindly man, and had ever a great affection for Bargany.

And Nell, when she heard it, went out and stopped the boys that played at ball and shouted in the tennis-court. Also, to keep them sober, she set them to learn their religion —of which, in common with all in that country side (save perhaps my master) they had great need.

But strange to tell, after the grief for Bargany's death was a little by-past among us, there befell the quietest and most gracious time that ever had been in the house of Culzean. It was like the coming of joy after the rain— the warm rain of pity which thawed our winter-frozen hearts.

Yet the things that happened during these months were many. First of all there was the marrying of my pretty cruel Kate to Robert Harburgh, who had at last gotten leave to depart from the Earl, and the down-sitting to settle on. So the day came that I had looked for to be so bitter to me, and lo! it was not bitter at all; for I stood beside Nell Kennedy in white, who was Kate Allison's best maid, and it was indeed a sight comely. Then it was that for the first time I honestly judged Nell to be more beautiful than her sister Marjorie, of which I have often thought since.

When all was over, and Nell and I had done racing and throwing of old shoes after them, as they rode away together to their well-furnished house of Chitterlintie, it chanced that she and I walked home together. We were silent a long while.

Then said I, 'Nell, do you remember how it was our daily use to quarrel?'

'And so it may be again,' she said, tossing her head.

'I wonder where the rope is, and the tow-steps that used to dangle from the White Tower?' she asked after a moment.

'They are e'en there yet,' I said, 'if it be that you desire to go and see your lad. But be more timely, I pray you, in your homecoming, for now you have no excuse in the way of sisters—'

Then I remembered, and was shamed. However, Nell paid no heed, but seemed to be thinking of something else.

'Nor have you now any excuse for going down by to Sandy the Grieve's,' she said, giving me tit for tat.

'Nell,' said I, 'we are very good friends, are we not?'

'Ay,' said she, drily, 'brawly do I ken the reason of that.'

'And what may the reason be?' I asked of her.

'Just that I am all there is left,' she said, so quickly that I declare the saying took the wind from me, like a sudden blow where one's breath bides. Nor do I yet know the answer to that, for on the surface of the thing there was certainly some reason in what she said.

'Oh, I am not proud,' she went on, 'and you and I are good friends and good company. I am e'en content to be Mistress Do-no-better!'

'Nell,' said I, going nearer to her, and taking her hand, 'Nell, you and I are now to be more than that.'

But she drew her hand away with a jerk.

'Try a new way of it,' she said; 'I am not taking Mistress Katherine Allison's cast-off sweet speeches!'

So that base little wretch Kate Allison had been at the telling of tales!

After this I saw no better way out of the bog than to withdraw myself from her, and walk apart in that silent dignity, which, upon occasion, I have at my command.

'No, Launce,' she said, standing up with her hands behind her and her mouth pouted, 'you are a good lad enough, but simple. I knew that I would send you into the sulks. That was the reason I said it. If you take me for a sweet confection that melts in the mouth, you mistake me sorely!'

But I made no answer, not indeed having any to make, and so marched off by myself. Yet for all Nell's ill-treatment and scorning of me, I did not grieve any more for that minx Kate. For, as I was no long time in discovering, the pretty traitress had told Nell many of those sweet things I had said to her. I never imagined that girls told such speeches and love-makings the one to the other. I had always believed that a lass kept her own secrets, and only told other people's. It was, indeed, most true what Nell had cast up to me. I was but a simple lad.

CHAPTER XXVII

ON THE HEARTSOME HEATHER

Now I must tell during this time of Sir Thomas Kennedy. He seemed altogether another man. He had ever, indeed, been kindly and generous, forgiving and unsuspicious. But during these spring months of the year after Bargany's death, he seemed to ripen like a winter apple when it is laid by, till there was no more sourness in him anywhere.

Oftentimes he would come and cause me to read to him out of the Gospels. Aforetime it had always been from the Old Testament, which I had ever thought the more interesting, till Sir Thomas that spring showed me other of it, making me read through the Holy Gospels.

Indeed, to talk with him and watch his life was better than any sermon. I declare that before I understood his character and thought, I knew not that religion was aught more than the colour of a faction—a thing to fight about, like the blood feuds of Cassillis and Bargany, concerning the wrong and right of which not one in a thousand knows anything, and still fewer care.

Yet for all his increasing gentleness there was naught unmanly about my lord, but ever the bearing and speech of a most courteous knight. He had a great love for noble and sweet music, and often diverted himself on the viol, upon which he played most masterly. The scurril jest, indeed, he would sharply reprove; but his heart still inclined to wit and mirth, and his countenance was constantly cheerful.

Specially this was so when he and I, with Nell and little David, rode south to Galloway, where we were to abide a long season with Sheriff Agnew. For Marget Kennedy, his eldest daughter, was married to the young Laird, the Sheriff's son, and abode at the castle of Lochnaw. Now in these days the air of Galloway, brisk yet kindly, suited my master better than the sea winds which were ever blowing about Culzean. And what was more to him than all Galloway was not so torn by feuds as Carrick and Kyle. And a man held not his life ever in the palm of his hand, as a tavern drawer does an unsteady cup which at any moment may be spilled. Nevertheless my good master found an infinite sadness in this, that in a wide realm of men that are called Christians, I, Launcelot Kennedy, should have come to the years of manhood with no better opinion of religion than that it was the rag of fiction. And this, too, with ministers in mostly every parish, with preachings and communings, and all the outer husk of godliness.

But during this springtime, Sir Thomas showed me quite other of it. But yet I gave not in to all his argument about the Kingdom of Peace. For I answered that I was his soldier and servant, and that time and again it had been so ordered by Providence that fight I must—for the safety and honour of my master and eke for mine own, this being the sphere of life in which my lot had been cast.

'I object it not,' said Sir Thomas; 'defence and the appeal to arms are lawful. But I have lived many days, and I think shall not live many more. Yet never have I seen the lasting success of them that make the appeal to the sword. Truly does Holy Writ say, that they that flee to the sword shall perish by the sword.'

And as we paced together he read to me much from his little Bible, and bemoaned his sins and evil life, especially how that he had been overtaken in the house of Sir Thomas Nisbett on the New Year's night of the attack. I wished that I dared tell him that I had arranged the matter with his host for the saving of his life. But I judged that repentance is no bad thing for young or old, so I e'en let him repent his fill and bemoan as he would.

Few places more heartsome have I seen than the tower of Lochnaw. First, it stood near to an inland loch, where ducks squattered and splashed, instead of being like Culzean, set amid the thresh of winds and the brattle of the sea.

Then the Sheriff and his children were well agreed, and friendly with their neighbours, so that it was a proverb, that the wolves and the lambs lay down together in that countryside. For if you stirred an Agnew, you had all the wolves of Galloway on your back! But in truth the Agnews were somewhat strange 'lambs,' though their name bears that signification.

'We are called Agnews because we have so often been fleeced,' said the Sheriff once in his pleasantry.

But I told him that was bad sense though good wit—because in the hills we shore not the lambs till they had grown to be sheep.

'Ay, well,' said the Sheriff, twinkling with his eyes, 'shear my son Patrick there, for he is now sheep-muckle, and has been so silly as to mix himself with the unruly folk of Carrick.'

I had indeed great pleasure in the house of Lochnaw. It is a fair place, with walls, moats, and drawbridges all about—very proper for defence—so that there be no artillery set against it. But to my thinking the mounds might now very well be levelled and turned into walks and terraces, as had been done at Culzean.

I sat down daily with the family at table, and was in all respects as one of them. For the Sheriff said, 'Ye are not to be strange with us—for my wife comes from within sight of Kirrieoch Hill, and likes dearly to listen to the tongue of the muirland border folk.'

'Ay,' said my Lady Agnew, for I will not call her the old lady, seeing that she had kept the heart that was within her young, 'ay, and I have not seen any folk to better them on these fat, profitable Rhynns.'

'That,' said the Sheriff, 'was what I thought when I went to the Minnoch side for a wife.'

And very gallantly he lifted his wife's hand to his lips, like the noble and courtly gentleman he was. And to this day the Agnews have ever been proud of their wives. And with reason.

'Hearken to these young folk,' said Lady Agnew, as the noise and tumult of much laughter and daffing came up to us. 'Hark to them. Is it not good to be young?'

'And therefore it is good to be my Lady of Lochnaw!

said I, for I determined to show that there were folk in
Garrick that could be gallant as well as Galloway Agnews.

'Hoot, Culzean,' cried the Lady Agnew, 'how have ye
brought up your squire, that he cannot see a well-looking
woman, but on the instant he maun begin to court her?'

'What,' cried my master, 'the regardless loon—and that
before her husband's face, too!'

'That, at least, is not a Galloway fault, at any gate,'
said the Sheriff, smiling, 'for Galloway ever behaves itself
before folk, and courts only behind backs and slily by the
licht of the moon.'

'Ye talk havers, Andrew,' said his wife. 'Never did I
meet you behind backs all the days of our courting.'

'Na,' said the Sheriff, 'but your father, honest man, was
sair troubled with deafness, and your mother was blind, and
lame o' a leg forbye.'

'Haud your tongue, guidman. Have some mense afore
the young man, for he looks a sober chiel and blate. What
should he have to do with lasses? At his years!'

Here Nell Kennedy broke out in peal on peal of laughter,
and when they asked her the reason,—

'It was but at Launcelot's face when my lady praises
him for being blate. He looks as innocent as our grey cat
Grimalkin, when she has eaten all the fish for supper.'

I wish that I could dwell longer on these sweet, peaceful
days in Galloway, but the spring went on apace, and Sir
Thomas was summoned back to Culzean. His nephew the
Earl urgently needed his advice, and wrote to him to say so.

'The Earl makes you many compliments,' said the Lady
Lochnaw.

'Ay, ay,' said Culzean, 'Earl John was aye a great
spender with his tongue, even as was the daddy of him.'

So we were bound to ride away from this kindly and
merry house of Lochnaw, and much did I desire to return
thither. Never once did we speak of wars and stratagems
while we remained under that roof, but all of friendship, of
lusty daffing, and of leasome love.

But when we mounted I bade farewell to all with a wae
heart. I envied the Sheriff greatly, for he had a wife whom
he loved in age as in youth, and yet whom he knew wherein
to be the master of—a thing, I take it, which makes home

happier than all besides. I thought within me that Patrick, his son, had set himself a harder field to plough in his Marget. Yea, already methought he had let the reins slip from his hands—which, after all, is no strange thing, considering that she was own sister to Marjorie and Nell Kennedy, of whose stiff necks I had oft had experience.

Ere we went, the Sheriff said a word that amused us all.

'When I came to be Sheriff,' he said, 'I found my father at the horn, outlaw and rebel, for refusing to pay teinds to cover the back of a bishop's lady with silks and satins. And when I die it looks like that I shall see my son at the horn for cleading of his wife according to the degree of a queen.'

For young Patrick Agnew liked better than all to be for ever gadding about after the merchants of France and the Low Countries, who knew his weakness so well that they would come from far to sell him stuff for the decking of his lady—who, when all was said and done, was nothing to compare to Nell or even to Marjorie, her younger sisters.

So we departed, almost heart-broken to leave the sweet place of Lochnaw. And the Sheriff rode with us to the village of Stranrawer—a long, clarty, Irish-looking street with pigs and bairns running about it, set on the shore of a fine loch. Here Sir Andrew and his retinue bade us farewell, and so turned them and rode away back to the homely steading of Lochnaw.

Now, upon our homeward journey it was the great good pleasure of the knight, my master, that we should ride up the Minnoch Glen to visit my father and mother, whom I had not seen for long. Sir Thomas put it, that it would be well that we rode not directly by Ardstinchar and near to Bargany along the shore road, for the folk of Bargany were cruelly set against us. Nevertheless, I knew that the real reason was that he wished me to see my mother.

So we struck across the moorland country of Wigtonshire to the head of the Loch of Cree, which is a vast, wild, swampy place where many waterfowl congregate, and where duck and seagull build their nests.

As we breasted the swelling moors, we came in sight of the mountains that were dear to me, for I was hill-bred and loved them—so that I could have ridden on, carolling like a lark, had I been in any other company.

But Sir Thomas and Nell knew what was in my heart, for as we rode up Minnoch they looked at each little thatched cot-house, and asked what it might be called—which was most amiable of them, for I loved to tell over the well-kenned names, though the hearing of them could not possible have pleasured Nell or her father.

When we came to the brow of the hill, along the side of which runs the track to the Rowan Tree, I begged of them that I might ride a little way in front, in order to prepare my father and mother for their reception. Really, I went because I did not wish them to see me meet my mother, for I knew that I was bound to weep.

But it fell not out as I had expected, for the dogs that were about the farm came barking and youching round the corner, and I saw the rough head of our herd laddie looking out of the barn. Then he scudded across the yard like a hare, and, anon, there came my mother forth, with a white hood upon her head, and girt about with her apron—even as she had been when, as a boy, I used to come pelting home from the hills, hungrily looking for a piece and a slockening drink of milk.

So she came down the little loaning to meet me, nearly running in her eagerness, I declare. And there, at the gate-slap, I leaped down from Dom Nicholas and took my mother about the neck, greeting like a great silly bairn. But for my life I could not help it. Yet I need not have cared, for Nell and Sir Thomas were admiring something on the hills, with their heads close together; and over my shoulder I could hear him pointing out to her the road to Straiton, and the way across the hills to Girvan—so they observed not my weakness.

Then came Sir Thomas forward, and I presented him to my mother. Whereupon he greeted her by the name of Lady Kirrieoch, for that was a title of courtesy to a laird's wife. And though Kirrieoch is but a little place and a wild, uncouth holding, yet Sir Thomas walked by my mother's side, leading his horse and talking, with his hat in his hand all the while, as if she had been the Queen of Scots herself.

And as I looked steadfastly away towards the wind, so that they should not see that I had been weeping, and also to let the air dry my eyes (for such weakness is ridiculous in a man), Nell came riding by on her palfrey. She cast a little glance about her to see that none observed, a look quick and timorous. Then she leaned over and gave me a light little pat on the cheek with her hand—a thing she never did before, but which I liked very well.

Then came out my father to meet us at the door, and Sir Thomas took him by the hand heartily.

'You and I, Laird,' he said, 'are not so young as we were at the King's muster on the Boroughmuir, and when you held the colours of Cassilis, even as your son does this day.'

'No, Sir Thomas,' said my father, 'brittle bones, slack sinew, thin-sown hair have come to us both since that day, when it was my good fortune to serve with you and under you.'

'Ah, Kirrieoch,' replied the Tutor of Cassilis, 'I envy you here on your high and heartsome muirs, where the wild cats are your greatest enemies, and naught more dangerous than the erne ever stoops to slay.'

'It is a gye hard struggle at times,' replied my father, 'with Launcelot away and only two old bodies left with the serving men.'

'Ah, bide a wee,' said the Tutor. 'I have made it my business to see that in a little, when the lad has won his spurs, you shall have Launcelot back with something worth while in his pouch, and a handle to his name as good as the lave of us.'

'I am glad that you have such good reports to give of him,' said my mother.

'Oh,' said the Tutor of Cassillis, drolling, 'I am none so sure of that. He has enough conceit of himself, indeed. But in his presence we will not say more.'

And then my mother set the table for us with her own hands, though Sir Thomas insisted that she should not; but with all due acknowledgment of his courtesy, my mother continued the work with dignity and grace. Besides which, I question whether at the moment Susan, the byre lass, was dressed fitting to come into a room where there was the company of great folk.

But it was more than pleasant to see Nell rise to help my mother to spread the cloth and lay out the silver spoons.

We had the best of muirland fare—mutton of the sweetest, black-faced and small, toothsomely fed on the sweet, tender grasses that nestle among the heather-knowes. Also we had sweet milk, oaten cake of a rare crispness, a kebbuck of rich cheese, and butter, as the Scriptures say, in a lordly dish, for the vessel was of silver, and had upon it the ancient arms of the Kennedies.

The Tutor picked it up and looked at it.

'These are the bearings of my great-grandfather!' he exclaimed, much astonished.

'Yes,' said my father; 'and he was also my grand-father.'

'Bless me!' cried the Tutor of Cassillis; 'I knew not that we were so nearly related.'

And all through the remainder of our stay he called my father 'cousin.' And as for Mistress Nell, there was no end to her merriment on the subject.

'Now we shall fight more than ever,' she said, 'for we Kennedies always fight with our cousins. And I must find the handle of the hayrake with which I used to beat my cousin Philip. It will serve excellently for drubbing Launcelot, my new sweet coz!'

At last we rode away, and Nell Kennedy kissed my mother lovingly when we bade farewell, so that my heart warmed more than ever to the lass.

Waeheartedly enough we left the little white housie behind us, sitting blythsome on its brae above the white stones of the burn. And in my imagination to this very day, whenever I am away from the Minnoch for long, rises a clear picture of the water-side as we saw it that morning —a wide valley filled to the brim with sunshine and the stir of breathing airs, the whaups and peesweeps beginning to build, and keeping up all the time above our heads a brave welter of crying and the whistle of eddying wings.

'I wonder not that sometimes you grow homesick,' said Nell Kennedy. 'When you are distracted and morose, I shall now know the reason.'

So we came in due season to the house of Culzean, and there we found all well, with James playing tennis con-tentedly in the court; and Sandy, up at the stables, acting the big man and giving his orders as large as my lord.

CHAPTER XXVIII

WARM BACKS MAKE BRAW BAIRNS

IT was the morning of the 11th of May, and we were on the morrow to take our journey to the town of Edinburgh. I had advertisement the night before that I was to ride to the town of Maybole to meet John Mure of Auchendrayne, and on my master's account to appoint a tryst with him at the Duppil, not far from the town of Ayr, for my Lord desired not to pass through that place, knowing that many of the faction of Bargany abode there. But Sir Thomas ever believed that Auchendrayne was of those that wished him well, because of the marriage and of all that had passed between them.

So I had to ride on this mission that I loved not over well. But I had nought to say. For whenever I spake to the Tutor concerning John Mure, he would clap me on the head and say, ' Ye are overcareful and suspicions, Launcelot. John Mure and I are fathers of the same pair of bairns, wherefore, then, should we not be as one—even as they?'

Poor man—I could not find it in my heart to tell him of the happening beneath the town-gate of Maybole, when James Mure's wife bade farewell to Gilbert Kennedy of Bargany, as he lay there dead on his enemies' spears.

So at early morning I rode as I was bidden to Maybole to meet the Laird of Auchendrayne, who, as my master knew, had some business there. But it so fell out that I missed him, for he had lodged all night in the town at the Black House, which belongs to one Kennedy of Knockdone, a friend of his and of the Laird of Newark's.

I was loath to ride all the way after him to Auchendrayne, and so bethought me that I should get the loan of a laddie from my crony, Dominie Mure, out of his school at the foot of the Kirkwynd. My way led me by the Green, where it was sorely in my mind to try a stroke of the ball. But I remembered me that Sir Thomas bade me be soon back, that I might be ready to ride with him on the morrow's morn to the town of Edinburgh by Duppil and the Ford of Holmestone. So, though I saw some brisk birkies licking at the ball, one of them being Laigh-nosed Jamie

Crawford that had his nose flattened with the stroke of a
golf ball on the hills of Ayr, I refrained me for that time
and went to seek a boy.

But I saw none on the Green, saving some raggedy
loons playing kick-ball, whom I did not like to trust with
so important a message. I went on, therefore, to the schoolhouse. And as I went it cheered me to think on Dominie
Mure and his humours, for he and I had been gossips of a
long season.

The schoolhouse of Maybole was a curious building
tacked on to the rear of the kirk, with vaulted passages of
timber, in which were the doors which could on occasion be
opened, so that the school itself might be used as an
addition to the kirk should the latter be crowded. But in
my time the space was but seldom in demand. It was an
age of iron, and men's minds craved not naturally that
which was peaceable and good. The old Papistry had
passed away, but the new religion had not yet grown into
the hearts of the people.

I came to the schoolhouse door. The noise of conning
lessons that used to go humming all along the Kirk Vennel
was louder than it was wont to be. Indeed, I thought that
of a surety Dominie Mure had gone as far as the changehouse for his morning glass of strong waters, wherein I did
that worthy man an injury. The dominie's Highland pipes
lay on the desk before him, the great drones looking out
like eyes at the scholars. They were the recreation of his
leisure, for he had been in his youth in the savage North,
and had learned to be no ill-considered performer even in
the country of pipes and pibrochs.

I looked within, and there, mounted upon two desks
and a chair, stood the Dominie with his head through a
round hole in the boards of the roof, and all that one
could see of him convulsed with animation.

The bairns below were in a great consternation, crying
out that this one and that other was misbehaving—that
Robin Gibb was pinching, or that Towhead Kennedy
was in the act of some piece of villainy which remained
unexpressed, for the obvious reason that the heavy hand
of Towhead Kennedy had prisoned the information within
the mouth of the tale-bearer.

The school of Maybole was an apartment nearly square, with a dark, well-hacked oaken writing-desk running round two sides of it, and benches set cross-ways on the floor, where, when the peace was undisturbed by internal war, the bairns conned their tasks from worn copies of the Bible.

At the far end of the school was a wooden bar a foot from the floor, and a little behind it another. This was called the hangman, for it was the post of judgment to unruly boys, who were called upon to kneel over the first bar and grasp the second, thus putting themselves into a proper position for the operations of the fiery and untender little Dominie. The desk of the master had a framework behind it, in which were half-a-dozen birch rods, carefully kept and oiled, even as I keep my stands of arms,—for the callants of Maybole have ever been unruly, and so remain to this day.

Dominie Mure was in stature the least, but in learning, I can well believe, the greatest of dominies, for he was never without two or three scholars in the Latin. It was whispered by the malicious that he had been trained for a clerk in the old days of the Roman Church, but made a false step, and so had to turn dominie. Taking the words at their usual meaning, I utterly condemn and reject this lying, malicious explanation, for Dominie Mure was the least handsome man in Carrick. He was little, scarce bigger than many boys of twelve and fourteen who sat in his class in the New Testament—which was naturally the class beneath the Old Testament.

His hair grew all over his head and face, grey, wiry and rough, like burned heather. Out of this tangle a pair of humorsome eyes looked, and a stout nose projected like the angle of an overgrown and ruined building. His arms were long, and so strong that he could lift any lad in the school into the air with one of them, while he gave him 'paikie' with the other. So fierce and fiery was the little man, that no one of the great stalwart loons who came in the winter-time dared to try their pranks upon him. He would fly at them swift as the wild cat springs, and beat half-a-dozen black and blue before they had time to rally.

What he was now doing with his head through the ceiling I could not well imagine. But there was a great noise aloft and a rushing of feet, while the master made desperate dives hither and thither, like a man in deep water and not well able to swim.

Beneath, one little rascal of a bare-legged loon rose from the seat where he had been sitting squirming at his copy.

'The Dominie is lost!' he cried in great pretended alarm. 'Oh, sirs, where is our Dominie? Look in the ink-horns, lassies. Look in a' your pouches, laddies!'

And so all the ill-set vagabonds rose and began to search the ink-horns, the dinner wallets, and even in the rat holes for the master.

But at this moment there was a crash, and first one and then another pair of legs appeared dangling through the ceiling, wildly kicking. The head of the Dominie returned through the hole in the ceiling, and he cautiously descended. His face was damp with perspiration from his exertions aloft, and he had his longest and stoutest birch rod, which was of the thickness of one's forefinger, in his hand. There was a great streak of soot across his nose—which indeed was about all that there was for it to cross, the rest of his face being but a grey tangle of hair.

Dominie Mure came forward to where I stood by the door. He greeted me right heartily, and not the less when I told him on whose account I was there, for he had often been summoned over to drink a pint with Sir Thomas at the inn or in his own town house, because my master ever loved all learned men.

'Bide a wee,' he said, 'till I attend to these rascal loons. They climbed up through the hole in the ceiling, when I was at Deacon Gilroy's funeral, to get the store of balls, knuckle-bones, chuckie stones, and other things the bairns throw up there. I kenned well they would fall through.'

So the Dominie took a much thinner and suppler bundle of birch, gave it a draw through his hand and a swish or two in the air, which made the dangling legs kick more wildly than ever—it might be with pleasure and it might be with painful anticipation.

Dominie Mure walked to the place and set a chair for himself to stand upon.

'Wha belangs thae legs?' he asked of the scholars.

'They are Tammy Nisbett's,' said the school with one voice, 'we ken by his duddy breeks!'

'And whose limbs are these—to whom do these legs belong?' he continued, pointing to certain red objects that twinkled in frantic endeavours to be free.

'Jock Harrison's,' answered the school without a moment's hesitation; 'they are clouted wi' his mither's auld petticoat!'

Then the master did his office affectionately upon those parts of Tommy Nisbett and Jock Harrison which of their own accord the adventurous loons had exposed. The thwacks resounded through the school, but the yells mostly ascended through the roof. Then, when he had finished his pleasure—for I saw by his eye it was no unwelcome task—he put up an arm, and without circumspection pulled the squirming urchins through the rotten boards.

'Thomas Nisbett,' he said severely, 'your faither is an householder. He shall pay for the damage done to the ceiling of this schule, which is the property of the Session of the parish, of which I am clerk. And your faither can take the price out of your breeks himsel' at his leisure.'

He then hauled the other down in the same manner.

'Jock Harrison, I'll never trouble your puir mither about the siller for the repairs. She has enough to do with ten like you. But I'll e'en pay your hurdies the noo, and quit your mother and you too, at the one settlement.'

Which having done, he laid down his bundle of rods, dusted his hands, and commended himself to me to know how, and in what manner, he might serve my master. I told him that if he would write a letter to John Mure of Auchendrayne to bid him meet with Sir Thomas at the Chapel of St. Leonard's by the sandhills of Ayr, on the morrow's morn at ten of the clock, and send it to Auchendrayne by one of his most trustworthy lads, it would be no small obligation. And furthermore that I would await an answer here in Maybole, having other business to transact.

'Good faith, Master Launcelot, I will do that—and gladsomely,' said the little Dominie.

So, having brought the school to order and set the classes to their work, he squared himself at his desk, and wrote fairly and elaborately as I told him. For the little man prided himself on his penmanship—which, indeed, Sir Thomas ever said was better than that of any law scrivener in Edinburgh.

I reminded him of this, and Dominie Mure could hardly contain himself for pride. How strange that so small a thing should set up some men!

Then, when he had finished and addressed it in the Italian manner, he called out, 'William Dalrymple, come hither!' And, from the close-built ranks of the older scholars at the wall-desks, a plump-faced, ruddy boy arose.

'This,' the Dominie said, 'is the son of a widow woman, and a steady lad that will truly do your message and bring you word again without delay or falsehood. He is called for a nickname Willie Glegfeet.'

So to William was delivered the letter and sundry copper coins for running the errand. Whereupon he took up the Vennel and through the High Street on the way to Auchendrayne like a hunted hare, for, as his name imports, he was wonderfully nimble of his feet.

Having thus delivered my message, I thanked the Dominie very heartily, and went to the play of the golf green till the messenger should return.

I had an excellent game, but, not playing with mine own clubs, I was beaten (though not at a great odds), by the young Laird of Gremmat, whose chin was hardly yet better of the cleaving it got on the fatal day at the Lady's Carse. But this interfered naught with his putting. Now gaming on the green is uncommonly fretting to the temper, and more especially when you are losing with a man like Gremmat, who cries and shouts at every good stroke of his own and dispraises yours. Yet, owing to the well-kenned equality of my temper, and also because he was not yet fully recovered of his wound, I did not clout him over the sconce with my cleek, as I certainly was in a great mind more than once to do.

We were yet hard at it, and the afternoon wearing on apace when I saw the little Dominie coming toward us with the boy William Dalrymple by his side. The schoolmaster held the letter in his hand and gave it back to me.

'William Dalrymple says that he found not the Laird of Auchendrayne in his own house, and has therefore brought back the letter.'

I looked at it a moment, turning it over in my hand.

'It has been opened,' said I. 'See, the wax is gone, and there are finger-marks within.'

'So, indeed, it has,' said Dominie Mure. 'Boy, if you have opened it I will tan you alive, outside and in.'

Whereat the boy began to weep.

'I have said what I was told to say,' he cried, and for all we could do, nothing more could we get out of him— save that a dark man, faced like an ape or a wild beast, had come some way home behind him and sorely terrified him. So we sent the boy back to his mother, and, bidding farewell for that time to the Dominie and to young Gremmat, I fared along the way to Culzean to make me ready for the long journey of the morrow.

CHAPTER XXIX

THE MURDER AMONG THE SANDHILLS

IT was broad day and a pleasant May morn, when my master and I said our farewells at the gate of Culzean. With my own hands I had saddled for Sir Thomas his war-horse. But he, coming down arrayed in his plain suit of dark Flemish cloth, bade me take him back to the stable and get instead a pacing palfrey, which he loved because Marjorie had used to ride it.

Then he kissed his bairns, for the lads and Nell stood by the door on the landward side, watching us with earnest eyes.

'Keep the castle, James,' he cried, 'till I come back!'

'Ay,' said Sandy, 'we will keep it for you, faither.'

For Sandy came ever to the forefront, setting himself naturally before the slow and quiet Jamie.

Then Nell came near and kissed her father. But she and I only looked the one at the other as friends look, for at least before folk we did not so much as touch hands.

So down through the woods Sir Thomas and I went sedately and quietly, now into little caller blinks of morning sunshine which glinted straight and level between the trees, and anon coming out upon a bare knoll as into a room with a removed and spacious ceiling. For there at our feet was the plain of the sea, sparkling and blue, beyond it again the hills of Arran, and to the south the shoulder of the Craig of Ailsa, heaving its bulk skyward like a monster of the ocean stranded in the shoreward shallows.

Very pleasant was my master's discourse as we went, of the wonderful peace that he was going to bring upon the land of Carrick from his dealings with the King and Council in Edinburgh. Specially he spoke with thankfulness of the present friendship of Auchendrayne, of the young Bargany who should for long be under tutors and governors, and of our own Earl, now tired of the feud and eager for a lasting peace.

'It needs,' said he, 'but that one should take on him all the burden and heat of the day, and carry the matter through. And I, that am no warrior, but a quiet man dwelling in mine own house and fit only for daunering about mine own fields, may be able to do more in the matter than many battalions. For I have some influence with the King—a man that loves grave discourse upon occasion.'

So pleasantly talking together in this fashion, speaking ever the kindliest things of the enemies of his house, and all the time making many excuses for them, Sir Thomas kept his palfrey at the amble.

Presently we came to the castle of Greenan, which stands on a sea crag, and looks right bravely over the Bay of Ayr and down upon the little town thereof. It belongs to Kennedy of Balterson, a gossip and well-wisher of Culzean's.

'Now,' said my master, 'I must see if Balterson is at home. I think truly that he is, for there is a reek coming up very freely from the lum. Now John was ever a big eater and a long lier abed in the mornings. What a pleasantry if I should raise him from between the blankets! It would be a great cast-up all the days of his life.'

So we lighted down in front of the castle yett. I tied the horses together, and walked about the cliff edge, looking out to sea and over the sands of Ayr, thinking of many things. Mostly my thoughts ran on the treasure of

Kelwood, and whether I should ever win it. Of Nell, too, and what she meant by patting me on the cheek when we met my mother, of the Tutor's words to my father that one day I should have a handle to my name and a down-sitting as good as any. Plenty of pleasant things I had to think about that caller morn in May, as indeed a young man of spirit ought to have.

And it was not very long before Sir Thomas came forth arm in arm with John Kennedy of Balterson, a grave and portentous man of heavy figure, richly arrayed, more like the provost of a town than a country laird. And these two paced up and down the narrow terrace walk of Greenan Castle, turning and returning, wheeling and countering as on the quarterdeck of a ship. But of the matter of their discourse I know nothing, though I guessed it to have been concerning the making up of peace between the feudal enemies in the lands of Carrick and Kyle.

It was near to ten of the clock, and already close upon the time which had been appointed for the tryst with Auchendrayne, that we mounted at the yett of Greenan to ride on our way to Holmestone Ford.

'Sorry am I,' said my master, 'that I have not spoken a word with John Mure ere I go. But I know his loving desire for my success, and he well knows my affection for him.'

We rode down from the castle crag of Greenan, and presently came out upon the links. These are here all sandy, cast up into rounded mounds and hills, and bitten into by the little pits and dungeons, called of them that play at the golf, 'bunkers.'

'Launcelot, ride a little way in front. It approaches the hour of noon, and I would do my devotion and meditate a little alone,' said Sir Thomas to me. So I drew myself a bowshot before him, riding upon Dom Nicholas and taking my hat in my hand. I rode easily, enjoying the sea breeze that cooled my brow and tossed my hair. I wondered if ever the time would come, when I also should be thinking about my religion at noon of a fine heart-some day. It seemed a strange time enough for a hale, well-to-do gentleman to set to his prayers.

Presently I saw a man standing upon my right hand

somewhat above me upon the crown of a sandhill. And he raised his hand as one that cried to clear the course in the game, so I thought no more of the matter. But I looked round, thinking perchance that he cried to my master, who was riding with bared head and holding his little red Testament in his hand.

Suddenly, even as I looked at him, I heard the sound of shots behind me, and, turning Dom Nicholas, I saw my master reel in his saddle, with white blowing puffs of gunpowder rising all about him, from behind the desolate sandhills among which the murderers had hidden themselves. Drawing my sword, I set spurs to the sides of Dom Nicholas, and galloped towards them. I was aware, as I rode, of my master lying on his back on the sand, and his palfrey galloping away with streaming mane. A little black crowd of men stood and knelt about him, and I saw the flash of steel again and again as one and another of them lifted a knife and struck.

I yelled aloud to them in my agony and bade them wait till I came. So they hasted to make front against me, some of them leaping on their horses and others biding a moment to put as it had been booty into their saddle wallets.

It was Thomas Kennedy, called the Wolf of Drummurchie, that withstood me as I came thus furiously upon Dom Nicholas. With him I first crossed swords, while one, James Mure of Auchendrayne, held off a little warily, watching to win in at me when I should give him opportunity. With the corner of my eye I saw the same man whom I had at first observed making the warning signal. He held up his hand as before. Then he leaped on a horse which he had by him in a hollow of the sands. He was, as I noted, a tall man, with a hat pulled low over his eyes, and he wore about him the long grey cloak which had been so fatal a sign to us of Cassillis.

But ere I could see more, I was in the thick of the murderers with my sword. I struck and warded, not knowing what I did, but only striking, with the anger of blood in my eye, till I gave Drummurchie a cut on the shoulder, which made him fain to shift his sword arm. Then I wheeled and attacked Cloncaird as furiously, who was a great mountain of a fellow, red of face and brutal of heart. And I had readily enough done for him, too, had he been alone, for he was no man of his weapons. But I could see plainly enough three or four others charging pistols and training of hackbutts, making ready to take an aim at me. Whereupon I knew that there was no use of spending my life for naught. So, with my sword red in my hand, I rode over the sandhills straight at the tall man in the grey cloak; but such was the effect of an ill conscience that he took his mantle about his mouth as one that fears being known, and set spurs to his horse. I had not pursued far when I came to the top of a dune and saw a little cloud of citizens that played at the clubs beneath me. To them I rode as hard as I could, ·vith the murderers' bullets splattering here and there and throwing up little spirts of sand about me.

'Murder! Foul murder!' I cried. 'Come hastily, for the Tutor of Cassillis is done to death!'

One of the citizens held up his hand to me as if to bid me be silent, for it was the putting stroke which his neighbour played, and of its kind difficult, so that men held their breath. But when it was made and the ball holed, they ran to me quickly enough, for, alas! murder was so common in those days, that men took little notice unless he that fell was one who was some kin to themselves.

Nevertheless, they hasted when I cried who was my master, and who were the villains that beset him. For the players were all burghers of Ayr and feared that they should underlie the angers of the Earl and of the King, if they gave not ready help when this slaughter was done, as it were, at their very gates.

Thus very quickly we came to my dear master. He was lying alone on his back quietly gazing up to the sky, the red blood welling from many ghastly wounds. All his rich plain Flanders cleading was torn and disarranged by the villains, who had not disdained to despoil after that they had murdered him.

Yet there was some life left in him, and he turned his head, smiling as if thankful (after the hateful faces of his cruel enemies) to gaze at the last upon the countenances of friends. He was, as I thought, past speech; but he looked about him in a certain curious way he had when he had lost something, and, being absent-minded, knew not for the moment what. I showed him his empty purse; but it was not that. So I looked round and saw nothing but some discharged pistols lying with broken lingels abroad upon the sand, and the little book he had been reading as his palfrey paced along.

So as soon as I showed the latter to him he put out his hand for it. Then he held it a moment, kissed it, and gave it back to me.

'Be a good lad,' he said quietly and composedly. 'Fear not for me; I go in friendship with all men. Poor, poor Cloncaird!' he said, thinking of one of his murderers whom he had always befriended, 'it is a pity for his wife and young family!'

Then he closed his eyes and we thought he had already passed from us.

But presently he opened them again and looked toward me.

'Be kind to Nelly!' he said, smiling so kindly at me, that my heart nearly broke. He shook his head at seeing my grief and the tears running down, for, indeed, I could not withhold them.

'There is no need,' he said reprovingly, 'no need for the like of that ava'. Be a brave lad, Launcelot, and just as true to your God as you have proved to me, who have been a loving master to you here below. I am only wae for the poor, misguided lads, that were so far left to themselves as to lay me here like this.'

And with that there was but his body on the sands, for the spirit of the gentlest master that ever a man served had gone its way to its own Master.

But it was even as he said—for the end of such an one there is no need of tears.

Then I stood up, and the terrible thought came in upon me like Solway tide. How—how shall I take him home to Helen Kennedy—to his orphaned bairns, and to the stricken house of Culzean?

CHAPTER XXX

I SEEK FOR VENGEANCE

Ay, well might I say it. How was I to face Nell Kennedy —she that had with a long, kindly look committed her father into my keeping that very morning? Tenderly we lifted the body, which in life had been so noble and now was so pitifully mishandled. The villains had despoiled the dainty garmentry, torn the lace, and snatched the jewellery which Helen Kennedy had set in place as, daffing right merrily, she prepared her father (as she said) to 'gang worthily and bonnily before the King.' But the King he went before was One, as he himself would often say, that looked not on the outer appearance but on the heart. And concerning that last Thomas Kennedy need have no fear that his would not be well looked upon—for it was upright, and kindly, and true, nor did it ever move to the hurt of any man in all this world. And as I took him up, I saw still more clearly the black-hearted rage of the persecutors. For it showed as manifestly as any other fact the hellish intent of the murderers, that they had taken time, even while I was in the act to come at them, to despoil my master of his purse with a thousand merks of gold therein. Nay, his very ring of fine diamonds they tore from his finger, and his golden buttons of wrought goldsmith work were riven from his frilled sark—one murderous loon snatching one thing and the other another, worse than brute beasts of the field.

We laid him gently upon the back of wise Dom Nicholas, that all the time stood like a statue, and then when everything was ready, moved graciously and soberly away, as though he had been well aware of the melancholy burden he bore. Even thus we brought my dear master to the sea terrace of Greenan which he had so lately left.

And when John Kennedy of Balterson heard the trampling of the horse on the flags of the court, he came out crying loudly and heartily as was the manner of the man.

'Wi' what's this, Culzean? Are ye back again?'

So running to the door he stood with his table-knife in

his hand and a bit of his mid-day meal thereupon, astonished
beyond the utterance of words.

'What's this? What's this?' he cried. 'Oh, sirs, what
foul wark is here? Wha has done this?'

And I told him their names—at least so far as I knew
them.

'Thomas of Drummurchie!' he cried. 'It shall not be
the uplands of Barr parish that shall keep ye frae the stark
sword of John Kennedy of Balterson. And thou, Walter
Mure of Cloncaird, that has so often sat in this house of
the Greenan, by the grace of God I shall lay thee as low
as thou hast laid my friend this day.'

But I begged Balterson to think of something else than
the taking of revenge—of which all in good time. So
presently he got a horse litter with two steady-going
beasts, and I walked alongside it with Dom Nicholas arching his head and treading softly as if he also mourned.
Thus we came to the town of Maybole, which was as our
own place. And such dule and lament as there was that
day saw I never anywhere.

For the town had loved him as its liege lord, far more
than either John, Earl of Cassillis, or his father the King
of Carrick. Such a congregation as met us at the town
gate! The women all crying the cry of death, the men
cursing and calling vengeance. The minister was there
to pray, and all classes and conditions were moved to
tears.

And ere we were well past the Foul Alley there were
twenty men on horseback to chase the murderers, with
John Kennedy of Balterson at their head. But they might
as well have chased the wind, for by this time, with the
relays of horse that had been ordered for them, they were
safe among the wild Crauford country on the borders of Kyle.

Of the sad homecoming to Culzean itself I declare I
cannot write at length. At the entering in of the woodland I left them, and upon Dom Nicholas I rode drearily
forward to do the bitterest day's work of my life—to tell
Helen Kennedy that I brought only her father's corpse
home with me.

And, as the chance befell it, it was at least half-a-mile
before I reached the home gate of Culzean, just where one

sees for the first time the grey turrets sitting against the dimpled blue of the incoming tide, that I was aware of Nell Kennedy coming light-foot towards me, singing a catch of a song and swaying a flourish of sweet may-blossom daintily in her hand. I have never rightly loved the white hawthorn since that day.

But as soon as she saw me she stopped her song and clutched her fingers close upon her palm, for the flowery branch had fallen at her feet.

'What is wrong?' she cried, when I came near to her. But I could not answer till I had leaped from Dom Nicholas and taken her by the hand. She turned round, keeping me at the stretch of her arm so that she might read the news, good or bad, in my eyes.

'Is it my father? Tell me,' she said very calmly.

'Nell, it is your father,' I said as quietly. 'They set upon him and hurt him, even when he had sent me on a little way before him that he might be alone at his mid-day meditation—'

'Is he dead—tell me—is he dead?' she broke in. But I answered her not; for I could not. So she knew, and in an instant grew as pale and still as the man that was passed from us.

'Take me to him,' she said at length. And, seeing that I still hesitated, she said, 'Do not fear for me. I will do all that a daughter of Culzean should do.'

'They are bringing him hither now,' I said. 'I came hasting to tell you. The feet of the horses that carry him are even now upon the brae.'

Then, when I had told her all, I ended the tale with my tears and with crying out that which was in my heart, 'Oh, would to God I had died instead of him!'

'Launcelot,' Nell said, with a wonderful quiet, 'that is useless, and not well said. Be comforted. None would have done one-tenth so much as thou hast.'

'Bless you, Nell!' I said, for I had feared greatly she would have broken upon me with bitter railing.

It was by the great oak tree which sends its boughs over the road that we met the bier, and the horses stopped. Even thus Nell Kennedy met her father, and there was not a tear on her face, but only a great sweet calm. She silenced the noisy limmer wives that went behind crying and mourning aloud. So in this manner we went onward to Culzean, Nell walking on one side of the bier and I on the other, leading Dom Nicholas by the bridle.

And lo! as the body passed the drawbridge, a sudden gust out of the sea snatched his knightly pennon from the topmost turret tower of the battlements of Culzean, which was held a freit and a warning by all the folk of Carrick. But though the master had come home to his own, yet both Culzean and I were now masterless.

In due time we gave him stately funeral, carrying him forth upon a day so calm, so breathless, that the banners did not wave as they swept the dust. And thereafter all life seemed to stop, when we came home again to the darkened house. James and Sandy, the two young lads, played no more in the tennis-courts, but went about with linked arms speaking of revenge. But little David abode with Nell and went forth only with her, clinging winsomely to her hand; for we kept us close within bars and warded ramparts, with the drawbridge up, watching the fruit ripening on the walls of the orchard of Culzean all that splendid summer of the murder of our lord and master.

Slowly I thought over many things, till the resolve to bring the matter to a head came masterfully upon me. From the Earl as Bailzie of Carrick I got warrant, according to my dead master's word and direction, to be doer-in-ordinary for the young man James, who was now the heir of Cassillis. For Earl John knew that Launcelot Kennedy was no self-seeker; also they that stood about had told to him the Tutor's last words—that I was to be a good lad and to be kind to Nelly. It was Adam Boyd of Penkil, and David Somerville, hosier in Ayr, who told him this, and they were two of those that played golf by the sandhills on the day of that foul slaying under trust.

CHAPTER XXXI

THE BLUE BLANKET

YET because I needed advice and had none to give it, I rode one day to Edinburgh to see Maister Robert Bruce. I found the whole city in an uproar. There was the beating

of drums in all the streets and closes, and a great multitude
of the common folk crying out 'For God and the Kirk!'
Pikes danced merrily along the causeways, and good wives'
heads were thrust through all the port-holes in the windings
of the stairs. Their voices, shrill and vehement, kept up
a constant deafening clamour, each calling to her John or
Tam to 'come awa' in oot o' that,' or bidding them 'not
to mell wi' what concerned them not.'

'What concern is the glory o' God o' yours—you that
is but a baker in Coul's Close?' I heard one wife cry
to her man, and it seemed to me a mightily pertinent
question.

At last, after many inquiries, I heard how the Minister
of Edinburgh had bearded the King, so that he was gone
off to Linlithgow in great indignation, and how that in
a day or two Maister Robert Bruce would either be King
of Scotland or lay his head on the block.

Yet the minister was in his study chamber when I went
to seek him, reading of his Bible and writing his sermon,
as quietly as though there had been no King in Scotland
—save, as it might be, the King in whose interest he
had so often bearded King Jamie Stuart, sixth of that
name.

Robert Bruce looked up when he saw me.

'Ah, Launcelot,' he cried, more heartily than ever I had
heard him, 'ken ye, lad, that you are likely to be at the
horn for communing with a wild rebel like me?'

'To be "at the horn" is no uncommon thing in Carrick,'
I replied, 'and makes little difference either to the length
of a man's life or the soundness of his sleep. I have been
at the horn ever since I was eighteen years of my age.'

'Well, Launcelot,' he said soberly, 'so it has turned
out even as I said. I know—I know. It is not in man
that walketh to direct his steps. But I saw ye were all
"fey" at Culzean.'

Then I told him the purpose of my coming all the way
to Edinburgh to see him.

'What!' he said, 'ye have never come so far only to
have speech of poor Robert Bruce, that was yesterday
Minister of Edinburgh, and to-day is, I fear, doomed to
lay his head on the hag-clog?'

I told him it was even so, and that, being the man of wisest counsel I had ever known, I would have gone ten times as far to have his friendly advice.

'Ay me,' he said sadly, 'wae is the man that has such a rumour and report of wisdom, yet cannot counsel himself what he should do in his own utter need.'

But, for all that, he went over everything that had happened in Carrick, with a clearness most like that of a lawyer when he sets in order his case before the judge. Then he sat a long while silent, with his finger tips drumming idly upon his writing.

'So Bargany is dead,' he said at last. 'He was the only considerable man of his own faction. Who is there to succeed him?'

'But a child!' said I, 'one that plays with puppets.'

'As do we all, Launcelot,' said Maister Bruce, smiling on me.

'And after him in that faction, of his own house and kin who comes—?' he asked.

'There are none besides the Tutor's murderer, Thomas of Drummurchie, and Benane his brother, but he is a deboshed man and of no account,' I made answer, not seeing his drift.

'Who leads them then—?'

'John Mure of Auchendrayne is their only considerable man, and he has waxen great and greater within these months.'

The minister nodded his head and sat still as one that considers all sides of a question.

'And of you that stand by the gold and blue—who remains?' he went on.

I told him but John, Earl of Cassillis, and his brother the Master.

'And in whose friendship is the Master?' he asked.

'In our country of Carrick he has an auld friendship with Auchendrayne, and a good-going feud with the Earl, his brother; but recently he has taken up with the Lord of Garthland in Galloway, and married his sister.'

'Tell him from me,' said the minister of Edinburgh, 'to bide close in Galloway and get him bairns in peace. For gin he comes back to Carrick, of a surety his head shall be the next to fall.'

'And why so?' said I.

'Because,' said Maister Robert Bruce, 'John Mure designs that there shall be no power in Carrick nor in the Shire of Ayr besides his own and that of the Earl—till he get time to have him also killed. I tell you Auchendrayne hath the brains of any three of you.'

'And of the treasure of Kelwood, what?' said I.

'That,' said the minister, meditating, 'is a little forth of my province. But, if ye will know, I think it is in the keeping of some of Auchendrayne's tools. And I advise you, ere ye look for revenge, to go seek for it.' I was silent, for I hoped that he would tell me yet more.

'The treasure of Kelwood will lead you to your aim. I think ye will find that the same hands which reft it away are red with the blood of your master. And one thing I am sure of—that within that treasure chest lie your love, your land, and your lordship!'

I asked him what he meant, but he would not tell me more clearly. Only this he said, speaking like them that have the second sight,—

'James Stuart being what he is—a treasure-seeker— and John, Earl of Cassillis, being what he is—a treasure-gripper—if ye find the kist, ye have them both in your hand. And therein (or I am a false prophet) lie, as I say, your love, your land, and your lordship.'

Then I asked him if he had any counsel to give me ere I went.

'Be brave,' he said, 'read your Testament. Tell no lies. Carry no tales. Seek carefully for the man that wears the grey cloak, and then for the man that runs like a beast and carries the knife in his teeth.'

He went to the window as one that has spoken his last word.

'Hear ye that?' he said. 'That is the warrant for my heading.'

There circulated a great crowd of people without, apprentices and suchlike mostly, with here and there among them a decent, responsible man of the trades. They were singing at the utmost pitch of their voices:—

'We'll hae nae mair Jeems Davie-son,
    Davie's son—Davie's son!
We'll gie his loons the spavie sune,
    Spavie sune, spavie sune,
An' the deil may tak Jeems Davie-son.'

'They might as well shear my head at once as sing that song,' said Maister Robert Bruce. 'There is nothing that James Stuart likes so ill as to be called the son of Davie, unless it be the man who upholds the right of private judgment!

'Ah,' he cried again, 'the Blue Blanket—this waxes serious. I must put on my gown and sally forth.'

Then up the Canongate there came a great crowd of citizens all marching together and crying, 'God and the Kirk! God and the Kirk!' And in the midst there was borne the famous flag that has ever staggered in the front of a bicker, foretelling storms and the shaking of thrones —the Blue Blanket of the trades of Edinburgh.

Robert Bruce drew his black Geneva gown about him, and taking his little Bible and his oak staff in his hand he went out. As he stood forth upon his step, he was hailed with shouts of joy and rejoicing.

'Hearken Maister Bruce! Hear the minister! God and the Kirk! Doon wi' Jeemie Fat-Breeks!'

And the Blue Blanket wavered and waggled, being borne this way and that by the press. All about the skirts of the crowd, and down the closes angry drums were beating, and a hundred idle 'prentices thundered on great folk's doors and garred the window panes rattle on the causeway—which was a sin when glass was so dear, and to be seen in so few places besides the citizen houses of the great.

'Men of Edinburgh,' cried Bruce, 'hear your minister. Wherefore this tumult? I bid you to depart quietly to your homes. We have a difference with the King, it is true; but let us who are the servants of God and of the Kirk of Scotland settle our own affairs with the King. What is your concern in the matter?'

But the more he spoke of the King the more loud grew the tumult.

'God and the Kirk! God and the Kirk!' they cried,

and the Blue Blanket waved higher than ever, being held up by one man standing upon the shoulders of other two.

'Ay, ay, even so; it is a good cry,' said the minister; 'but it would set you better to be a little more ready to obey both God and the Kirk at other times. The most part of you know not for what cause ye are come together. Ye want to roll your minister's head in the dust——'

'No, no!' cried the throng; 'we will keep you safe, or know the reason why.'

'Depart—scatter instantly to your firesides!' cried Bruce. 'And so ye will the better serve the Kirk of Scotland and me, her unworthy servant.'

And with this he motioned to them with his hands, dismissing them. So great was his power that they went, scattering like peet reek on a windy day. In a minute or two there was not one of them to be seen on the street. The minister and I were left alone.

'What think ye, Launcelot? Why stand ye so moody?' my companion said to me.

I told him that I liked not much to tell him; that it was no fitting thought to tell a minister.

'Say on,' he said. 'I have listed to strange speeches in my time.'

'Well then, sir,' I made answer, 'I was thinking what a pity to see so many limber lads with stark pikes in their hands, and nobody a penny the worse! I would to God I had them in Carrick. John Mure of Auchendrayne would hear news of it right bliskly.'

The minister clapped me on the back.

'Ah, Launce, it will be a strange Heaven that you win to, unless you mend your ways. Ye are nocht but a wild Carrick savage. But ye maun e'en dree your weird, young Launcelot, and auld Robert Bruce maun dree his. Fare ye weel.'

So we parted there on the steps of his own house. And with that I betook me to horse, and forth through the turbulent city that could yet make so little of its tulzies; and as I went I thought, 'Lord, Lord, for one hour of Gilbert Kennedy and me to show them a better way of it; or even Robert Harburgh. And it would be like capturing

Heaven by violence, to enter Holyrood House in the way of stouthrief and spulzie!'

But I only thought these things without intent to do them, for I am a King's man and peaceable—besides which, I had but lately spoken good words to a minister of religion. Nevertheless, what a booty would there not have been in that place at the Canongate foot! Not that I would lay hand upon a stiver of it, even if I got the chance, but the thought of it was marvellously refreshing, I own.

CHAPTER XXXII

GREEK MEETS GREEK

THEN as I journeyed south I saw my work set out like a perspective before me. As the minister had said, the treasure of Kelwood and the death of my master hung by one string. The House of the Red Moss was very near to the sandhills of Ayr, and there could be little doubt that the hand which had sped the bloody dagger was the hand that had brought my master to his death.

As the drawbridge clanged down for me to ride once more within the house of Culzean, and lazy Gib stretched himself to cry that all was well, I took a resolve. It was to tell Helen Kennedy all that I knew, and ask her judgment upon it—though I have small notion (for ordinary) of women's discretion. So, when the greetings were said, I took my opportunity and came to her when she was walking in the garden apart, where the apple trees grow. When she had heard all, she said, 'Launce, you and I must ride to Auchendrayne.'

'Well,' said I, 'and what then? Shall we bid Grieve Allison have our coffins in readiness against our return feet first?'

'We shall see my sister Marjorie,' she said, without heeding my words, 'and take counsel with her. They will not kill us within the house of Auchendrayne while she is alive.'

'I believe not that we shall even have the chance of speech with her,' I replied, 'but we may at least go and see. Whether we ever win back to Culzean is another matter.'

But Nell was mainly set on it, and I did not counter
her, it being so that I was to ride in her company—for,
indeed, I myself desired greatly to see the famous tower
where dwelled a man so potent and so evil. The next
day it happened that I went to Maybole and found mine
ancient friend, Robert Mure, Dominie and Session Clerk
of the town. He sat gloomily in his school and bowed his
head on his hands, for he had never looked up nor taken
pleasure in life since they laid my master in the burying-
place of his folk within the kirkyard of Maybole. The
school hummed about him, but he took little heed. His old
alertness seemed quite gone from him. And when I came
in he only lifted his head a moment and nodded, falling
back again at once into his new melancholy. His pipes
lay beside him indeed, but so long as I was there I did
not see him recreate himself upon them—as had been his
ordinary wont, playing pibrochs for his scholars' delecta-
tion at every pause in the day's occupations.

'Dominie,' said I, 'there is one thing I want——'

'Say on,' said he, briefly, not looking at me.

'I want speech with William Dalrymple, the lad that
carried the letter to Auchendrayne the day before my
lord's death.'

'Of what good is the like of that?' said he. 'Will all
the speech in the world bring back him that's gane?'

'No,' said I, going nearer to him and speaking under
my breath, 'but it may help us to his murderer.'

'Eh, what?' said the master, sitting up as gleg as a cat
at a mousehole, '"His murderer," said ye? Are not Thomas
of Drummurchie and Mure of Cloncaird his declared
murderers?'

'Ay,' said I, 'exactly—his "declared" murderers.'

'Speak either less or mair—let us hae done wi' parables!'
quoth the Dominie.

'What think ye,' said I, 'of the Grey Man that stood
behind and waved them on, like a pilot guiding a ship
into a port? I mean the man that threw the dagger into
the Red House. I mean the man that let loose the scum
of the Tolbooth on us of Cassillis the day of "Clear the
Causeway."'

'And who might he be?' said the Dominie, breaking in

upon me, for some of these things he was not acquainted
with.

'First bring in the laddie,' said I.

So Dominie Mure brought Dalrymple in to a private
place, and having dismissed the school, we proceeded faithfully to examine him. I asked him to tell me all that had
befallen that fateful day, from the time I had seen him
run up the Kirk Vennel to the time when he came to me
again upon the green at my play, and making a poor
hand of it with another man's clubs.

The boy began his tale well enough, like one that says
a well-learned lesson; but in the very midst, when, somewhat severely, I bade him say over again what he had
already said, he broke out into a passion of weeping and
begging us to have mercy upon him—for that he was but
a laddie and had been commanded upon pain of his death
to tell the tale which he had told us at the first.

So we bade him to speak freely, to tell no lie any more
and all would yet be well. So he told us how he had gone
fleet-foot to Auchendrayne and had there found John
Mure, the master thereof, sitting in the great chamber
with Walter of Cloncaird. He described how that he had
given the letter into the Laird's hands, even as he had
been bidden. When Mure had read it, he handed it over
to Cloncaird. But he, swearing that he was not gleg at
the parson-work, bade Auchendrayne to read it aloud for
him. Which, when he did, they looked long and strangely
at one another. And at last John Mure said, 'I should
not wonder, Cloncaird, but something might come out
of this.'

Then the boy told how they had gripped him, set a
naked dagger to his throat, and afterwards made him swear
to take the letter back to them that sent him, saying that
he had gone to Auchendrayne, but had returned without
seeing the Laird.

'Say,' said Mure, 'that the servant bade you take back
the letter unopened, because that his master was afield
and he knew not when he would be home. So,' concluded
the boy, 'even thus I did! And this is all the truth, or
may God strike me dead!'

The Dominie and I looked each at the other in our turns.

'The Grey Man himself,' said I.

'The Black Deil himsel'!' said he.

'We will exorcise him, black or grey!' cried the Dominie. 'I am going direct to the bailies and elders to tell them that this school has vacation till it pleases me to take it up again.'

So he went out and I waited alone with the boy William Dalrymple, whose rosy and innocent face was all be-blubbered with weeping.

I slapped him on the shoulder and bade him take heart because he had found friends. Then I also told him that on the morrow he must come with me to the Earl of Cassillis, and by-and-by it might be to the King himself.

'Will the Dominie come too?' the boy asked very anxiously.

So when I told him that he would, he seemed more satisfied, and asked leave to go home to his mother.

I had, indeed, something to tell Nell Kennedy that night when I rode home from Maybole. And upon the head of it we two sat long in talk, and were more than ever set on riding to Auchendrayne. But first we decided that the Dominie and I should carry William Dalrymple to the Earl, that he might certify to him what he had already testified to us at the schoolhouse in the Kirk Vennel.

But on the morrow we, that is the Dominie and I, had it set to ride to Cassillis by way of Maybole. On the way we came to the little hut of the widow Dalrymple, for William was a town's bursar, and so got his learning from the Session as a poor scholar. The door was shut, and a neighbour's wife cried to us that both the boy and his mother had gone on to Cassillis before us. So we rode forward. Yet we must have missed them on the way, for when we came to the castle yett there was nobody there before us, and the Earl himself had ridden forth to the hawking by the waterside.

Then came out to us foolish Sir Thomas Tode with his long story, which began as usual with the Black Vault of Dunure, and was proceeding by devious ways when his wife came round the corner—whereat right briskly he changed his tune.

'And as I was saying,' he said, 'on Tuesday seven nights we had a shrewd frost that nipped the buds.'

'It is as well for you, old dotard,' cried his wife, listening a moment, 'I had thought ye were at your auld tricks again.'

So we went in, and were busily partaking of the cheer of Mistress Tode when we became aware of the noise of altercation without.

'Save us,' said the cook, 'it is a mercy that neither my lord nor my lady are within gate, wi' a' that narration of noise outbye! What can it be at a'?'

And she went out to inquire.

But if the disturbance was loud before, it certainly became ten times worse when Mistress Tode disappeared. I got up to look, and the Dominie followed me. We saw a tall, grey-haired woman stand upon the causeway of the courtyard, with one hand on her hip, and with the other tossing back the straying witch locks from her brow.

'Where's my boy, Mistress Tode?' cried the newcomer fiercely, to our friend the cook, who stood upon the steps. 'What hae ye dune wi' my laddie at the black house of Cassillis? He left his hame to come here, by command o' my lord and young Launce of Culzean, at five this morning. An' Jock Edgar met him set on a pony between twa men on horseback, and he declares that the puir lad was greeting sair. What hae ye dune wi' him, ye misleared, ill-favoured Tode woman that ye are?"

'Weel ken ye, Meg Dalrymple,' cried Mistress Thomas Tode, 'that I wadna steal ony chance-gotten loon of yours. Faith na, I wadna fyle my parritch-spurtle on his back. We shelter nae lazy gaberlunzie speldrons in the house of Cassillis. There is enough rack and ruin about the country-side as it is, withoot gatherin' in every gipsy brat and prowling night-hawk to its walls. Gin ye come here to insult my master, a belted Earl, I'll e'en set the dowgs on ye, ye gruesome ill-tongued limmer woman!"

I saw that this was to be altogether another kind of tulzie from those clattering bickers of the sword-blades, that I knew something about. So I signed to the Dominie to be silent, for here of a surety were two foemen worthy of each other's points.

'Ye shall cast no stour in my e'en, certes,' cried Meg Dalrymple. 'I ken ye, ye auld yeld crummie Tode. Ye hae nae bairns o' your ain, and ye wad kidnap the bonny bairn o' a decent woman.'

'I daresay no, "nae bairns o' my ain," quo' she,' cried Mistress Tode, roused to high anger. 'I micht hae had as mony as a clockin' hen, gin I had gane the gate ye gaed, Meg Dalrymple. I'll hae the law on ye, ye randy, casting up my man's infirmity to me.'

'Your "man," quo' she,' retorted Meg Dalrymple, 'ca' ye that auld bundle o' dish-clouts tied aboot wi' hippens— a *man!* Save us, one micht as soon bed ayont a pair of auld duddy breeks!'

'Ay, my man,' cried Mistress Tode, 'what hae ye to say, ye shameless woman, again Sir Thomas Tode, that has been Earl's chaplain for forty year and my lawfu' wedded man for ten?'

Mistress Tode rang out the titles like a herald now, when her husband was gainsayed and made light of. But we know that on occasions she could treat him cavalierly enough.

'I wad as sune mairry a heather cow for soopin' the rink at the channel stanes,' cried Meg Dalrymple. And this implication bit deeper into the feelings of the lady of Sir Thomas Tode than all the other reproaches, for the brush of tonsure hair was a sore subject of jesting with her, as I well knew.

'I hae telled ye,' Mistress Tode cried, pausing a moment with her hand on her side, as if to keep command of herself, 'I hae telled ye, woman, that we only deal with kenned and authenticate folk in this hoose—no wi' orra loons, that nane kens wha belangs them! And I wad hae ye ken also that I am no to be named a liar by the likes o' you, Meg Dalrymple—me that has been keeper o' the larder keys o' this Earl's castle for fifteen year, me that has had the outgiving o' all plenishing, the power o' down-sitting and on-putting, and never has been checked in a boodle's worth. Gang hame, ye Canaanitish woman, and I doot na ye'll find your brat safe in the town's bridewell. It will learn ye to bide from decent folk's houses, making such a cry about your wastrel runnagates.'

'Keep your ill tongue for that disjaskit, ill-put-thegither rachle o' banes that ye hae for guidman,' cried the widow Dalrymple. 'Weel do I ken that ye hae my bairn hidden awa' somegate amang ye. Sic a trade as has been hauden wi' the puir bit laddie for carryin' a letter to the Laird o' Auchendrayne. An' the like o' you to stand in my road, Tode woman, you that is weel kenned in sax parishes for an ill-tongued gipsy. I'll hae ye proclaimed at the market cross, a lord's cook though ye be, gin ye dinna gie me hame my bairn wi' me!'

'Na,' said Mistress Tode, more quietly, 'an' you'll no. Ye'll e'en ask my pardon and gang quietly away to your hame by yoursel'.'

'And wha is gaun to gar me to that?' said Meg Dalrymple.

'Just me and this bonny wee bit mannikie here,' said Mistress Thomas Tode, turning round unexpectedly and catching the Dominie Mure by the arm. She pushed him forward and clapped him in a knowing way on the shoulder. 'Just this decent snod bit mannikie!' she said again.

'Woman,' said the Dominie, very indignantly, 'what have I to do with your quarrels and tongue-thrashings?'

'Just this, honest man,' said Mistress Tode; 'ye keep the Session records o' the parish o' Maybole. And if this ill-tongued woman disna gang hame doucely and quaitly, ye are the man that is going to gie me a sicht and extract o' them, under date fourteenth o' Januar, fifteen hundred and aughty years.'

The stroke told. Meg Dalrymple grew silent. The anger faded out of her face suddenly as the shining on wet sea sand when you lift your foot. The warlike crook of her elbow flattened to a droop. For the Session records of the Kirk of Scotland are the nearest thing to the Books of the Recording Angel, and the opening of them is a little Day of Judgment to half the parish.

But we could not let the poor woman depart in this fashion. I stepped to the door from behind the pillar where I had been listening for the ending of the fray.

'Mistress Dalrymple,' I said, very quietly, 'your lad has never come to Cassillis at all. We came here to meet him. He must have lost his way.'

'Maister Launcelot,' said Meg Dalrymple, in a changed voice, 'ye come o' a guid, kind hoose, and ye tell no lies. I am free to believe you. But my bairn is tint a' the same. What will I do! Oh, what will I do?'

'Go home and bide quiet,' I bade her, gently. 'I shall myself speak to the Earl. And fear not but we will find your lad if he be in the land.'

CHAPTER XXXIII

THE DEVIL IS A GENTLEMAN

BUT William Dalrymple was not to be so easily gotten. High and low he was sought for, but no trace of him was found. A girl had seen him taking the road to Cassillis with the dust rising behind him, as was his wont. For, as I have said, he was the best runner in the school of Maybole, and in the winter forenights he kept himself in fine practice with out-running Rob Nickerson, the town's watchman.

So on a day, since no better might be, Nell Kennedy and I rode out to Auchendrayne. At first we had it trysted to go by ourselves, but Dominie Mure declared that he would come with us—'and wait in the hall, if ye were asked to gang ben',' as he said, meaningly.

'For they might put you and the lassie awa', and never hear mair of it. But even John Mure and his son would think twice before they either sequestered or murdered the Dominie o' Maybole, and the Clerk of the Kirk Session thereof.'

So, though his coming with us wearied Nell and myself somewhat and hindered our discourse on the journey, it all turned out for the best in the end, as things that are bitter in the taking often do.

I was, I will own, monstrously curious to see the tower of Auchendrayne and the surroundings of it; for there were strange rumours in the countryside concerning gangs of wild, savage folk that sometimes camped under the trees, and tales of horrid faces which might at any moment glower at you from the dark bole of a gnarled oak.

But this fair sunshiny day we that rode saw nothing but the leaves rustling and clashing above us, and heard nothing but the sough and murmur of the Doon water beneath us. Auchendrayne is a place hidden among woods—set on a knoll, indeed, but with trees all about it, not conspicuous and far-regarding like the Newark or Culzean.

When first we saw it the grey battlements looked pleasantly enough out of the greenery, basking as peacefully in the sun as though they had risen over the abode of some hermit or saint. We saw nought of the customary stir and bustle of an habited house about the mansion of Auchendrayne. None ran to the office houses. None carried bundle nor drove cattle about the home parks. It was a peace like that of a Sabbath day. 'A black devil's Sabbath!' said the Dominie, grimly. And in truth there was something not altogether canny about thus coming to a dead and silent house, with the sun shining hot and the broad common day all about and above.

Nor even when we dismounted did any servant or retainer come forth to meet or challenge us. We did not see so much as the flutter of a banner or the gleam of a steel cap. Only there about us was the silent courtyard, with the heat of noon trembling athwart it, and the very paving stones clean swept like a table before the feast is set.

I tied our horses to the iron ring of a louping-on stone which stood at the angle of the wall by the gate, thinking as I did so that if only these foot-worn steps could speak, they could tell a tale worth hearkening to of strange venturings and bloody quests.

Also I loosened my sword, and I think I saw the Dominie lay his hand to his hip, ere Nell and I set forward together. We went up the steps of the outside stair, and as we did so we came within hearing of a little continuous murmur of hoarse sound. The doors were all open, and I wot well that we walked softly and with our hearts in our mouths, for the silence and the strangeness of the deadly house of Auchendrayne daunted me more than the clash of swords or the crack of pistols. But I had Nell Kennedy by me, and I would have gone to destruction's pit-mouth for her sake—because, saving my father and mother, she was the only friend I had.

Suddenly, in our advance, we came to the door of a great hall, where, at the upper end, was a table in the midst. The windows were narrow and high, throwing down but a dim light upon the rush-strewn floor. There were many

servants and others sitting in the hall, and at the further
end stood one who read from a book. As soon as our
eyes became accustomed to the cool duskiness after the
white equal glare without, I perceived that the reader
was none other than John Mure himself. About him there
sat all his servants and retainers, both men and women.

It was the crown of my astonishment to hear that the
book from which he read was the Bible, and also that as he
went on he made comments like a minister expounding
his morning chapter, speaking very seasonably and fitly,
and eke with excellent judgment and sense. Or so at least
it seemed to me, for I am not enough of a clerk to be a
judge of expositions, though my father has the two great
leather-bound volumes of Clerk *Erasmus his Paraphrases*,
on the shelf over the mantel. But though he is fond of
these himself, he never rubbed any of his liking into me.

But we were hearkening to the reading of John Mure
in his own hall of Auchendrayne.

'"Fill ye up, then, the measures of your fathers,"'
somewhat in this fashion he read from his place. ' "Ye
serpents, ye generation of vipers, how shall ye escape the
damnation of hell? Wherefore behold I send unto you
prophets and wise men and scribes; and some of them
ye shall kill and crucify, and some of them shall ye scourge
in your synagogues, and persecute them from city to city
—that upon you may come all the righteous blood shed
upon the earth, from the blood of righteous Abel unto
the blood of Zacharias, son of Barachias, whom ye slew
between the temple and the altar. Verily I say unto
you, all these things shall come upon this generation." '

Having read this word, which, knowing what I knew,
I had thought would have made him sink through the
earth with the fear of condemnation, John Mure commented upon it, showing how it applied to such as refused
the right gospel way and walked in devious courses,
careless of God and man. Then he went on with his
reading in the same clear and solemn voice, though he
must perforce have seen us stand in the hall door.

So soon as the reading was over, the great company
of the retainers decently took their departure, walking
out soberly and without hurry. Then came John Mure

down from the dias with the Bible yet in his hand, and welcomed us with a condescension that was quaint and uncanny.

'Ye have gotten us at our devotions, Mistress Helen, and you Master Launcelot, and Dominie Mure—my good cousin. You could not have found us better employed.'

'Do ye believe what ye read?' asked the Dominie, quickly.

'Whatever is a means to an end, that I believe in—even as you believe in your taws and birch twigs. The reading of Scripture threatenings makes quiet bairns, and so does the birch.'

'What think ye of the blood of righteous Abel?' said the Dominie—with, methought, more boldness than discretion. 'Will it cry from the ground, think ye?'

The Laird of Auchendrayne looked at the little Dominie, as one might upon a fractious but entertaining bairn.

'It is a point much disputed. Ye had better ask our Launcelot's friend, Maister Robert Bruce, Minister of Edinburgh, if perchance his head be yet upon his shoulders.'

Which saying showed me that John Mure knew more than I had given him the credit for.

Then he turned to Nell.

'You would wish to see the young Lady Auchendrayne?' he said courteously.

Nell replied coldly enough, 'I should like to see my sister.'

'I think,' said Auchendrayne, with a wiselike and grave sobriety that set well on his reverend person, 'that she is presently in the orchard house.'

'Will you bide here, or will you go with Mistress Helen?' he asked of me.

'We would all go together,' said Nell, 'if it pleasure you.'

So with a courteous wave of the hand, he led us through stone passages and along echoing corridors, till we came to a door in the wall, from which we entered upon a pleasant prospect of gardens and orchards. Here again there was the same curious silence, and, as it seemed, an absence of the twitter and stir of a Scottish garden in the season of summer.

We came presently to a stone building like a tomb, all overshaded with trees.

'This is the orchard house of Auchendrayne,' he said. 'I believe the Lady Marjorie is within.'

The Dominie and I stayed without with John Mure, while Nell went in alone to greet her sister. We heard the faint murmur of voices and now and then a pulsing check as of a slow, smothered sob. We that were without, stood with our backs to the cold, heavy, white stones under the green shade, while John Mure discoursed learnedly and pleasantly of flower-beds and tulips and the best form of dovecot tower for the supply of the table with pigeon pie.

At last Nell came to the door.

'Launcelot, Marjorie wishes you to come in,' she said. Whereupon I entered and found a large room finished in oaken panelling and moulded archings. Roses looked in at the windows, and a stir of pleasant coolness was all about. Marjorie was sitting by a table with many books spread upon it.

My dear lady was pale and white as a lily. She leaned her head wearily on her hand. But there burned a still and unslockened fire in her eye.

'Launcelot,' she said to me, 'this is not so wide a place to walk within as the pleasaunce at Culzean, nor yet can we see from the garden house of Auchendrayne the rough blue edges of Arran or the round Haystack of Ailsa.'

I bade her look forward to happy days yet to come, for, indeed, I knew not what to say to her. She smiled upon me wistfully and indulgently, as one does upon a prattling child.

'I thank you, Launcelot,' she said, 'but I was not born for happiness. Nevertheless, you were ever my good lad. I see you still wear my favour, but doubtless long ere this you have found another lady. Is it not so?'

I told her no, blushing to have to say so in the hearing of Nell—who afterwards might flout me, or, as like as not, cast up again the old matter of Kate Allison.

Then through one of the windows I saw John Mure pacing up and down the path with the Dominie at the other side of the garden, so I knew that it was our time to speak.

'Ye have heard of your father's death?' said I. 'What think ye? How was it wrought and how brought about? Can you help us to unravel it?'

'Nay,' said Marjorie, 'not at present. But in good time I shall yet clear the matter to the roots, and that before I die.'

'Wherefore will you not come back to us at Culzean? We need you sorely,' pleaded Nell, who stood holding her sister's hand.

'Nay,' said Marjorie, 'my work is not yet done at Auchendrayne.'

It was the self-same answer she had given when she rode away from the gate of Maybole on the day of the death of Gilbert Kennedy of Bargany.

'Are they cruel to you here, Marjorie, tell me that?' I said, for I saw that the old Laird was approaching, and that our further time would be but short.

'No one of them hath laid so much as a finger upon me!' said Marjorie. And this at least was some comfort to carry back to the sad house of Culzean with us.

So with that, little satisfied concerning the thing which we came to seek, but with somewhat more ease in our hearts for Marjorie's sake, we went back through the passages and into the great hall. While we waited there for a servant to show us forth to our horses, my eye rested upon a large, closely-written volume, with the quill pen laid upon it, and ink-horn set in a hole in the desk above it.

'I see that my clerkly work has caught your eye,' said John Mure. 'It is a nothing that I amuse myself withal, yet it may live longer than you or I. It is but a slight history of the mighty sept whose name you, Master Launcelot, so worthily bear, with all their branches and noble deeds at arms. For me, I am but a useless old man, past the labour of fighting. Yea, I know it was your own lance that put me there. But I bear no malice, it was the fortune of war. You know me better than to suppose that John Mure bears a grudge for that shrewd thrust you dealt me on the day of the quenching of our hopes in blood by the gate of Maybole.'

I bowed and thanked him for his courteous words.

'It was indeed the gallantest charge that ever was made,' said I, 'since that of Norman Leslie, when, on the day before Renti, he drave into the midst of sixty Spaniards with but seven Scottish lances at his tail.'

'Ah, Master Kennedy,' replied the Laird of Auchendrayne, smiling, 'I knew not that you also were a historian.'

'Sir,' said I, 'I am no historian, but a soldier. Yet it is a part of the training of a good fighter, that he should know the great deeds which have been done in the wars before him by brave men, so that he may emulate them when he himself is launched upon the points.'

'It is well said, sir squire,' said Auchendrayne, bowing to me.

So, with a courteous farewell, in which there was to be seen no grain of hate nor as much as a glint of the teeth of the wolf, he bade us go our ways. 'And, above all things,' he cried after us, 'mind your prayers. 'Tis a good lesson for the young to remember.'

CHAPTER XXXIV

IN THE ENEMY'S COUNTRY

Now, through being over-careful with my chronicle, I have spent too much time on our conferences. But we were, indeed, at the parting of the ways, and needed all advice. On our way to Culzean we met one who told us that the Earl had gone home that day to Cassillis. Nell besought me to ride thither, for she had a request to make to the head of her house ere she went her ways back to Culzean.

So to Cassillis we rode, and at the gate encountered Robert Harburgh, dressed, as usual, in his dark, close-fitting doublet, and with his long, plain sword by his side. With him I abode while Helen went within to pay her duty and service to the Countess—who, as Nell told me afterwards, never stopped praising the ancient days when she was the Chancellor's wife, and had one of the ladies of the Court to attire her.

'Now,' she said bitterly, 'John grudges it if I take a milkmaid half-an-hour from the butter-kirning to help to arrange my hair.'

Presently the Earl came out. He showed himself well pleased and kind, as, indeed, he ever was with me—perhaps because I never asked aught of him in all my life.

'Helen, our cousin,' said he, 'desires that she may go and bide among the heather with your good mother at Kirrieoch. What think ye of that?'

I told him that I had not heard of it—that she had spoken no word to me.

'See to the matter,' he said with significance. 'I have been

advised concerning Sir Thomas and his last words. And if
you prove worthy, I know no reason why ye should not have
the lass. But first ye must find the treasure of Kelwood or
bring down her father's murderers—one of the two. And
then, when that is done, I pledge you my knightly word
that ye shall have both the lass and a suitable providing.
Besides which, if I am in favour with the King, ye may
even get a clap on the shoulder from the flat of a royal
sword. But that,' said he, 'I can nocht promise ye, for with
King Jamie no man's favour is siccar.'

I told him that I kenned not rightly if the lass would
have me; that I never spoke a single word of love to her
but what she lightlied me.

'In good time,' said the Earl, smiling and nodding. 'The
lass that wants in time of stress to gang and bide with the
minnie, will draw not unkindly to the son in times of ease.'

Then came Nell with a knitted shawl from the Countess to
wear among the hills, for Earl John and she were kind folk
enough in all that touched not the getting or spending of gear.

I asked my lord also for the company of Robert Harburgh
to help me in the escorting of Nell fitly to the little tower
of Kirrieoch on the side of the Minnoch water.

'Ay, ay; let him gang,' said the Earl. 'The honey-
moon is by, and his wife will be the fonder of him for lying
her lane till he comes hame to her again.'

So Robert Harburgh and his long sword went southward from Cassillis along with us, riding mostly with the
Dominie, while I rode behind with Nell.

I told her all our plans as we went. How we must seek
the treasure; and how we must, above all things, find the
boy Dalrymple.

'I will go with you upon your quest,' the staunch little
Dominie had said to me, when he heard of our adventure.
And so it fell out that we four rode steadily to the south,
till we came in the evening to my own hill-land, where the
whaups cry, where the burns go chuckling to themselves
and clattering over the pebbles, and where all the folk's
hearts are kindly and warm. My mother took my lass in
her arms when we told her our purpose and Nell's request.

'And I will help you with the kye?' said Nell, blithely,
to her.

'Ay,' answered my mother. 'Ye will help with the drinking of the milk, and that will e'en bring some roses back into your cheeks, my puir bit shilpit lassie.'

And though there passed not a look by the common between us when we parted, I think my mother shrewdly jaloosed what were my hopes.

Thus we left them standing by the loan dyke, the two old folk and Nell with her yellow hair a-blowing in the midst. And I, that knew not whether I might ever see them again, waved a hand, and resolved to return with a name and a barony at the least; or, if my lot were perverse, to leave my bones in some stricken field.

It is hard for a man to part from a lass—and in especial from one to whom he dares not make love as he has done to others, all because those others have told upon him, till he fears the ridicule of his real love more than rapier thrusts. Right bitterly did I regret that I had done my by-courtings so near home; because, on my very life I dared not venture a sweet word to Nell Kennedy for fear of her saying, 'That is even what you said to Kate Allison, the Grieve's lass.' Or as it might, 'Keep to your customs. It is not your usual time yet by a quarter-of-an-hour to put your arm about our waists.'

Now this is monstrously unfair to any man, who, after all, is compelled to conduct his affairs with some sort of rule and plan of attack. I was a fool—well do I know it. I ought to have gone further afield than the Grieve's house. I am sure there are plenty of lasses in Carrick fairer to look upon than Kate Allison, though I am free to admit that I thought not so at the time.

So as we went back it was arranged that Robert Harburgh should ride to the woodland country about Auchendrayne, and there, from his headquarters at Cassillis, keep his eye upon the doings of the Mures, because his person was unknown to them of Auchendrayne's household.

The Dominie and I undertook the more uncertain work, but we had made our plans and were not to be put off. The neighbourhood of the Benane was well known to all that trafficked about the town of Girvan. It was a dangerous and an ill-famed place, and many innocent people had very mysteriously lost their lives there, or at least disappeared to return no more. In order, therefore, that we might be more free to pursue our wanderings, we left our horses behind us. Indeed, Dom Nicholas was even now cropping the sweet grasses on the side of the Minnoch water, with my father to show him where they grew thickest and my mother to give him oats between times, till the brave beast was in some danger of being overfed.

As we neared Girvan, we came into a country of the bitterest partizans of the Bargany folk. Here dwelt James Bannatyne of Chapeldonnan, one of the great intimates of John Mure, and much beholden to him. Here also was Girvan Mains, over the possession of which much of the black blood had arisen. So, for our safety, we gave ourselves out to be plain merchants travelling to Stranrawer in order to get a passage over to Ireland.

When we came to the farmhouses where we were to stay for the night, we always asked of the good man, in the hearing of his wife, concerning the state of the country. Was it peaceful? Were the bloody feuds staunched, and could honest men now live in peace? We heard, as was natural, a great deal of abuse of the Earl and of our faction, as the greediest and worst-intentioned rascals in the world. That from the goodman; but when the wife got her tongue started, she would tell us much that was no credit to Drummurchie and others on the side of the murderers. Soon we were fully certified that we were already in the country where Drummurchie and Cloncaird and the rest of their party were being secretly sustained by their friends. Yet we could not come at them, which perhaps was as well, seeing that my person was well known to them.

I found the little Dominie a right brave companion. When we sojourned at houses, he had a way with the bairns that kept them on the trot to do his will, and pleasured to do it—a manner also of cross-questioning the parents about their children which showed them his interest and his knowledge. Then he would most wisely and soberly advise them to see and give this lad Alec a good education, to make that one a merchant because of his cleverness with figures, and this a dominie or a clerk, because he did not give promise of being fit for anything else. It was as good as a play to hear him, and made us much thought of wherever we went.

Yet he was ready with his fighting tools also. Once when we went by Kildonan and a pack of dirty vagabonds bade us stand, what was my surprise to find that Dominie Mure having laid down his pipes and out with his blade, was already driving among them before I had got so much as my hand on the sword blade. And I am no laggard, either, with the iron, as all may know by this time. But with his great bristling fierce head and his rapier that thrust up unexpectedly from below (yet which with the length of his arm reached as far as a tall man's), the Dominie gave the rascals a fright and a wound or two also, which started them at the run. Even then he followed, thrusting at them behind till they shouted amain, and took across the fields to escape the pricking of his merciless weapon. And ever as they ran he cried, '"Halt and deliver!" did ye say? I will give you a bellyful of "Halt and deliver!"'

CHAPTER XXXV

THE OGRE'S CASTLE

So being wearied with the chase we went to the nearest farm, which, as it happened, was that of Chapeldonnan. It stood quite close by the roadside. A tall, large-boned woman came to the gate with a pail of pigs' meat in her hand.

'What seek ye?' she said. 'We want nae travelling folk about Chapeldonnan.'

We told her that we were merchants going to Ireland, and that we had been attacked by a set of rascals upon the way, whom we had made flee.

'They are no that ill in this pairt o' the country. They wad only hae killed ye,' she said, as if that would have been a satisfaction to us. 'It is doon aboot the Benane that the real ill folk bide.'

I told her that killing was enough for me, and that I was puzzled to know what worse she could mean.

So with some seeming reluctance she bade us come in. The wide quadrangle of the farm buildings was defended like a fortress. The gate was spiked and barred with iron from post to post, as though it had been the gate of a fighting baron instead of the yett of a tenant, devised only to keep in the kye.

We asked civilly for the master of the house, and somewhat hastily the woman answered us,—

'The guidman's no at hame. He has been away ower by at the Craig trying to win the harvest of the solan geese and sea-parrots.'

'Your husband is tenant of the rock?' I said, for it is always worth while finding out what a man like James Bannatyne may be doing, or at least how much he thinks it advisable to tell.

'Ow ay,' she said, 'and a bonny holding it is. Gin it werena for the Ailsa cocks, the conies, and the doos, it wad be a mill-stone aboot our necks, for we have to pay sweetly for the rent o' it to my Lady of Bargany.'

'But,' said I, 'it belongs to the Earl, does it not?'

The mistress of Chapeldonnan looked pityingly at us.

'Ye are twa well-put-on men to be so ignorant. Ye maun hae been lang awa' frae this pairt o' the country no to ken that the neighbourhood is very unhealthy for the friends o' the Earl o' Cassillis to come here. Faith, the last that cam' speerin' for rent and mails in this quarter gat six inch o' cauld steel in the wame o' him!'

'And what,' said the Dominie, 'became o' him after that? Did he manage to recover?'

'Na, na. He was buried in Colmonel kirkyaird. The good man of Boghead gied him a resting-grave and a headstone. It was thought to be very kind o' him. It was Boghead himsel' that stickit him.'

'Ye see what it is to be a Christian, good wife!' said the Dominie.

'Ow ay, lad,' said the woman, placidly. 'That was generally remarked on at the time. Ye see, Boghead was aye a forgiein' man a' his days. But for a' that, it was the general opinion o' the pairish that the thing might be carried ower far, when it cam' to setting up my Lord of Cassillis's folks wi' graves and headstones!'

She continued, after a pause,—

'I hae been deevin' at our guidman to gie up the Craig, for it keeps him a deal from hame, and I aye tell him that he carries awa' mair than he brings back o' drink and victual. But he says that the rock is a maist extraordinary hungrysome place!'

'It has that name,' said I, unwarily.

She stopped and looked at me with sudden suspicion. 'What ken ye aboot the Ailsa?' she asked, looking directly at me.

'Nocht ava,' I replied, 'but a' seaside places hae the name o' making you ready for your meal of meat.'

'Hoot, no,' said Mistress Bannatyne. 'Now, there's mysel'. I canna do mair than tak' a pickin' o' meat, like a sparrow on the lip o' the swinepot. Yet Chapeldonnan is but a step frae the sea.'

She was at that moment lifting a heavy iron pot off the cleps, or iron hooks by which it hung over the fireplace in the midst of the kitchen floor.

'I hae aye been delicate a' my days, and it is an awesome thing for a woman like me to be tied to a big eater like James, that never kens when he has his fill—like a corbie howkin' at a braxy sheep till there was naething left but the horns and the tail.'

I thought we might get some information about the Benane, which might prove of some use to us when we adventured thither.

'Good wife,' said I, 'we are thinking of going by Ballantrae to the town of Stranrawer. The direct way, I hear, is by the Benane. What think ye—is the road a good one?'

'Ye are a sonsy lad,' she said, 'ye wad mak' braw pickin' for the teeth o' Sawny Bean's bairns. They wad roast your ribs fresh and fresh till they were done. Syne they would pickle your quarters for the winter. The like o' you wad be as guid as a Christmas mart to them.'

'Hoot, good wife,' said I, 'ye ken that a' this talk aboot Sawny Bean's folk is juist blethers—made to fright bairns frae gallivanting at night.'

'Ye'll maybe get news o' that gin Sawny puts his knife intil your throat. Ye hae heard o' my man. James Bannatyne is not a man easily feared, but not for the Earldom o' Cassillis wad he gang that shore road to Ballantrae his lane.'

And, indeed, there were in the countryside enough tales of wayfarers who had disappeared there, of pools of blood frozen in the morning, of traveller's footsteps that went so far and then were lost in a smother of tracks made by naked feet running every way. But I kept on with my questions. I wanted to hear the bruit of the country, and what were our chances.

While we were thus cheerfully talking, and the Dominie by whiles playing a spring upon his pipes to gain the lady's goodwill, there came in a man of a black and gruesome countenance. We knew him at once for the master of Chapeldonnan, James Bannatyne, for he came in as only a goodman comes into his own house. He was a man renowned for his great strength all over Carrick. He turned on us a lowering regard as he went clumsily by into an inner room, carrying an armful of nets. I noted that the twine had not been wet, so that his sea fishing had not come to much. But behind the door he flung down a back-load of birds—mostly solan geese and the fowl called 'the Foolish Cock of the Rock,' together with half-a-dozen 'Tammy Nories.' So I guessed that he had either been over the water to Ailsa, or desired to have it thought so.

His wife went ben the room to him. We could hear the sulky giant's growling questions as to who we were, and his wife's brisk replies. Presently she came out looking a little dashed.

'James has come in raither tired,' she said, 'and he will need to lie down and hae a sleep.'

'In that case, mistress,' I said, 'we will e'en thank you for your kindly hospitality and take our ways.'

She followed us to the door, and I think she was wonderfully glad to get us safe away without bloodshed.

'Be sure that ye gang na south by the Benane,' she said, 'the folk that bide there are no canny.'

So we thanked her again and took our way, breathing more freely also to have left the giant behind.

We had not gone far, however, when we spied her husband hastening after us across a field. He came up with us by a turn in the road.

'We harbour no spies at Chapeldonnan,' he said, bending sullenest brows at us, 'and that I would have you know.'

'We are no spies on you nor on any well-doing man,' I said. 'We are honest merchants on our way to Stranrawer, and but called in to ask the way.'

'Ye speered ower mony questions of my wife to be honest men,' he said threateningly.

'And why,' said the Dominie, birsing up as one that
is ready to quarrel, 'in this realm of Scotland may not a
man without offence ask his way, from the honest wife
of an honest man, so long as he soliciteth no favour more
intimate?'

At this the giant made a blow at the little Dominie.
He had a large cudgel in his hand, and he struck without
warning, like the ill-conditioned ruffian that he was. But
he fell in with the wrong man when he tried to take
Dominie Mure unawares, for the little man was as gleg
as a hawk, having been accustomed to watch the eyes
of boys all his life, ay, and often those of lads bigger
than himself. So that, long before the hulking stroke of
the fellow came near him, the Dominie had sprung to
the side, and was ready, with his whinger in his hand, to
spit Bannatyne upon the point. For myself I did not
even think it worth my while even to draw—for I had
only brought my plain sword, fearing that in some of the
company which on our wanderings we might have to keep,
the Earl's Damascus blade might overmuch excite cupidity.

But instead I ordered the fellow away as one that has
authority. It was not for Launcelot Kennedy to mix
himself with a common brawling dog like Chapeldonnan.

'It wants but the tickling of a straw,' cried the little man,
'that I should spit you through, like a paddock to bait a
line for geds. And but for your wife's sake, who is a civil-
spoken woman by ill-fortune tied to a ruffian, I should do it.'

Then seeing that together we were overstrong for him,
James Bannatyne took himself away, growling curses and
threatenings as to what should happen to us before we got
clear of Carrick. However, we took little heed to the empty
boaster, but went our ways down into the town of Girvan.

Here it came to my mind to hire a boat and provision
her as it were to go to the island of Arran. And nothing
would set me till I had it done. So on the south beach
we found a man cleaning just such a boat as we needed,
with a half-deck on her and a little mast which would go
either up or down. For three merks in silver we got the
use of the boat for a month, and with her both suitable
oars and sails. He was going to the haying in the parish
of Colmonel, the owner said, but lest we should lose her,

we must deposit with the minister or the provost of the town other thirty merks as the value of the boat, which money should again be ours when we returned to claim it. So to the provost we went, whom we found a hearty, red-faced man, a dealer in provisions and all manner of victual. Of these we took a sufficient cargo on board, and having paid down our thirty merks, early one morning we laid our course for the Isle of Arran.

But when we had gone screeving well across with a following wind, we lay to under Pladda till it was dusk, and then with a breeze shifted to our quarter we bore down on Ailsa. I knew not very well what we should find there, but I judged that we would at least come on some traces of the murderous crew, which might help us to clear up some of their secrets. For I judged that James Bannatyne did not spend his nights out of bed in order to wile a few solan geese off the rocks of Ailsa.

CHAPTER XXXVI

THE DEFENCE OF CASTLE AILSA

Now the Isle of Ailsa is little more than a great lumping crag set askew in the sea. Nevertheless, it has both landing place and pasturage, house of refuge and place of defence. The island was not new to me, for I had once upon a time gone thither out of curiosity after the matter of Barclay, Laird of Ladyland—who, in his madness, thought to make it a place of arms for the Papists in the year of the Spanish Armada, but was prevented and slain at the instance of Andrew Knox, one of the good reforming name, minister of Paisley. This last was a wonderfully clever man and accounted a moving preacher; but on this occasion he showed himself a better fighter—which upon Craig Ailsa, at least, is more to the purpose.

It was the dusk of the morning when we ran into the spit of shingle which is upon the eastern side and, watching our chance, we drew the boat ashore. The sea was chill and calm, only a little ruffled by the night wind, and the sun was already brightening the sky to the east, so that the Byne Hill and Brown Carrick stood black against it.

With great stealth and quiet we climbed up the narrow path, seeing nothing, however, save a pasturing goat that sprang away as we came near. It was eerie enough work, for the seabirds clanged around us, yammering and chunnering querulously among themselves on the main cliffs at the farther side of the isle. It grew a little lighter when we came out upon the narrow path which leads to the castle.

Suddenly the dark door of the tower loomed before us, very black and grim. I declare it was like marching up to the cannon's mouth to walk up that little flight of stairs which led to the door in the wall. Nevertheless, I clambered first, with a curious pricking down my back and a slackness about the knees. So all unscathed we entered. There was only emptiness in all the chambers. The castle had been almost wholly ruined and spoiled, for since its taking by the Protestant party, it had not been touched nor put in defence. 'Now I will bring up the provender. Keep you the castle,' said I to the little Dominie, as soon as we were certified that we were first in possession.

So I went down and made first one backload and then another of those things which we had bought at Girvan and placed in the boat. I brought up also all the ammunition for the hackbutt and the pistols. Before I had finished the sky grew grey and clear, the day breaking nobly with only a rack of cloud racing up the far side of Kilbrannan Sound to hang upon the chill shark's teeth of the mountains of Arran. Upon my return I was glad to find the castle intact, and the little man seated calmly with a book in his hand.

'Did you never so much as shut the outer door?' I asked him.

'And shut you without,' said he. 'Is it likely? Ye might have had to come along that footpad with only your limber legs to keep your tail, and Tam o' Drummurchie or Sawny Bean jumping ahint ye!'

So before we went to examine the nooks and crannies of the Craig either for enemies or treasure boxes, we resolved to put the castle into as good a state of defence as we could.

First we drew in the rough wooden steps which led to the door in the wall by which we had entered, so that only the little projections whereon the wood had rested were left to afford foothold to any besieger. Then we closed and barricaded the door, for the huge iron bolt was yet in its place and ran securely into the stone of the wall itself for quite two feet.

When the day broke fully, I went up to the turret top to look about me.

'Save us!' I cried down to the little man. 'Come hither, Dominie. Is not that our boat out there with men in her?'

The Dominie ran up and looked long and earnestly.

'Ay, deed is it that,' he made answer. 'We are trapped, Launcelot, for all our cleverness. And if these chiels be our enemies, I doubt that we are as good as dead men in the jaws of the Wolf of Drummurchie.'

The men in the boat kept leaning back and looking up at the cliffs as if to get sight of something. Sometimes they went completely out of view, as it had been close into the bulk of the isle, mayhap to examine more carefully some cave or lurking-place.

'We had better look well to our priming, and set a watch,' said I. 'We shall have visitors this day at Castle Ailsa, or my name is not Launcelot Kennedy.'

But the hours passed slowly on from nine till noon before we heard a sound, or saw a living creature beside the geese and the gulls. After the boat had gone westward out of sight, we waxed weary at our posts on the top of the turret. I went down to look at the cupboards of the chambers. There I was rooting and exploring, when I heard the Dominie whispering loudly to me to run up hastily into the tower.

He told me how that a stone had come pelting against the wall, on the side towards the hill. Now the castle sits on the verge of the precipice, and only a narrow path leads to it along the cliff. But behind there is a little courtyard to landward, now mostly ruined and broken down. It was from this side, so Dominie Mure whispered to me, that the stone had come.

'Tut, man,' said I, 'you are losing your nerve with this playing of hide-and-seek. It was but a billy-goat's foot that spurned it, and so naturally it came bumming down the hill side.'

'Then,' he replied grimly, 'it was a billy-goat as big as an elephant, and it will ding over this castle into the sea, for no ordinary goat could have stirred the stone I saw; I tell you it popped over the heuch like a cannon-ball.'

But we were soon to have other company besides that of the stone.

For presently there came in sight a man walking daintily and carefully along the path which led to the door of the tower. Now he would pull wantonly at a flower, and anon he would skip a stone over the cliff—for all the world as if it were a Sabbath afternoon, and he was waiting for his lass. But I knew better, for I heard his harness clattering under his loose coat of blue.

'Where gang ye so blythe, my bonny man?' cried the Dominie suddenly from my elbow. The man started back, and set his hand beneath his cloak, but the Dominie cried,—

'Keep awa' your hand frae your hip, young man—ye may need it to preserve your balance on the footpath—and give me your attention for a wee.'

The man did as he was bid, and cast his eye aloft, where the black mouth of a hackbutt looked discouragingly down upon him.

"Your name, friend?' said the Dominie.

'I am James Carrick from the parish of Barr,' said the man at last.

'Aye, aye, slee Jamie—Drummurchie's man,' said the Dominie, with meaning. 'When the man is pooin' gowans and skytin' slate stanes, the maister is no that far awa'. Noo, James, e'en turn you aboot and gang your ways, and tell your maister that his black murder is found out, and that there are those on their way to this isle that will put the irons on his heels.'

So the man who had called himself James Carrick turned obediently about, and marched away the road he had come. Probably he had been sent for nothing more than to know if we had stolen a march upon them, and taken possession of the strength of the castle. They had our boat—there was no question of that. We were, therefore, set here with only two backloads of powder and provisions to stand a siege in a small and ruinous tower upon a barren cliff.

Nor was it long before we had news of the enemy, for as we strolled up and down the battlement walk, which as is common in such little fortalices, went round three sides of the tower—that is, round every side except that which looks inward to the cliff-edge—a number of scattering shots came from all about, but chiefly from above.

We could hear them whistling over us as we ducked our heads. We got ready our guns to fire in return so soon as a man showed; but the many bowders and rocky humps about gave the enemy great shelter, so that it was no easy thing to take aim at them. However, I did get a steady shot at an incautious leg, and on the back of the crack of the hackbutt came a great torrent of swearing, and this I took for a good sign.

All we could do was to keep the little courtyard clear, and to shoot whenever we saw a bonnet rise up or a limb carelessly exposed. But we both yearned for something more lively to put an end to our suspense.

Nor had we long to wait.

From the east side of the tower which looks to the sea, there came the sound of a loud report, a tumble of stones, and then a loud, continual, and most pitiful crying, as of a man hurt unto death. I ran up into the battlements above and set my head through a loophole. Beneath me lay a fine-looking young man, with his red bonnet fallen aside, clad in a short white coat, with doublet and hose also of red. He was unarmed so far as I could see.

'Who are you, and what brought you there?' I cried to him from the turret loop.

A massy corner-stone fallen from the castle lay on his chest, and a pile of other rocks and stones was heaped about his legs. He turned his eyes upward at me and tried twice to speak.

At last he said, with many pants and piteous groans, 'I am Allan Crosby, from Auchneil. I brought you a letter from my Lord Cassillis. I landed below and came up by the path, but when I got near I heard firing and saw the door shut. So I tried to clamber up the castle wall to cry in at the window to you, because you were my friends. And even as I climbed, the stones of the castle fell upon me, and now they are crushing the life out of me.'

'Where is the letter from my Lord?' said I.

The man cast his eyes about him as if to look for it.

'I had it in my hand just now,' he said.

I saw a scrap of parchment a little way from him, and asked if that were the letter.

'Tie it to a cord for me,' said I, 'that I may see it.'

But, by reason of his wounds, he was not able to reach it, and the stones pressed so bitterly on his breast that he could do nothing but lie and groan most waesomely.

'Oh, help me, or else end my misery—for the love of God,' he cried earnestly, 'for I am at the point of death in this agony.'

I went all round the top of the tower and looked about every way. Our enemies had retired further up the cliff, and were contenting themselves with firing an occasional shot, which fell harmless against the walls, buzzed among the battlements, or else sang past us into the sea.

I called the Dominie.

'Come to the door,' said I. 'I cannot bide still and see that poor man suffer. He says that he has come with a letter from my Lord Cassillis. It may be so. I will at least go and see. Drummurchie's thieves have gone up the face of the rock, and the wounded man cannot hurt me much, even if he were willing.'

Then the Dominie pled with me to bide where I was 'because,' said he, 'you know not whether it be not an ambush.'

'I cannot let a fellow-creature be crushed to pieces before my eyes and abide to hear his death-cries,' I answered. 'Come down and hold you the door open.'

So with that I undid the bolts and put the Dominie behind it. I set my feet upon the jutting stones on which the wooden stair usually rested, and so scrambled perilously down, holding on to the wall with my right hand the while. When I came to him the lad was lying gasping on his back with the stones edgewise on his breast. I asked him how he did. He seemed past speech, but was able to motion me round to the further side. There I stooped gently in order to raise the great block that lay upon his bosom.

I stepped carefully about and turned my body to render him my aid as tenderly as I could. But I got a sudden and terrible surprise, and though I am not one much given to fear, I own that it shook my heart. Even as I stooped over him, the fellow flung off the stones as if they had been featherweights, leaped upon his own feet with a bended pistol in his hand, and stood in front of me, striding across the path which led back again to the castle door.

At the same moment I heard a loud shout of warning from the Dominie, that the enemy were again coming down the brae. I had no time to draw my dagger, and for greater lightness I had left my sword behind. I saw the rascal make him ready to fire at me, aiming at my heart. So I remembered a French trick of high kicking which Robert Harburgh had once taught me, for he had been in France at the schools with his master the Earl, and had learned much there besides philosophy.

So I gave the fellow my foot, shod with toe-plates, full upon his wrist, which knocked the pistol up against his chin with a stunning crash. In the next moment I leaped at his throat and overbore him, spurning him with my heel as I passed. I can remember leaping upon him with all my weight from the top of one of the very stones the traitor had pulled down upon himself.

Then I ran fleet-foot for the entrance of the castle. Others of the enemy were just coming about the corner when I reached the projecting points of stone. With my heart in my mouth I sprang up the little juts of rock. I was almost within and in safety, but I had not counted upon the swiftness and resource of my gentleman of the fallen stone. He was hard upon my heels in spite of the thundering clout he had gotten on the jaw from the pistol. But luckily my brave little friend the Dominie stood ready behind the door, and as soon as my hindmost foot was over the threshold, he set his strength to the iron handle and sent the massy oak home to its fastenings with such force that it struck the pursuer fair on the face with a stunning crash. As a stone is driven from a sling, so he fell whirling over the stair head, and, unable to stop himself, he went, gripping vainly at the rock-weeds, headlong over the cliff.

This, however, being behind the door and fully employed in securing it, we did not know at the time. But when we hurried again to the top of the tower, we saw the enemy swarming down the cliff side to render him some assistance, or it might be to recover his body.

'Ask him, when you get him, if he has another letter from my lord the Earl,' cried the Dominie after them.

'And serve him right well, the treacherous hound,' muttered the little man to himself, ' if you find him in pound pieces!'

But I said nothing, for I thought the fellow would mind the kick that I gave him.

That night Thomas of Drummurchie and all his folk removed from the cave where till now they had dwelt. They went over in our boat and in that of James Bannatyne of Chapeldonnan to the mainland, being frightened (as I guess) by our declaration that there were those coming who would deliver them to justice. And also being dismayed, as I make no doubt, by our staunch and desperate defence.

Thus we were left alone on the muckle weary rock which men call Ailsa, and which thousands of free men and women look at every day without a thought of the poor prisoned folk upon it.

CHAPTER XXXVII

THE VOICE OUT OF THE NIGHT

Now, so long as provisions last, Ailsa is none such a bad sanctuary, and we might have passed the time there very well, had we possessed minds sufficiently at ease for enjoying such a hermitage. The spring was but a few yards above the castle, and it ran crystal clear into a little basin which I cut in the rock. We had enough victual to serve us for a month with the provision we had bought in Girvan, and with what I shot of the puffins or Tammy Nories, which ran in and out of their holes all day like conies in a warren.

Sometimes we would climb to the top of the crag and look long at the sea, which from there seemed like a great sheet hung upon Cantyre and Arran on the one side and upon the hills of Galloway and Carrick on the other—with Ailsa itself, on which we were sitting, in the deepest trough of it.

A few boats crept timidly about the shore, and a little ship sometimes passed by. But otherwise we had for companions only the silly guillemots that couped their tails uppermost and dived under, the fishing-gulls that dropped splash into the water, and the solan or solemne geese which, when they fell, made a bigger plunge than any, even as on the cliffs of the island their keckling and crying are the loudest.

One day the Dominie and I were sitting on the roof of all things (as the summit of Ailsa seemed to be), picking at the grasses and knuckling little stones for the idlesse which comes with summer weather, when it came in my head to rally Robert Mure, because he had a cold hearthstone and half empty bed.

'You, a burgess and a learned man, with an official rent and a yearly charge on the burgh, yet cannot get so much as a cotter's sonsy bit lass to keep you company, and to sit, canty like Jenny or Jock, on the far side of the chimbley lug. Think shame of yourself, Dominie. Any questing lout that can persuade a tow-headed Mall of the byre to set up house with him, deserves better of his country than you. Were all of your mind, Maybole school might have none to attend it but dotards and grandmothers! And where were your craft then, Socrates?' I asked him, for just before he had been speaking to me of a certain wise man, a Greek of that name.

And at first he made a jest of the matter, as indeed I meant it.

'Never fear,' he said, 'there will always be enough fools in Ayrshire to get more. Maybole shall have its share of these.'

And indeed that hath been the repute of our town and countryside ever since Ayr water first ran over its pebbles!

Yet when I pressed the Dominie further upon the matter, he waxed thoughtful. His face, which was not naturally merry, took on a still sterner expression. Presently he put his hand within his blouse and pulled out a little string of beads, such as Catholics wear to mind them of their prayers. It was suspended about his neck. This, I own, was a great marvel to me, for the Dominie was a strong Reformer, and showed little mercy in arguing with men still inclined to the ancient opinion.

He gave the brown rosary into my hand, and I turned it curiously about. It was made of the stones of some foreign fruit, most quaintly and fantastically carven and joined together with little links of gold. Between two of the beads there was a longer portion of the chain, and upon it two rings of gold were strung.

'Once,' said the Dominie, 'there was a maid who had promised to share my hearth. One ring of these two was mine, to wear upon my finger, and one was hers. Upon the night before her marriage day we met at our place of tryst. I tried the ring upon her finger and wished her to wear it that night. 'To-morrow will serve—it is not so far away!' she said, and slipped from my arms. Under a new-risen moon she went homeward, singing by the heads Benane. And that was the last that these eyes ever beheld of bonny Mary Torrance—save only this necklace of beads which she wore, and the stain of her blood upon the short grass of the seashore!'

The Dominie looked long to seaward at the flashing birds that circled and clanged about our rocky isle, each tribe of them following its own orbit and keeping to its own airy sphere.

'And what happened to her?' I began, but got no further.

'Murder, most foul,' he cried, rising to his feet in his agitation, 'horrible, unheard of in any kingdom! For all about the spot where these things were found, was the trampling of naked feet. And some of these were small and some were great. But all were naked, and the print of every foot was plain upon the sand of the shore. Each footprint had the toes of the bare feet wide and distinct. Every toe was a pointed claw, as though the steads were those of birds. And the fearsome beast-prints went down to the sea edge, and the blood marks followed them. And that was all.' Then the Dominie fell silent, and I also, for though Ayrshire was full of blood feuds and the quest of human life, this was a new kind of murder to me— though by all accounts it seemed not rare in the neighbourhood of Benane, for I minded the warning words of the Mistress of Chapeldonnan.

'And she had no enemies, this Mary Torrance?' I asked.

'She was but young, and of birth too lowly for feuds and fightings. Besides, who in Carrick would harm a maid going homeward from her love-tryst?'

The Dominie rose and walked away to the other side of the Rock of Ailsa, where for long he sat by himself and fingered the necklace of beads. His face was fixed, as if he were making of the rosary a very catena of hate, a receptacle of dark imaginings and vengeful vows. Scarcely could I recognise my quaint and friendly Dominie.

It was that night, as the blackness grew grey towards the morn, that I yielded my watch upon the roof of the little Castle of Ailsa to the Dominie. Too long I had paced the battlements, listening to the confused and belated yawping and crying of the sea-birds upon the ledges, and to the mysterious night sounds of the isle. For I began to hear and to see all manner of uncouth things, that have no existence except on the borderlands of sleep.

The Dominie said no word, good or bad, but drew his cloak about him and sat down on the rampart. I bade him good morning, but he never answered me a word; and so I left him, for I judged that his thought was bitter, and that the tale he had told me of Mary Torrance lay blackly upon him.

Yet, when I went below, it was not with me as cn other mornings. I lay down upon the plaids and composed me to sleep. Yet I remained broad awake, which was an unaccountable thing for me, who have been all my life a great sleeper. I lay and thought of my friend, sitting gloomy and silent above in the greyness of morn, till my own meditations grew eerie and comfortless. Often and often I started upon my elbow with the intention of going to him. As often I lay down again, because I had no excuse, and also (as it seemed to me) he had not desired my company.

But once, as I lifted me up on my elbow, I seemed to hear a shrill crying as it had been out of the sea, 'Launcelot —Launcelot Kennedy!' it said. And the crying was most like a woman's voice. My very blood chilled within me, for the tale of the lass murdered upon the morn of her marriage day was yet in my mind. And I thought of naught less than that her uneasy spirit was now come to visit the man, aged and withered, who sat up there waiting and watching for her coming. Yet why it should cry my name passed my comprehension.

It was, therefore, small wonder that I listened long, lying there among the plaids upon the floor. But the night wind soughed and sobbed through the narrow wicket window, and there was no further noise. Thinking that I had dreamed, I laid my head upon the hard pillow and composed me to sleep, but even then I caught as it had been the regular beat of a boat's oars upon the rullocks. And anon I heard my name cried twice and

thrice, 'Launcelot Kennedy! Launcelot Kennedy! Launcelot Kennedy!' Whereat, with a thrill of horror, I rose,
cast the wrappings from me, and, with my naked sword
in my hand, I went up to the roof of the castle.

The Dominie was sitting with his face turned seaward.
He heard me come behind him. Without turning he put
out his hand.

'Did you hear it too?' he said. 'Go below. That which
shall come is not for your eyes to see!'

'But I heard a woman call my name!' I said. 'I heard
it twice and thrice, plain as I hear you speak!'

'Nay,' he said, 'not your name—mine!'

And once more we listened together. As for me, I
strained my eyes into the darkness so that they ached and
were ready to behold anything. I gazed out directly
towards the sea, from which the sounds had come; but
the Dominie looked along the path which led precariously
between the wall of the isle above and the precipice below.

Thus we watched as it seemed for hours and hours.

Suddenly I heard him draw in his breath with a gasping
sound, like that which a man gives when he finds himself
unexpectedly in ice-cold water. The twilight of the
morning had come a little, and as I looked over his
shoulder, lo! there seemed to me as it had been a maid
in white coming along the path. I felt my heart stop
beating, and I, too, gazed rigidly, for it seemed to me to
be Nell Kennedy, coming towards us, robed like an angel.

'She is dead!' I thought. 'Mayhap the clawed things
out of the sea have devoured her, even as they took Mary
Torrance!'

But I heard the Dominie say under his breath, 'It is she!
It is she!'

For in the moment of terror, when the soul is unmanned,
everyone hears with his own ears and sees with his own
eyes, according to his own heart's fantasy.

But the figure came ever closer to us, stepping daintily
and surely in the dim light. Again I heard the voice which
had spoken to me from the sea, and at the sound my very
bones quaked within me.

'Launcelot—Launcelot Kennedy!' it said.

And for a long moment the figure stood still as if waiting

for an answer. But my voice was shut dumbly within me.
The Dominie stood up.

'Art thou the spirit of Mary Torrance, or a deceiving
fiend of hell that has taken her shape? Answer me, or I fire!'

And the Dominie held out his pistol to the white-sheeted
ghost, which even then appeared to me a mightily vain
thing, for how can a spirit fear these things which are only
deadly to flesh and bone?

'I have come to see Launcelot Kennedy,' answered the
voice, and it appeared awful and terrible to me beyond the
power of words. I could not so much as fix my mind on
a prayer, though I knew several well enough. 'I have come
to seek Launce Kennedy. Is he within?' said the voice.

'What would you with him? He is no concern of yours,'
said the Dominie.

'I ken that,' said the voice. 'Nevertheless, I have come
to seek him. I greet you well, Dominie Mure. Will you
open and let Helen Kennedy within?'

And with that the light came clearer. The veil of the
fantasies of that fearful night fell like a loosened bandage
from my eyes. And lo! there at the tower's foot was my
dear quipsome lass, Nell Kennedy, in her own proper
body, and I knew her for good, sound flesh and blood.
Nor could I now tell how I had so deceived myself. But
one thing I resolved—that I should not reveal my terror
to her, for very certainly she would laugh at me!

But the Dominie was too firmly fixed in his thought.
I saw him grip his pistol and lean over the parapet. It
seemed that he could not even believe the seeing of his eyes.

'Come not nearer,' he cried in a wild voice, 'for well do
I know that you are a fiend of the breed of the sea demons,
whatsoever you may pretend. I will try a bullet of holy
silver upon you.'

But I threw myself upon him and held his arm.

'It is but our own Nell Kennedy,' I said. 'What frights
you, Dominie?'

For I resolved to make a virtue of my courage. And,
indeed, as I came to myself first, and had done no open
foolishness, I thought I might as well take all the credit
which was due to me. 'See you not that it is only Helen
Kennedy of Culzean?' I repeated, reasoning with him.

'And what seeks she with you?' said he, still struggling in my grasp. 'I tell you it is a prodigy, and bodes us no good,' he persisted.

'That I cannot tell,' said I. 'I had thought her safe upon the moors with my mother. But I will go down and open the door to her.'

So when I had run down the stairs of the small keep and set the bolt wide, lo, there upon the step was Nell Kennedy, her face dimpled with smiles, albeit somewhat pale also with the morning light and the strangeness of her adventure.

I held out my hand to her. Never had I been so moved with any meeting.

'Nell!' I said, and could say no more.

'Ay, Launce—just Nell!' she said. And she came in without taking my hand. But for all that she was not abashed nor shame-faced. But she remained as direct and simple in her demeanour as she had been about Culzean, in the old days before sorrow fell upon the house, and, indeed, upon us all.

'Take me up the stairs to the Dominie,' she said. And I took her hand and kept it tightly as we went upwards. But I tried after no great favours at that time, for I knew that her mood leaned not towards the desires of a lover.

'Ah, Dominie,' said Nell, when she reached the top, 'this Ailsa is a strange place to keep school in. Yet I warrant you that geese are not more numerous here than they were in Maybole!'

But the Dominie could only gaze at her, thus daffing with him, so fixed had he been in his fantasy. Then when he was somewhat come to himself, we waited expectantly for Nell to reveal her errand and to relate her adventure, and she did not keep us long waiting.

'You must instantly leave Ailsa and come back with me,' she said. 'My sister Marjorie is lost from Auchendrayne, and we three must find her. I fear that the Mures have done her a mischief, being afraid of the things that she might reveal!'

'How knew you of that, Nelly?' I asked, for, indeed, it was a thing I could make no guess at myself.

'It was one morning at Kirrieoch,' said Nell, 'as we were bringing in the kye out of the green pastures by the waterside, that a messenger rode up with a letter from Marjorie. She asked me to meet her at Culzean and to bring you and any other faithful men whom I could trust along with me. And thus the letter ended: *"For gin I once win clear out of Auchendrayne, we have them all in the hollow of our hand. I have found him that carried the letter."*

'She means the letter to John Mure that took your father to the tryst of death,' I said.

The Dominie seemed to awake at the words.

'That will be young William Dalrymple she has fallen on with,' he cried, in much excitement.

I rose, and hastened down to put our belongings together, which were scattered about the castle. As soon as I returned Nell went on with her tale.

'Then because I knew not where you were,' she said, 'I was in much distress. But your father donned his war graith and rode with me to the house of Culzean, where he yet abides. As for me, I could noways rest, so I set myself to trace you. And here I have found you. Pray God we may find our Marjorie as safely!'

'But how did you manage to trace us!' I asked, for the Dominie and I thought that we had well hidden our tracks.

'Oh, I got the kindly side of the goodwife of Chapeldonnan,' said Nell, lightly. And when I heard that, I did not wonder any more, for she could get the kindly side of anyone, if she chose. Because Nell Kennedy, in spite of her taunting and teasing, had ever a coaxing, winsome way with her which was vastly taking.

Then we fell to making our plans. It would not do for us to be seen leaving the Craig by day, for our position was plainly in view of keen eyes along all the Girvan shore and at Chapeldonnan or Girvanmains as well. And worse enemies than these might put out a dozen boats to intercept us, or simply lie in wait to take us as we landed. Besides, all this day and part of the night there befel a storm which lashed the waves to white foam about our abode.

With more than a woman's ordinary forethought in adventure, Nell had left her boat in a cove to the right of the landing-place. And indeed I, that somewhat prided myself upon my wisdom, had not taken as great precautions myself—which, among other things, was the

cause of our present position on the Craig. So we three
spent all the day in cheerful talk, thinking that so soon
as we could find Marjorie, we should come to the end of
our perplexities, and have the guilty in our power. But in
this we spoke without knowledge of the manifold shifts
and stratagems of our arch enemy.

CHAPTER XXXVIII

A RESCUE FROM THE SEA

WHILE we thus waited and planned, Nell told us how that
she had remained at Culzean till there seemed no more hope
of Marjorie's coming. Then there arrived a lass of the
Cochranes who had been Marjorie's tiring maid at Auchendrayne. From her Nell learned how, after a fierce and
bitter scene with the elder Mure, Marjorie had fled from
Auchendrayne none knew wither, escaping all their toils
and passing the inner and outer guard under silence of
night. Then so soon as she had heard this, fearing all
evil to her sister, Nell set out to find me—believing that,
in the absence of any hope of help from her brothers,
I might aid her to find her sister and to clear some of
the ever deepening mysteries.

It was the dusk of an evening, sweet and debonnair,
when we left the castle which had been so long our home,
and descended the perilous steeps to the foot of Ailsa. Here
we found Nell's boat safe in its cove, and immediately we
pushed out, having placed therein all our weapons and belongings. Nell sat in the stern, and the Dominie and I took the
oars. The storm of the night and morning had abated, and
there was now no more than an oily swell upon the water.

There was little talk between us as we went, for we
felt that our lives were in our hands and that we might
be only running into greater perils. I supposed that the
Dominie was thinking of the love he had lost by black,
unnatural murder, on that dangerous shore to which we
were making our way. We kept well to the south of
Girvan, because I had twice gone there on errands which
did not tend to make us favourites with the Bargany
Kennedies and their supporters, of whom the townsfolk
were mostly composed. Besides, I remembered the

word of the rascal whom I had held at my mercy
in the house of Mistress Allison, the Grieve's wife at
Culzean. 'The treasure of Kelwood is in the cave of Sawny
Bean on the shore of Bennanbrack over against Benerard.'
And this, though not a clear direction, pointed to some
promontory south of Girvan and north of Ballantrae.

And though the discovery of my master's death was, I
trust, first in my mind, I need not deny that I was also
mindful of the treasure for which so much had been
adventured first and last.

It was a high tide and a calm sea when we got over
into the loom of the cliffs. We had a making wind and
the tide was with us, so that we had been able to set the
sail part of the way—for a little mast which would carry
a lug sail lay snugly under the thwarts of the boat.

The Dominie, who in his rambling youth had followed
the sea, both steered and managed the sheet as we drew
nearer the shore, while I lay over the bow and kept a look-
out ahead. We steered towards a light which went wavering along the top of the rocks, for we opined that it must
be some shepherd wandering with a lantern to look for a
lost sheep. Now it dipped into clefts, now it mounted
to the summit of the crags, and anon it was lost again
behind the screes and tumbled cliffs of the coast.

Suddenly from high above us, where we had last seen
the light, we heard sounds as of pain and despair—a
woman's cry in her extremity—not weeping or beseech-
ing, but crying only, being, as it seemed, utterly in distress.

''Tis our Marjorie! I ken her voice!' cried Nell, and
we all strained our eyes upwards to the dark heuchs. The
lantern had come to a standstill almost directly above us.

The Dominie silently took down the mast and let it rest
in the bottom of the boat. Our speed slackened till we
floated without motion on the gently heaving water. I
continued to peer into the gloom. Yet how Marjorie
Kennedy could have come to be in danger upon the shore
of Benane was far beyond my comprehending at that time.

'Marjorie! Sister Marjorie!' cried Nell, as loudly as
she could. And almost as she spoke I saw something white
descending towards us from the cliff, like a poised bird that
closes its pinions and dives into the water. The smitten

waters sprang up white not twenty feet from our bows.

I stood erect on the stern, scarce knowing what might hap, yet to be ready for anything, balancing on both feet for a spring. And as soon as I had a glimpse of something white which rose from the black water, I sprang towards it ere it had time to sink again. For Nell was with me in the boat, and it was my opportunity to let her see that Launce Kennedy did not do all his deeds standing thread-dry on the solid land. I declare, so much was I affected and worked upon by her crying to her sister, that had it been Sawny Bean himself I had grappled with him there in the salt water.

But it was a braver weight and shape that I held in my arm—even the slim form of a woman. I felt a thrill run through me when I found that her arms had been tied closely behind her back both at wrist and elbow. Nevertheless, I gripped the cords which confined her, and struck out for the boat, which I saw black like a rock above me.

It was no more than a minute that I supported the girl in the water,but to me it seemed to be a year for I was hill born, and had learned the swimming since I came in my youth to Culzean. And this never makes a strong nor yet a long swimmer like the shore-bred boy, who has been half in and out of the tide all day long every summer season since he could walk.

But the Dominie speedily brought the boat about, for indeed there was little way on her at anyrate. In a moment more his strong hands and long fingers were lifting Marjorie Kennedy on board, and laying her, all wet as she was, in the arms of her sister Nell.

Then he gave me a hand over the bow, and we cowered low in the boat, letting her drift inward with the tide till we were close under the loom of the land and in the very darkest of the shadow. We knew well that they who had tied Marjorie's hands would be on the look-out for her rescuers. So on the black water we lay and waited.

Nor had we long to wait, for in a short time voices echoed here and there among the rocks, and the lantern, with others which we had not previously seen, appeared far down near the edge of the sea. At the same time, from the other direction, came the noise of oars roughly thrown into a boat and the clambering of men over the side. Then

we were, indeed, in sore jeopardy, for the wind had died
to nothing under the land, and the grey sea lay outside
the shadow of the cliffs with quite enough light upon it
to trace us by, if we rowed out in that direction.

And all the while Marjorie lay silent in her sister's arms.
I had cut the cords and chafed her hands as well as I could,
but still she did not speak.

The pursuers closed rapidly upon us from both sides, and
ere we could think of a plan, we saw the boats pushing out
with torches held at their prows by the hands of dark and
stalwart men. And then the Dominie and I looked to our
pistols and swords, resolving, if it came to the sharp pinch,
to make a good fight for it. For when the two boats came
together they could not choose but find us.

CHAPTER XXXIX

THE CLEFT IN THE ROCK

'LET us get in nearer to the land,' said the Dominie; ''tis
the sole chance that remains to us.'

So seizing each of us an oar, the sea being perfectly
calm and a full tide lapsing as smoothly upon the cliffs
as the water in a tub wherein good wives wash their duds,
we risked the matter and rowed in closer to the rock.
We sought if by good chance there might be found some
inlet where we could land, or some cave which might conceal us from the cruel men who were seeking our lives.

Nor was our adventuring in vain, for as we cautiously
advanced into the blackness, the wall of the cliff seemed
to retire before us, so that the prow of the boat actually
appeared to push it steadily back. A denser darkness, a
very night of Egypt, surrounded us. Gradually the noise of
the pursuers dulled, sank, and died away. We lost sight of
the grey, uneasy plain of the sea behind us, and continued
to advance through a long water passage walled with
rock, the sides of which we could sometimes feel with our
hands and sometimes fail to touch with our oars. This
I took at the time to be a marvellous dispensation of
Providence on our behalf, as without doubt it was. But
now we know that all that shoreward country, owing to
the abundance of soft stone by the seaside, is honeycombed

with caves, so that it was well-nigh impossible to miss at least one of these in every half mile of cliff all about the Heads of Benerard. Yet that we should strike this one of all others appeared a thing worthy of admiration, as presently you shall hear, and showed the same dispensing and favourable Providence which has throughout been on the side of Culzean and against our enemies of Bargany.

Marjorie and Nell still sat together in the stern, but so dense was the dark that we could see nothing of them. The Dominie and I took our oars from the rullocks and pushed onward into the cave, hoping to come in time to some wider space,. where we could either disembark or find a passage out upon the land above us.

And so presently we came to a place wonderful enough in itself, yet no more than the gateway to other and greater marvels.

The waves which had scarcely been visible out on the open sea ran into the cave at regular intervals, and in the narrow place formed themselves into a considerable swell of water. Before us we could hear them break with a noise like thunder upon some hidden strand or beach. This somewhat terrified us in that place of horrid darkness, for the noise was loud as is a waterfall in the time of spate, the echoing of the cave and the many contracted passages and wide halls deceiving the ear.

So our boat, being poised upon the crest of one of these smooth steeps of water which rolled onward into the cave, advanced swiftly into a more spacious cavern, where the oar could be used without touching the rock at either side. The sounds now came back to us also from high aloft, and we had the feeling of much air and a certain spacious vastness above us. Yet the imprisoning darkness, confused with the lashing of the waves, wrought a kind of invincible melancholy which weighed down all our spirits.

Presently, however, the prow of the boat took the slushy sand in a coign more retired, where the waves did not, as in other places, fall with an arching dash, but rather lapsed with a gentler wash as upon a regular beach. Being in the bow, I lost no time in leaping ashore, and in a few moments I had the boat fast to a natural pier of rock, behind which the water was quiet as in a mill pond.

Here in the darkness we helped each other out, and feeling ourselves now somewhat more safe from our enemies, we shook one another by the hand and made many congratulation on our escape, which had indeed been marvellous.

Even thus we waited for the day to reveal to us whether there were any passage by which we could ascend from the deeps of the Cimmerian pit wherein we were enclosed, without adventuring out again in our boat upon the water, where our enemies watched for us.

We drew close together upon the rocky pier, and Marjorie told us of her escape from the Auchendraynes, the strange tale of which shall hereafter be given at length in its own place. Also she confirmed the message which she had sent to her sister, that she had discovered all the wickedness and certain guilt of the Mures in the death of her father, and in many other crimes. So we saw before us in plain case their condemnation, if once we could escape from this snare and bring their iniquity to light before the King and the Council. Yet all the while it was a marvel to me how Marjorie had so completely forgotten James Mure the younger, who was her wedded husband, even though she had never rendered to him the love and duty of a wife.

But we were by no means yet won out of the wood. And, at the best, our case was not a particularly comfortable one. The Dominie and I had, indeed, provided Marjorie with such wrappings and covertures as were in our power, which we had brought with us from the isle. But we had mainly to trust to the virtues of the strong waters of France, which the Dominie always carried about with him, as well as to the mildness of the night, that she should take no harm from her fearful plunge from the cliffs into the salt water.

But it is certain that the perturbation of one's spirit at such a time is so great, that many things pass without penalty to the health which at another season might induce disease and death.

Presently we found that our boat was being left high and dry, the water ebbing swiftly away from us towards the mouth of the cave. We had, as it happened, entered at the height of the tide, and now the water was upon the turn. But this affected us little, for we judged that either it would go so far back that we might find a way of escape by clambering over the rocks out upon the land; or else, at the worst, we knew that, by waiting till the next tide, we should be able to return the way we had come. At all events, for that time at least, we thought ourselves to have outwitted our pursuers and to stand no longer in their danger.

But we were briskly to learn another way of it, for the oftenest slip is made upon the threshold of safety.

Marjorie and Nell bore themselves through all these dangers and discomforts with the greatest courage. Never had this come home to me so strongly before, for the maid's shamefacedness had died out of Marjorie Kennedy; and now she seemed wholly set with a fierce jealousy of hate to compass the punishment of her father's enemies.

The water being in this manner retired, and our boat lying high and dry upon a shelving beach, I proposed that the Dominie and myself should attempt some exploration of the place where we found ourselves—while we left Nell and her sister by the boat to make such dispositions of their cleading as would countervale the discomfort of Marjorie's rescue from death.

So the Dominie and I felt with our hands all round the wide amphitheatre which had so lately been filled with the salt water. We had no difficulty in discovering the narrow passage by which we had come, for down its narrow gullet the water was now retreating with great swiftness. But we seemed to be at the sack's end in every other way, so that we looked for nothing else but having to return to the same place, and in the same way by which we came, after our enemies had retired. So swiftly did the tide run back, that it seemed as if it might be possible for us to walk out upon our own feet. And so indeed we did, but in a very strange fashion.

For in one of my gropings I came upon a projection of the rock, which caught my foot and threw me forward upon my face. As I fell, my hands touched something like a flight of rough steps which led up from the sanded floor of the cavern. Without waiting to call out to Dominie Mure I mounted, with my heart beating fast with antici-pation, and at the top I came into a narrower passage than any we had yet entered, which led me forward a long way. As I went the air felt unaccountably lighter. It smelled most like a well-fired room, dry and pleasant, so that I waited only to ascertain that the passage ended in another apartment before going back to communicate my fortunate discovery to Marjorie and Nell.

When I reached the boat I found that, by the skilful management of her sister, Marjorie had been made somewhat more comfortable, and that the Dominie on his part had discovered nothing of importance, of which I was glad, for it became me to be the leader of our expedition. So I bade him take his weapons, and with what provender we could carry upon our backs we proceeded all of us together to the rocky stairway leading to the drier inner cave.

The Dominie had as usual brought his pipes over his shoulder, from which, indeed, he refused to be parted even for a moment. And but for the fear of the noise reaching our enemies, I think that there and then he would have played us both reels and strathspeys—that is, if we had given him any encouragement, so pleased was he, and, indeed, all of us, to leave the dark cavern and oozy sand upon which we had first landed.

We were not long in ascending the stairs, and, as I had foretold, we found ourselves speedily in the warmer and drier air, like that of a habited house, which was so great a change from the dripping damp of the lower sea-cave that we rejoiced greatly, though quite unable to discover the cause.

Yet there was something—we knew not what—about the inner cavern which took us all by the throat. Indeed, we had not gone far when Marjorie Kennedy gasped for breath and said, 'Let us go back! I do not like the place!'

But this I took to be no more than the dashing of her spirit by the adventures of the night, and the terrors through which, as she had already told us, she had come in the dreary and dangerous house of Auchendrayne.

For the passage broadened out into a wider hall with a firm floor of hard earth, as if it had been beaten or trampled. We had hardly been in this place longer than a few moments when a strangely persistent and pervading smell began to impress us with the deadliest loathing. It was sharp, pungent, and familiar. Yet could none of us tell whence it came, nor in what place we had smelled it before.

'I am faint unto death,' said Marjorie, leaning heavily on me. 'Let me go back, Launcelot, while I can.'

But this, for the sake of the dryness and comfort, I was not willing to do. So, stumbling now over one thing and now over another in the darkness, I made shift to find a further passage.

I chanced to put down my hand, when my foot struck something heavier and more massive than before, and, lo! to my horror, I touched the side of a wooden tub or vat. And scarce had I moved from the place where I was, before something cold and soft brushed my face, as if it had been suspended from the roof. My heart trembled, for we were plainly in a place of habitation of some unknown and terrible sort.

'Stand still where you are,' I cried to my companions. For I was afraid that they also might come against one of these obstructions, which were good evidence of others having been in this abode of horror and darkness as well as ourselves.

Immediately I set to the groping again, and went stumbling from one thing to another till I came to a branching passage which ascended away from the hall. And since here, in the roomy alcove high above the floor of the cave, there were (so far as I could find) none of the vats or other furniture which I had encountered about the sides of the greater cave, I decided to use it as a place of temporary shelter.

So I made my way back to where they were all standing close together, and I pinched the Dominie's arm in token that he was to ask no questions. Then very slowly and stealthily we felt our way to the little alcove which I had found. And as often as I stumbled against anything, I pretended to clatter some of the stuff which I carried upon my back, having laden myself with it at the boat. And so passed the matter off.

At last we came to the hiding-place which had been my latest discovery, and found that the rock was cut, as it had been, into seats all round about, while the path ascended upwards at the back yet higher into the stone, by which I judged that we had not yet come to the end of the cavern. Here in the high alcove or gallery above the main cave we accommodated ourselves, and disposed our belongings as well as we could for the darkness. The Dominie set himself to arrange them, while Nell and Marjorie lay covered up together in our plaids upon the stone bench which ran about the place, and which appeared to have been hewn out at some past time by the rude art of man. But I myself, to whom it came as natural to be stirring as to breathe, set about making a further exploration.

Now my disappointment was great when I found that we had indeed come to the limit of the cavern. Search which way I would, my hands encountered nothing but rock. Nevertheless, I continued my circuit, standing upon the stone ledge and groping above me, for it was possible that there was some fresh passage which from this alcove might lead to the outer air.

Suddenly, while I was searching with my hands at the top of the steps of stone, and, without the least warning, my finger tips fell upon something which felt colder than the stone. I touched metal—then the projection of a keyhole, then the iron corners of a chest. I ran my hand along the pattern of the metal bands which bound the lid. What wonder that my heart beat vehemently, for I knew in that moment that I had my hand upon the Treasure of Kelwood!

CHAPTER XL

THE CAVE OF DEATH

For a moment there in the darkness I stood dazed, and my head swam, for I bethought me of the Earl's words, as well as of the words of the Minister of Edinburgh, and I knew that my fate stood upon tip-toe. For here in the finding of this box lay all my life, and it might be my love also. But again another thought crossed the first, damming back and freezing the current of hot blood which surged to my heart. The caird's words in the Grieve's kitchen also came back to me, 'You will find the Treasure of Kelwood in the cave of Sawny Bean in the head of Bennanbrack over against Benerard.'

If this were so, there was little doubt but that we stood in the most instant and imminent danger of our lives. Yet I could not bring myself to leave the treasure. Doubtless I ought to have done so, and hastened our escape for the sake of the girls, Nell and Marjorie. But I thought it might be possible to convey the chest out, and so bring both our quests to an end at once—that for treasure, by the recovery of

the box which had been lost and found, and then lost again
upon the Red Moss, and that of vengeance, by the certain condemnation of the Auchendraynes upon Marjorie's evidence.

The next moment mighty fear took hold on me. All that
I had heard since my childhood, about the unknown being
who dwelled upon the shore-side of Benane and lived no man
knew how, ran through my mind—his monstrous form, his
cloven feet that made steads on the ground like those of
a beast, his huge, hairy arms, clawed at the finger ends like
the toes of a bear. I minded me of the fireside tales of
travellers who had lost their way in that fastness, and who,
falling into the power of his savage tribe, returned no more
to kindlier places. I minded also how none might speak to
the prowler by night, nor get answer from him—how every
expedition against him had come to naught, because that he
was protected by a power stronger than himself, warned
and advised by an intelligence higher than his own. Besides,
none had been able to find the abode, nor yet to enter into
the secret defences where lurked the man-beast of Benerard.

And it was in this abode of death that I, Launce Kennedy,
being, as I supposed, in my sane mind, had taken refuge
with two women, one the dearest to me on earth. The
blood ran pingling and pricking in my veins at the thought.
My heart cords tightened as though it too had been shut
in a box and the key turned.

Hastily I slipped down, and upon a pretext took the
Dominie aside to tell him what it was that I had found.

'Ye have found our dead warrant then. I wish we had
never seen your treasures and brass-banded boxes!' said he
roughly, as if I had done it with intent.

And in troth I began to think he was right. But it
was none of my fault, and, so far as I could see, we had been
just as badly off in that place, if I had not found it at all.

After that I went ranging hither and thither among all
the passages and twinings of the cave, yet never daring to go
very far from the place where we were, lest I should not
be able to find my way back. For it was an ill, murderous,
uncanny abode, where every step that I took something
strange swept across my face or slithered clammily along
my cheek, making me grue to my very bone marrows. I am
as fond of a nimble fetch of adventures as any man, as

every believing reader of this chronicle kens well by this time, but I want no more such darkling experiences— specially now that I am become a peaceable man, and no longer so regardlessly forward as I once was, in thrusting myself into all stirs and quarrels up to the elbows.

Then in a little I went soft-footed to where Marjorie and Nell had bestowed themselves. When I told them how we had run into danger with a folly and senselessness that nothing could have excused—save the great necessity into which, by the hellish fury of our enemies, we had been driven —it was indeed cheerful to hear their words of trust and their declarations that they could abide the issue with fortitude.

So a little heartened, we made such preparations as we could—as preparing our pistols and loosening our swords. Yet all had to be done by touch, in that abode of darkness and black, un-Christian deeds.

It was silent and eerie beyond telling in the cave. We heard the water lapping further and further from us as it retreated down the long passage. Now and then we seemed to catch a gliff of the noise of human voices. But again, when we listened, it seemed naught but the wind blowing every way through the passages and halls of the cave, or the echoed wing-beatings of the uncanny things that battened in the roofs and crevices of this murtherous cavern, unfathomed, unsounded, and obscure.

But we had not long to wait ere our courage and resolution were tested to the uttermost. For presently there came to us, clearly enough, though faintly at first, the crying and baying of voices fearful and threatening. Indeed they sounded more like the insensate howling of dogs or shut-up hungry hounds in a kennel than kindly human creatures. Then there was empty silence, through which the noise came in gusts, like the sudden deadly anger of a mob. Again it came, more sharp and double-edged with fear, like the wailing of women led to unpitied doom. And the sound of this inhuman carnival, approaching, filled the cave with shuddering.

This direful crying came nearer and nearer, till we all cowered paleface together, save Marjorie alone—who, having been, as it were, in hell itself, feared not the most merciless fiends that might have broken loose therefrom.

She stood a little apart from us, so far that I had not known her presence but for the draught of air that blew inward, which carried her light robe towards me, so that its texture touched my face, and I was aware of the old subtle fragrance which in happy days had well-nigh turned my head in the gardens of Culzean.

But Nell Kennedy stood close to me, so close that I could hear her heart beating and the little nervous sound of the clasping and the unclasping of her hands—which thing made me somewhat braver, especially when she put both her palms about my arm and gripped it convulsively to her, as the noises of the crying and howling waxed louder and nearer.

'I am vexed that I flouted you, Launce,' she whispered in my ear. 'I do not care a docken what you said to Kate Allison. After all, she is not such a truth-telling girl, nor yet by-ordinary bonny.'

I whispered to her that I cared not either, but that I was content to die for her.

'Oh, but you might have lived for me,' she moaned, 'if I had not led you into all this trouble.'

'Nay, Nell, my dear,' said I, hastily, 'speak not so. You have ever been our saviour and our best fortune hitherto, and so shall be yet.'

Then (mock us not) in the darkness of the cave we kissed each other one or twice, amorously and willingly, and the savour of it was passing sweet even when we looked for naught but death.

'Give me a dagger,' Nell said to me, and I gave mine own to her, which she put away in her bosom, as I judged, and again took my hand.

Then the horrid brabblement filled all the cave, and sounded louder and more outrageous, being heard in darkness. Suddenly, however, the murky gloom was shot through with beams of light, and a rout of savages, wild and bloody, filled the wide cave beneath us. Some of them carried rude torches, and others had various sorts of back-burdens, which they cast down in the corners. I gat a gliff of one of these, and though in battle I had often seen things grim and butcherly, my heart now sprang to my mouth, so that I had well-nigh fainted with loathing. But I commanded myself, and thrust me before Nell, who from where she sat could only see the flickering skarrow of the torches upon the roof and walls—for the place seemed now, after the former darkness of Egypt, fairly bursting with light.

Then I knew that these execrable hell-hounds must be the hideous crew who called Sawny Bean lord and master. They were of both sexes and all ages, mostly running naked, the more stalwart of them armed with knives and whingers, or with knotted piece of tree in which a ragged stone had been thrust and tied with sinew or tags of rope. The very tottering children were striking at one another, or biting like young wolves, till the blood flowed. In the corner sat an old bleared hag, who seemed of some authority over them, for she pointed with her finger, and the uproar calmed itself a little. The shameless naked women-crew began to bestir themselves, and heaped broken driftwood upon the floor, to which presently a light was set.

Then the red climbing flame went upward. The wood smoke filled the cave, acrid and tickling, which, getting into our throats, might have worked us infinite danger, had it not been that the clamour of the savages was so great that it never stilled for a moment. But in time we became accustomed to the reek, and it disturbed us not.

More by luck that good guiding, the place where we sat was, as I have said, favourably situate for seeing without being seen—being a kind of natural balcony or chamber in the wall, like a swallow's nest plastered under the eaves of a barn. We learned afterwards that it was a place forbidden by Sawny Bean, the head of the clan, and so kept sacred for himself when it should please him to retire thither for his ease and pleasure, with whomsoever he would of his unholy crew. And to this no doubt we owed our safety, for the young impish boys roamed everywhere else, specially swarming and yelling about our boat, which they had just discovered. I noted, also, that when any of these came in the way of the men, he was knocked down incontinent with a hand, a knife, or a stick, as was most convenient. Sometimes the lad would lie a minute or two where he had been struck, then up again, and to the playing and disport he fell, as though nothing had happened.

All this was horrid enough, but that was not the worst of it, and I own that I hesitate to write that which I saw. Yet, for the sake of the truth, tell I must and will. The cavern was very high in the midst, but at the sides not so high—rather like the sloping roof of an attic which slants quickly down from the rooftree. But that which took my eye amid the smoke were certain vague shapes, as it had been of the limbs of human beings, shrunk and blackened, which hung in rows on either side of the cave. At first it seemed that my eyes must certainly deceive me, for the reek drifted hither and thither, and made the rheum flow from them with its bitterness. But after a little study of these wall adornments, I could make nothing else of it, than that these poor relics, which hung in rows from the roof of the cave like hams and black puddings set to dry in the smoke, were indeed no other than the parched arms and legs of men and women who had once walked the upper earth—but who by misfortune had fallen into the power of this hideous, inconceivable gang of monstrous man-eaters. Then the true interpretation of all the tales that went floating about the countryside, and which I had hitherto deemed wholly vain and fantastical, burst upon me.

But there was that nearer to me which smote me down like a blow taking a man at unawares. As I stood up to look, gripping nervously at my sword and peering over, there came a gust of the sea, roaring up the passages of the cavern. For with the moon the wind had risen without. The fire on the floor flickered upward and filled the place with light. I felt something touch my cheek. Speedily I turned, and, lo! it was a little babe's hand that swung by a cord. The wind had caught it, so light it was, and it had rubbed my cheek. By the Lord, it was enough and more than enough. I sank down and the spirit within me became water because of that soft, sliding little hand. Had the naked devils come on to me then, I declare I had not found power to lift my hand against them, not so much as to set a finger to the latch of a pistol.

But in a little while I was strengthened, for now, as though I had never seen her before, I saw the true face of the brave lass Nell Kennedy. And it is passing sweet, even in the presence of death, to see the eyes of the beloved for the first time after declared and unashamed love had come into them. She never took her sad, steadfast

regard from my face, and, as I say, I was infinitely strengthened thereby.

I could also mark Marjorie Kennedy. And since she
stood erect, I knew that she had seen all the blasting horrors
I had witnessed—except, perhaps, the babe's hand a-swing
by its cord. Yet there was no blanching of her face.
Rather, she stood and eyed the scene with a calm and
assured countenance, like to a stake-kissing martyr ere
the flames are lit.

If ever any soul had cast out fear it was that of Marjorie
Kennedy, for unfathomed hate can do that as well as
perfect love—and especially in a woman.

But when my eyes fell on Dominie Mure, I got a yet
greater start. The little, thickset man, who had been my
brave companion through such a multitude of dangers,
seemed to be transformed. A still and biting fury sat in-
exorably on his lips. He gripped his blade as if he would
spring straight over the wall of rock upon the bestial crew.
So afraid was I to look upon him and read his intent in his
burning eyes, that I undid for a moment the clasp of Nell's
hand upon my shoulder and crawled to him.

'Have a care what you do, Dominie,' I whispered in his
ear. 'Remember, it is of the women we have to think.'

For as clearly as if I had read it in print, I saw his desire
and his determination. He thought of young Mary Torrance, the lass that had been spirited away. And the red
stain on the grass, and the ghastly garniture about the walls
of the monster's cave, had revealed to him the conclusion
of the untold tale.

But my words stopped him dead, like a bullet in the
heart of a springing wild cat on the bough. He looked
just once at me, and his eyes had the same wild glare. But
there came that into them which told me of a thought
greater than the stark revenge on which he had been all
intent but a few moments before.

I bent still nearer to his ear.

'Dominie,' I said, 'if they come at us, mind that we are
not to leave the lasses alive to fall into their bloody hands.'

He looked at me with a haggard face and shook his head.

'I cannot do it!' he said, and set his hands over his eyes
to hide the torches' flare.

When he looked up again I pointed to the loathed things that decked the walls in the eaves of the cave, and to the pickle barrels that stood in the corners.

The Dominie understood and nodded.

'Surely you can if *I* can,' I whispered to him. 'I will take care of Nell—my love, if you——'

And I looked at Marjorie so that he understood fully. Then came my eyes back to Nell. They felt hot and dry.

For I was taken with the reek in them, and my heart rose within me to think that in a swift tale of moments I might have to take away the sweet life from my own heart's love. But when I went back to her, there was a new light of understanding in the face on which the flicker of the fire was reflected from the roof. I knew that she had seen and understood the import of my colloquy with the Dominie, and our looking from the one to the other of them.

Yet the fear had strangely gone from her face. I declare she looked almost glad. She set her lips to my ear.

'Launce,' she whispered, 'I want none but you to do it—if so be that it comes to that. You will, will you not, Launce?''

Then I knew that she had understood all the love she had seen in my face. For, indeed, I would rather had killed my sweetheart a hundred times, then let her fall alive into the hands of such a ghastly, bestial devil's crew.

So Nell Kennedy, trusting me with the manner of her death as though it had been a little love-tryst between ourselves, sat looking up at me with such eyes of love and trust that they went nigh to make me forget that Cimmerian den and the ghoulish beasts that rioted in it.

CHAPTER XLI

THE WERE-WOLF OF BENERARD

Thus we sat a long time, waiting. Suddenly there was a pause in the noise which filled the cavern below. I thought for a moment that they had discovered us. But Marjorie moved her hand a little to bid me keep down. And very carefully I raised my head over the rock, so that through the niche I could as before look down upon them.

The water-door of the cave was now entirely filled

by a black hulk, in shape like a grizzly ape. Even in the
flickering light I knew instantly that I had seen the
monster before. A thrill ran through me when I remembered the man-beast, the thing with which I had grappled
in the barn of Culzean the night I out-faced the Grey Man.
And now by the silence and the crouching of the horde
beneath me, I learned that their master had come home.
The monster stood a moment in the doorway as though
angered at something, then he spoke in a voice like a beast's
growl, certain things which I could not at all understand—
though it was clear that his progeny did, for there ensued
a tumultuous rushing from side to side. Then Sawny
Bean strode into the midst of his den. It happened that
by misadventure he stumbled and set his foot upon a lad
of six or seven, judging by the size of him, who sprawled
naked in the doorway. The imp squirmed round like a
serpent and bit Sawny Bean in the leg, whereat he stooped,
and catching the lad by the feet, he dashed his head with
a dull crash against the wall, and threw him quivering like
a dead rabbit into the corner.

The rest stood for a moment aghast. But in a trice, and
without a single one so much as going to see if the boy
were dead or only stunned, the whole hornet's byke
hummed again, and the place was filled with a stifling smell
of burning fat and roasting victual, upon the origin of
which I dared not let my mind for a moment dwell.

When Sawny Bean came in, he had that which looked
like a rich cloth of gold over his arm—the plunder of some
poor butchered wretch, belike. He stood with this trophy in
front of him, examining it before the fire. Presently he threw
it over his shoulders, with the arms hanging idly down in
front, and strode about most like a play-actor or a mad person
—but manifestly to his own great content and to the huge admiration of his followers, who stood still and gaped after him.

When he had satisfied himself with this posturing, the
monster looked towards our place of refuge. A great spasm
seized my heart when I saw him take the first step towards
us, for I guessed that it was his forbidden treasure-house
in which we lurked.

So I thought it had certainly come to the last bitter
push with us. But something yet more terrible than the

matter of the boy diverted for the moment the monster's attention. The lad whom he had cast to the side had been left alone, none daring to meddle. But now, as he passed him, Sawny Bean gave the body a toss with his foot. At this, quick as a darting falcon on the stoop, a woman sprang at him from a crevice where she had been crouching —at least by her shape she was a woman, with long elf-locks twisting like snakes about her brow and over her shoulders. She held an open knife in her hand, and she struck at the chieftan's hairy breast. I heard the point strike the flesh, and the cry of anger and pain which followed. But the monster caught the woman by the wrist, pulled her over his knee, and bent back her head. It was a horrid thing to see, and there is small wonder that I can see it yet in many a dream of the night. And no doubt also I shall see it till I die—hear it as well, which is worse.

Then for a long season I could look no more. But when I had recovered me a little, and could again command my heart. I saw a great part of the crew swarm thick as flies —fetching, carrying, and working like bees upon spilled honey about the corner where had lain the bodies of the lad and the woman. But it was not in the ordinary way that these were being prepared for burial. In the centre of the cave sat Sawny Bean, with some of the younger sort of the women pawing over him and bandaging his wounded shoulder. He was growling and spitting inarticulately all the while like a wild cat. And every time his shoulder hurt him as the women worked with the wound and mouthed it, he would take his other hand and strike one of them down, as though it was to her that he owed the twinge of pain.

Presently the monster arose and took the gold brocade again in his hand. I thought that of a certainty now our time was come, and I looked at Nell Kennedy.

God knows what was in my eyes. My heart within me was ready to break, for the like of this pass had never man been in. That I should have to smite my love to the death within an hour of my first kiss and the first owning of her affection.

But she that loved me read my thought in mine eyes.

She bared her neck for me, so that I could see its tender whiteness in the flicker of the fire.

'Strike there,' she said, 'and let me die in your arms, who art my own heart's love, Launcelot Kennedy.'

I heard the beast-man's step on the stair. I looked from Nell's dear neck to her eyes and back again to her bosom. Then I lifted my hand with the steel in it, and nerved myself for the striking, for I must make no mistake. And even in that moment I saw the gleam of a dagger in Marjorie's hand also.

Suddenly a tremendous rush of sound filled the cave. The blade fell from my hand, and by instinct, not knowing what we did, Nell and I clasped one another. The clamour seemed to be about us and all round us. Roaring echoes came back to us. The bowels of the earth quaked. Yet methought there was something strongly familiar in the sound of it. I turned me about and there, standing erect with all his little height was the Dominie. His cheeks were distended, and he was blowing upon his great war-pipes such a thunderous pibroch as never had been heard east of the Minch since the island pipes skirled on the Red Harlaw.

What madcap possession had come upon his mind, I know not. But the effect I can tell. The pack of fiends that caroused and slew beneath, stood stricken a moment in amaze at the dreadful, incomprehensible sounds. Then they fled helter-skelter, yellyhooing with fear, down the narrow sea-way from which the tide had now fully ebbed. And when I looked again, there was not a soul to be seen. Only over the edge of a lappered cauldron the body of the murdered woman (or, at least, a part of it), lay doubled—a bloody incentive to make haste out of this direful Cave of Death.

The Dominie stepped down from our hidden alcove as though he had been leading a march, strutting and passaging like the King's piper marching about the banqueting table at Holyrood. I declare the creature seemed 'fey'. He was certainly possessed with a devil. But the very fearlessness of the deed won into our veins also, for with steel or pistol in each of our hands we marched after them—ready, and, indeed, eager to encounter aught that might come in our way. Ay, and even thus we passed out of the cave, hasting down the long passage without a quiver of the heart or a blenching of the cheek—so suddenly and so starkly, by way of unexpected hope, had the glorious music brought the hot blood back to our hearts, even as it had stricken our cruel foes with instant terror.

Thus dryshod we marched out of the cave of Sawny Bean, and, as I am a true man, not so much as a dog barked at us. But when we emerged into the grey of a stormy morning and reached the cliff's edge, we heard nland the wild voices of the gang yelling down the wind, as though their furies of fear were still pursuing them and tearing at their vitals. What they expected I know not, but I conceive that they must have taken the Dominie's pipes for whatever particular devil they happened to believe in, come to take them quick to their own place. Which, after all, could not be much worse than the den in which we had seen them at their disport. Nor could all the torturing fiends of lowest hell have been their marrows in devilish cruelty.

CHAPTER XLII

ANE LOCHABER AIX GIED HIM HIS PAIKS

So once more the world was before us, and strangely peaceful it seemed, as if somehow or other we had died in stress and riot and been born again into an uncanny quiet. There remained for us now only the bringing to pass of righteous judgments upon the wicked ones who had compassed and plotted all this terrible tale of evils—these murders without end, these hellish cruelties and death-breeding deceits. For the vengeance must not fall alone on the crazed outlaw and his brood, since the chief criminals were those that were greater and wiser than Sawny Bean and his merciless crew.

It was, as I say, the breaking of a stormy morrow when we faced up the brae, sword in hand, finding none to withstand us, for all had fled before the music of the wild Highland drones. Then in the sustaining quiet I asked the Dominie by what inspiration he had thought of such a mad thing as thus blasting upon the war-pipes.

'Oh it just came to me!' said he, lightly. And with that he wiped his chanter and set the drones under his arm, letting them hang down as though they had been the legs of a lamb which a herd has found on the hill.

But our troubles were not yet over, for we had to pass through many miles of Bargany country ere we could reach our own folk. I proposed to turn landwards, for that, as the crow flies, is the shortest road. But the Dominie denied me, saying that since those cruel monsters of the were-wolf's band had fled that way, the closer we kept to the coast, the safer we should be.

We made, therefore, only such a detour as would enable us to escape the town of Girvan, which was a strength of our foes, and passing by Killochan, a pleasant and friendly tower, well set in a wooded valley with a view of our old strength of Alisa, we hastened as fast as we could march with the women in our company to Culzean.

Now near by Killochan there was a school and a school-master, the name of him John Guid. He had been for a long season a friend and crony of our Dominie Mure. To him we resorted, or rather the Dominie went alone to seek him, while I abode with Marjorie and Nell. It was over in the afternoon when he came back, and what was our joy to hear behind him the trampling of a pair of hardy ponies, for with the weariness of her terrible quest and the stress of the night in the Cave of Death, Marjorie looked dismally near to her end. And, indeed, I am not sure that Nell was greatly better.

Marjorie had passed some part of the long march in telling us in bits and snatches the tale of her sufferings, her flight and capture, and how by evil and hateful hands she had been flung into the water from off the Heuch of Benerard.

It was a tale of most tyrannous wrong, and shall be kept for its own place, when Marjorie came to tell it to a greater and more powerful than either Launcelot Kennedy or Dominie Mure of Maybole.

I shall, therefore, let the reader wait yet a brief space for the explanation of many things which are dark to him now, and which had been equally dark to me till that gusty, rain-plashing morning.

So we four fared northward over the moors of Carrick, with Marjorie and Nell riding upon the garrons, and the Dominie and myself hasting along by their side with a hand apiece in their stirrup-leathers. We were just by the edge of the Red Moss, and going straight and snell for my Lord Earl's house of Cassillis, when Nell, who was ever our most keen-eyed watcher, cried out that we were pursued. And when I had turned me about and looked, I saw that of a surety it was so.

Then I thought that if it should happen that we were attacked, it might be as well to have the advantage of position. So I posted our party on a little heathery mound, having an open lairy moss in front with dangerous quags, trembling bogs, and square black islands of moss and peat standing in the midst, all gashed and riven. Here we waited, the two men of us under arms in front, and the maids standing close behind the horses, with the bridles loose in their hands.

I had cast my cloak over the shoulder of Nell's sheltie to clear my arms for the fray, if indeed it should come to the clash of blows; and it pleased me well to see her catch it without a word, and fold it like a wife who watches her husband and is pleased to anticipate his need. This indeed (I say it twice) pleased me well, for I knew that she had done with daffing with me any more, and that she had at last forgotten all the matters concerning that pretty tell-tale Kate Allison.

The three men who rode toward us were at first to our sight like ships low down on the sea-line. But they mounted steadily, spears and pennons first, after that the shine of armour, and then the heads of their horses, becking and bowing with the travail of the moss.

Then verily we that stood had anxious hearts, for we knew not whether they might chance to be friend or foe, and, indeed, it was well that we looked for the worst. As they came nearer we saw that the two who rode ahead were armed in a knightly way, and gripped lances in their hands. But the third, who came behind and held a little aloof, was plainly clad in a grey cloak and hat.

'It is Auchendrayne and a younger man, with the Wolf of Drummurchie in their company; it could not well be worse,'' said the Dominie. 'We are like to be hard bested.'

And I knew that Marjorie Kennedy looked once more upon the man who, in cold blood, had slain her father, and also upon the man who according to the law, was her husband.

I had looked for them to call a parley, and had set myself in front to acquit me well in the barter of words before the damsels; but I was not prepared for the event as it happened.

For without a word of preamble, warning or speech-making, John Mure of Auchendrayne (he in the cloak of grey) cried out, 'Have at them! Slay them everyone!' Tis now too late for whimsies. It is our lives for theirs if we do not.'

So with that the two younger men-at-arms came on, couching their long lances and riding directly at us. I stuck my sword downward by the point, naked in the soft moss at my side, so that I should not have it to draw out of my sheath when it came to the pinch. And for the last time I looked at my pistol priming, and longed horribly for one of my lord's new hackbutts of the French pattern out of the armoury of Cassillis.

But wishing would not bring them or I had had a dozen, each with a good Culzean man behind it, with his finger on the touch. But yet you may depend that my imagination bodied them forth, standing there useless in the press, oiled and burnished, as I had seen them. And all the while the two villains came on.

Now, in a plain place we had had but little chance to stand against them, cumbered with the women as we were; but the peat hag I had chosen for our defence on the edge of the Red Moss favoured us. When, however, I had fired my pistol and made nothing of it, save only the clink of the bullet whizzing off the plate metal, they got time to ride round the main obstruction. Then it had gone hard with us indeed, but that the Dominie Mure, as the horses came forward, blew so sudden a snorting blast upon his pipes, that one of the steeds swerved and stumbled, almost throwing his rider to the ground. Then, ere, he had time to recover the Dominie was upon him with his sword, springing upward and striking like an angry etter-cap ever at the face, so that it took the horseman all his time to defend himself.

The other drave at me full tilt with his long spear, and though I leapt aside from the lance-thrust, I, with only my pistol and sword, had been no better than a dead man at the next turn. But Marjorie Kennedy, giving the bridle reins of both horses to her sister, seized the Dominie's Lochaber axe. She sprang behind the visored man, and, hooking the bent prong in his gorget collar behind, she pulled him down from his horse with a clash of armour. Then, after that, there remained nothing for me to do, but to set my sword to his throat and bid him yield himself.

By this time the frightened horse which had stumbled

first became perfectly mad, and turning in spite of all that Thomas Drummurchie could do, it galloped away with him belly-to-earth, across the Red Moss.

Then the man in the grey cloak also put his horse to its speed, so soon as he saw how the matter was like to go. For he had kept at a distance and taken no part in the fighting. We were therefore left alone, victorious, without a wound, and with the man in the visor, our prisoner.

He seemed to be stunned with his fall, so Marjorie stooped and undid his laced steel-cap, shelling his head as one shells the husk of a nut from the kernel.

The man whom she revealed was James Mure the younger of Auchendrayne, her wedded husband.

We stood thus some time in wonderment what should be the upshot. Marjorie Kennedy (I cannot while I live call her by any other name) stood looking down at the man to whom in foulest treachery she had been given. Then after a while Nell touched my arm, and lo! on the Moss, there was yet another man on horseback coming towards us. I knew the beast. It was the same on which the Wolf of Drummurchie had ridden. But the man was other than the Wolf.

The thing was a mystery to us.

But at last Nell, whose eyes were like an eagle's for keenness—though, as I have before observed, of heavenly beauty cried out, 'It is Robert Harburgh—we are saved!' Which was no great thing of a saying, for I myself had saved her ten times during that last night and day, if it came to any talk of saving. Yet I think from that moment she began to draw away a little from me. Whether as remembering some of my old ploys with that tricksy lass who was now Robert Harburgh's wife, or partly lest she should have seemed to be over-ready in owning her love for me.

At any rate, after I had thought over her unkindness and sudden chill a little while, I was not sure that it might not be after all the best sign in the world. For as the reader of this chronicle must have gathered, I am a man of some penetration in these matters, and it is not given to any woman to twine Launcelot Kennedy in a knot about her little finger.

Also I have had very considerable experience.

'Faith,' cried Robert Harburgh, when he had ridden up, 'whom have we here?'

I answered him with another question.

'Where gat ye that horse, Robert?'

'I got it,' he replied, readily and also calmly, 'from a man that is little likely to need it again, at least for a tale of months.'

'From Thomas of Drummurchie?' I asked.

'Who else?' said Harburgh, simply, as though the fact had been sufficient explanation; as, indeed, it was—in the way he said it.

But all the while Marjorie stood looking calmly down at James Mure. He recovered little by little from the stunning knock, and presently made as if he would sit up.

'Tie his hands,' said Marjorie Kennedy. And then seeing that we hesitated—'nay, give me the halter,' she said, 'I will do it myself.' And there on the open moor, with the bridle of his own beast, I declare she did the binding featly and well.

'Now listen, James Mure,' she said, raising her voice, 'ye have steeped your hands in my father's blood. Ye have shed yet more blood to cover that crime, even the blood of an innocent young child. With these hands that are tied, you did these things. I am your wife. I will never leave you nor forsake you till you die. I will see that you have fair and honourable trial; but be assured that I shall testify against you truly as to that which I know and have seen.'

She turned to us with her old easy way of command, imperiously gracious, but sharper a little than her ordinary. 'Mount him on that horse,' she said, like a queen who issues commands to her court.

And this was she who had walked gladsomely with me in the garden at Culzean, and who in smiling maidenly condescension had given a love-sick boy her favour to wear. What agony of hell had passed over her spirit thus to turn the sweet maiden to a woman of stone?

'Whither shall we take him?' said I, for it seemed to me not at all expedient to delay longer than we could help in that disturbed and fatal part of the country.

'To the Earl, on his way to the King!' replied Marjorie Kennedy.

'If ye bide still half-an-hour where ye are, ye will see the Earl come hither,' said Robert Harburgh. 'He rides to the south to hold his yearly Court of Bailiary on the borders of Carrick.'

For since the great defeat of the Bargany faction, and the death of the young chief at the gate of Maybole upon that memorable day of snow, my Lord Cassillis had gained more and more in power, so that none now was able to make any head openly against him. The death of Sir Thomas, my good master, had also thrown all that additional weight of authority upon his shoulders. Indeed Earl John bode fair to be what his father had been before him—the King of Carrick.

His titular jurisdiction had always included the southern parts of the district. But it was only of late that he had made himself so strong as to be able to enforce his authority there.

Now, however, Earl John was riding to hold his Court near Girvan, in a country which not a great while ago had been purely a stronghold of his enemies, and which still swarmed with the disaffected and rebellious.

So even while we stood and waited there, Nell cried out that a cavalcade rode southward toward us by the edge of the Red Moss. It was not long before we could discern the fluttering pennons of blue and gold, which denoted the presence of the Earl. He had with him a noble retinue of well-night four hundred—all handsomely armed—many of them knights and gentlemen of his own name.

We waited for them to come up with us, I meanwhile keeping close by Nell's side, and Marjorie Kennedy standing steadfastly at her husband's head and looking at him, while Robert Harburgh marched up and down with his hands under his points and whistled the 'Broom o' the Cowden-knowes.'

When the Earl John, riding first as was his custom, perceived who we were, he lighted down with much courtesy to salute his cousins.

'How do you, ladies? And what, by the grace of God, brings you hither with so small a company in such a dangerous place?''

Then said Marjorie, 'Earl of Cassillis, you are my cousin; but you are also Bailzie of Carrick and hold the power of life and death. I take you and all your company to witness that I deliver over to you this man, called James Mure of Auchendrayne. He is twice a convict murderer—

right cruelly he slew my father and your uncle, and I charge him also with the fact of the murder of William Dalrymple, a poor boy of tender years, whom he killed with his own hands to cover the first deed—both which accusations I shall in due time make good.'

The Earl was manifestly mightily astonished, as well he might be, at the Lady Marjorie's declaration; but he was glad also, because it was no light thing for him to lay the enemy of his house by the heels, and, seeing good prospect of getting the Mures attainted and denounced to be able to make himself omnipotent in all the lands of the south.

'Bring the man along with us!' he commanded. 'Let him have all tendance and care; but let a double guard be placed over him.'

'I will be his guard!' said Marjorie, firmly. 'I, and no other!'

Nevertheless, Earl John named a retinue to ride with Marjorie and her husband, in the name of a guard of honour; but really because he felt his fingers already on the throat of his house's enemy.

And as we rode back the way we had come—now no longer in fear and trembling, but in manifest state and pomp—Marjorie sate humbly upon a sheltie by the side of the man who was lawfully her husband, and yet whom she had most sacredly vowed to bring to the gallows.

And for the present the Dominie and I resolved to keep the secret of the Cave of Death, and of the fearsome inner place where was bestowed the Treasure of Kelwood.

But immediately after the Court of Justicaire I resolved to make it known to the Earl, for so Nell and I had made our compact. And as for the Dominie he might be relied upon to speak or to be silent even as I bade him.

CHAPTER XLIII

THE MOOT HILL OF GIRVAN

As may well be imagined, two hundred gentlemen with their retinue of as many more of the commonalty made a gallant stir, and required almost the providing of an army. So that as we went southward the people were well warned to repair to the Court of my Lord Bailzie of Car·ick, for the

office of Earl John was the greatest of the Lowland heredi-
tary jurisdictions. Though the house of Cassillis has never
been so beloved of the people nor yet so careful of their
rights as that of the Agnews of Lochnaw, who from very
ancient times have been Sheriffs of Galloway.

Nevertheless, it was a right solemn gathering which
assembled on the little hill outside the town of Girvan,
where such feudal courts had always been held. Within the
enclosure, formed by the fluttering blue and gold pennons
of the Earl, there was set a high seat for Cassillis himself. In
front of him, at a draped table, sat his adviser and assessor,
Lawyer Boyd of Penkill, while all round the gentlemen of his
house and name sat or stood according to their degree, just
outside the line of pennons, within which none might come
save the accused and they who gave their evidence.

Then the trumpeter from the summit of the Moot Hill
of Girvan made proclamation with three blasts of his
horn that the session was open, and that all men's causes
were to be brought to the probation.

First there came sundry usual complaints of stouthreif
and oppression, for the country was yet very unsettled. A
woman cried for vengeance on Thomas of Drummurchie,
called the Wolf, for the carrying off of her daughter. But
as Drummurchie was already ten times attainted, it seemed
as though little would come of it.

But Robert Harburgh strode forward and cried out,
'By your leave, Earl of Cassillis, the Wolf of Drummurchie will carry off no more tender lambs, neither mell
with other men's wives any more. The dainty ladies of Ayr
need no more draw their purses to rescue him, neither to pro-
vide him with costly gear. For he has gone to a country where
he shall be keeped bien and warm, beiking forever fornent
the hottest fires of Satan, so lately his master here on earth!'

And with that he threw the arms and accountrement of
the Wolf on the green with prodigious clatterment.

'But this,' said the Earl John, 'though greatly creditable
to our squire and of excellent omen for the peace of Carrick
from this day forth, gives not this poor woman again her
daughter.'

For he did not wish to assign any reward to Robert
Harburgh besides the lands which had already been given

him, perhaps desiring to retain so valiant a sworder near to his own person and estate.

'I had been to the house of Drummurchie ere I settled accounts with the Wolf himself,' replied Robert Harburgh, in the same manner of exceeding quiet, 'and there have I set all things in order, sending every man's daughter to her father's house and every man's wife back to his keeping.'

'Retaining none for yourself!" cried Earl John, for daffing's sake. For that was his idea of a jest.

'Whatever my desires, I have married a wife that sees to that—even as hath also my Lord Earl!' quoth Robert Harburgh.

And so the laugh was turned against the Earl John, because all knew how carefully the ancient Countess kept the valleys about Cassillis and the Inch clear of buxom dames and over-complacent maids. For, in his youth, Earl John had the name of being both generally and most subtly amorous.

Yet, strange to say, the jest thus broken at his expense, put the Earl into a good key, for it was only the outlay of money that he grudged. So he cried out, 'Robert Harburgh, your tongue can be as sharp as your rapier. You have rid us of a great curse here in the south, and there is muckle need in these parts of such a sword and such a tongue as yours to keep the landward oafs in civility. You shall have the lands of Drummurchie, with ten men's fighting charges to hold them against all evil folk till such time as the land be quiet.'

And Robert Harburgh bowed low to his lord and retired. As he went I clapped him on the back, and said, 'Robert, I would that my long sword had done as muckle for me.'

"Steady on the hilt! Keep your point low, your tongue silent, and it shall do more!' he answered over his shoulder as he went by.

Then was brought forward James Mure of Auchndrayne, clad only in the suit of russet leather which he had worn under the mail wherein he had been taken. He was ever a hang-dog, ill-favoured oaf, and now looked sullenly and silently upon the ground.

His names and titles were first declared.

'Who accuses this man, and of what?' cried Earl John in loud tones.

And every man in the assembly moved a little, as
though he itched to be the accuser himself. But since there
was none that directly knew of our adventure no one
stood forth save our Marjorie and Nell, till I myself stepped forth with them, with Robert Harburgh and the Dominie
a little behind us.

'Now speak out,' whispered Harburgh of the Long Sword
to me, 'and let your nimble wit win you a wife.'

And I looked at Nell, and resolved that if she slipped
through my fingers, it should not be the fault of my lack
of address.

'Who accuses this man?' cried the herald, taking the
word from his master, for the Lords of Carrick and Cassillis
were beyond the paltry fashion of pursuivants.

'I do!' said Marjorie Kennedy, and all men set their
eyes on her. Neither, so long as the case lasted, did they
withdraw their eyes from her face. Then she opened her
mouth and spoke firmly and sternly her accusation.

'I, Marjorie, daughter of the Tutor of Cassillis, in law
wife to this man, charge James Mure the younger of
Auchendrayne with the murder of my father, committed, as
all men know, upon the sandhills of Ayr. I also accuse him of
the murder of William Dalrymple, the lad who carried the
message to Auchendrayne concerning my father's journey.'

'Cousin,' said Earl John, 'you have doubtless abundant
proof to support these strange charges?'

Marjorie Kennedy stood up among us, tall like a lily
flower, and she held her head erect.

'Hear you, John of Cassillis, and all men,' she said. 'I will
tell my tale. Of my own griefs I will say naught, for in no
realm do a woman's heart-breakings count for a docken's
value. It is enough that my father in the simplicity of his
heart gave me to this man, as an innocent sacrifice is cast to a
monster to appease his ravening. These many months I
dwelt in this man's castle. I have been prisoned, starved,
tortured—yet all the Mures in Auchendrayne could neither
prevail to break my resolve, nor yet could they close my
mouth concerning the things which I saw.

'And now I, that am no more bound to this man than
I was when he took me out of my father's house of Culzean
—I, who have never looked upon him that is my wedded

husband save with eyes of hatred, never lain by his side, stand here to denounce James Mure and his father for black, cruel, repeated, defenceless MURDER!'

CHAPTER XLIV

THE MURDER UPON THE BEACH

MARJORIE KENNEDY rang out the last words like a trumpet. Not even the Earl's herald could have been heard further.

'All men hear my tale before they judge,' she went on. 'It was the morn before my father's death-day. From my window in the house of Auchendrayne I had seen this man and his father, with Thomas of Drummurchie and Walter of Cloncaird, come and go all day with trappings and harness, because they knew that the time was nigh at hand for my father's riding to Edinburgh. It chanced that I was looking down through the bars of my prison-house, for there was little else to do in the house of Auchendrayne. It was about eleven of the clock when I saw a young lad, dusty from head to foot, venture a little way within the castle yett and stand as one that looks about him, not knowing where to turn. The court was void and silent, and the lad seemed distressed. But while he thus stood James Mure and his father came down the turnpike stair and stepped, talking whisperingly together, out into the flagged court.

'It was John Mure the elder who first saw the lad and called him. I saw the boy put a letter into his hand, the which he opened carefully and read, passing it to his son, who read also. Then James Mure stepped back and called Thomas of Drummurchie and Cloncaird. They came both of them, and the four bent their heads together over the writing.

'Then in a little John Mure closed the letter again as it had been and gave it with certain charges to the boy.'

'Saw you that letter or knew you aught of its contents?' asked the Earl John.

'Nay,' said Marjorie Kennedy, 'my window was too far from them, and they spoke low and with privity among themselves.'

Then was my time.

'My Lord Bailzie of Carrick,' said I, 'may it please you it was I, Launcelot Kennedy of Kirrieoch, some time squire to Sir Thomas of Culzean, who sent that letter. I sent it from Maybole by the hands of William Dalrymple, the lad whom the Lady Marjorie saw come within the castle yett of Auchendrayne.'

The Dominie stood forward.

'And it was I, Robert Mure, schoolmaster in the town of Maybole, who wrote that letter. I wrote it as Launcelot Kennedy set me the words, for he is a man readier with the sword than the pen, though he hath some small skill even of that. But that day he was hot upon his game of golf (which I hold to be but a foolish sport which rapidly obscures the senses), so I, having, as is mine office, pen in hand, wrote the letter for him. Also I sent one William Dalrymple, called for a nickname Willie of the Gleg-foot, with it to John Mure at his house of Auchendrayne. I bear witness that after a space this boy came back, with the story that he had found John Mure from home. But when we charged it upon him that the letter had been thumbed and opened, he grew confused and confessed that he had been compelled to bring back that message by Mure himself, who had broken the seal and given it again to him, even as the Lady Marjorie has said.'

'And what further proof do you offer of all this?' asked the Earl, bending forward with eagerness to catch the Dominie's words.

The Dominie put his hand into the inner pocket of his coat and pulled out, among various pipe reeds and scraps of writing, a letter which he kept carefully folded in a leathern case by itself.

'There is the thing itself; may it please your lordship to look upon it,' said he, calmly. And as soon as he had said that, the Earl rose eagerly to see the famous missive which had brought about all this turmoil. There was also a stir among the folk that were gathered about, for all strained their eyes as if they could see that which was going on, and read the writing at that distance.

'It is a most notable proof,' said the Earl, 'and so we receive it. But can you not produce the lad William Dalrymple?'

'That can we not,' said the Lady Marjorie; 'but I, and I alone, can tell you all the story of his death—blacker even than the other, because done to a young lad against whom even these cruel murderers could allege no quarrel.'

And again there could be heard the sound of men settling down to deep attention throughout all the crowd at the diet of Justiceaire. And they even crowded in a little past the pennons, so that the heralds had to beat upon the ground with the butts of their halbards, as though to bruise their feet, before they could force them to give back. But James Mure abode stupidlike and sullen before his judge, while his accuser stood not three feet from him and told her story.

'It was just when the bruit of my father's death began to go abroad against the Auchendraynes,' so Marjorie Kennedy again took up her tale, 'and when John Mure the elder began to fear that the matter of the letter would be made manifest, that I again saw the little lad William Dalrymple. One night I observed James Mure leading him rudely by the neck into one of the barred cells which underlie the stables. And to that place with his own hands he carried food and water once every day thereafter.

'Then came to visit John Mure one Sir Robert Montgomery, the Laird of Skelmorlie. And with him they sent the lad, on pretext to be a page at his house of Loch Ranza, which he keeps for the King's hunting lodge on the Isle of Arran. What befell there I cannot tell, but it was not many weeks before William Dalrymple was back again. And this time they sent him (as he told me afterwards) to the Lowlands of Holland, there to serve in the Lord Buccleuch's regiment, which, first as a trumpeter and after as a soldier, he did. Nevertheless, being but young, he wearied easily of the stress and chance of foreign war, and so returned as before.

'Then when, in spite of all, the boy came back, and it was told to John Mure that William Dalrymple was again in his native town, he was neither to hold nor to bind. He neither rested nor slept till he had again brought the lad to his house, where he abode for some weeks, but not so closely shut up as before, so that it was often my chance to see him as he came and went about the court, and even to converse with him. But in a little while he vanished, and from that time I saw him no more.

'Now, the bitterness of my life and my desire to bring

to justice the murderers of my father caused me at last
to quit the house of Auchendrayne. For now I held, as
I thought, the strings which would draw mine enemies
to their doom. So upon a night I had it set to escape, she
that was my maid helping me, with one other that was a
body servant of Auchendrayne's and my tire-woman's lover.

'When I came out I found a pony waiting for me, and
it was my purpose to ride to the house of my kinsman, the
Earl of Cassillis. But, as I journeyed, what was my great
affrightment to come upon a company of two, who rode
some little way before me. I could easily have turned
bridle-rein and ridden another way, but for something
which came into my heart to make me follow on. For in
a trice I recognised the riders to be John Mure and his son,
the father being wrapped in his great cloak of grey, as is
his custom. And by this I knew him.

'So I followed them, but not very near. And because
my beast was a stable companion of their horses, he went
after of his own accord—till, by the first breaking touch of
morn we came to a waste place upon the edge of the sea,
where in a secret dell I dismounted and tied my pony to
a broom-bush which shot out over a sandy hollow.

'Then, yet more secretly, I followed them across the
sandhills, and on the very edge on the links, where the
turf ceases underfoot and there is only sand, John Mure and
his son, this man before you, waited. For a while they
stood listening and talking low together, so that, though
I lay hidden behind a whin which overgrew a little turfy
dell, I could neither hear what was said, nor yet by reason of
the bareness of the sand, dared I to adventure nearer them.

'But they waited not long before one came down to
meet them over the turf, bringing a lad with him. Then,
immediately James Mure whistled a call, and the reply
came back in like manner.

' "You are late, James Bannatyne," I heard John Mure
the elder say; "what has taigled you?"

' "My sea cloth is not so well accustomed to night ploys
as your cloak of grey!" the man growled as he came along
sullenly enough.

'Then the three men of them walked a little apart, and
came in their circuit very near to the hollow where I lay.

While down on the shore the young lad stood and yawned, with his hands in his pockets, like one that shivers and wishes he were back in bed. Nor had he, I am confident, even then any thought of evil.

'But the talk of the three, as I heard it in snatches, was black and bitter.

'The darkest counsel was that of the man who stands here, for James Mure said only, "The dead are no tale-pyets." And again, "We have had enough of this silly, endless, hiding-and-seeking work. Let the earth hide him, or the sea keep him—and be done with it!"

'Now John Mure the elder, and the man whom they called James Bannatyne, seemed at the least inclined to discuss milder councils. Bannatyne was all for sending the lad over to Ireland. And John Mure listened as though he might be persuaded. Yet I knew his guile, for even when he stood with his back to his son, I saw him lift up his hand for a signal. And with that and no more, James Mure rushed at the poor lad and overbore him to the ground. And there upon the sands of the seashore, this James Mure set his knee on the bairnie's breast, and with bloody hands choked and worried him till there was no life left in the lad. And his father also went and held the lad when he fought, his white, reverend beard waggling in the wind, till at last the bairn lay still. But James Banna-tyne stood by and clasped his hands, as the boy tossed and struggled for his dear young life, for I think he was now mainly sorry that he had brought the lad to his death.

'Then I could stand the vileness no longer without protest. So I, Marjorie Kennedy, even though I well knew that they would certainly do the like to me, rose from my hiding-place in the sand-hollow, and cried, "Murderers, cease from your cruel work. God will come and judge you!"

'Whereat John Mure came hastily to where I stood and gripped me. "You have seen all," he said, "then you must die. Let us see if God will come and help you!"

'So I defied them to do their worst with me, for madness had come upon me at the sight of the monstrous cruelty to an innocent bairn. And for the time I cared not what should become of myself.

'Then I called to James Bannatyne requiring of him

to declare if he too were a murderer like the other fiends, and to call upon him to protect the innocent.

'"We will settle all that in the one payment, mistress," said John Mure to me.

'So by force I was compelled to abide with them, John Mure the elder taking me cruelly by the arm, while he sent the others to cast into the sea the dead body of the lad. But even so oft as they threw him in, so often the waves cast him out again upon the shore; and that though there was a strong wind off the land, which blew the tops from the waves and drave the sand in hissing streams into the sea.

'So when for the third time the boy had been tumbled upon the beach, John Mure bade Bannatyne bring his boat, saying that they would cast the loon afloat in the deeps of the bay, so that the outerly wind might drive him to the coast of Ireland. After that they would return betimes to attend to other matters—by which I took him to mean that they would do that for me, which I had so lately seen them do for the young boy. And, indeed, I looked for no other mercy at their brutal hands. So in a little space James Bannatyne brought his boat, and with hard endeavour they launched her, and compelled me to accompany them. There was a strong wind from the east, and we were soon blown far out into the wild sea. There they cast the body of the lad overboard, and turned to make again for the shore. But though they all took oars and laboured in rowing, James Bannatyne taking twain, they could make nothing of it; but were rather worse than they had been before they started.

'So they began to be afraid, and I was right glad thereat, for I looked that the doom of the twice guilty murderers should speedily come. And so the pain of this trial and my witnessing might have been spared.

'Now the Mures were the most fearful of the quick-risen storm, being as it were inland bred. It was all that James Bannatyne could get them to do to sit still.

'"Ye will wreck us all and send us red-hand before our Maker, with the lad's body not cold in the water, and his spirit there to meet us at the Judgment seat!" said he.

'And with that John Mure rose in his place, and in despite of the swaying and plunging of the ship, into which the water came lashing, he cried out, "The Wraith, the Wraith! It is following us—we are doomed!"

'And lo! when I looked, I saw that which chilled me more than the whistling tempest. And if it feared me to the soul, judge ye what it must have been to the guilty men whose hands were yet red with the blood of the innocent.

'For there, not thirty yards behind the boat, and following strongly in our wake, as a stark swimmer might do, now tumbling and leaping in the wash of the seas and now lunging forward like a boat that is towed, was the murdered boy himself. And thus he followed with a smile on his face, or what looked like it in the uncertain light of the morning.

'So with that the men who rowed fell on their faces and could not look any more, though the prodigy followed us a good while. Only John Mure sat wrapped in his grey cloak steering the boat, and I sat beside him. Little by little we came to the land, but as it had been sideways, having been driven by the wind to the other side of the wide bay.

'There we disembarked and the Mures kept me close all that day in a place of strength on the seashore, till it was night. They plied me to promise silence, for they believed that I would keep my word if once I pledged it. They offered me all that they had of honour or place in the country. There was nothing, they said, that was not within the power of their compassing. For since the death of Gilbert of Bargany the King needed someone in Carrick strong enough to count spears with the Earl of Cassillis.

'But very steadfastly I withstood them, declaring that I should certainly reveal all their murder and treachery, both in the matter of the death of my father, and in that which I had seen done upon the sands to the young lad William Dalrymple.

'So finally seeing that they could prevail nothing, they went out and kept silent watch by the door till the even. Then as soon as it was dark they opened the lock and bade me come forth. And this I did, knowing for a certainty that my last hour was come. Yet my life had not been so pleasant to me as to be very greatly precious. So I followed them with no very ill will, nor yet greatly concerned. Then on the craggy top they gave me, for the sake of their house and good name (as they said), one more chance to swear silence. This I would not accept, and they, being startled with the approach of a boat upon the water which steered towards our light, pinioned my arms, and thrusting something into my mouth, forthwith threw me over the cliff into the sea. And as to the mode of my rescuing and standing here before the Earl my cousin, young Launcelot Kennedy, my father's squire, can tell. And also my sister and Robert Mure of Maybole.'

CHAPTER XLV

THE MAN IN THE WIDE BREECHES

SHE ceased suddenly after this long account of her adventuring, and the folk stood still in amazement, having held their breath while she told of the killing of young William Dalrymple and of the Wraith. And then there arose a great cry from all the people,—

'Tear the murderer in pieces—kill him, kill him!' So that Cassillis had to summon men-at-arms to keep back that throng of furious folk, for the death of my master seemed to them but a·little thing and venial, compared to the killing of a lad like William Dalrymple. And this was because the people of Carrick had been used all their days to family feuds and the expiation of blood by blood.

The Earl was about to call me up to give an account of my part in the affair, and I was preparing myself to make a good and creditable appearance—a thing which I have all my life studied to do—when there was heard a mighty crying in the rear of the Bailzie Court. Men cried 'He comes! He comes!' as though it had been some great one. And everybody turned their heads, to the no small annoyance of Earl John, who when on his Hill of Justice loved not that men should look in any other direction than his own.

The ranks of the men-at-arms opened, and there strode into the square of trial, which was guarded by the pennons of blue and gold at the four corners—who but John Mure of Auchendrayne himself, wearing the same cloak of grey and broad plumed hat which had been his wont when he went abroad upon dangerous quests! With him was another shorter man, whose face was for the time being

almost hidden, for he had pulled the cloak he was wearing
close about his mouth. He walked with an odd jolt or
roll in his gait, and his breeches were exceedingly broad
in the basement.

It was small wonder that we stood aghast at this sudden
compearing of the arch criminal, whose misdeeds throughout all the countryside had filled the cup of his wickedness
to the brim.

'Seize him!' cried the Earl, pointing directly at John Mure.

And his Bailzie's men took him roughly by the shoulders
and set him beside his son. Then it was to be noticed, as
the two stood together, that there was a great likeness
between father and son. The elder man possessed the same
features without any evident differences in outline. But so
informed was his face with intelligence and power, that
what was simply dull cruelty and loutishness in the one
became the guile of statecraft in the other.

'Wherefore, my Lord Earl,' cried John Mure of Auchendrayne, 'is this violence done to me and to the heir of my
house? I demand to know concerning what we are called
in question and by whom?'

Then the Earl of Cassillis answered him,—

'John Mure of Auchendrayne, know then that you are
charged, along with this your son, with the bloody murder
of Sir Thomas Kennedy of Culzean, Tutor of Cassillis; and
also with the cruel death of William Dalrymple, the young
lad who brought you the message to your own house of
Auchendrayne, telling at what hour the Tutor should pass
the trysting place, where he was by you and yours foully
assaulted and slain.'

'And who declares these things?' cried Mure, boldly,
with a bearing more like that of an innocent man than
that of any criminal that ever I saw.

The Earl bade us who had accused them so justly to
stand forth. Then John Mure eyed us with a grave and
amused contempt.

'My son's false wife, whom sorrow has caused to dote
concerning her father's death—her night-raking rantipole
sister, and her paramour, a loutish, land-louping squire—
the Dominie of Maybole, a crippledick and piping merry-
Andrew that travelled with them—these are the accusers

of John Mure of Auchendrayne. They have seen, heard, noted what others have been ignorant of! Nay, rather, is it not clear that they have collogued together, conspiring to bear false witness against me and mine—for the sake of the frantic splenetic madness of her who is my son's fugitive wife, whose wrongs exist only in her own imaginings.'

'You have forgotten me!" said Robert Harburgh, quietly, stepping forward.

'I know you well,' said John Mure, 'and I would have remembered you had you been worth remembering. You are my Lord of Cassillis's squire and erstwhile a gay cock-sparrow ruffler, now married to the Grieve's daughter at Culzean.'

'Well,' said Harburgh, 'and what of that? Can a man not be all that and yet tell the truth?'

'That I leave to one who is greater, to judge,' said John Mure.

'And I do judge, John Mure,' cried the Earl, rising in his chair of state. 'I judge you to be a man rebel and mansworn, a traitor and a man-slayer. For a score of years ye have keeped all this realm of Carrick in a turmoil, you and they that have partaken with you in your evil deeds.'

'Loud, swelling words are but wind, my lord Earl of Cassillis,' answered Mure of Auchendrayne, a dry smile of contempt coming over his features.

'Now I will show thee, bold ill-doer,' said the Earl, fiercely, 'whether I speak the words of a dotard or no. Forward, men, take him up and bind him. Methinks we have yet engines within the castle of Dunure that can make him declare the rights of this murderous treason!'

Then I rejoiced, not for the torture of our enemy, but because at last the Earl saw fully with our eyes, and would right us against the cruel oppressor of Marjorie Kennedy, and for the murder of my gentle and courteous master.

But ere the men could carry out the orders of the Earl, the broad-breeched man who had accompanied Auchendrayne, and who had all the while stood still and watchful, dropped his plaid, which like a mask he had held beneath his eyes. He was a middle-sized, fleshy man, with no great dignity of face, and with a weak mouth that dribbled perpetually at the side as if the tongue were too large for it. He wore a slashed doublet very full at the sleeves, baggy trunks, and a sword in a plain scabbard hanging at his side. I saw nothing further very particular about the man save the shambling inward bend of his knees.

But it was with dumb amaze that the Earl looked at him, standing there arrested in the act of pointing with his hand at John Mure. He stood with his jaw fallen, and his eyes starting from his head.

'The King! the King!' he muttered in astonishment, looking about him like one distracted.

'Ay, Baron Bailzie of Carrick, even your King,' said the man in the wide trunk hosen, 'come to see how his some-time High Treasurer of Scotland executes just judgment in his own regality!'

The Earl came quickly to himself, and he and all the people took off their hats. He stepped down and made his obeisance to the King, bending humbly upon his knee. Then he ushered the King to the throne whereon he himself had been sitting, and took a lower seat beside Adam Boyd of Penkill, his accessor in ordinary.

The King rose to speak.

'My Lord Earl and gentlemen of Carrick,' he said, with dignity enough, but with a thick and rolling accent as if his tongue had been indeed too big, 'I know this case to the bottom. I am fully persuaded of the innocence of our trusty councillor, John Mure of Auchendrayne—who is besides of the fraternity of learned men, and one that hath a history of this realm in script ready for the printers, wherein he does full justice both to myself and to my noble predecessors. He hath, as I should nominate it, an exactness of expression and a perspicuity of argument that have never been matched in the land. I propose shortly to make him my historiographer royal. Also I, the King, do know him to be a man well affected to the right ecclesiastical ruling of this kingdom, and minded to help me with the due ordering of it.'

The King puffed and blew after his speech, and we and all that were there stood silent, for to most of us he might as well have spoken in the Hebrew of which he boasted himself so great a master. Then he went on:—

'I have left my Lord Mar and my retinue some way in

the rear. For we go to hunt the deer in whatever forest the goodwill of our loyal subjects may put at our disposal.'

'You are right welcome, my liege,' said the Earl John, starting up and standing bareheaded, 'to my hunting lodges and retinue, both in the Forest of Buchan and also at my house of Cassillis.'

The King bent towards him royally, for James the Sixth had manners when he liked to show them—which, in truth, was not always.

'I thank you, trusty councillor,' said he; 'it is nobly and generously done—qualities which also marked your all-too-brief tenure of the office of High Treasurer of Scotland. But for the judging of this our worthy subject, I propose to take that upon myself, being wholly persuaded of his innocence. And as for those that have falsely accused him, let the men underlie my will in the prison most convenient, and the women be warded meantime in their own house and castle, till I cause to be known my whole pleasure in the matter.'

We stood aghast, and knew not what to say, so completely had Auchendrayne turned our flank with the King. Not a word had we found to allege when the officers of the court, to whom the charge was given, came to put the iron rings on our wrists and march us off, even as we had hoped and expected to see Auchendrayne and his son taken.

And as the Dominie and I were haled away we could see Auchendrayne bending suavely over the King's high seat, and His Majesty inclining to him and talking privately back and forth, with many becks and uncouth graces such as he had used in his address to the Earl and his people.

'He is the very devil himself,' said the Dominie, meaning Auchendrayne and not the King; 'he hath not halted to cozen the greatest man in this realm with his lying tongue!'

But I said nothing, for what had I to say? I had seen lands, honours, love, and consideration vanish at a stroke.

CHAPTER XLVI

THE JUDGMENT OF GOD

THE court of the Baron Bailzie of Carrick broke up in confusion. It had been arranged that we should ride all together to the north, even to Culzean, where His Majesty might have due entertainment provided for him nearer than at my lord's castle of Cassillis. Also it was upon this shore-side road that he had left the Earl of Mar and the favourite attendants with whom James the Sixth ordinarily sallied forth to the hunting.

Those of the Auchendrayne and Bargany party who hated us, clamoured that the Dominie and I should be left warded in the lock-fast place of Girvan, where our enemies would soon have ta'en their will of us. But Robert Harburgh moved my lord, who went about dour and heart-sick for the failure of his plans in the matter of the Mures, to have us brought on, with purpose to lodge us within the ancient strengths of Dunure.

So that as I rode hand-tied at the tail of the King's retinue, I was yet near enough to have sight of Marjorie and Nell who rode before us. And this was some comfort to my heart.

The way lay for miles along the seashore, which is here sandy, with a broad belt of fine hard beach whereon the horses went daintily and well, while at our left elbows the sea murmured.

The King and John Mure rode first, and His Majesty constantly broke into loud mirth at some witty saying of his companion's. Level with them, but riding moodily apart, was the Earl, while James Mure the younger rode alone by himself behind these three.

I groaned within me for the exaltation of our enemy and at the shortsightedness of anointed kings.

'Is there a God in heaven,' I cried aloud, 'thus to make no sign, while the devil is driving all things headlong to destruction according to his own devising?'

There was a God in heaven.

For, quick as an echo that answers from the wood, there before us upon the sands, just where the levels had been overflowed at the last tide, lay a thing which halted the advancing cavalcade as suddenly as an army with banners. The men crowded about, and, having in the excitement forgotten us their charges, we also were per-mitted to look. And this is what we saw.

There upon the ribbed sea sand lay the dead body of the boy William Dalrymple. I knew him at a glance, for all

that so much had come and gone since that day when I
played at the golf game upon the green of Maybole. He
lay with his arms stretched away from his sides, his face
turned over, and one cheek dented deeply into the sand. It
was a pitiful sight. Yet the lad was not greatly altered—
wind-tossed and wave-borne as he had been, and now
brought to cross the path of the unjust at the very nick
of time, by the manifest judgment and providence of God.

'What means this?' said the King. 'Some poor
drowned sailor boy. Let us avoid!' For of all things
he loved not gruesome sights nor the colour of blood. But
James Mure suddenly cried aloud at the vision, as if he
had been stricken with pain. And as he did so, his father
looked at him as though he would have slain him, so
devilish was his glance of hate and contempt.

But a woman who had coming running hot-foot after
the party, now rushed to the front. She gave a loud
scream, ear-piercing and frantic, when she saw the tossed
little body lying all abroad upon the sand.

'My Willie, my ain son Willie!' she cried. For it was
Meg Dalrymple. All her ignorant rudeness seemed to fade
away in the presence of death, and as she lifted the poor
mishandled head that had been her son's, each of us felt
that she grew akin to our own mothers, widowed and
bereaved. For I think that which touches us most in the
grief of a widow, is not our feeling for a particular woman,
but our obligation to the mother of all flesh.

So when Meg Dalrymple lifted her son's head, it might
have been a mourning queen with a dead kingling upon her
knee.

'My ain, my ain lad!' she cried. 'See, lammie, but I
loved ye. Ye were the widow's ae son. Fleeter-footed than
the mountain roe, mair gleg than the falcon that sits yonder
on the King's wrist, ye were the hope o' thy mither's life.
And they hae slain ye, killed my bonny wean, that never
did harm to nae man—'

She undid a kerchief from about the white, swollen neck
of her son.

'Kens ony man that image and superscription?' said she,
pointing to an embroidered crest upon it. John Mure
strode forward hastily. He had grown as pale as death.

'Give it me. I will pass it to His Majesty,' he said, holding out his hand for it.

But the woman leaped up fiercely.

'Na,' she said; 'the butcher kens his knife; but he would only hide it in the day of trial. I will give it to my ain well-kenned lord.

And she put the napkin into the hands of the Earl of Cassillis, who looked at it with the most minute attention.

'This kerchief,' said the Earl, gravely, 'has the crest and motto of John Mure of Auchendrayne.'

The King looked staggered and bewildered.

'Let all dismount till we try further of this thing,' he said.

But John Mure would have had him go on, saying that it was yet more of the plot. But the King would not now hearken to him; for he was an obstinate man, and oftentime he would listen to no reason, though his ear was ever open enough to flattery. Besides, he thought himself to be the wisest man in all the islands and kingdoms of the world—wiser, even, than Solomon the son of David.

So His Majesty commanded his inclination, and went up to the body. There was also a rope around the neck with a long end, which was embedded in the sand. With his own hand the King drew this out.

He held it up.

'Kens any man this length of rope?' he asked, looking about.

Now, one strand of sea-cordage is like another as two peas; but this was our Solomon's way of judging—to find out the insignificant, and then pretend that it told him a mighty deal.

Yet it so happened that there was a man there from out of the shore side of Girvan. He was a coastwise sailor, and he took the rope in his hand.

'This rope,' he said, turning it about every way, 'is Irish made, and has been used to tie bundles of neat hides.'

'And who,' again asked the King—shrewdly, as I do admit, 'who upon this coast trades with Ireland in the commodity of neat hides?'

'There are but myself and James Bannatyne of Chapeldonnan,' replied the man, honestly and promptly.

'And this is not your rope?' said the King.

'Nay,' said the man, 'I would not buy a pennyworth of Irish hemp so long as I could twine the hemp of Scotland— no, not even to hang an Irishman would I do it. This is James Bannantyne's rope!'

Then said the King, 'Bring hither James of Chapeldonnan!'

And they brought him. He stood forth, much feared indeed, but taking the matter dourly, like the burly ruffian he was. Nevertheless when put to question he denied the rope, and that in spite of all threats of torture. Yet I could see that the King was greatly shaken in his opinion, and knew not what to think. For when John Mure drew near to touch his arm and as before say somewhat in his private ear, the King drew hastily away and looked at Auchendrayne's hand as though there had been pollution upon it. So I knew that his opinion was wavering. Also the poor body in the mother's arms daunted him.

Suddenly he clapped his hands together and became exceedingly joyous and alert.

'I have it,' he cried, 'the ordeal of touch. It is God's ordinary and manifest way of vindicating His justice. Here is the dead body of the slain. Here are all the accused and the accusers. Let it be equally done. Let all touch the body, for the revealing of the secrets of the hearts wicked men.'

Then John Mure laughed and scoffed, saying that it was but a freit, a foolish opinion, an old wives' fable.

But for all his quirksome guile he had gotten this time very mightily on the wrong side of the King. For His Majesty was just mad with belief in such things as omens and miracles of God's providence. So the King shook him off and said, 'It is my royal will, that all who are tainted with the matter shall immediately touch or be held guilty.'

And the sayings comforted King James, being, as it were, easily pleased with his own words and plaiks.

So they brought us forward from amongst the crowd bound as we were, and first of all I touched fearlessly the poor dead body of the lad. Yet it was with some strange feeling, though I knew well that I was wholly innocent. But yet I could not forget that something untoward might happen, and then good-bye to this fair world and all the pleasant stir of life within it.

Then after me the Dominie touched—even Marjorie and Nell doing it with set faces and strange eyes.

It was now the turns of the real murderers, and my heart beat little and fast to see what should happen.

'Let Auchendrayne the younger touch first, being the more directly accused!' cried the King.

But James Mure seemed to flame out suddenly distract, like a madman being taken to Bethlem. He cried out, 'No, no, I will not touch. I declare that I will not go near him!'

And when John Mure stove to persuade him to it, he struck at him fiercely with his open hand, leaving the stead of his fingers dead white upon his father's cheek. And when they took his arm and would have forced him to it, he threw himself down headlong in the sand, foaming and crying. "I will not touch for blood! I will not touch for blood!'

But in spite of his struggling they carried him to where the body lay. And, all men standing back, they thrust his bare hand sharply upon the neck where the rope had been.

And, it is true as Scripture, I that write declare (though I cannot explain) it, out from the open mouth of the lad there sprang a gout of black and oozy blood.

Whereat a great cry went up and James Mure fell forward on the sand as one suddenly stricken dead. All crowded forward to see, crying with one voice, 'The Judgment of God! The Judgment of God!'

And I shouted too, for I had seen the vindication of justice upon the murdered. The blood of Abel had cried out of the waste sea sand. The mark of God was on the guilty.

Then suddenly in the midst of the push I heard a stirring and a shouting.

'Stop him! stop him!' they cried.

I looked about, and lo! there, sitting erect upon his horse and riding like fire among heather, was John Mure. He had stolen away while all eyes were on the marvel. He had passed unregarded through the press, and now he rode for his life southward along the shore.

I gave one mighty twist to the manacles on my wrists, and whether those that set them had been kindly, being of my own name and clan, or whether the gyves were weak, I cannot tell. At all events, my hands were free, and so, with never a weapon in my possession, I leaped on a horse

—the same, indeed, which the King had been riding—and set it to the gallop after the man whose death was my life.

It was the maddest, foolishest venture, for doubtless my enemy was well armed. But I seemed to see my love, and all the endowment of grace and favour I was to receive with her, vanishing away with every stride of John Mure's horse. Besides, there was a King and an Earl looking on; so upon the King's horse I settled down to a long chase.

I was already far forward ere behind me I heard the clatter of mounting men, the crying to restive horses to stand still, and the other accompaniments of a cavalcade leaping hastily into the saddle. But when I looked at John Mure upon his fleet steed, and saw that I upon the King's horse but scarcely held mine own, I knew that the stopping of the murderer must be work of mine, if it were to be done at all. So I resolved to chance it, in spite of whatever armoury of weapons he might carry.

But first I cleared my feet of the stirrups which the King used, so that if it came to the bitter pinch, and I was stricken with a bullet or pierced with steel, I should not be dragged helpless along the ground with my foot in the iron, as once or twice I had seen happen in battle.

And that, though an easily memorable, is, I can bear witness, not a bonny sight.

My charger stretched away as though he had been a beagle running conies of the down into their holes. But John Mure's horse went every whit as fast. I saw well that he made for the deep, trackless spaces of Killochan wood. The oak trees that grew along its edge stretched out their arms to hide him; the birken shaw waved all its green boughs with a promise of security. I shortened my grip upon the stout golden-crowned staff which the King carried at the pommel of his saddle.

Yet as John Mure drave madly towards the wood, and sometimes looked over his shoulder to see how I came on, I was overjoyed to notice a wide ditch before him which he must needs overleap—and at that business, if at no other, I thought to beat him, being slim and of half his weight.

So I kept my horse to the right upon better ground, though it took me a little out of the straight course for the wood. His horse at the first refused the leap, and I counted upon him as mine. But I counted too soon, for he went down the bankside a short way to an easier place, where there was a landward man's bridge of trees and sods. Here he easily walked his horse across, and, having mounted the bank, he waved his hand at me and set off again toward the wood.

But now while he had an uneven country to overpass I had only the green fields, rich in old pasture and undulating like the waves of an oily tide when the sea is deep, and there is no break of the water. He was at the very edge of the wood before I came upon his flank. Then I gave a loud shout as I set my horse to his speed and circled about to head him off. But John Mure, though an old man, only settled himself firmer in the saddle, and with his sword in his hand rode soldierly and straight at the wood, as though I had not been in front of him at all.

It was wisely enough done, for his heavier beast took mine upon the shoulder and almost rolled me in the dust. He came upon me, not front to front as a rider meets his foe in the lists, but, as it were stem to side, like two boats that meet upon converging tacks.

Yet I managed to avoid him, being light and supple, though he leaned far over and struck savagely at me as he passed. Again at the third shock he had almost overridden me and made me die the death. But I had not practised horsemanship and the art of fighting in the saddle so long for nothing. Indeed, on all the seaboard of Ayr there was no one that could compare with me in these things. Therefore, it was easy for me, by dint of my quickness and skill, to swerve off to the right and receive the sword stroke on my cloak, which I carried twisted about my left arm.

Then keeping still between the wood and John Mure, I met him this time face to face, with my eyes watching the direction of his eye and the crook of his elbow, that I might know where he meant to strike. For a good sworder knows the enemy's intent, and his blade meets it long ere thought can pass into action.

So it was no second-sight which told me that he meant to slash me across the thigh when he came a-nigh me. I knew it or ever his blade was raised. So that when he struck I was ready for him and measured his sword, proving my distance as it had been upon parade. And as the blade whistled by me, I judged that it was my turn, and struck him with all the force I could muster a crashing blow upon the face with the heavy butt of the King's stave, which stunned and unsettled him so that he pitched forward upon his horse, yet not so as to lose his seat.

Nevertheless, owing to the swing of my arm, the stroke fell also partly upon his horse's back, which affrighted the beast and set him harder than ever to the running. So that I was passed ere I knew it, and the wood was won. But I was not thirty yards behind him, and looked to make the capture ere we reached the further side. And but for a foul trick I should have done it. It so happens that there is a little hill in the woods of Killochan, and I, seeing that John Mure was riding about one side, took round the other, thinking that I had the shorter line of it.

But he, so soon as he saw me make round the corner, turned his horse into its own hoof-marks and sped away back again—as it had been to meet them that pursued, but at the same time bearing enough to the south to clear them easily. So that when I came round the hill I saw no quarry, and only heard the boughs crashing in his wake.

Nevertheless, without the loss of a moment, I took the line of his retreat (as I thought), yet not so correctly but that when I issued forth from the wood I saw him nigh half a mile in front. Again he waved a contumelious hand which made me so fiercely angry that I tightened my waist-belt, and vowed to go no more to sunny Culzean if I took not back the head and hands of John Mure at my saddle-bow.

So, with set and determined brow, I rode ever forward. It was the cast of the die for me, for Nell herself, our life together, and our green pastures and lavender-scented napery cupboards were all to come out of the catching of this enemy of our house. It is small wonder therefore that I was passing keen upon the matter.

Yet, in spite of my endeavours, I gained but little. And it was already greying to the twilight when I came to a place by the seashore, waste and solitary, where there were but few houses about. I had seen John Mure ride in thitherwards. And so I followed him full tilt, reckless of danger, being weary-heart with the ill-fortune of my riding and quest.

But as I entered the narrows of the pass, a stone flew

from an ambuscade. I felt a hot, stunning blow upon the head, and with the pain I remember laying hold of my horse's mane and gripping tight with the hand on which a broken manacle still jangled. Something warm flowed over my brow, and suddenly I saw everything red, as though I had been looking through the stained glass of some ancient kirk red— flowers, red grass, red sand, and red sea.

That was all I saw, and I do not remember even falling to the ground.

CHAPTER XLVII

THE PLACE OF THE LEGION OF DEVILS

WHEN I woke it was exceedingly dark, but a darkness with shooting lights and hideous sounds. At the first start I thought that I was dead and in the place of torment. And when I grew a little more awake, I wished to God that I had been. For all about were swart naked men and harpy-clawed women dancing round me, while on a cask or keg at my head sat John Mure himself, wrapped in his cloak and regarding me with gloating, baleful, bloodshot eyes.

Then I knew that I was lost indeed. For by the flickering light of a dying fire of driftwood I could see that I was again in the cave of Sawny Bean, in the same wide hall with the strange narrow hams a-swing on the roof, the tubs of salt meat festering under the eaves, and the wild savage crew dancing about me.

What wonder that my heart fainted within me to be thus left alone in that den of hideous things, and especially to think of the free birds going to their beds on the cliffs above me and the fishing solan geese circling and balancing home to the lonely rock of Ailsa.

'Ha, Sir Launcelot Kennedy,' said a mocking voice, as the deafening turmoil quieted a little, 'you are near your honours now—that is, if there be such bauble dignities either in heaven or hell. The Treasure of Kelwood in hand, John Mure's life out of hand—and there on the shelf (as it were) are your broad acres and your bonny lady!'

I was silent, for I knew that nothing could avail me now. It was useless to waste words.

'But ere all that comes to pass,' he went on, 'there are sundry little formalities to be gone through.—Oh, we

are right dainty folk here in Sawny Bean's mansion.
You shall be kept warm and cherished tenderly. There
are here twenty sonsier queans than the one whose heart
you desire. Warmly shall they welcome, sweetly shall
they cherish handsome Sir Launcelot. Their embracements
shall sting you more than all sweetheartening raptures.'

Again he pauses to observe the effect of his words.

'You that so lately held me in chase, like a steer that
has escaped from the shambles. Now you yourself are in
the thills. You that have crossed me a thousand times
in my plans since that frore night in Sir Thomas Nesbitt's
yard in Maybole, you shall now be crossed in a new fashion.
You that wagged tongue so merrily at another's expense,
you shall see your tongue wag the redhot brander to an
unkenned tune.

'You that have ridden so fast and so far, you shall ride
your last ride—ride slowly, very slowly,' cried the fiend in
my ear, 'for I shall hoard every drop of your blood as
John of Cassillis hoards his gold rose nobles. I shall
husband every minute of your life, as though they were
the hours of young bridal content.

'Ye have bruised my old face indeed with your oaken
staff, but I will cherish yours, that is youthful and bloom-
ing. Tenderly shall we take off the coverture of hide,
the tegument of beauty. Sawny Bean has famous skill
in such surgery. Gently will we lay you down in the
swarming nest of the patient ant. We have read how
Scriptures bids the sluggard go to the ant, for it that makes
him not lively, nothing will. I have ofttimes commented
on the passage at family worship. And I must see that
the young and headstrong, like you, my Lord Launcelot,
give heed to that which is commanded.'

But in spite of all his terrible threatenings, I bode still
and answered him never a word. They laid logs of driftwood upon the fire, till the whole inside of the cave grew
bright and clear; and all the monstrous deformity of the
women and the cruel hideousness of the men were made
apparent as in broad daylight. Some of them were painted
and stained like demons, and danced and leaped through
the fire like them, too. For such monsters have not been
heard of, much less seen, in the history of any country

as were Sawny Bean and his crew in the cave upon the seashore of Bennanbrack.

'Bring me a knife,' cried John Mure from where he sat, for he appeared like a chief devil among a company of gibbering lubber fiends. He had still his grey cloak about him. His plumed hat was upon his head, and he looked, save for the eyes of him in which the fires of hell burned, a civil, respectable, well-put-on man of means and substance. As, indeed, save for his evil heart he might have been, for he came of as good a family as the Earl of Cassillis, or, as it might be, as I myself, Launcelot Kennedy of Kirrieoch.

So when Auchendrayne asked for a knife, Sawny Bean himself, the ruffian kemper, low-browed, buck-toothed, and inhuman, brought it to him with a grin. He made as if he would have set it in me to the hilt. But John Mure stayed him.

'Bide,' he said, 'not so fast. There is long and sweet pleasuring to come before that—such slow, relishing delight, such covetous mouseplay of the brindled cat, such luxurious tiger-licking of the delicate skin till it be raw, such well-conceited dainty torments as when one would bite his love and be glad of it. He shall taste them all, this frolic squire of errant-dames, this gamesome player upon pipes, this curious handler of quaint love tunes. Ere we pluck the red rose of his life, he shall sate himself with new delicious experience—rarer than the handling of many maidens' tresses.'

I was moved to speak to him.

'I ask not mercy,' said I, 'for I own that I would have killed you if I could. But as you are a valiant man, give me a sword and let me make a stand for it against you all, that as I have lived so I may also die fighting.'

But he mocked me, hurrying on his heady turmoil of words.

'"If I be a man," you say—who said that I was a man? Do I act as other men? Is my knowledge like that of other men? Do I company with other men? Call you that a man?' (He pointed to Sawny Bean, who for wantonness sat on an upturned tub, striking with a keen-edged knife at the legs of all that came by for mere delight of blood, storming at them meantime with horrid imprecations to approach nearer and be flicked.) 'Or call you these men? (He showed me some of the younger cannibal race gnawing like kennelled dogs at horrid bones.) 'Nay, my dainty wanton, you shall not enter Hell through the brave brattle of warring blades, nor yet handling your rapier like a morris-dancer. But as the blood drains to the white from the stricken calf, so shall they whiten your flesh for the tooth, and so reluctantly shall your life drip from you drop by drop.'

And I declare that this scornful fiend telling me of tortures in choice words made me scunner more than the prick of the knife. For the abhorred invention quickened the imagination and set the nerves agate.

So that I was honestly glad when he took knife in hand—a shoemaker's curved blade with a keen cutting edge.

'Strip him naked!' he cried. And very cheerfully so they did, smiting me the meantime with the broad of their hand.

Then John Mure leaned over me delicately, and made as though he would have traced with his knife the jointing of my limbs, saying, 'Thus and thus shall the she-tribe dismember your body when the torture of the ant's nest is ended.' And again 'Here is toothsome eating, Sawny Bean, thou chief lover of dainty vivers.'

Then, as the evil man went on with his pitiless jestings, his grey cloak began to waver before me, his face to glow like fire, and I fainted or dwamed away till the sharp knife pricked me into consciousness again.

Yet Auchendrayne overdid his threatening, for the too sharp relish of the words issued in tranced dulness ere the matter came to action. And of torture there was none that I can now remember or bear the mark of—save only the slight scores of the knife which he made when he showed me where they would joint and haggle my body.

Indeed, I mind no more till I came to myself, lying on my back, with the cave all empty save for John Mure—who sat, as before, with his hand to his ear listening.

But there sounded a great and furious uproar down by the cave mouth, the deep baying of bloodhounds, the fierce cry of many voices striving for mastery, and above all the shrieks of the smitten.

Surely, I thought, there is a battle fierce and fell at the cave's mouth. John Mure sat and listened for a long space, and presently he looked over at me.

'I will even make sure of him, come what may,' he said.

And with that he took the knife and came nearer to smite me in the breast, and I lay as one dead already, waiting for the stroke.

But even in that moment as I held my breath a ravening hound darted within the cave, overleaped the embers of the fire, and pinned the grey-haired murderer to the earth by the throat. He struck out desperately, but the dog held him fast. Another and another came in, till, as it seemed, he was in danger of being torn to pieces of dogs.

But me they minded not at all, for (as I say) I lay as one dead.

. . . . .

And this is the story of the chase as Nell told it to me when all was over.

As they of the King's company looked from the shore towards the south, there in the distance was John Mure on his horse disappearing into the wood, and I (as it seemed) at his very heels. Both of us were leaning far forward, like men that run a race. And because she knew that I carried no equipment with me, Nell leaped upon a horse with a sword laid before her crosswise on the saddle.

Whereupon I turned to Nell and called her the bravest maid in broad Scotland, with other names as I could mind them. But she set her head aside, and would content me nothing (though I was minded for kindness), saying only, 'If you do not desire to hear the tale, then I am saved the fash of telling it. 'Tis no time for fooling,' said she, 'when I am speaking of the saving of your life.'

'Nell,' said I (for I was nettled at her indifference), 'thou art an unseasoned lass, skilless in love's mysteries.

'I want none of Kate Allison's love-skilling at second hand,' said Nell, harking back like a pretty shrew on her former taunts. 'Since ye are so wise, unriddle me the manner of your saving from the cave of Sawny Bean, and I am content to yield me to your teaching in the mysteries.'

Yet even with this fair promise I could not, but desired her instead to continue her tale-telling.

'Well,' said she, 'Robert Harburgh it was who, next after me, took horse—and not far behind either. For he had but to disentangle the bridle from his arm, while I had to beguile another to lend me his horse.

'So, in a little, we were all after you, and we took the wood in the very place you entered. But naught could we find save the trail of you all confused among the trees. Then what a chasing hither and thither there followed. Even the King searched for you like any common man, and puffed and blew upon his purple cheeks like the Dominie on his pipes. And he that had been our companion, this same Dominie, went about everywhere, seeking and crying each time that he came near to me, ''Reckless loon, reckless loon, well he deserves to be unbreeched and soundly paid for this hardiness.''

'Then we utterly lost you, and I believe they would have given up the search. But I minded me of the dogs that James of Chapeldonnan keeps for his own purposes, which on my way to Ailsa I had seen his wife feed. So I told the Earl John of them, and he had James Bannatyne brought, and bade him bring them to set on the trail, promising him his life if the matter were brought to a good issue.

'And so Robert Harburgh and a few swords were sent to Chapeldonnan with James Bannatyne—with his life upon it if he played them false, and Robert Harburgh's sword near his ribs each time that he faltered or failed to remember. And the good wife, seeing her man in such deadly case, came back herself to plead with the King for him.

'So the Chapeldonnan pack was laid on the trail, and fine well-hungered blood hounds they were. But so soon as I heard the first deep bay, when, with noses on the ground, they took the line of the shore, it went to my heart that since you were the last to enter the wood the dogs would first seize you. So I cried a word to Robert Harburgh, and we two that loved you spurred horses and sped on well-nigh level with the dogs.

'And through all the windings and wimplings of you path we followed till we came to the shore, where, together with the King's oaken staff which had been in your hand, we found the place all trampled with naked feet and stains of blood. So we traced you across the shore grass to the sand and over the sand into the sea, with a company of bare feet and many stains of blood.

'Then for a moment I knew not what to think. But Marjorie, my sister, cried out, "It is the vile wretches of Sawny Bean's band who have taken him to the Cave of Death!"'

'Then I remembered that the entrance to the cavern **was** among the rocks, and yet because of the gladness that **was** in our hearts when we issued forth, I had taken no **very** great pains to mind the exact place. Nor was the Dominie aught the wiser. For he had been wholly intent on blowing upon his pipes. But Marjorie minded better than any of us the cleave in the rocks, and showed us to a nearness where the cave entrance was. But the tide had flowed in, and we had perforce to wait and calm our impatience as best we might till it went back again, ere we could follow into the cave mouth. But by this time it was dark, so that the men-at-arms had to find rosin torches and set them alight.

'Thus with the flambeaux blazing and the smoke wavering red overhead we took our way along the wet edge of the sea. But the tide had washed away all traces of blood and feet. Up and down the coast we wandered trying every covert. And yet for our lives we could not hit upon the right cave's entrance. The dogs ran yelping and nosing here and there, but for long nothing came of it.

'Then Earl John and the King himself threatened James Bannatyne to reveal the place. But he denied that he had any knowledge of the cave. And whether he spoke truth or no I cannot say. But his wife went to the King and holding his bridle rein, she said, "Well do I ken, your Majesty, that my man's life is forfeit, but he is my husband. And at least, so far as it concerns him and me, betwixt barn-door and bed-stock I can rule him as a wife should. Gin I persuade him to lead you to the spot, will ye on your word, give me my ain man's life?"

'So the King promised, though Earl John hung a little on the form of the words. Then went the goodwife of Chapeldonnan to her husband. And what she said to him I know not, for they spake privily and apart. But though at first he shook his head and denied, as I could see, that he had any knowledge of the Cave of Death, yet in a little while he took some other thought and ran forward to grip one of the dogs.

'Then went James Bannatyne on ahead, with all of us hotfoot after him, with the torches and the swords.'

'And you also, Nell,' said I, 'were you lurking with the men-at-arms, and which had you, a sword or a torch?'

'I had both,' said Nell Kennedy, shortly. And went on with her tale as if she had been speaking of milking-stools.

'James Bannatyne took the dog into all the wide cave mouths and made him smell the walls and floor above the tide mark, talking to the brute all the time and encouraging him. But for a long time it was still in vain.

'At last the other dog which had been left to itself, bayed out suddenly from among the rocks, where it had found a dark and dismal archway with a wide pool of water in it, which we had passed time and again without suspicion. And at the entrance to this place we found the second hound, with tail erected, baying up the cave mouth from the edge of the pool.

'Then so soon as James Bannatyne brought in his well-taught dog, it began to smell hither and thither with erected ears and bristling hair. Presently it swam away into the darkness. And because the men hesitated to go after the beast, I took the water to show them the way.'

Hearing which, I had made my acknowledgments.

But Nell said, 'No, no; hear my tale first.'

'Then with me there came Robert Harburgh, and after him the Earl and all his company with their torches. The pool proved shallow, and after many turns and windings we came to a wide place—indeed, to the same beach with sand and dripping fingers of stone where we had first found ourselves. And here also we passed the remains of our boat, for it was to this point that we had rowed that night when we took refuge in the lion's den. The savages had broken most of it up for firewood, yet enough remained so that I knew it again.

'But ere the men-at-arms had time to gather behind us, a host of wild creatures armed with stones, knives, and sheath-whittles burst upon us, yelling like demons of the pit. Women also there were, some half clad and some wholly without cleading. And then and there was a fight such as you, Launce, love to tell about, but I have no skill in. For the men-at-arms shot, and we that had but swords struck, while the wild folk shouted and the savage women bit and tore with their nails till the cavern was full of confused noise and the red reek of burning torches. But ever as the slain rolled among our feet they gripped to pull us down, so that in the intervals of his fighting Robert Harburgh went hither and thither "making siccar," as he said, with a *coup de grâce* for each poor clawing wretch.

'And in the narrow doorway through which you found the way, stood the chief himself, with his eyes fiery-red, and his hair about his face. He gripped a mighty axe in his hand, and with it he stood ready to cleave all that came against him. Even the men hesitated at his fearsome aspect. And it was small wonder. But I knew that there was no other way to the innermost cave, so I cried to them to overpass the rabble and drive forward at all hazards.

'How it came about I know not, but a moment after I found myself opposite to Sawny Bean himself and engaging him with your sword—just for all the world as if it had been in the armoire room of Culzean on a rainy day, and you again teaching me the fence of blade against Lochaber axe. But though I had not wholly forgotten my skill, doubtless the giant had soon made an end of me, for he struck fiercely every way. But sudden as the heathcat springs on the hill, the little Dominie leaped upon him and drove his sword into his heart. So that Sawny Bean fell with Dominie Mure upon his breast. Then because he was not able to pull out his sword again, being too close, the Dominie gripped his dagger and struck again and again, panting. And between each blow he cried out the name of a lass—"Mary Torrance! Mary Torrance!" he said.

'Then it was that the hounds over-leaped the two of them struggling there in the arch and sprang on, and after them came Robert Harburgh and I. We two first entered the murky place of death. The dogs were mouthing and gripping the Grey Man. But you lay naked upon the sand as it had been dead.'

This was the matter of Nell's tale, and I will now in turn take up mine own part in it, from the time at which the dogs gripped my remorseless enemy, and as it had been, the life went out from me.

CHAPTER XLVIII

THE FINDING OF THE TREASURE OF KELWOOD

WHEN I came to myself the cave was filled with armed men and the confused clamour of voices. The torches spluttered and reeked, and I could feel that my naked body was covered with a woman's cleak wrapped well about me. Someone was binding up my head; and as she examined to see if all been rightly done, I saw that it was Nell Kennedy. So I called her softly by her name.

But she bade me not try to rise; and looked again to my head to see that it had no serious wound.

Then came John the Earl and asked how I did. Whereupon, minding, as is my wont, to have old Time by the forelock, I spoke of his promise.

'Here', I said, 'is the murderer John Mure. Here is the gang of monsters, and now I will put you in the way of obtaining the Treasure of Kelwood, if you will fulfil the promise which you made to me.'

'What was that?' he said shortly. For although Earl John liked promising well enough, he was not so fond of performing if it cost him aught, as in this case it was like to do.

'My sweetheart here, my knighthood, and a suitable down-sitting of land,' said I, knowing that it was now or never with me.

Then he demurred a little, and hesitated, so that for a moment I thought all was lost.

'Your sweetheart you shall have,' he said at last, 'but the others are not in my gift—save a holding of hand, perhaps, which I can let you for a trifling return when it falls vacant.'

And so rejoiced was I to think of getting my lass that I might have consented to this; but Nell was behind me, and upon pretence of arranging a knot of the bandage upon my forehead, she whispered in my ear, 'Threat him with telling the King about the treasure.'

So, knowing her wisdom, I obeyed her.

'Well then, Earl John,' said I, 'if that be so, and a knighthood and suitable heritages are not in your power to bestow, here at hand is the King. Give me leave to speak with him. He is fond of treasure, and I can put a brave one under his hand!'

'Hush!' said the Earl, looking about him with apprehension. For the King was yet in the place with Mar and Lennox, ordering the taking down and burying of the strane, white, narrow-shaped hams, and the other things that turned the gay, squeamish folk that came with him pale and sick only to look upon them.

'Hush!' he said again, 'above all things beware what you say to the King. Show the Kelwood treasure to myself alone, and you shall have Barrhill—ay, and all Minnochside from the Rowan-tree to the forks of Trool, and I will even speak to the King about the knighting!'

'Will your lordship please to declare it before witnesses,' said I, Nell prompting me as before, for my head was dazed; but hers was singularly clear.

So he called to him certain honourable men of his name, and promised faithfully. 'Are you content?' said he.

So I said, 'Nelly, show them the treasure. Here is the key!'

And she rose and took them to the box—which, by the blessing of God remained still where we had left it in the recess—and she fitted the key in the lock, and it turned without a sound. And there the Earl bathed his hands in the set jewels, the loose stones of price, and the coined, golden money, plashing them through his fingers with a sound like a spout of water, till for fear of the King, I advised him to close it again.

'It is worth the bargain,' said he, 'though I am sorry to have promised away fair Minnochside. I trow it was woman's wit that guided you in the asking, and not that thick-bandaged head-piece of thine, Launcelot Kennedy.'

But I answered not, knowing how to leave well alone when a man is pleased with himself. So the Earl placed Robert Harburgh to guard the chest, and to lie discreetly concerning it if any of the King's men should come near, saying that it was but some foulness appropriate to the den.

But none came asking, and thus was the Treasure of Kelwood conquest for ever to the family of Cassillis.

As for Sawny Bean's monstrous brood, is it not recorded how they were carried through the country to Edinburgh, and as how they went the folk flocked in from leagues away

to see and execrate them. They were hurried straight to the
sands of Leith, where, without process of trial or pleading, and
in the manner prescribed for such fiends, they were executed
out of hand as enemies to the human race in general.

Thus, mainly through my instrumentality, was the
country rid of a monstrous foul blot such as no land since
the flood has ever been cursed with. Though I deny not
that Dominie Mure and Nell Kennedy helped well according
to their possibles, yet the most part of the credit was
rightly given to me, who had twice adventured my life
within the Cave of Death—though, as I admit, on both
occasions against my will.

·　　·　　·　　·　　·

Once more the City of Edinburgh swarmed with
Kennedys, come thither to the great trial. There had not
been so great a concurrence of Westland folk in Edinburgh, since the memorable day when young Gilbert of
Bargany cleared the causeway of us of the house of Cassillis
—for which afterwards we were one and all put to the
horn, to our great and lasting honour, as hath been related.

At the West Port I met Patrick Rippett, he who had
taunted Benane at the Maybole snowballing.

'Whither is your eye gone?' I asked him, for he had a
black patch where his left eye should have been.

'A fause loon pyked it out and offered it me back on
the end of his rapier!' said Patrick Rippett, with the
utmost unconcern.

'And what said ye to him?' I asked of Patrick, because he
was not a man to take a jest (and such a jest) for nothing.

'Faith, I juise bartered him fair. I offered him his heart
on the point of mine!' said Rippett, and so strolled away,
ogling the snooded maids at the windows of the high
lands as best he could, with the one wicked orb which was
left to him.

I was walking with my father at the time. He had
ridden the long way from Kirrieoch on a white pony, all to
pleasure my mother,

'Ye maun gang and hear the laddie gie his evidence,'
she bade him. 'They will fright him to deid else, amang
thae Edinburgh men o' the law. They are no canny. So

long as Launce gets striking at them with the steel I ken
he is safe and sound. For his hand can e'en keep his head,
as a Kennedy's ever should. But wha kens what they may
do to my laddie when he stands afore the justicers, and the
lawyer loons come at him wi' their quips and quandaries?'

'Faith then, good wife,' said my father, 'ye shall come
too. And thou and I shall ride to Edinburgh like joes that
are newly wed.'

And though at first she denied, yet at the last she
consented, well-pleased enough—having a desire to
purchase garmentry more suitable for the wife of a laird and
the mother of one who was to be made a knight.

When my mother went out for the first time, she held
up her hands and exclaimed at the noise and bustle of
the High Street—the soldiers who were for ever marching
to and fro in companies with drums and pipes, the lasses
that went hither and thither with a shawl about their
heads, and bandied compliments—and such compliments
—with swashbucklers and rantipole 'prentice lads. 'The
limmers, they need soundly skelping!' said my mother,
'for a' that they carry their heads so high, and their
kirtles higher than their heads!'

'Surely scantly that!' said my father.

'But ay,' continued my mother, not heeding him in her
press of speech, 'such hair-brained hempies wad be dookit
in the Limmers' Dub on Saturday in every decent country,
and set on the black stool of repentance ilka Sabbath day.
I wonder what the King and the ministers o' Edinburgh
can be thinkin' o'?'

There was, however, for most of us a long and weary
waiting, ere in the town of Edinburgh the High Court of
Justiciary was ripe for the hearing of the case against the
Mures. But when at last the great day came the whole
West Country was there.*

And though many a face was joyous as were ours, eke

*Sir Launcelot Kennedy, of Palgowan and Kirrieoch, appears
somewhat to have confused the dates of the first and second
trials of John Mure of Auchendrayne. Indeed, weakness in
exact chronology is common to his record and to the con-
temporary Historie of the Kennedies, which was written
about the same time by a partisan of the other side—it may
even be by John Mure of Auchendrayne himself.

many were sad and lowering. For it is strange that such ill men should have some to love them, or at least so it was with John Mure the elder. And so there were in the city Mures by the score, fighting, black-avised MacKerrows, cankered Craufords, with all the disbanded Bargany discontents from the south of Carrick, Drummurchie's broken band from the hill-lands of Barr together with many others. So that we kept our swords, as at our first visit to the town in the days of Gilbert Kennedy, free in their scabbards while we ruffled it along the pavement.

And I mind what my mother said, the first time she went down the plainstones with me. We met young Anthony Kennedy of Benane, and I perceived that it was his intent to take the wall of me. So I squared myself, and went a little before with my hand on my rapier hilt and my elbows wide, also cocking fiercely my bonnet over my eye—which assurance feared Anthony so greatly that he meekly took the pavement edge, and I went by with my mother on my arm, having, as I thought, come off very well in the matter.

But my mother stood stock still in amazement.

'Laddie, laddie, I kenned na what had taken ye—ye prinked and passaged for a' the world like our bantam cock at Kirrieoch, when he hears his neighbour at Kirriemore craw in the prime of the morn. Gin ye gang on that gait, ye will get your kame berried and scarted, my lad. So listen your auld mither, and walk mair humbly.'

At this I was somewhat shamed, and dropped behind like a little whipped messan; for my mother has a brisk tongue. My father said not a word, but there was a look of dry humoursomeness upon his face which I knew and feared more than my mother's clip-wit tongue.

CHAPTER XLIX

THE GREAT DAY OF TRIAL

At last, however, the trial was set, and we all summoned for our evidence. It was to be held in the High Court of Justiciary, and was a right solemn thing. A hot day in midsummer it proved, with the narrow, overcrowded bounds of the town drowsed with heat, and yet eaten up with a plague of flies. The room of the trial was a large one, with a dais for the judges at the end, the boxes for the prisoners, and a tall stool with steps and a bar on which to rest the hands, for the witnesses.

And in the long, dark, low, oak-panelled room what a crush of people! For the report of the monstrous dealing of the Mures and the strangeness of their crimes, had caused a mighty coil in the town of Edinburgh and in the country round about. So that all the time of the trial there was a constant hum about the doors—now a continuous murmur that forced its way within, and now a louder roar as the doors were opened and shut by the officers of the court. Also, in order to show themselves busybodies, these pot-bellied stripe-jackets went and came every minute or two, pushing right and left with their halberts, which the poor folk had very peaceably to abide as best they might.

But the disposition of the rabble of the city was a marvel to me. For being stirred up by the Bargeny folk and by the Earl of Dunbar, Mure's well-wished, it was singularly unfriendly to us. So that we were almost feared that the criminals might, after all, be let off by the over-awing of the assize that sat upon the case. But finally, as it happened, those who were chosen assize-men were mostly landward gentlemen of stout hearts and no subjection to the clamour of the vulgar—such, indeed, as should ever be placed upon the hearing of justice, not mere bodies of the Luckenbooths, who, if they give the verdict against the popular voice, are liable to have their shops and stalls plundered. And James Scrymgeour of Dudhope, a good man, was made the chancellor of the jury.

There were many of the great Lords of Session on the bench. For a case so important and notable had not been tried for years, and the Lords of Secret Council appointed my Lord President himself to be in the chief place in his robes, as well as five other justices in his company, that the dittay might be heard with all equal mind and with great motion of solemnity.

It was eleven by the clock when the judges were ushered in, Sir John Fenton of Fentonbarns, Lord President, coming first and sitting in the midst.

Then the crier of the court shouted, ' Way for His Majesty—for King James the Sext make way!'

And all the people rose up while King James was coming in. He sat upon the bench with the justices indeed, but a little way apart, as having by law no share in their deliberations. Nevertheless he was all the time writing and passing pieces of white paper to them, whereat they bowed very courteously back to him. But whether they took any notice of their import I know not.

Then the prisoners were brought in. John Mure the elder, with his grey hair and commanding presence, looked out of from beneath his eyebrows like a lion ignominously beset. James Mure the younger came after his father, a heavy, loutish, ignorant man, but somewhat paled with his bloody handling at the instance of the Lords of Secret Council. Also in accordance with the promise of Earl John in the matter of the finding of the cave, James Bannatyne of Chapeldonnan was not set up for trial along with them, which was a wonder to many and an outcry to some of the evilly affected.

Then the court being set, the dittay was read solemnly by a very fair-spoken and courteous gentleman, Thomas Hamilton of Byres, the King's advocate. He spoke in a soft voice as if he were courting a lady. And whenever he addressed a word to the prisoners, it was as if he had been their dearest friend, and grieved that they should thus stand in jeopardy of their lives.

Yet, cr so it seemed to me, John Mure was ever his match, and answered him without a moment's hesitancy.

Then, after the advocate's opening, the evidence was led. They called upon me first to arise. And I declare that my knees trembled and shook as they never did before the shock of battle. So that only the sight of Nell's pale face and my mother holding her hand, at all gave me any shred of courage. But, nevertheless, I went, with my tall, blue-banded hat in hand and my Damascus sword by my side, to the stance. And there I told all that I had seen— first of the murder at the Chapel of St. Leonards, with the matter of the Grey Man who sat his horse a little way apart among the sandhills. Yet could I not declare on mine oath that I knew of a certainty that this man was the accused John Mure of Auchendrayne. Though as between man and man I was wholly assured of it.

I told also of the sending of the letter and of the confusion of the lad upon his return from the house of
Auchendrayne, and of all the other matter which came
under my observation, even as I have detailed them in
this history, but more briefly. Then a tall, thin, leathery
man, Sir John Russell the name of him, advocate for the
Mures, stood up and tried to shake me in my averments.
But he could not—no, nor any other man. For I wasted
no thought on what I ought to say, but out with the
plain truth. So that he could not break down the impregnable wall of the thing that was, neither make me
say that which was not.

Then there came one after the other the Dominie,
Meg Dalrymple, Robert Harburgh, and lastly my own Nell.
But they had little more to tell than I had told at the
first, till the herald of the court cried out for Marjorie Mure,
or Kennedy, called in the pleas the younger lady of
Auchendrayne.

Then, pale as a lily flower is pale, clad in white, and with
her hair daintily and smoothly braided, she rose and gave
her hand to my Lord Cassillis, who brought her with all
dignity and observance to the witness stance. So firmly she
stood within it, that she seemed a figure of some goddess
done in alabaster, the like of that which I had once seen
at the entering in of the King's palace at Holyrood House.

There was the stillest silence while Marjorie told her
tale. The King stood up in his place, with his hat on his
head, to look at her. The judges gazed as though they had
seen a ghost. But in an even voice she related all the terrible
story, making it clear as crystal, till there stood out the full
wickedness of the unparalleled murders.

'You are the wife of James Mure, the younger prisoner,'
said the man of leather, the advocate Russell,; 'how then
do you appear to give evidence against him?'

'I was first the daughter of Thomas Kennedy of Culzean,
whom these men slew!' said she.

And this was her sole answer. The lawyers for the
defence, as was their duty, tried to make it out that her
evidence was prejudiced, and so to shake it. But the King
broke out upon them, 'No more than we are all prejudiced
against foul murder!'

So they were silenced. But the judges were manifestly ill at ease, and shifted in their seats—for even the King had not liberty of speech in that place. Yet no man said him nay, because he was the King, and, save it were Maister Robert Bruce, not many cared to brook his sudden violent rages.

Then was entered James Bannatyne, who had been brought to confession (in what fashion it boots not to inquire), and he in his turn detailed, line by line, all the iniquity. So it seemed that now the net was indeed woven about the cruel plotters. But my Lord President, by the King's authority, was instant with the prisoners to confess the murdering of Sir Thomas and of the other—yea, even offering his life (but no more) to either of them who would reveal the matter, and tell who were complices in the conspiracy.

And I think James Mure the younger was a little moved at this offer, for I saw him very plainly move and shift the hand that was upon his head. His father watched him with a sharp eye, and once set his manacled wrist upon his son's shoulder, as it had been to encourage him to remain firm. He himself stood erect and undaunted all the time of the trial, like a tower of ancient strength, while his son sat upon a stool with his back against the bars of the box, as it seemed careless of the crimes which were alleged against him. He had not even lifted his eyes when his wife Marjorie went into the place of witnessing.

At last it was all over, and the men of the jury spoke earnestly together, while John Mure watched them with his lionlike eyes shining from under his hassock of grey hair. The King sat impatiently drumming his hands upon a rail. He would have liked, I could see, to go over to confer with them. But even King Jamie had hardly dared so much as that.

After a short space for consultation their president of assize, Sir James Scrymgeour, stood up in the body of the court with a little paper in his hand,

'King's lieges all, are ye agreed in your verdict?' asked my Lord President.

'We are,' said Sir James, firmly.

'And what is your finding?'

There was a great and mighty silence so that the anxious tapping of the King's fingers on the wooden bench could be heard.

'We find them both GUILTY—' said Sir James.

He would have said more in due form, but there was a thunderous shout from all the Westland folk that were in the hall, so that no more could be heard. But the King was seen upon his feet commanding silence, and the macers of the court struck here and there among them that shouted.

Then when the tumult within was a little hushed, my Lord President rose to pronounce sentence. But he had scarce opened his mouth, when there came through the open windows the angry roaring of the mob without. For the news had already reached them, and Dunbar and others were busily employed stirring them up to make a tumult on behalf of the murderers. My Lord President had a noble voice and the words of condemnation came clear and solemn from him, so that they were heard above the din by every ear in the hall—ay, and even as far as the outer port.

'We discern and adjudge John Mure of Auchendrayne and James Mure his son and apparent heir to be ta'en to the Mercat Cross of Edinburgh, and there their heads to be stricken from their bodies—as being culpable and convict of many treasonable and heinous crimes. Which is pronounced for DOOM!'

And when the officers had removed the prisoners, Marjorie Kennedy walked forth from the hall of judgment, as silent and composed as though she had been coming out of the kirk on a still summer's morning with her Bible in her hand.

CHAPTER L

THE LAST OF THE GREY MAN

IT was the morn of the execution. Justice, delayed for long, was that day to let fall its sword. We of the Cassillis colours mustered in the dead of the night, for there was no force save the City Guards within the walls. And we had recently had overly many proofs how little these men could do with the unruly commons of Edinburgh if it pleased them to be turbulent. So it had come to be bruited abroad, that there was an intent to prevent the execution and deliver the murderers out of the hands of justice.

But we were resolved that this should not be. So, as was our bounden duty, we armed us to support the right and to keep the King's peace against all riotous law-breakers.

The Earl gave to me the command of one half of the band, reserving the other for himself. And already he called me Sir Launcelot, though I had not yet received the acknowledgment of knighthood from the King.

At the first break of day it was to be done. Of this we had private notice from the turnkey of the Tolbooth.

I had worked earnestly upon my mother and Nell that they should abide from the business—which was, indeed, not for womankind to see. Though I knew that there would be many there, ay, even dames gentle of degree. But my father marched with me.

' Shall I put my harness off me,' said he, 'when there is a chance of a tumult, and of defeating of the solemn justice of Providence and of King James? God forbid! Wife, help me on with my jack.'

So I placed my father in my own command, and I set him in the second rank with Hugh of Kirriemore beside him and Robert Harburgh in front of him, where I judged he would not come to any great harm. And we Kennedies had the King's private permission thus to come through the town under arms. When we arrived at the place the tall scaffold had already been set up at the cross, and even ere we arrayed us first about it, many a candle had begun to wink here and there in the tall windows of the High Street.

The Earl was to command a second strong guard from the prison port to the scaffold, lest the rabble should try to overwhelm the City Guard and the marshal's men as they convoyed the prisoners to the place of execution.

Thus we of the first band stood grimly to our arms a long time after the gloaming of the morning began. The hum of the folk gathering surrounded us. There was, however, little pleasance or laughing, as there is at an ordinary heading or hanging; and that did not betoken good, for when the populace is silent, it is plotting. This much I had learned in my long service and afterwards as a knight-at-arms. Therefore I hold it the true wisdom to strike ere the many-headed can bite. That, at least, is my thought of it.

Slowly and slowly three or four dark figures on the scaffold grew clearer to our eyes, till we could see the headsman and his assistants waiting patiently for their work to be brought to them. The chief of these was a man mighty of his arms. He had a black mask upon his face, and was naked even to the waist. A leathern apron like a smith's was done about his loins, and he stood leaning his broad axe upon the block. The sun was just beginning to redden the clouds in the east, when the door of the Tolbooth fell open with a loud noise. At the very same moment the rooks and jackdaws arose in a perfect cloud from the pinnacles of St Giles as well as from the whole city. And in a black clanging cloud they drifted seaward. Which was looked upon as a marvel by them that watched for freits. For they said, 'These be John Mure's devils that have forsaken him.' And, indeed, whether there was aught in it or no, certain is it that the birds came not back for many days. At least, not to my seeing, but then I was much occupied with other matters.

As the procession came out, the Earl John and his men filed on either side in a triple line, with the axe-men of the guard marching close about the prisoners. John Mure walked first in his grey cloak, but bareheaded, striding reverend and strong before all. Behind him came his son. And hand in hand with him (O marvel of marvels!) was she that had been in name his wife, even Marjorie Kennedy. And as they came, the light grew clearer. There seemed to be almost a smile upon the Lady Marjorie's face. And James Mure listened intently as she spoke low and steadily to him.

For Marjorie had in these days become (as it seemed) a woman removed from us, supported by no earthly food. For none touched her lips, her strength being upheld by some power from above; at least, so I think. She had received permission from the King to be with her husband in his last hours.

'I have fulfilled the Lord's justice, for my duty was laid upon me,' she said, 'but I would not kill both body and soul.'

How she effected it I know not; but certain it is that during the weeks of waiting she had won James Mure in some sort to contrition and prayer. And now with his hand in hers, they walked together along the short way to the scaffold foot; but old John Mure strode scornfully on before, heedful neither of man nor woman. And I swear that I could not but in some measure admire at him, devil of cruelty as he was.

They climbed the scaffold—John Mure calmly as though he were leading a lady to a banquet table—but his son faltered and had fallen at the ladder foot, save for the hand of Marjorie, who walked in white by his side, accompanying him faithfully to his end.

'I am his wife,' she said. 'It was I who brought him to this.' Ye will not twain me from him on this day of shame. Never have I owned James Mure as my husband before, but I own him now.' These were her words, when the captain of the guard was instant with her to depart home.

And I declare that the doomed man looked at her with something like a beast's dumb gratitude in his eyes, which, when you think on it, is a thing marvellous enough. And I ask not that it shall be believed. Yet I saw it, and will at any time uphold the truth of it with my sword if need be.

At last they stood upon the scaffold platform, and the headsman made ready. Then there sounded above the mingled roar of the multitude the blowing of a trumpet. And the King's gay favourite, the Duke of Lennox, rode to the foot of the stage. He had a paper in his hand.

'A pardon! A pardon!' yelled the people.

My heart gave a great leap and stood still.

'They never dare!' cried I. 'Lads, stand firm. If the King hath pardoned the murderers, shall we of the West? Will ye follow me, lads?'

And they whispered back, 'Ay, that we will. We will help you to do justice upon them. The Mures shall never leave this place alive, though we all die also. We shall not go back to Carrick, shamed by these men's lives.'

So we arranged it, if by chance there should be news of a reprieve. For it was by singular good hap that we were the only company under arms in the city, save the few men of the Town Guard.

But when Lennox made his way to the scaffold, we heard another way of it. I was almost underneath the staging upon the front, and heard that which was said, almost every word.

'The King to you two traitors about to die,' he read. 'His Majesty desires greatly to be informed of the certainty

of these things whereof you have been accused, and for
which you have been justly condemned—the murder of
Sir Thomas Kennedy, the matter of the bloody dagger
thrown at the Red House, the Treasure of Kelwood, and
its taking out of the changehouse on the Red Moss. His
Majesty the King offers life and his clemency in a perpetual
exile upon some warded isle, to the first of you that will
reveal the whole matter.'

The King's favourite ceased his reading, and looked at
the condemned men.

And John Mure in his plain grey cloak, which he had
not yet laid aside, looked askance at Lennox, who shone like
a butterfly in gay colours, being tricked out in the latest
fitful extravagancies of fashion.

'We shall be grateful to His Majesty all our lives,' said
he, sneeringly, 'but the Solomon of Scotland is so wise that
he can easily certify himself of the truth of these things
without our poor aid.'

But James Mure the younger, where he stood with his
wife by his side, seemed a little struck with the message, and
began to listen with interest.

'Read that again,' he said to Lennox, abruptly.

And Lennox, prinking and preening him like a gay-
feathered Indian bird in my lady's bower, read the King's
mandate over again.

John Mure watched his son with the eye of a crouching
wild cat. The younger man was about to utter something,
when his father said quickly to Lennox, 'I pray thee, my
Lord Duke, may I speak with you for a moment apart?
I am the first to accept the offer!'

And with that they came both of them to the side of the
scaffold where I was on guard, leaving James Mure standing
with drooping head by the block.

'Hark ye, my lords,' said Auchendrayne the elder, 'thy
master's terms are fair enough to be offered to a dying man
on the scaffold. I will take them. But on condition that
my son be executed before I reveal the secret. For there are
but two of us left, and we have been close to one another
all our lives. I would not, therefore, have my son think
that I, being an old man, for the sake of a year or two of
longer life, would reveal those matters for which he has

already suffered the torture of the extreme question, with
so great constancy both in the King's inquest chamber and
before the Lords of Secret Council.'

'That is easily arranged,' said Lennox, dusting at his
doublet. 'I have but to give the word to the executioner,
and he will do his duty first upon your son. Then he will
halt till you have accepted the King's mercy, and given
pledge and earnest of full revelations concerning these
hidden and mysterious matters.'

This was Lennox's customary manner of speaking—as
he had learned it in the English Court, with womanish
conceits and a flood of words and gestures. And as he spoke
he smiled upon John Mure, as though the old grey man in
the cloak and reverend beard had been some young and
easy virtued dame of the Court.

And so taken up with himself was he, that he did not
observe the basilisk look which the arch-conspirator turned
upon him.

Lennox held up his hand to the executioner.

'In the King's name,' he cried to the man in the mask,
'do thine office upon the younger first, and speedily.'

'These are not my orders!' quoth he in the mask, curtly.

Lennox flashed a little ebon staff, with a golden crown
set upon the summit, before his eyes.

'Would'st thou argie-bargie with me?' he said, 'then
right soon another shall take thy bishopric and (as thou
dost others) shalt shepherd thee to Hades.'

Whereat Marjorie, robed in her clear-shining white, took
the hand of James Mure, the man that was about to die.

'Husband,' said she, calmly, 'I have asked pardon for
thee from God—do thou also ask it now, ere swift death
take thee. Ask it both from God and man.'

For she had been his ministrant angel in the prison.
And her own heart being changed—vengeance in the drinking not seeming so sweet a cup as it had appeared in the
mixing. She had also won the sullen mechanic heart of
him, who, according to the law of the land, had been so
long her husband. She had showed him the way to a
certain sum of faith, penitence, and hope. Which, perchance, he snatched at, not so much for themselves, but
as the best things which were left to him.

'James, won thou forth on thy way. Fear not! Thou shalt not be long alone,' she said to him.

And, staggering a little, he moved across the scaffold. He would have fallen but that Marjorie set his hand upon her shoulder and put her arm about him. So he came forward stumbling like a man in sore sickness, as doubtless he was.

'I am a sinful man,' he said, so that some, at least, could hear him. 'Pray for me, good people. Keep your hands from blood, as I have not kept mine. And, Marjorie, though thou didst never love me, love me now, and bide with me till I die.'

'Fear not,' she said; 'I will stand beside thee, and not only here. I have a message that I shall right soon be called to journey with thee further, meeting thee somewhere by the way that thou must go.'

And calling him again 'sweet brother' and 'James,' she laid down his neck upon the block, and with one blow the headsman featly did his office. But Marjorie stood still and received the poor head in a decent napkin after the masked man had held it up.

John Mure looked at her and at her son all the time, and an evil and contemptuous light shone in his eyes.

'Madam,' he said, 'it had done no harm had you begun your care and attendance somewhat earlier. Ye might have made a decent preacher out of James. He was never muckle worth for aught else.'

Then Lennox came forward again with his paper.

'Now, John Mure,' he said, 'we have done according to your desire. Ye will now, I doubt not, having seen the end and reward of iniquity in the person of your son, accept His Majesty's so marvellous clemency, and be content to reveal all the matter.'

He came a little near to the old man, airily whisking his paper with his forefinger.

John Mure waved him aside with one hand, and held his nose with the other.

'Pah! Get apart from me, civet cat!' he cried. 'Think ye that I will have any dealings with you or with your dullard fool master, King Baggy-breeches. I saw that ye might, perchance, were I first turned to dead clay and lappered blood, chance to get something out of James there.

I saw him look somewhat too eagerly on your reprieve, for much belated domesticity had turned him soft. So I played with you. And now, wot ye well, ye shall know nothing from me that your precious Solomon of asses cannot divine for himself!'

He took off his cloak of grey and lace collar, baring his neck for the dead stroke.

'Stay,' he said to Lennox. 'Since your wise King is so curious. Here is a history of divers matters that may interest your master. It may do him some good.'

The new minister of Edinburgh, a soft-spoken, King-fearing man, came near. John Mure looked at him.

'Of what religion art thou?' he asked. 'Ay, verily, of the King's religion. Were my time not so circumscribed, I would have at thee with texts, thou time-serving rogue. Ay, and would swinge thee with them soundly, too.'

'In what religion dost thou die?' said the minister. For it was a customary question in those days, when men were forced to live and die on the borderland of many creeds.

John Mure smiled as he bent his head to the block.

'Of the ancientest persuasion,' said he, 'for I am ready to believe in any well-disposed god whom I may chance to meet in my pilgriming. But in none will I believe till I do meet him. Nevertheless do thou, like a wise, silly bishop, stick to the King and thy printed book!'

Which saying was remembered when the minister was afterward made a bishop by the King's favour.

With these words, John Mure threw out his hands with a sharp jerk—for that was the customary signal. The broad axe rose and fell, flashing in the sun a moment ere it crashed dully upon the block. The Westland men gave a shout, and the heathen spirit of John Mure of Auchendrayne, carrying such a load of sin and bloodshedding as never soul did before or since, fared forth alone to its own place.

CHAPTER LI

MARJORIE'S GOOD-NIGHT

EVEN as the axe was falling, Marjorie Kennedy sank down upon the platform of the scaffold, as though the stroke had fallen upon her. I sheathed my sword, and sprang upon the slippery stage to hold her up. When I took her in my arms she was soft and pliable in all her limbs like a little child. Till now she had been like a woman of steel, or rather like one carven in alabaster, as I have said. But now she lay in my arms like a new-born babe on the nurse's lap.

We carried her homeward, making strangely enough for some distance but one procession with the bodies which were going to be buried without the wall, while the heads were taken to be set on the pikes of the Nether Bow.

To the Earl John's own lodging we brought her, and in a room with a wide north-looking window we laid her down on a bed. Then we stood silently about her, Nell and I being nearest.

In a little while Marjorie turned her head to the window. The sun had risen on the sea. A north wind was blowing. All was very blue, and smacked of the morning freshness, for the window was open, and the sea air blew off the firth almost as salt as it was wont to blow in at the windows of Culzean.

Thrice she moved her lips to speak, but till the fourth time no word came.

'I have done the work appointed,' she said, 'I ken not if I have done it right.'

She paused a little, and her eyes, as she looked at the sea, were very wide and wistful.

'It is a hard saying that "Vengeance is His." I thought it would be sweet—sweet,' she said, 'but now in the mouth it is bitter.'

'Hush thee, Marjorie,' whispered my Nell; 'it was the justice of God upon the murderers of our father.'

And I thought that she spoke well.

But Marjorie waved her aside.

'Like enough,' she answered, quietly, as one that has not strength to argue, but yet holds the contrary opinion. 'Done, at least, is Marjorie's task. I journey forth to take my wages. Fare you well.'

She turned her face a little outward so that she could look upon the sea and the Fife Lomonds.

'A dearer shore,' she said, softly, and then she started a little, quickly as if she had waked from sleep.

'Where am I?' she asked.

But ere we could answer—even Nell, who stood close beside her and stroked her brow with a soft hand, she went on,—

'Oh, what am I saying? I was thinking on our garden at Culzean, with its rose walks and the sweet dreaming scent of the sea?'

She looked up at me, as it had been almost archly, yet so as almost to break my heart.

'Launcelot, lad,' she said, 'hast thou thy gage that I gave thee there? Ye thought me once to be sweet. And I liked you, laddie, I liked you—with something just an inch on the hither side of loving. But now Nelly will love thee a mile on the further side. Come you, Nell,' she said, beckoning her, 'brave, sweet sister! Let not thy sharp tongue longer injure thy warm heart. Give me your hand, little sister Nelly. Where is it? I cannot see—for the bright shining light.'

And finding Nell's hand she put it into mine across the bed.

'Good-night, bairns,' she said, 'even so keep them till the world ends!'

Then for a short space she was silent, and when she spoke again it was very low, so that none save Nell and I could hear. But the words made us tingle as we caught them.

'Gilbert,' she was saying in a whisper, clear and distinct, 'is it not sweet to walk thus hand in hand on the green meadows? Are not the spring flowers sweet, lad of my love? Shall I sing thee a song about them? For, though thou know'st it not, I can sing both high and low.'

Then she spoke as it had been liltingly and gladsomely.

'Gilbert, let me set this spray of the bonny birk above thine heart. Methinks it hath a strange look. I kenned not that it grew in this countryside.'

She broke into a weird lilt of song that sent the tears hasting to our eyes. But Marjorie was smiling as she never smiled on me, and that made me weep the more.

> *It neither grew in syke nor ditch*
> *Nor yet on ony sheuch,*
> *But at the gates o' Paradise,*
> *That birk grew fair eneuch.*

'Gilbert, Gilbert,' she said lovingly, crooning like one that is caressed, 'is not this right winsome? That we are

walking here together on the living green—with all our
fashes, all our troubles left quite behind us. There was
surely something long ago that wearied us, something that
parted us and twained us. I cannot mind what it was. I
shall not try to remember. But, love of mine, it shall
separate us no more for ever and ever!'

Her voice had almost gone. But once again it came
louder.

'Keep my hand, Gilbert,' she said, trembling a little,
'there is a mist coming over the green betwixt me and
the sunshine—a cold, cold mist from the sea. But keep
thou my hand, dear love, clasp it tighter, and it will pass
over.'

I saw the death sweat break on her brow.

'Gilbert, Gilbert,' she whispered, searching above her
with her hands and opening her arms, 'clasp me closer. I
cannot see thee, love, for the mist. I cannot feel your
hand.'

I bent my ear. I thought she was gone from us. But,
as from an infinite distance I heard the words come to me.
They were the last, spoken with great relief.

'The mist has gone by, dear love! The mist has quite
gone by!'

And she lay still, smiling most sweetly.

CHAPTER LII

HOME-COMING

THE snows of another winter had fallen, frozen, and lain
long ere they were at last whisked away by the winds of a
brisk and bitter March. It was now again the springtime
upon the face of the earth—the time of the earliest singing
of the mavis, of the sweet piping of the blackbird on the
tree. The grasses were green, too, over the unforgotten
grave of our Marjorie. But we who loved her had won to
a memory that was not now wholly sorrow. Specially we
remembered the sweet and profitable end she had made,
when after many days of bitter winter in her heart, forgive-
ness and love at last unsealed her bosom.

It had been a long winter for us all, because it behoved
that I should go to London, there to be made one of His

Majesty's new knights. For I had told all my tale to the King, being so charged by the Earl John.

'Yet,' said he, 'keep ever your thumb upon the matter of the Treasure of Kelwood. And I will keep mine right effectually upon Currie, the ill-conditioned thief thereof.'

And so he did, and for the same Laird of Kelwood's sake chiefly, he set to mending and patching our old tower of defence on Craig Ailsa, in which he gave one Hamilton the charge of him as prisoner, together with John Dick the traitor and two or three more.

'It was a fine, quiet place,' said the Earl John, 'and would give such rascals time and opportunity for repentance—which,' added he, 'seems more than I am ever likely to get with all this throng of business on hand.'

For the Earl John was now waxen one of the greatest men in broad Scotland, and withal he had all the power worth considering in the shire of Ayr. So that even the Craufords, wanting now their ancient chief, and broken with bickering among themselves, sent an embassy of peace and goodwill to him.

It chanced that it came when the Earl was in a good humour.

'Ah, John Crauford,' said Cassillis, ''tis a changed day since Bargany and you chased us off Skeldon Haughs. It looks as if the sow had not been flitted so far after all. But ye shall have the peace ye ask. For we live under a gracious King who loves quietness as much as when he dwelt there in our kindly North. And he is now the better able to enforce it. Therefore, look ye to it. I will maintain you Craufords in your heritages of Kerse—which by my power as Bailzie, I might legally declare forfeit.

'But I will tell you what ye must do in return. Ye shall render me place and precedence at kirk and market. Ye shall build up your private door in Dalrymple Kirk, and ye shall abide from taking your places there till ye have seen me seated.'

To this, dourly enough, the Craufords perforce agreed. For, indeed, they could make no better of it, so great a man was our Earl grown.

But to me he was ever kind, and proved none so ill-given when it liked him. For he said, 'Build you the house of

Palgowan and I will plenish it for you, and that not meanly. And you and my cousin Nell shall rear me routh of lusty knaves to protect my south-western marches, and keep down the reivers of the Dungeon!' Which, indeed (so far as I was concerned), I was right willing to promise.

So it came about that the Earl would have it that our wedding must be held in the ancient strength of Cassillis, which sits by the waterside not so far from the town of Ayr. And a bonny, well-sheltered place it is—not like Culzean, which stands blusteringly on the seabrink, over-frowning all. And because the Earl of Cassillis said it, so it was bound to be.

For he was our Nell's guardian, and besides we that were to live under him, were none the worse of keeping in with him.

When I went to do my courting, as often as not I found Nell walking with him, and ofttimes flouting him. And when I would have cautioned her, 'Tut,' she said, 'he likes nothing better. If his own wife flouted him, he might stay better at home.'

'Cousin,' Nell would say to him sometimes, 'Cousin John, ye think ye are such a great man, yet a little musket-ball, or a woman's finger-long bodkin, might let all thy greatness out. Ye should think oftener on that.

'What, Nell,' said he, 'is it that the hour of thy marriage grows so near, that thou must test thy preaching on me. Keep the proof of the pudding for thine own goodman.'

'Ah,' said she, 'perchance my cousin, the noble Countess, has already given thee thy fill of it.'

'Thou art a forward chit,' said he, wringing her ear between his finger and thumb. 'I hope Launce will swinge thee tightly with a supple birch for thy often naughtiness.'

It was, indeed, a notable day when Nell and I were married. All the morning my heart was beating a fine tune, lest something should happen ere I got my lass carried off to our home. Alone I rode from the Cove of Culzean to the house of Cassillis. I started brave and early, and my good old horse, Dom Nicholas, rode for once the right road and the ready, the gate that I longed to go. I had a rare fine coat of blue silk upon me, belted about the waist with the King's belt, and with the King's order of knighthood all a-glitter upon my breast. Silver-buttoned was my coat, and of solid silver, too, were the accoutrements of Dom Nicholas—ay, to the very stirrups and the broidery on his blue saddle-cloth. I wore the Earl's Damascus sword, his first gift, swinging at my side. And as Dom Nicholas and I went through Maybole, wot ye, if we kept not our heads up. For the lasses ran out in clouds to watch us go past, and what was even better, the lads sulked and turned their backs, saying that they would be shamed to lay a leg across a horse's back thus apparelled. For I knew well what they were thinking. Had I been trudging afoot in hodden, and they riding by all in silk with a gold-hilted sword, that is just what I should have said. So the black envy eating into their hearts and lowering on their brows cheered me like old French wine on a cold day.

I had not gone far across the bent when I spied a cavalcade before me. It was the men of Culzean, whom I had so often led in battle, come to give me a right gay sending off. And at their head rode James (now the heir), mirthful Sandy, and mine own little Davie, dressed like a page-boy in satin of blue and gold.

They gave me boisterous welcome, and they that dared would have broken many jests of the time-honoured sort upon my head. But on such a day a lover's head is helmeted alike against the hand of war and the strife of tongues.

The Earl himself met us at Cassillis Yett. Whereupon I dismounted and bent upon a knee. He raised me right courteously and led me within, conversing all the while as to an equal. Such a repair of folk I never saw before in Carrick or in Kyle. And sweetest of all to me was to see my father, for my mother had bidden at home to welcome us when we should ride southward.

And among the first that came to bid me good fortune were Robert Harburgh and his wife. Now so soon as the eyes of my ancient love crossed mine, I perceived well that there was yet wickedness lurking in them.

And whensoever her husband was called away on some business of the Earl's I had proof of it. For Kate Allison

came near to me, and, setting her hand on the silver buttons
of my coat, as though to pick a thread, she said,—

'So, Launcelot—or, I should say, Sir Launcelot—is it
come to this? You see there is none so disdainful but in
time their fall will come.'

'Nay, Kate,' I made answer, 'it was not I that was first
disdainful, for do you mind who it was that told me certain
truths in the Grieve's house at Culzean?'

'Ah Launce!' said Kate Allison, 'own it now. Was
not I a kind leech, to bite one I loved so healthily all for
his good and for the cooling of his blood?'

'Kate Allison,' said I, 'thou wast ever a minx, a teasing
rogue of rogues. But thy disdain might have gone near to
costing me my life!'

'Go to, Sir Want-wit,' said she. 'Did not I know all
the time that thy love for me was no more than a boy's
fondness for kissing comfits, and to be made of by a bonny
lass? Why, even then thou wast fonder of Nell's little finger
than of my whole body.'

I knew that Kate spoke true—for, indeed, it was many
months since I had so much as thought upon her. But this
I told her not. The Lord knows how seldom she had
thought upon me. But when they meet together, old
sweethearts take pleasure thus in dallying with the past,
when all wounds have been healed and no hearts broken.

But she saw my eyes wandering, as I guess, every way
about, and she must needs tease me concerning that also.

'Nay,' she said, 'you will not see your posy, till she comes
in to the minister and you. So e'en content ye for a little
with an old married wife and the mother of a family. Ye shall
have time and to spare with your bonny bride or all be done.'

'Kate,' I said, 'ye will be my friend as of yore.'

'Ay, and hold my tongue,' answered she quickly.

'That you did not always, then,' said I, 'for there never
was such an uncouth love-making in the world, as with
your tell-tale tongue ye made mine. I dared not lay my
lips to a tender word nor so much as seek a favour, as it
might be innocently betwixt man and maid, but it was
"That you said to Kate on such a night!" or "Think ye
that I count so little on myself as to be content with Kate
Allison's cast-off sweet speeches."'

And the pretty besom laughed. For though a married wife, she was not a whit sobered, as one might see by her eyes.

'It served you greatly right,' said she, 'but do me some justice. Did you ever hear of my telling of the night of the fair at Maybole, and of our home-coming by the woodland way?'

'No,' said I, curtly. For indeed I liked not that memory specially well, and wondered that she did.

'Then,' said Kate Allison, 'rail no more against woman's tongues. For they are moveable yard measures, and let out no more than likes them.'

At this moment they called to me from the great door, and Kate Allison waved me off with a gay 'Up and away, Sir Knight!'—which pleased me more from her than many a *Benedicite* from another.

The minister had come, they said, and was waiting for me. I went in, and lo! to my wonder, who should he be but Maister Robert Bruce, the sequestrated minister of Edinburgh, with whom the King had at last wholly fallen out concerning the matter of the Gowrie riot.

The Earl smiled at my wonderment.

'Art thou astonished,' he said, 'thus to see our ancient friend in Carrick? Thinkest thou that thy marriage will not stand? Truth it will, for even King James will think twice, or he bids his bishop unfrock a man that bides with me in my defenced house of Cassillis.'

'Sir Launcelot,' said Maister Robert Bruce, bending to me with his ancient grace and most reverend dignity, 'this is the happiest hour with me since I quitted my high town upon the Long Ridge. It is true that I wander like a restless ghost seeking abode; but as yet the King hath not bent me —yea, though thrice I have met him in dispute and conference.'

Then went the Earl out to bring in my Nell, and I listened to the minister of Edinburgh speaking. Yet, on my life I could not fix my mind on a word he said, for there was a jangling as of many bells in mine ears, and all the pulses of my life beat together. Then knew I of a surety that none had power to touch my heart like Nell Kennedy, the lass that would not need to change her name.

At last the door opened and she entered—leaning on the Earl's arm she came. There was a rim of gold about her hair like a coronet. And John of Cassillis bent over to me, as he gave her into my hand. 'Take her,' he said, 'I have set a coronet about her brows for to-day. She is in haste to be wed, or I might have put a real one there. And what had Sir Launcelot done then, poor thing?"

And I think the cold, tall Earl John was more than a little fond of our Nell, concerning which I often rally her now.

So Nell and I were married. And as though he had known her and her teasing temper, Maister Robert Bruce paused long on the promise to 'obey' when he came to put the questions to her, and also upon the words 'obedient wife.' Wherefore I have ever held him to be a man gifted above most with the second sight.

It was between the sweet hazel and the flowering May that we rode south—we two alone. For Robert Harburgh had led a company of men with flower-wreathed lances and of young maids on palfreys as far as the crossing of the roads which come from Culzean, where there met us a party with the loving cup.

But now at long and last we were won clear, and ever as we rode we caught hands and laughed and loosed them again—all for gladness to be alone. And we looked in one another's eyes, and nigh brought ourselves and our horses to destruction by thus looking and overlooking. Till I felt mine old Dom Nicholas, a horse that loves not philandering, grow restive and sulky under my thigh, tossing his head up as one slighted for the unworthy. And ever as we went she charged it upon me that then and then, and at such another time, I loved her not. And ever I swore that I did. Thereafter, being beaten on that point, she fell to declaring that she had loved me first and most—but I only reluctantly and, as it had been, at second-hand.

Thus we made the miles and the hours go by, redding up all our past life and planning our future, wondering the while if the stir and clangour of war had indeed passed away for ever. For already there had come a new look upon the land. Whether it was the union of the crowns and the new English wealth which made money more plenty, I know not, at any rate certain it is that there had arrived a security to which we in the lands of Carrick had been strangers for many generations.

Then it was that the farmer began to set his oxen to the plough in teams of a dozen or more, not fearing any longer that there might come a glint of steel-harnessed riders over the hill, who should drive his cattle before them and leave himself lying in the furrow a-welter in his blood.

The wind blew sweet about us. It seemed that never had there been a spring like this one since the world began, never such delicatest airs as those that stirred the crisps about Nell's white neck when she bent it sideways to hearken to my speeches. I declare that were I not an unlearned Scot, who takes to his pen only when work for the sword waxes slack, I could praise my love in similitudes of Arabian birds and ferny sprays, as well as Euphues' Delight or even as in the gentle Sydney his Arcadia.

But as it is I waste time, for already I have spoke too long, and must haste me to the end. Though this is a part of my life that I could love to linger on. For what is pleasanter than sunshine after storm and the bolts of ruin.

I declare it was five years since I had had time to look at a robin. But there seemed to be time for everything this fine May day.

And ever as we went, it seemed that we had been a long time alone, and that it would soon come time to be turning back again. Then to which soever of us the thought came, that we were now on the long lane that has no turning (save that which turns in at the kirkyaird loaning), there would also come the desire to touch and to look. And even thus did Nell Kennedy often, reaching her hand across to me from her gentle, equal-pacing steed.

Then would she fall back on the things that had been, and which now were passed away.

'Yesterday, at such a time,' she would say, 'I thought that to-day would never come. And now—'

Whereupon with her eyes she would look the rest.

Then I told her how that I had seen the Dominie but yestereven, when she was sewing at the pearling of her bridal dress and thinking of me. He had gone back with his pipes to the school by the kirk at Maybole.

'And what said he of our wedding?' asked my dear.

'Why I was instant with him to come and bide at Palgowan,' I made answer. 'Shall I tell thee what he said?'

'Ay, tell it me, indeed!' quoth she, blithely, stopping a moment on a high-lying moorish summit, with her hand above her eyes and looking to the Spear of the Merrick towards which we rode.

'Well, then, he said that those that were but newly wed had no use for carven negro-heads, wherein to put the ashes of their loves.'

'He is none so ugly as that!' said Nell—with, I think, a look at me which I took for a certain complaisance it pleased me to see.

Then I told her how the Dominie had added that it was not yet time for men of his profession to come about the house of a newly-wedded knight. But that if prosperity should come to Palgowan and the din of bairns' voices, we might ask him again in ten years or somewhat less.

'Oh,' said Nell, shortly, and rode a little further off. Yet I flattered myself that I had said the thing pretty well. For it was not at all in these terms that the Dominie had put his offer. Indeed, I was in a quandary how most discreetly to deliver his message.

So, in the long twilight of May, we came riding down Minnoch Water. For, with the sun-setting, we had fallen silent, and we looked no more so frankly at each other. But with one accord we turned our eyes across the water to watch for the light of my mother's candle in the little window.

She heard us as we came; and there, lo! before I knew it, she was at Nelly's saddle leather, helping her to dismount, and the tears were running steadily down her face. I think she minded the day when she, too, had come home a bride to the little house of Kirrieoch among the hills.

'Oh, my bairn—my bairn,' was what she said, 'come awa' ben!'

And it was to Nell that she said it. Me she minded no more than a cock-sparrow under the eaves. Then came Hugh of Kirriemore out to take the horses. But I went, as is my custom, to the stable with Dom Nicholas, for he never slept well otherwise. And when I came in again I found that my mother had Nell already seated by the fireside, for it is chill among the uplands in May. The peats were burning fine, and on the white board there was a supper set fit for a prince and princess.

But all the time my mother never minded me at all, save to rage on me for bringing the lass so far and so fast.

'But, mother,' said I, 'remember that if I had not made some haste, all your fine supper would have been wasted.'

And indeed it came not far from being that as it was, for we could eat but little. The finest of muirland fare seemed somehow or other to stick by the way, tasting strangely dry and sapless. And after we had done we drew apart and looked at the red ashes, while my mother rattled on about the simple concerns of the sheep and the calves, which mountain-bred folk vastly love both to speak of and to hear about.

Presently she leaned over me and took down the burnt Bible out of the wall aumry.

'Here, Launce,' she said, 'read you the chapter this night ere ye sleep. It becomes a man wedded and the head of a family. Besides, your father is from home.'

I declare I would sooner have charged upon the level spears. But I had no choice with my mother, speaking as she did when I was a boy, and my Nell sitting there cross-ing her pretty ankles by the fireside. So I manned to read a portion. It was about Jonathan clambering up a rock (and a good soldier he was). But the prayer fairly beat me. However, ere we rose from our knees we said the Lord's prayer all of us together. So to rest we went, without other word spoken. And through the little window of the room in which I was born, Nell and I could hear, ere we went to sleep, the brattle of the burn hurrying down through the peace of the hills, past our own new house of Palgowan and so on toward the silence of the outermost sea.

THE END

Printed in Great Britain by offset lithography by
Billing & Sons Ltd, Guildford, London and Worcester